THAT YOU REMEMBER

a novel

ISABEL REDDY

BELLE ISLE BOOKS
www.belleislebooks.com

ISBN: 978-1-958754-05-4
Library of Congress Control Number: 2022918580

Designed by Sami Langston
Project managed by Grace Albritton

Printed in the United States of America

Published by
Belle Isle Books (an imprint of Brandylane Publishers, Inc.)
5 S. 1st Street
Richmond, Virginia 23219

BELLE ISLE BOOKS
www.belleislebooks.com

belleislebooks.com | brandylanepublishers.com

Praise for *That You Remember*

"Brilliant pacing, characterization, and imagery. *That You Remember* is a universally worthy, socioeconomic tour de force. It is fiction resonating as fact."
—Peter Kilborn, *New York Times* correspondent and author, *Next Stop Reloville*

"Isabel Reddy has written a big, sweeping novel with a big, beating heart. An entire mountain community comes to life in this epic story of a Kentucky mine disaster told from both sides as it follows the star-crossed love between an absentee mine owner from Connecticut and a beautiful local waitress. *That You Remember* could not be more relevant today, carrying an important message for our own time. Deep characterization and important themes mark this engrossing novel as a major achievement—as well as a page-turner."
—Lee Smith, author, *The Last Girls*

"With this novel, Isabel Reddy has given us a landscape so dramatically rendered we can almost walk around in it. As thoughtful as it is evocative, *That You Remember* is an ode to a region, an elegy for a tidal wave of destruction, vivid and haunting, full of life and loss alike."
—Judy Goldman, author, *Child: A Memoir*

"The characters in *That You Remember* are decent, humble, salt-of-the-earth types who, frankly, don't much get written about. Isabel Reddy allows them their dignity, their struggles, their humanity. This is, for my money, what the novel does best of all—takes situations that we think are so foreign to us and reminds us of our shared humanity, of all the things that unite and link us: wishes for love, family, safety. It's a big-hearted and compassionate view of the world, and I think that's immensely valuable, especially now."
—Mark Sarvas, author, *Memento Park*

"A moving, imagined story of coal miners and their families leading up to a coal mine disaster in Appalachia."
—Gerald M. Stern, author, *The Buffalo Creek Disaster*

"In this strongly felt, highly compelling debut novel, Isabel Reddy finds romance in the hardscrabble world of Appalachian coal mining."
—Michael Shnayerson, author, *Coal River*

For Bill

Disclaimer

This book is a work of fiction. The extraction industries have resulted in disasters, and continue to result in disasters, both in the United States and around the globe. This novel is loosely based on historic events worldwide, but all names, places, specific incidents, and details of occurrences during historic events are a product of the author's imagination. All characters depicted here—including inspectors and other officials—and the specific actions and conversations attributed to them, are fictional.

Chapter 1

2019

My father never saved anything. That's why it surprised me when the large box arrived filled with his desk diaries. I lugged the box into the living room. When I was ready, I sat cross-legged on the floor to delve into this intriguing cache, written documents of my father's life, a bittersweet pursuit, at best. Tipping the box on end, I spilled out some books. Choosing the years that had relevance to me, I glanced briefly through a few of them. *Flight to Chicago. Dinner at the Sky Club.* Boring stuff. Not many minutes had passed when I noticed a small piece of torn paper on the floor next to my foot. It appeared to have come from the 1970 book. On it was written: *Sara, Sara, Sara.*

That was how this all began.

* * *

A couple of months later, I was standing at her front door. I breathed deeply the sweet, acrid smell from the English boxwood bushes bordering her brick house, the fragrance melding with autumn's decaying leaves. I was uninvited and probably the last person in the world that she wanted to see; that is, if I was even right about who she was. But everything in me wanted to stay. I had to get this final answer. I knocked.

In a moment she was before me, the door half open, shadowy dark wood beyond. I could see, even in her loose, short-sleeved summer dress, that she was strong. The thickness of her arms and the way she stood made me think that she gardened. Her gray hair was pulled back loosely.

"Yes?" she said.

Seconds ticked away. I needed to identify myself before she slammed the door in my face. I wouldn't say "Fitzgerald," my married name, the name I'd used for twenty years. My marriage was over. I'd have to use my maiden name to jog her memory.

"I'm Aleena Rowan."

Her face went white, and then magenta splotches began to spread like beet juice.

When my husband Stephen walked out, my life had collapsed around me. It was finding Sara's name on that piece of paper—not really paper, but what looked to be a torn piece of a paper placemat from a restaurant—that relieved some of my inner turmoil and fueled my need for more answers. Had my father only written her name once, I wouldn't have thought anything of it. Perhaps he was trying to get his pen to work and wrote his favorite name, or the name of an actress in a movie he'd recently seen, or the name of someone he was about to interview for a job. One *Sara* could have been anything. But *Sara, Sara, Sara*—that was so much more.

At first I looked at it as further evidence of everything I'd always accused him of. My father was such a mystery to me, and therefore easy to take potshots at. Sympathizing with my mother was more straight-forward, as she was the one who showed the suffering. He was always gone. Heartache and turmoil had riddled our house. I kept looking at the *Sara, Sara, Sara*. Seeing this paper with the dust of fifty years, could I really be so sure that it was more evidence that he was a schmuck, a jerk, a miserable SOB, like I'd called him in my head a million times?

Finding myself facing the shards of my marriage, the dome I thought so solid collapsing about me, I had to go to the back of the judgment line. Even without infidelity, I was painfully discovering the pieces of the puzzle that were on me, my role, what I did. I had perpet-uated my own fantasy, and in the end, it choked off all life. It was my refusal to be honest, to talk to Stephen, to try to make things better, that landed me here. I could now see the many ways of destroying love.

She waited for me to say something else: perhaps why I was stand-ing on her doorstep. I rallied my nerve, as I'd come too far to turn around now.

"Are you Sara, without an *h*?"

Now I was sure she'd slam the door in my face. She didn't answer, but I could see her struggle, going through the reams of files in her mind, over the past fifty years, the dead files, or maybe the files she'd hoped were dead.

"Are you related to Frank Rowan, of Rowan Coal?" she finally asked.

I told her he was my father, and she asked how I'd found her.

"I found a piece of paper with your name on it. Well, to be honest, just your first name. Sara without an *h*."

"Found it where?"

"In my father's desk diaries."

"You'd better come in."

Chapter 2

1970

The conical mountains of Appalachia around the eastern Kentucky coal mines bunch up haphazardly, as if pulled by a drawstring. Steep valleys crisscross this formidable landscape in serpentine tracks. Rivers and railroad tracks creep along the floor of the narrow valleys. In these valleys, claiming any bit of flat land, lie smatterings of towns known as hollows (pronounced "hollers"). Houses, churches, stores, and baseball fields are thrown out like a cup of Yahtzee dice, climbing the foothills until they are forced to give way to the vertical grade.

For centuries, families flocked to these hollows to settle in what were known as "coal camps." However, much had changed since those times. There were hard-earned improvements in terms of salary and benefits, and most houses were refurbished and expanded. Suffice to say that in 1970, neighbors knew one another and had a feeling of connection to their community. If someone had a flat tire and needed to get to work, they could count on a neighbor providing either a tire, a car, or a ride. Word traveled so fast that children who got into mischief were often scolded all along their walk home and scolded again when they met their parents. A Shangri-La it wasn't, but to many this was a happy time that never would return.

It was a comfort for Sara Stone to wake to the sounds of her brothers, coal miners in the Number 5, rustling in the kitchen like a couple of bears biffing and banging away. But this morning, to her surprise, when she attempted to look out the window next to her bed, she found that her curtain was frozen to the window frame. She pulled it free, releasing small shavings of ice. Dawn was a long way off on this leafless January morning. Through the dark and perhaps mostly from memory, she could make out the mountain's humpback silhouette, the spiky ridgeline of spruces, black against the smoky gray predawn sky. She loved her mountains. This little peek fortified her for the day. She pulled on a large sweater, a reject from one of her brothers, over her flannel nightgown, along with a pair of wool socks that had long ago lost their elastic, before heading into the kitchen.

"Darryl, I knew it was cold in my room, but today there was ice on my curtain! I thought you fixed that thing."

"The duct again? Oh, man. I'll look into it, Frisky."

"You can connect the damn duct, Sara. You got nothing to do all day," Benny said, a cigarette hanging from his mouth.

"I'm not going into that crawlspace. You know I have claustrophobia." She poured herself a coffee and blew into it, warming her face. "If I had to go into a mine, I'd croak in the first five minutes. I'd rather go in a rocket ship to the moon than go in a mine. But really, that wouldn't be much better."

Giving her a sympathetic smile, Darryl handed her a plate of scrambled eggs. "Then it's a good thing you don't have to."

Benny, at twenty-four, three years older than she was, was her constant nemesis. On the other hand, Darryl, four years her senior, was the opposite. He was one of those guys who was just there when she needed someone, like when she was carrying too much, or reaching for something from atop a chair.

When Sara was sixteen, her mother had walked out, no note or explanation. It was like the kingpin of the chain was gone, or the one thread that, when pulled, causes a complete unraveling. That's when Sara started questioning everything. She even began to wonder about her siblings. Clay, the oldest, and the only one not still living there, looked like their dad. But she, Benny, and Darryl didn't resemble their father, didn't resemble Clay, and looked absolutely nothing like one another. She had strawberry blonde hair, while Benny was dark-haired and dark-eyed and looked to be cut from a spool of wire. Darryl was brown-haired and soft as a teddy bear. Clay and his wife Linda Lee lived up the hollow toward Elliston. Their son, Baby Jake, who just had his first birthday, was the spitting image of his daddy, which was nice because Clay was the cutest of Sara's three brothers. So much for genotypes and phenotypes, which Sara had mostly taught herself because she'd missed so much of high school taking care of their dad before he died of black lung. Sara had learned, from experience, not to bring up anything to do with their mother. Darryl would quietly walk out and Benny would yell at her to "shut up about Mom, because she ain't here!" Whatever the truth, though, they were her brothers. And that was that.

Bonnie, Sara's dog, happily followed her to the table; Sara always let the dog lick the crumbs off the plate. Sara bent down to snuggle her.

"You ought to try it with a man. More fun than kissing that mangy mutt," Benny said.

She looked at him for a long moment, then said, "I'm not going to flatter you with a response."

It was just last month, on her birthday, that Brian had broken her heart. He'd come down from Louisville, where he was in his second year at the university. They were talking in the driveway and she was about to ask him if he could stay over when he broke up with her.

She had gone inside, making up an excuse as to why he left, even though it was only Aunt Betts who'd noticed he wasn't there. Knowing Aunt Betts, she probably read right through Sara's excuse of a headache. Sara wrote in her journal that night until her hand ached. She wrote until she realized that it wasn't so much that she loved Brian—she wasn't even sure if she did—it was just that he was the best thing that had come along. Being with him was comfortable. They'd go for walks, find a place to sit; he'd sketch and she would write.

"He's through with this holler," she'd said out loud, putting her journal between her mattress and the box spring. "And who can blame him?"

The subject of her dating again had come up, but everybody knew that Sara would never date a miner.

Just then the doorbell rang. Benny got up and leaned toward Sara. "Why don't you get dressed and put on some mascara? This red hat is from up north."

"In two weeks, he'll be the one wearing mascara," Sara said. She meant miner's mascara, the coal dust that bore into the skin around the eyes of miners.

Sara didn't have time to change even if she'd wanted to. In a minute, Benny walked back in with the new guy. "This is Griff's grandson," he said, then turned to the guy. "I'm sorry, man, what's your name again?"

"Pete. Pete Griffith."

"Hungry?" Benny asked. "Some joe?"

"Coffee would be great. My grandfather made me this big breakfast, then he poured gravy all over it and sat there to watch me eat it." Pete patted his stomach and made a full face. "I'm not used to heavy food in the morning. I'm a Cheerios kind of guy." He was a string bean under his baggy clothes but had a sweet baby face, which Sara liked. She pitied him, though, going into the pit. Pete joined them at the table, and Bonnie sniffed around his legs. Sara whistled for the dog to stop, but the dog seemed intent on getting attention from a new person.

"Oh, I love dogs," Pete said, petting Bonnie's head while she leaned her body against his legs.

Darryl extended his hand across the table. "I'm Darryl. And this is my sister, Sara."

Curious why anyone would move to their holler, Sara asked Pete where he was from.

"Lowell, Massachusetts. It's near Boston."

Benny handed him a mug of coffee and took a seat.

Sara looked at him with a smile, a smile that wasn't really a smile. She tilted her head as if wanting an answer, but her eyes were incredulous. "You left out of Massachusetts to come here to work in the pit?"

Pete's hair was windswept, some across his forehead, and some sticking up, like he just pulled off a sweater. He glanced at Sara, and then looked across the table toward Darryl and Benny, with a goofy smile spreading slowly across his face. "That's about the size of it."

"How's your grandfather doing?" Darryl asked, rolling his eyes at Sara.

"He's good. I'd never met him till a week ago. My mother and I didn't really . . . we never visited him. I like him though, and I feel really lucky to be able to come here and start a new job. He told me stories from his mining days, but he says that things are so different now with the machinery. He talked about undercutters and dynamite as if the older days were better, but I kinda doubt that."

Lighting a cigarette, Darryl said, "Wouldn't want to go back to dynamite and donkeys, with breaker boys picking stones."

Benny laughed. "Hand-loading and pickaxes. No way. But we could do with a couple of canaries. You can't disconnect a canary. Better than those good-for-nothing gauges we got."

"My grandfather said the continuous miner took a lot of jobs," Pete said, "but I don't know anything about coal mining. And I didn't want to ask too many questions. Came this far, so I can't lose my nerve now. He seemed happy to have me, which says a lot, and he didn't mind giving me a ride here."

Sara thought she saw fear in his eyes, but fear with willingness. A mixture of seriousness and courage. She was puzzled, and despite her desire not to like him, she was impressed.

"He tell you about the rats?" Benny asked, cupping his cigarette with his fingers as he lit it.

"Rats'll save your life," Darryl said. "Don't underestimate a rat."

"They got feelers on their tiny feet," Benny said, pointing his cigarette at Pete for emphasis. "Can feel things no human can detect."

In a mocking voice, Sara said, "When the rats run, *everybody* runs."

Pete burst out with a laugh, but quickly stifled it, looking around. No one else laughed.

There was a pause, which Sara hated. She chimed in with, "It was nice of your grandpa to drive you here. I've always felt a little sorry for him, up there in Davie Holler living all alone. And now come to find out he has family. I thought I knew just about everything there was to know about this holler."

Benny mumbled, "There's a lot you don't know about this holler."

Sara went on. "One time he was crossing the street with those spindly legs, looking like he could topple over if you breathed on him. Anyway, he did trip and almost fell. I think I said 'Jesus' or something, because it about scared me to death. Ooo, the look he gave me! I thought my cussing would do him in. Whew, he's got a stern side, and that's no joke."

Pete smiled. "Oh yeah, he reads the Bible every night. It's the only book in the house."

Sara began to gather the dirty dishes. "Does that bother you? The Bible reading, I mean?"

"Not one bit. He's already asked me to go to church with him, which I'm happy to do. One thing that does surprise me is how cold it is here." Pete chuckled. "I moved eight hundred miles south, and it's colder here than home."

"It's the mountains," Sara said. "Traps the cold." She scrutinized his hands, the soft skin on his long, thin fingers. "Nice hands."

Benny brought his chair down hard and put his cigarette out in the ashtray. "Baby's butt. Looks like we'll be stopping at Underwood's for a pair of White Mules."

"Blue Boys are better." Darryl pushed himself out of the chair, his stomach filling but not stretching his striped button-down shirt. "Didn't your grandpa loan you some gloves?" Pete looked confused. To Sara, Darryl said, "I'll pick up a clamp at Underwood's. That'll fix your heat duct."

While the brothers got their dinner buckets, Pete asked Sara, "Blue Boys and White Mules?"

"You'll find out."

"C'mon." He gave her a half smile.

She was about to carry the dishes in but put them down. "Gloves. You can't work in the pit without gloves. Miners go through a pair of gloves faster than we go through a gallon of milk, and that's fast. Mostly because Benny doesn't bother to use a glass." Her brothers were at the front door. "Better watch yourself today."

"What do you mean?"

Pointing to the front door, she said, "You're about to miss your ride."

"Whoops!"

Goofy guy, Sara thought. Then, as Pete left, she kissed the palm of her hand three times and blew across it toward the door, remembering what her mother would say:

"You always kiss a miner goodbye.

Chapter 3

The absence of songbirds wasn't unusual for a January morning. The birds wouldn't rise until the there was something to eat, so they stayed nested down, conserving their energy. When the three men walked to Benny's car, the only noise was the ever-present whining and groaning of the tipple. Fog snaked through the mountain ridges and the sky was a heavy gray-black blanket.

As Pete got into the backseat, Benny at the wheel and Darryl in the front passenger seat, he asked about the make of the car.

"A '64 Polara. Rebuilt the carburetor and put a new starter in it, and it cranks fine." Benny turned over the engine and it started right away. "See?"

"Yeah," Pete said. "I'm going to need a car. Never owned one."

"Oh, I can get you a 318."

"Yeah? What's that?" Pete asked.

Benny and Darryl looked at each other. Darryl said, "The size of the cylinders. A V-8. I have a '65 Dodge Coronet. It's a 318. It's a good engine. I bought it off a preacher, 109 thousand miles for 450 dollars."

"And you don't do a damn thing to it," added Pete. "Have you even changed the oil?"

At that point, they pulled into the parking lot of the Number 5 mine. Benny smoothly navigated the potholes, ice-crusted puddles, and piles of snow, as if he was afraid to get a single splash on his car.

Pete said, "I'm starting to worry."

Darryl looked back at him. "You don't seem like the worrying type."

"That's what worries me. I'm not the worrying type." He opened the car door but made no move to get out. "So, tell me something important. One thing. Like the most important thing I should know, just so I can live through the day."

Benny laughed. "Whatcha worried about? It's just a black hole—unless it catches fire, then it's a hell hole. But don't worry, you'll go quick. Oh, and don't be fooled. We bottom dwellers got manners, so get some toilet paper from the shower room to put on your shit so no one will step in it."

He walked off, still laughing.

"I can tell he's gonna be a true friend." Pete got out of the car with his dinner bucket and newly purchased White Mule gloves.

"You could do worse," Darryl said as they started across the parking lot. "You'll be on Donny Atkins's crew, which is lucky. You can trust him. Do whatever he says. And no drinking."

"Shit no. I don't really like to drink."

"Well, there's not much grass here. Hard to come by. But you gotta keep your wits about ya." Darryl stopped Pete. "One more thing," he hesitated, then waved it off. "Forget it."

"What? C'mon. There is something; Sara hinted at it. C'mon, tell me."

Darryl slapped his back. "You'll be fine, kid."

Pete pointed ahead to a low, dark hole on the side of the mountain, five feet in height and eight feet wide, framed with rotten-looking four-bys. "Is that the mine?"

"Yeah. That's the pitmouth."

Pete's courage returned and he gave a little laugh. "We go into that little place?" This was the big bad mine he'd been anxiously awaiting? He realized that he'd been expecting something grander, more ominous, something foreboding. Where was the giant, fanged mouth of a dragon?

"It doesn't look like anything," he said. "Looks like something me and my friends might have dug out when we were kids."

"Let me tell you something," Darryl said, turning to face Pete. "There's only one thing worse than a red hat ready to shit his pants with fear. Do you know what that is?"

Pete shrugged.

"It's a red hat with no fear. The office is over there," Darryl said, pointing. "They'll show you to the showers, lockers, and lamp house. That's where you'll get your cap, battery pack, and ID tag."

"ID tag?" This was sounding more like Vietnam every minute.

"Yeah." Darryl slapped him on the back. "How else will they be able to identify what's left? That is, if there's anything left to worry over."

Pete mumbled, "Thanks, friend. Maybe Vietnam would've been better."

"Uh, I'd keep that to myself. They don't take too kindly to draft dodgers around here. Get going. Donny don't wait for no one."

The next thing Pete knew he was on the mantrip, an open railcar with two long metal benches, sitting between Donny and another miner. A man in a white miner's cap, standing off to the side, gave a signal. As the thing started off at a pathetic crawl, Pete noticed that the rest of the miners had black caps. Pete's was the only red hat; he was told that he would have to wear it for a year, then pass a test before getting a black cap.

The mantrip entered the rocky underground world. As soon as the earth and all things familiar fell away, something cold smashed Pete in the face.

"What the fuck?" he shouted. He swiped toward the thing that had hit him, but there was nothing there.

Donny laughed. Donny Atkins was the section boss and operator of the continuous miner. He was skinny and withered-looking, his rugged face like a dried-up prune. But Pete saw a light in his brown eyes, and there was something about him that Pete found reassuring.

"It's the fans," Donny said. "They keep the air moving so we can breathe."

"Are you kidding? It felt like I was hit in the face."

Still laughing, Donny said, "I'm glad we brought you along. You're worth your weight in entertainment so far."

"You'll get used to it," said the miner on the other side of Pete. "Right there it's blowing about thirty miles an hour." He was an older guy and, Pete thought, had a sad look in his eyes, or maybe a look of worry, or just tiredness. "Half the time they ain't working." He gave a sort of pathetic grunt.

"That doesn't sound good." Pete's nervousness was extending past jitters in his legs and beginning to involve his stomach. "I guess I was kind of hoping to breathe all the time."

Donny asked, "So, you're Griff's youngin', right? From up north?"

Pete introduced himself. "From Massachusetts. Boston area."

"Boston? You're a Harvard man." Pete started to reply but Donny went on. "Okay, Harvard. Don't mind if I call you Harvard, do you?" Again, Pete started to speak, but Donny didn't wait for an answer. "Where you been working?"

Pete had been actively counting the dim passageways they passed in case he needed to find his way out. He was up to five, but he might have missed some. None of his previous jobs were even remotely relevant to this. He'd worked as a lifeguard, which was great for his social life—that is, his sex life—and then at a bookstore emptying boxes and stacking shelves. He knew not to mention those two jobs. For a brief time he had pumped gas, another good way to meet girls.

"Pumped gas," he mumbled.

Donny looked intent. "You work machines?"

"Not really."

"Know any electrical work? We do just about everything in the pit."

"Better warn him about bug dust, right, Donny?" the older miner said. "Bug dust will blow faster than gasoline."

Pete knew that he couldn't ask too many questions about everything coming his way, but this older guy seemed a better candidate for getting information. "Bug dust?"

"Yeah, coal dust. It'll work into every crack and pore of your skin, into your hair and nose and lungs. And your dreams. Just need a little orange spark from a cigarette to kill us all. No smoking in the pit."

"I don't smoke." Pete stuck out his hand. "Pete Griffith."

"Kenny Sheldon."

Pete noticed that Kenny's eyes weren't as red as some of the others' were. But he still had what looked like black eyeliner.

"You been mining long?" Pete asked.

"On Donny's crew for just two years. I was a motorman for twenty-some years. Shuttled things in and out. I liked it because I could get outside and have a smoke. I haven't had a cigarette in two years. The doctor said I got that empherzeema."

"How do you find your way out of here? I mean if you get lost."

Donny overheard that and laughed again. "Yeah, go on out that way." He pointed straight ahead, the way they were going. "Might be shorter, and you can bring us back some hamburgers. I'll take mine with fries."

Kenny explained that this was a room-and-pillar mine with crosscuts. They were going down the main tunnel, referred to as the mains, heading west. The crosscuts headed north–south and were called 1N, 2N, and so on. The pillars were columns of coal left to support the roof. Today they'd be mining in 7N.

"What are those carved-out spaces for?"

"Shelter holes. To get out of the way of a vehicle or a runaway tram. You know, a few years back, a miner dropped a tool on a frayed wire. They'd walked into a pocket of gas. Boom! Four men dead. If you want to worry, don't worry about getting lost. Some of them try to get lost, do anything they can to get out of work. If you want to worry, worry about burning up in a ball of fire. You heard about Farmington, didn't you?"

Pete realized then his short sightedness; in his usual leap-before-you-look way, he'd thought he could just waltz in, learn on the job. Maybe part of that was because he didn't want to chicken out. But how arrogant! There was already more to this than he'd expected, and the mantrip hadn't even stopped. He had minimized and underestimated the entire occupation. It was not only arrogant; it was dumb. Funny that Donny called him Harvard. The irony stung. He made a mental note to ask his grandfather about this Farmington thing. He mumbled, "Yeah, of course. Terrible."

Donny chimed in, "So if you don't want to see us all go the same way, then keep them trailing cables away from the continuous miner. That's your job today."

Finding a sympathetic ear in Kenny, Pete asked him how to use his self-rescuer. Kenny explained, saying it had about a day's worth of oxygen. "Longer if you breathe slow." Then he said, "And they told you about your ID tag? It's so—"

"Yeah, I've been told."

"Most things ain't under our control. Weather, for instance."

"The *weather*?" Pete laughed. "Now, how can there be a problem with the weather? There's no weather underground."

"Oh yes there is. To the rocks there is. And it's worse in the winter, with the cold."

Donny said in a surprisingly serious tone, "Rocks are alive. Don't forget it."

Pete looked around at the dark rock walls and ceiling, wondering if it was the temperature or the humidity they were talking about.

"The mountain feels the storms and pressure changes," Sheldon explained. "A drop in the pressure loosens the seals and cracks, and methane seeps out of them gas pockets. The silent killer."

Donny looked hard at Pete. "So, you got to stay alert. We rely on each other."

What surprised Pete even more than the complexities and dangers of underground mining was Donny's matter-of-fact attitude, his easy smile, and the light in his eyes. Yet there was nothing cavalier about him. It seemed to Pete that there was no other job in the entire world that would have suited this man better. It was like Donny knew how to look danger in the eye: somewhere along the way, they'd reached a truce.

"Donny, you ever even read that monitor?" Kenny asked.

Donny was picking breakfast out of his teeth. "When I remember."

Kenny turned to Pete. "The continuous miner's got a methane reader. Newfangled thing—the monitor, not the miner. The continuous miner has been around for a couple of decades. Anyway, Donny's supposed to cut the power if the methane is at one percent or higher. Isn't that so, Donny?"

"Don't matter because it don't go below two percent, no way. I never seen it at no one percent, much less lower."

"That's what I'm saying. Except when an inspector's coming. Then we jiggle things, if you know what I mean."

"Christ," Pete said. Two percent, one percent? None of it sounded good. Pete decided not to ask more questions; the answers provided little comfort. He was too far in to turn back. He'd save his questions for his grandfather. If he made it out alive.

The slow-moving cart chug-chugged farther into the deep. Pete had lost track of the many tunnels and passageways. Now they were passing pieces of junk and rust-covered equipment backlit by single lightbulbs, making them look like corpses. The mantrip slogged through pools of water covering the tracks. Pete half got up the first time they approached one, thinking the water would prevent their passage. But they went right on through. His mouth was sandpaper, and his bowels felt like someone was in there pushing around furniture. The other miners seemed to be enjoying themselves, making jokes, even standing up, jostling around like puppies.

Then Pete thought of an easy, straightforward question. "Donny, why was that guy back there wearing a white hat instead of a black one? I know mine is red because I'm new, but everyone else has black ones."

"He's the fireboss. Supervisors and operators wear white."

Answers led to more questions. "What's the fireboss do?"

"He's supposed to check the face for methane before the start of each shift. The face is where we'll be mining. My guess is he just takes a leak."

Finally, after about an hour, the mantrip came to a stop. Pete had one more question: "How far did we come?"

"Why? Leaving so soon?" Donny jumped down. "About four miles. All right, boys! Let's run some coal!"

The other miners started yelling and hollering. "Let's crush Hoot Owl! C'mon, you sons of bitches!"

Four miles into a mountain and, like 'Nam, Pete guessed, you had no choice but to stick with your battalion. He certainly couldn't stay home pumping gas or emptying boxes of books. He eased his way off the bench.

"Harvard, get this trailing cable." Donny pointed toward a cable the thickness of a python, connected to a mammoth orange machine with a long arm bearing a wheel with steel teeth, each two feet long and as thick as a man's leg. "That's your job. Keep that cable from getting under the miner."

Pete tried to move but the muck sucked at his boots. He noted a gluey white paste on the walls, swiped his finger through, and smelled it. Could that be from methane? Only a few lousy light bulbs on the walls. How could a mine—in 1970—be so dimly lit? Wasn't that a safety hazard? Their very lives depended on him chasing around a cable while slipping and sliding in the muck. He'd done some stupid things in his life, but he was beginning to think that this was the stupidest.

The black coal seam, a dark layer in an otherwise gray rock wall, looked to be only about two yards thick. *They're going to all that trouble for that little bit of coal?* Pete couldn't believe it. *Why not turn around right now and go out and light candles? To hell with electricity!* Plus, the insanity of chewing into the wall of a cave while you were in it. *How could any sane person be doing this?*

He said to a guy next to him, "Is that all the coal there is?"

"Each cut gives sixty tons of coal. You have a better plan?"

Pete saw one of the miners shooting the white stuff onto the walls. "What's that for?"

"Keeps down the bug dust. It'll save your life."

How could they do this, every day, knowing there were countless ways they could die? Pete was amazed. He couldn't understand their attitude—such resignation. He, on the other hand, was terrified. He looked at the sweating walls, the dripping roof, and tried desperately to find something especially dire or treacherous, some proof that would convince the group they were going to die and should all get back on the mantrip and exit the mine, pronto.

Donny started up the giant continuous miner and the confined space filled with black smoke and deafening noise. Pete attacked the black, slithery cable, wrestling it as if it were a live tiger. But there was no need for his exuberance because Donny wasn't doing anything. A couple of miners hung a tattered yellow cloth across a passage. Pete figured it would control the direction of the air toward the giant fans. Pete didn't know why Donny wasn't moving the machine, but he hoped it was a problem that would end this madness, at least for the day. He yelled to Donny, "Is there a problem?"

Donny laughed, pointing to the cable.

Pete yelled again. "I was just wondering why you're waiting here!"

Donny pointed up ahead and yelled, "Roof bolter. They got to pin the top."

Pete then picked out the sound of drilling from the other noises and saw a couple of men sitting on a rubber-tired vehicle, inserting metal posts into the roof.

Over the rumble of the idling miner, Pete decided to joke, but he actually meant it. "Can I go stand under that?"

Donny cracked up laughing. "You're funny, Harvard. Those are resin bolts, best in the industry." The roof bolter waved to Donny.

Moving the levers, Donny yelled, "All right, boys, let's beat the boneyard crew!"

Hoots, hollers, and catcalls filled the space. A miner adjusted the fans and Pete felt cool air across his face. The miners yelled, "Let's run some coal! Wahoo!" and, "Let's beat Hoot Owl!" The lighted hats scurried about their duties, fellow warriors in this war with the rock.

Donny maneuvered the levers, and a cloud of black smoke—pulverized rock—filled the small space. The giant metal teeth spun and clawed into the rock wall. The coal then shot out onto the first shuttle buggy, which, when full, would leave the mine for the tipple. Despite the dust, because his life depended on it, Pete yanked the cable while also ducking out of the way of the jerking machine. It went back and forth with no pattern or regularity, and Pete hung on with a wild energy he hadn't known he was capable of. He fought the cable, sliding around in the muck, while the giant blasting machine jerked four feet forward and three feet back. They went out of one cubbyhole into the next with only a few minutes of rest in between. Hours passed. Pete's eyes stung, his head pounded, and his throat burned. But he didn't notice. He also didn't notice that his fear was gone.

He was having fun.

Chapter 4

On the same day, six hundred miles away from Otter Creek Hollow, Frank Rowan grumbled to himself as he hunched over to board the little plane at Westchester County Airport to fly to Lexington, Kentucky. Things were still a little slow from the holidays, so he'd figured it was the best time to look into their newest acquisition, Otter Creek Mining. He dreaded it. Yet another glorified truck mine teetering on the edge of bankruptcy in a backwoods ravine. Vern and his feeding frenzies, leaving Frank to straighten them out and try to make them profitable.

He lit a cigarette as the small propeller plane shook down the runway for takeoff. At least his new waders had fit into his suitcase, along with his fly rod. If the hotel seemed decent, he'd stay the night and try out the waders on the Red River or its tributary. Otherwise he'd drive back to Lexington and stay there.

Frank Rowan worked at Rowan Coal, which had its main office in the Pan Am building in New York City and a satellite office in Goshen, Virginia. Rowan Coal also had interests in oil, transportation, and warehousing. Other than a summer stint in a coal mine, where he'd done mostly office work, Frank had no working knowledge of mining practices and protocols. After he'd graduated from Princeton, he'd worked for a year at one of Rowan's subsidiaries.

Why *should* he know about mining coal? Frank knew people, and he knew how to close a deal. *Catch 'em when they're asleep*. It was almost a game to him, one where losing was not an option. In fact, he really didn't care what he sold; it could be ballpoint pens, as long as he made money. Within five years of joining Rowan, Frank had become vice president, and just a year before he had become president, succeeding his uncle, Vern, who was now the chief executive officer. As CEO, Vern had relinquished oversight of day-to-day operations but kept ultimate control of the company. Yet the one thing Vern couldn't let go of was buying up small mining companies. In Frank's opinion, this was no longer a recipe for success.

Vern—Vernon Floyd Rowan—had started the company on a dime and a prayer. Before he'd even graduated from Columbia, he'd started his own transport and coal delivery business. It was a popular enterprise, with little to no start-up costs, and he sold it for a profit. From there, Vern learned to dream big, buy big, act big. By 1939, he had started a coal brokerage company, and was approached by a couple of big-shot businessmen who were seeing their stock in the Pennsylvania Coal Company plummet. They wanted him to take over the company, which was in debt to the Erie Railroad to the tune of eight million dollars.

Frank knew the history, how Vern and Frank's father, Francis Sr., consolidated and bargained their way out of debt. In less than five years they were able to purchase sixty percent of Alleghany Coal, giving Rowan 150,000 total acres of bituminous reserves. The postwar years were great. Vern conquered the bituminous coal demand for the steel industry as well as the electricity market.

Sadly, those years are over, Frank thought, as he looked through his little window in the plane. He could see rivers gleaming in the sun. He was pretty sure they'd passed the Delaware and the Susquehanna. But then some clouds prevented him picking out the Potomac. He checked his watch. They'd be landing in ten minutes.

Once in his rental car, Frank checked his map. He calculated the route to be roughly 150 miles to the south and east, mostly on small roads. He headed east on Interstate 64.

Patches of dark clouds contrasted with the frozen white sky. To the east and south, near the horizon, black clouds were forming. With any luck they wouldn't produce much snow. Oncoming coal trucks barreled past him, making his pathetic rental car shake. Frank hadn't noticed the make of the car, which interested him not one bit, but now he wished he'd gotten something heavier. Giant tipples jutted out of the mountainsides, their cantilevered trams and tracks like bones from a compound fracture. In Prestonsburg, the road got very curvy past Coal Run Village then on to the Otter Creek Mining Company. This was more backwoods than any of the other mines they owned, and Frank wondered how he'd ever convince Vern that you don't have to own a mine to buy and sell its coal.

After missing it twice, he finally found a modest and somewhat run-down white house with a sign outside that said "Otter Creek Mining Company." The neighborhood looked neat and well cared for. But he doubted if he could get a cocktail, and he began to rethink his plan to stay there. The waders could wait. Frank stepped on his cigarette in the parking lot and went inside.

The wood frame structure had a dank smell, mixed with stale coffee and tobacco, and the thick air was heavy with dust. Various chairs were scattered about, and a small selection of old framed photos hung on the wall. The calendar hung askew.

A short man with a toothy smile came around his desk and greeted Frank with an eager, outstretched hand. He had a formidable belly, and was dressed in pressed chinos and a gray wool pullover sweater.

"Bart Sweeny. You must be Francis Rowan. Welcome to Otter—oh, pardon me. It's now Rowan Coal. But you know that. Okay, welcome."

Frank shook his hand. "We're keeping Otter Creek Mining as a subsidiary. Nice to meet you." Frank gave the ancient wooden chair a shake before sitting, testing its durability.

Sweeny poured two coffees and handed him one. "Did you have trouble finding us? The sign is down. We're having kind of a bad winter."

Frank mumbled that it was not too bad. He was surveying the room, noting the bookcases filled with stacks of *Coal Age* magazines. Looking up, he saw that the ceiling was blackened around the heating vents.

"You heat with coal?"

Sweeny looked at the ceiling too. "I think they did—the former owners. Oil furnace now, but it's most likely in need of service. I was the fireboss. Got promoted when they cleared out. Never had a desk job, but it suits." He leaned back and swiveled in his chair, and to Frank he looked like a teenager left home alone for the first time. Frank guessed he was under thirty. His face looked baby soft, and his longish hair, almost to his neck, did nothing to improve Frank's opinion of him.

"I think I saw a motel at the corner. One-story brick building."

"Yes, that's Todd's. It's a motel and diner. One of the few places to eat around here, but the food is good. Predictable, he doesn't change the menu much, but good. I mean if you like meatloaf, pot roast, chili—that kind of thing."

"Book me a room, would you? Those clouds in the west might bring snow. I drove down from Lexington, and the last twenty miles were not clearly marked. I wouldn't want to try them in a fresh snowfall." He paused to light a cigarette. "I certainly hope I can get a cocktail."

"Just pay your dollar and you're in the club," Sweeny chuckled.

"Well, that's a relief." Frank asked to see the minutes from the Otter Creek board of directors meetings.

"Board of?" Sweeny made a sour face. "Well, the former owners ran kind of an informal operation, if you know what I mean." He reached for a box on the table behind him. "Hey, we got donuts here. Got a few jellies left. Want one?"

"No thanks. About the former owners?"

"Jim Simpson and Wes Curley. They were buddies who pooled their resources. No prior experience with owning a mine, which I know because they were both close friends of my father. At my house all the time. They had a construction company before this."

Frank looked hard at Sweeny. "No corporate records at all?"

Sweeny scratched his neck, then opened the top drawer of the desk. "These are the production records. Number 5 is our best. Tonnage is consistently high. Well, not with third shift. They're always having something go wrong. Simpson was forever threatening them. Well, just a few miners, he really had to ride their tails. Problems like coming in late, sitting out. But they also just seem to have bad luck; belt problems, electrical shorts, you name it. I don't get it. Now Donny's crew, they're great."

Frank reached for the binder, then began pacing as he read. His legs were stiff from the drive. All handwritten and hardly legible records. What a shoddy enterprise, worse even than he'd imagined. Vern had outdone himself, buying this truck mine. Frank returned the book, drawing on his cigarette and slowly blowing the smoke. "What's your background?"

"I have an engineering certificate."

"What kind of engineering?"

"Mining engineering. Got it at night school, and that's why they promoted me. I will work hard and do whatever I need to do to for this job."

"Well," said Frank, "I guess there's not a big selection to choose from, so we'll keep you as General Superintendent of Otter Creek Mining. By the way, the two former owners, why'd they sell?"

Sweeny leaned back in his chair, put his hands behind his head. "I couldn't say."

Frank figured they'd run out of money and couldn't keep up with the regulations. He leaned over and put his cigarette out in the ashtray on Sweeny's desk. "And before the Curley and whoever it was?" Frank asked.

"Started way back as Henderson Coal. Went belly-up in the early '60s. Simpson and Curley bought it and changed the name to Otter Creek Mining."

"Tell me about the tipple."

Sweeny took a sip of his coffee. "Sir?"

"The capacity. There's a number of underground mines here, and we have strip plans. Any upgrades over the years that you recall? Any problems?"

The tipple was where water, under a terrific force, washed and separated the coal from shale, slate, and debris, creating massive amounts of waste, both in solids, known as slag, and black liquid, called slurry. To handle strip mining, the tipple had to handle a massive increase of rock and debris. For most of these small mines, the tipples hadn't been upgraded in decades.

Sweeny slowly shook his head. "It's the same tipple we've always had. As far as I know, Curley and them used to dump the slurry into Otter Creek. The politicians put a stop to that. Gotta save those trout." He laughed. Frank did not.

"That was probably in '48 with the Federal Water Pollution Control Act."

Sweeny continued. "Yeah, exactly. So they started the gob pile, up past the Number 5. It is a little big." He slurped his coffee. "And the tailings impoundment, well I guess you could say it's a little big too."

"Give me the whole story. When was it built? How big is it?"

"Probably started around '60, before my time here. But by '68 it filled up, so they started another a ways up." He sipped his coffee again. "This one is big. Real big."

"And who designed these impoundments?"

"I wouldn't know." Sweeny was looking at some papers that had been under the production binder. He quickly put them back into the drawer. "Curley and Simpson, I guess."

While pacing, Frank had still been watching him. "Listen, we purchased this mine with strip ops in mind. We can anticipate getting a strip permit, am I right?"

"Well, I'm new in this position."

Frank sat down again.

Sweeny shifted in his chair. "Of course, nowadays everybody's got a hand in the pot. All these new laws and rules, they've got the system so jammed. You know the expression 'too many cooks'?" He scratched his head. "Well, I like to say it's too many kooks!" His smile showed tobacco-stained teeth. "The Kentucky Water Resource Commission, the Department of Natural Resources, and the Public Service Commission. We're waiting on a big powwow. With this new Coal Act, they're all the time looking over your shoulder."

"What was the upshot from the geological inspection from the Feds?"

"Something about a spillway, as I recall. And raising the haul road. I can't see stopping production for that. Could take months in good weather, and longer in bad. I don't think you'd want that."

It definitely smelled fishy. Frank lit another cigarette, and pointing with it, said, "By the way, what is that?"

"What is what?"

"I'm referring to that folder from under the binder that you put back in the drawer."

Sweeny froze. Frank had suspected he'd cave. Instead, a steely look came over his face, and his small eyes narrowed.

Frank had trained his own hunting dog, Sugar Plum, a German shorthaired pointer. First he'd used apples. The dog retrieved the apples, which taught him not to bite down too hard on what he retrieved. In the field, though, Sugar had trouble letting go of the bird, whether pheasant, duck, or quail. No use repeating a command and wasting your breath; if you do, you're just teaching the dog not to do the very thing you want him to do. Frank would wait, his hand right next to the bird, grasped in the dog's mouth. Saliva would begin to drip. Frank wouldn't move. Eventually the dog would drop the bird, and that's when Frank would say, "Drop. Good drop!"

Neither of them moved. After a few minutes, Sweeny opened the drawer and handed over the folder.

It was a Federal Notice to Comply, dated 1969. Rowan Coal had a new engineer on board, and Frank wondered, with the changeover, if perhaps Vern had made this purchase sight unseen, with no engineer's inspection at all.

"And this is because the refuse water is filling the streams, is that right?" Frank handed it back. "Do you have other notices like this?"

Sweeny rustled through the desk, pulling out other papers. "It's not the creeks this time. It's the dam they're squawking about."

"The dam? Give it to me in a nutshell, will ya?"

"I'd say the tipple produces about eight hundred to a thousand tons a day of refuse rock, solid waste, that goes on the gob pile. The liquid refuse, black water, comes to about four to five hundred thousand gallons a day."

Raising his voice, Frank said, "I don't mean all that gobbledygook. What's the problem with the dam?"

His mouth contorted. "It's a little bigger than industry standard. Made of bulldozed tailings. Very solid, that's for sure. Honeycutt goes over them twice daily. He's our dozer operator." He scratched his neck and paused. "As far as I know it wasn't much of a problem until this Coal Act."

"This is serious, right? The notice to comply."

"No teeth."

"Just how much water in this impoundment?"

"About a half a mile."

Frank jumped in his seat like something bit him. "Half a mile!"

"Look, I wasn't in charge of anything. I had nothing to do with it." He shook his head. "It's never been a problem. Kind of nice, really. In the summer, they take their boats out on it."

Frank had had enough. He stood and so did Sweeny. "Now you listen very closely. Every correspondence, no matter how insignificant, from the PCS or the PSC or the DNR or FDR. I don't care if it's from the queen of England, I want to see it. Is that clear?"

Sweeny opened his lips slightly. "Yes, of course. I—"

"I want every piece of correspondence copied and sent to me."

Frank would need to get their lawyer and engineer on this. The situation was worse than he ever could have imagined.

He got in his car, checked his map, wanting to follow the Levisa Fork, then find a smaller tributary where he could fish. He found a small dirt road, perhaps an old logging trail, where he parked. There he found a path leading down to the river.

Time to try out his new waders.

Chapter 5

About the time Pete was mucking with the cable and Frank was boarding his plane, Sara had finished with her housework. It was only nine in the morning and the hours yawned before her, with nothing to do and no one to talk to until five. Her usual activities were: hanging out with her sister-in-law, Linda Lee; going to Underwood's General Store for some ground beef and cans of Manwich; or borrowing a car to go shopping. But stores didn't open until ten, Linda Lee was usually busy, and she didn't want to walk the gauntlet of out-of-work miners who also had nothing to do, sitting clumped together in rickety chairs at Underwood's.

Sara decided to go fishing. Never mind that it was January. She loaded up her backpack with a sandwich consisting of the remaining breakfast bacon between two pieces of white bread with mayo, an apple, a jar of water, and her container of frozen caterpillars. She'd collected the caterpillars the previous May from the catalpa tree in their backyard. Those fuzzy things could eat every leaf on the tree, so she figured she was doing a service by killing them. With a rake she'd knocked them off the branches laden with white blossoms, and they'd fallen like rain. When she was younger she'd climbed trees all over town, climbing to the smallest branches until the wind made the tree sway and she felt like the worm on the end of a fishing line. When people drove by, they'd give her a wave and go back to whatever they were paying attention to. Nothing unusual about Sara Stone up a tree.

With her peacoat bought at the army and navy store, her backpack, and her fishing pole, she headed out, but at the last minute she went back for her copy of *Walden*, thinking, *If my hands aren't too cold, I'll read it by the river.*

The air was bracing as she shut the door to the empty house and to the loneliness that at times felt suffocating. The blanket of night was retreating, and the sun was licking the top of the mountains with gold. Sara turned left on Otter Creek Road, where woodsmoke from chimneys rose and lingered, imparting that warm, cozy, family feeling that she longed for. Thin layers of ice and white crusty patches lined the banks of Otter Creek, but winter was not enough to stop the flow. The tops of bushes had a dusting of snow, making them look like powdered sugar-frosted cupcakes, and the roof of the Methodist church had snow in the corners and on the north side. No one had been inside the sanctuary since Sunday, but they'd be in there that evening for their Wednesday night service of songs and praise, making enough heat to seep through the leaky insulation and melt the stubborn patches of snow from the roof.

One of her neighbors stopped to ask her why she wasn't wearing her hat. Sara smiled and waved, knowing Mrs. Cantrell was right. The temperature felt like it was in the twenties.

Sara loved fishing, but she hated catching fish. She hated killing them or even hurting them, and catching them often meant both. That glassy eyeball staring, the flipping and flopping in distress, the slimy gills and poking scales, the breathing slowing down to no struggle, the fish giving up. She'd work hard and fast to remove the hook and throw it back, where it would lie near the top of the water on its side. Holding her breath, she'd wait. Most times, life would zing through its body and it would disappear into the depths; then she'd exhale.

Down the road she came upon the three Morgan boys. The older two boys were waiting for the school bus, but Mickey, the youngest, was perched on the split rail fence, swinging his legs in the cold air. The bus pulled up and Nancy Monroe, the driver, leaned out the window. "Mickey, why's your coat unzipped?"

He cried, "I want to go to school!"

His two older brothers climbed into the bus.

Grinding the gears, Nancy shouted, "Go inside, Mickey! It's freezing out here."

"When is it my turn?" He yelled at the departing bus.

Sara walked over. "It won't be long, Mickey. Find yourself a book. You can learn whether you're in school or not. And if you get a book and read it, you can tell me the story."

He jumped down, complaining that he didn't know what book to get.

"Get Miss Bickford to help you find a book. Maybe *Stuart Little*. He's a mouse who lives with a family in New York City. He's very small but he has adventures."

The little boy ran into his house, brimming with excitement. It was dazzling to see a kid's mood change in a matter of seconds.

From an empty field, Sara turned onto an overgrown logging road that ended at a footpath that zigzagged up a steep ridge. The familiar sounds of her holler—the low roar of the tipple, its whining steel cables, the groan of coal trucks downshifting—were now blocked by the belly of the mountain. Only one sound found its way around every obstacle. She could always hear it, as if it were lodged in her ears, as if it were coming up from inside the earth, as if it were the hum of the sun and moon. It was the percussive metal-on-metal clacking, squealing brakes, and that aching, mournful horn of the coal train. It pushed into her chest. It followed her. It punctuated her life. It teased her with its allure of going.

Sometimes, though, in the heart of a night, maybe on Christmas, or in a bad snowstorm, or when there was a strike, a heavy silence would awaken her. Obedient to its summons, she'd go outside. It was as if a vacuum was placed near her ears, sucking any sound away. Her ears quivered for a noise, as eyes in a dark room search for light.

Other noises were less welcome, like sirens. When they happened, everyone stopped. Cars stopped, shoppers stopped, storekeepers froze in midsentence. Phones jangled. Little groups of people formed out of nowhere. Panic rippled and spread. People running. Vehicles speeding toward the Number 5, where everyone knew someone. Worry-stricken children cringing in their fearful mothers' arms. Whispers while waiting: *Was it a rockfall? Gas explosion? Water burst?* And the question, like a lightning bolt shot through the minds of wives, mothers and fathers, sisters, brothers, daughters, and sons: *Did I kiss my miner goodbye?*

The holler huddled.

Sometimes it ended in a sigh of relief. Other times the collective horror of sheet-covered bodies.

That was why, so long ago, Sara had sworn she'd never marry a miner.

When she was eighteen, her father had died of black lung. He'd spent a year at Pine Valley Hospital, and during that year, her mother had left without a note; packed up and left during the night, leaving only her bathrobe, the bathrobe that now hung in Sara's closet. It used to have her mom's scent, but that was gone now too.

Years before she'd left, though, Sara had already taken on the chores, the cleaning, the wash, and even dinner preparation (however simplistic) that her mother, who loved to lay on the couch, failed to do. And it gave Sara a feeling of accomplishment, even joy. When her father came home from the hospital, and for that year that he survived, she took on his care. But after he passed, the chores became loathsome. She was cleaning up after Darryl and Benny, the smell of their sweat, the dirty ashtrays and beer cans and pull tabs all over the house. Sara lived there too, but sometimes she felt invisible, like someone at a bus station waiting to leave. She tried to fight back with flowers in warm weather months, washing and ironing the curtains, opening windows, and constant cleaning, but her home still felt to her like a mixture of a locker room and the Sunday morning after a wild party.

Today, though, she didn't have to be there.

The trail was thick with fallen trees and limbs. Last summer's precocious thorny branches were sharper in the winter without the protection of leaves. Wobbly, ice-covered rocks could cause a sprained ankle. Each step was a tentative experiment rather than a commitment, and she often wedged her feet between two rocks for stability. But it was all worth it when she reached the flat ridge, where she quickened her pace for the last half mile or so before making the descent to the Levisa Fork River.

At the river, she cast her line out, white against the black water, with the partially frozen caterpillar dropping into the current. Fishing was like a bet, a wager, a hope thrown out onto a surface of darkness, with the possibility it would come back with a prize. This was what she liked, the nothingness and the hope, cleansing her lungs and head by the river. It slowed her breathing, relaxed her. She enjoyed the solitude. It resonated with her deep well of optimism of which she was still unaware.

Often she would sing. Not words, not a song, just tones. These tones emerged with a life all their own. She never knew what would come out. She gave herself to it, became a channel, emptying her worries and her mind into the song. Her voice then followed the song, alone there with no one to hear, no one to criticize. She sang until she felt one with the water and trees. She sang until she didn't know where she ended and everything else began.

After a few hours of fishing, Sara, who was wearing no watch, looked up to guess the time. Some sunlight still caught the tops of the pines, so she guessed that it was a little after midday. She'd eaten her sandwich hours ago. Under a hemlock tree she found a dry place to sit. She breathed on her hands to warm them. A chipmunk chattered above her, making some debris fall on her head.

"Hey, bud, I was here first," she said, but he was undeterred and chattered on, his little body quivering with the effort, shaking the bough and dropping more needles on her. She was obviously a little too close to his nest, and she didn't mind letting him win. As she got up, she heard a branch snap. She froze. A couple of crows called. Then she heard the rustling of dry leaves. She grabbed her backpack and hugged it to her chest.

Sara knew that woods are never silent. There are always noises. Animals rustling, their sounds echoing. Birds forage, hopping around, scratching and kicking under leaves for insects and worms. A single squirrel can make a good bit of noise. Sara hadn't yet determined the source of the noise she'd heard, so she waited, motionless. Another few minutes and she'd be able to distinguish the difference between a human walking and animals foraging, the stops and starts of deer or squirrels or foxes. Their noises were intermittent, irregular, erratic. Human footsteps were deliberate and rhythmic. She looked up for the chipmunk, but he was gone. There was now no doubt. The steps were those of a human.

Sara and her brothers had often hunted in the woods around Levisa Fork, looking for deer and turkey, and if they were lucky, woodcock, which were the hardest to find. They brought her along because she could spot the game without scaring them. She could find the turkeys in small groups foraging together, the woodcock with its jerky, back-and-forth pecking, blending so well with its surroundings that her brothers kept saying, "Where? Where is it?" She was always the first to hear the distant croak of the pheasant. Her brothers had nicknamed her Frisky because she was quick and lively and tireless. In all the times she'd been here, alone or with her brothers, she had never seen anyone else.

This person, whoever they were, must have come up from the bridge. There was a small parking area, and a footpath to the river, but it was hard to find unless you knew where to look. Over the years, the only people who'd known to park there were teenagers, who went there to do what teenagers do. Sara had never been one of them. Fending off some pimply-faced guy's wandering hands wasn't her thing. Besides, there was little time left after her chores and caring for her father.

She reviewed in her mind the various people who could be way out there in the woods. She wondered about Mimi Blackstone. Mimi gathered wild herbs and mushrooms, but nothing grew here in the winter. It was probably a hunter, which did nothing to ease her anxiety. Too late to run; she'd have to face this.

A second later, from under a cedar bough, emerged a man carrying a fishing rod. He wore a funny vest with hooks all over it, a red ball cap, and ridiculous green rubber boots up to his thighs. He was good-looking though, which surprised her.

"Damn!" she said, with her hand on her chest. "You gave me a start."

"I didn't mean to scare you," the man said, carefully putting down his long fly rod and shoulder bag.

Out of breath, she asked, "Who are you?" It came out as more of an accusation than a question.

He gave a little laugh. "Well, if you're surprised, that makes two of us." He held out his hand. "Frank Rowan. And you?"

Ignoring his hand and his question, she said, "You've been fishing? Well, I'm glad to know I'm not the only one who fishes in the winter. This is kind of an out-of-the-way place. How'd you find it?"

"The usual way, as it happens. I took that logging road and then found the pull-off spot and from that I found the trail. I was just walking up the river looking for good places to cast."

"Not an easy trail."

"You're right. A deer path mostly." He looked around. "So, no one's here with you?"

She was trying to figure him out. He seemed friendly enough. A handsome, friendly fisherman, but not your ordinary fisherman and definitely not local. She gave a shrug in response. "How is it you know your way around in the woods so well?"

"I guess from my years of hunting. Who parks up there?" He tilted his head in the direction of the pull-off.

"Teenagers, mostly. But they don't go into the woods too far. Some don't get out of their car." She blushed a little. Frank gave a smile of understanding. He seemed about Benny's height, but older. Maybe older than Clay, who was thirty-two. From his bag, he pulled out a thermos and offered her some coffee. She declined.

"Catch anything, Miss—uh—"

"Sara." She thought a moment and then decided he seemed nice enough. "Sara, without the *h*, Stone. No, I haven't caught anything today. Too cold, I guess."

"Why no *h*?" He poured himself some steaming coffee.

"I guess Mama wanted to save me the bother of having a silent letter at the end of my name. Her name's Claire, with an *e* at the end. But that's just a guess, because I never thought to ask her and now I can't ask her because she's gone."

"I'm so sorry."

"Not dead. Just gone." Sara gave a shrug, and stared at the river. After a minute she looked back at him, then pointed at his boots. "Expecting a flood?"

"They're hip waders. I admit they are a bit much for this river. I have a salmon fishing trip coming up in June, on the Miramichi, and wanted to try them out."

"The mirror what?"

"A river in New Brunswick." Then, as an afterthought. "In Canada." He pulled a trout out of his shoulder bag. "Caught this today."

Sara noticed his dimples, kind of sweet and childlike, along with the small gap between his front teeth. "Is that a brookie? I've never seen one that big. Where'd you catch it?"

"Half a mile back, in the big pool under the falls. Big for a brook trout—looks to be about eight or nine inches." He deposited it back in his bag. "What are you using for lures? I imagine with your casting rod you're getting catfish or bass."

"Lures? I take it you mean bait. I use the caterpillars from our catalpa tree. We get redhorse suckers, hornyheads, sometimes creek chubs." She walked around the small clearing and tossed a stone into the river. He took out a cigarette and offered her one, but she shook her head.

"Where are you from?" she asked, turning to him again. "I know you're not from around here."

"I'm here on business, from New York. Well, actually I live in Connecticut, and commute to New York. I don't often—"

"Business? Oh no!" she said, with a start. "You're a coal operator!"

"Guilty." But he looked amused, and took a long drag on his cigarette. "C'mon, now. Is that really so bad?"

"In this holler? Are you kidding? I could get fried alive just for talking to you. I hate to think of what my brothers would do if they saw me talking to you right now." Pacing now, she added more casually, "Course, I personally have nothing against operators. But I'm not like other people in my holler." She turned and put her hands on her hips, with a stern look in her eyes. "I hate everything to do with coal."

"I can easily believe you're not like other people in Otter Creek, but I am a little surprised to hear your position on coal. I doubt if there are a lot of others in your county or even in Kentucky who'd share that position."

Sara chose a rock to sit on, and Frank did likewise, although his rock was too small for him and it wobbled, and his knees were bent like a grasshopper's.

"Well," she continued, "that's true. Not many do share my opinion and it's not an opinion I advertise."

"Do you like electricity?"

"What do you think?"

"Then you like coal."

Sara tried to hide her smile. "Got me there, I guess." Leaning back on the tree behind her, she said, "All right, then. I don't like coal *mining.*"

Crows had landed in the trees around them, cackling. Frank looked up and said, "Might be a hawk, or an owl. Probably a hawk at this hour."

She didn't notice a hawk, but she did notice that the sun had dropped. Long silver rays were shining on gray tree trunks. She asked him the time. He told her it was 2:40. She didn't have to be at work until five.

"The operator now," she said, "Mr. Sweeny. He isn't so bad. I guess you know him?"

"Well, I could hardly call it knowing him, but I did meet him today." Frank took off his cap and ran his hand through his hair. His dark hair was short, his face tanned. "Do you—are you related to any miners?"

"About everyone I know works in the mine in one way or the other."

A few minutes passed and neither of them spoke. Then she asked, "Did you see those big falls up yonder?"

"Yes, I heard them before I found them. Beautiful."

"I love those falls."

"Yeah?"

"Yes, it's the Big Hole. That's what we call it. Our swimming hole. My brothers and I go there in the summer, and I go right underneath the falls. It pounds on my head with cold, blasting water, but it doesn't hurt. Chases away my worries."

"What could worry your pretty young head?"

"Oh, I get it." Her eyes hardened as her face tightened with tension. "You don't think I have worries? Of course, because we're all *hillbillies* here, I presume?"

"Pardon me, young lady. That's Kennedy you're talking about, not me."

"Well, you said I have no worries. What did you mean, then? You think my biggest worry is how to find the outhouse!" She got up and started marching around.

"Look." He stood too. "I don't think anything of the sort—not in the least. And I had no intention of insulting you. Quite the opposite."

She stopped. "The opposite!"

"I was trying to be nice, but I admit, it may have sounded patronizing. I do apologize. Everyone has worries, of course they do. No doubt about that." In a quieter voice, he said, "I hope you'll accept my apology."

This was a new experience—a man apologizing. She made a mental note to look up "patronizing," but decided to believe him. There was a low branch, and she pulled it toward her, examining the curled translucent leaves.

"I worry about my brothers every day," she said.

"Your brothers are miners?"

"All three work in the Number 5. My oldest brother, Clay, got promoted recently. He's a roof bolter now. Better pay."

"Do you work?"

"I wait tables at Todd's." She stripped the leaves off the branch. "I wonder why these leaves don't fall off like all the others. They stay on sometimes till the new ones come out in the spring."

"Beech trees," Frank said. "They have high levels of tannic acid. It's true for oaks and ironwoods too."

"How do you know about that? I thought you were a *coal operator.*"

"Now maybe it's you who's insulting me."

She laughed a little. "Hmm, well, you might be right."

"I took dendrology, a course in tree identification, in college. It was my favorite course. We'd pile into these cattle trucks, on the floor in the back, and then go to the woods. My professor would save me till the last and if no one else got the answer he'd call on me. I always knew the answer. It just stayed with me. For the final exam we had a bunch of twigs on our desks. One was the American beech, *fagus grandifolia*— we also had to learn the Latin names. It has lance-shaped buds, and the bark is smooth and gray like the sand on a beach. It's often the tree that lovers carve their initials into. Little do they know it hurts the tree."

"I've seen that, but I didn't know that it hurt the tree." She scrutinized him, then took a few minutes before speaking. "How old are you?"

"Well, you've no qualms about being direct. How old do you think I am?"

"Oh, I don't know." A chilly wind blew the tops of the trees and the cold filtered down. Sara buttoned her coat. Shadows were lengthening through the woods, and the sky was turning a milky apricot color. She had to be at work, but there was something interesting about this man. She looked at his boots and smiled. "But I'll tell you one thing: you fall into that river with those boots on, and they'll find you a mile down river if they find you at all." She chuckled. "Face down."

"You got me there, Sara without the *h*." He smiled. "I'm thirty-six."

"Are you, like, the owner of Otter Creek Mining or something?"

"Something like that, yes. But it's owned by Rowan Coal now. By the way, how old are *you*?"

She ignored the question. "What do you mean, 'something like that'? You're either the owner or you're not."

They were standing on the riverbank watching the water.

"I'm not the owner, but I work for Rowan Coal in Manhattan. We just acquired Otter Creek Mining as a subsidiary."

"Huh." Sara was trying to piece together what she'd learned about this man. She would have thought a man like that, an operator, wouldn't give her the time of day. But Frank was the opposite. He seemed interested, genuinely interested in her. He was in no hurry to leave. He hunted and fished. And there was nothing creepy about him. "I'm twenty-one. I heard once that 'old' is fourteen years older than you are."

"So I'm old, is that right?"

"Maybe."

"Are you married, Sara? I don't see a ring."

"Nope. No ring on my finger. No way." Then she changed the subject again. "I recall hearing that Otter Creek Mining sold out. Why haven't I seen you at Todd's?"

"It's a recent acquisition. Just got here this morning." He lit another cigarette and, with a long exhale of smoke, said, "So, you're a waitress, huh?"

She threw a stick into the river. "And just what do you mean by that?"

"Well, I guess there aren't many options around here. But—"

She turned toward him. "But what?"

"It's just that you seem to be a very intelligent young woman."

"A lot of people would kill for my job."

"Of course. I think it could be a useful stepping stone."

"Stepping stone! I'll tell you what, you really are insulting me now."

Frank looked concerned. "I hope you understand that I had no intention of insulting you. In fact, I think waitressing would be a good thing, a way to make a good wage while going to night school, perhaps. Plenty of smart women go to night school and then get a good career. There are so many possibilities. You could get a job in something you're interested in. You're interested in fishing and the outdoors; you could find a job at an outdoor recreation company, or you could work for the Audubon Society."

"How many outdoor recreation jobs do you think there are between here and Lexington? And that's two and a half hours away!" Her throat clamped up, and she felt the flush in her cheeks. "Anyway, who are you to tell me how to live my life? First of all, you just met me. Second, it's not that easy."

He looked at her. "I'm not saying it'd be easy. You might have to move. But most things in life aren't easy, at least the things worth having."

Neither spoke for a few moments. At last, she looked away. "You're right. I do hope to leave the holler someday. Maybe get a job in a city or something."

Sara sat down again and leaned back against the tree, arms around her knees. Talking like this left her feeling that something big was lying there on the ground, and it had come from her chest and left a hole. She wanted it back. Yet his face looked kind, his eyes interested. She hadn't decided whether Frank was kind or rude. Maybe both.

"I don't know why we're talking about this," she said after a moment. "It's not really any of your business."

"I'm just trying to be nice."

"Nice! They might have taught you about trees in college, but you missed the course on manners."

"That I did." He sat on a different log. "You don't learn manners in college. Let's see, you're twenty-one? If you strike out, get a job in a city, and go to college or night school, you'd have so many options. And, I might as well add, so many suitors. I'm sure you have them lining up already."

"Just skip off to a city. Right. So simple. There's nothing simple about it." But she thought about Pete. It was exactly what he'd done. He had a grandfather at least. But she had her aunt and uncle in Lexington.

"No, you're right. It wouldn't be that easy. The money, I guess, is the most challenging part. Maybe you could get a scholarship. And work for your living expenses."

"Frank, do you know what a kettlebottom is?"

"I think I've heard the term. Why?"

"Bug dust?"

"Yes, I know about that. I worked in a mine, at least for a summer."

"Then you know about miner's mascara?"

"What's your point?"

A recurring dream had haunted her for years. She was on a dirt road in a long white wedding gown. No cars, no people, no noise, no groom even. Just her, in a clean white dress, all alone in a dust-brown world. Her nightmares were stronger than her dreams.

"Do you know what it's like to have a dream that will never come true?" she asked.

"What is your dream?"

She stood and walked to the edge of the river. "Why don't we drop it?"

Frank walked near to her. "Sorry, maybe it's not my business."

She turned to him, and they were very close. "My dream is to get as far away from coal as possible."

"Dreams—I suppose I don't put much stock in them. After college I went to work for my uncle, and I got married." He tossed a stick into the river, watched it get sucked away. "Both held promise, but they haven't quite turned out the way I thought. I just try to focus on my little corner."

She stared at him. "But in your corner, you've got power. You're the owner of the company."

"Not the owner, not at all. There's a lot I can't control."

"You've more control than we have. You don't know what it's like to live here. Kettlebottoms drop out of the roof of the mine. Crush a miner in a second. The worry every morning when you see them leave, not knowing whether you'll see them again. You live in New York, Frank, and you don't live under the dams."

"The filtration ponds?"

She sneered at him. "The Big Lagoon is right over our heads!"

"They're all over Appalachia. Nothing at all unusual."

"Have you even seen them?"

"Not yet."

"Bet that Sweeny didn't tell you about the flood either."

Wind clicked though the branches. "I just met Sweeny today. He couldn't tell me everything. What about this flood?"

"It's not that it was so bad. It's what could happen in the future."

Frank looked concerned. "They're inspected regularly."

"Yeah, by the dozer operator."

"Have *you* seen them?"

"Are you kidding? And get arrested for trespassing? But I live downstream from them. We all do. Whereas, *you* go home to New York, or Connecticut, or wherever you live."

"Well, I'm staying at Todd's Motel tonight, so I'll be downstream too."

The cold was turning her back into a washboard. She pulled her coat tighter around her. "I have to go to work. I'm going to be late as it is."

"Sara, I've enjoyed meeting you," Frank said in a conciliatory tone, "and I plan to look into these impoundments that you're talking about."

She wasn't sure if she could trust him. Yet he seemed like he listened. He seemed nice, and maybe she could influence him to do something about the dams. "Could I get a sip of that coffee before I go? When the sun dips below the ridge, it really cools things off." He poured her the remaining coffee in the cup that also served as the thermos lid.

She drank the warm coffee, and handed him back the lid. "Thanks."

"You're welcome. You said you're going to be late for work. Can I give you a ride? My car is just up there on Route 4."

With a dubious look, Sara said, "Frank, not if you want to save your life and keep my brothers out of the penitentiary. If they found out, they'd kill you." She began to leave, but turned and said, "I guess I'll see you at Todd's?"

"I'll be there."

"Pretend you don't know me."

Then she disappeared up the trail.

Chapter 6

Sara ran the whole way back, partly because of how late she was, but mostly because she felt like a gazelle, a flying weightless deer, a nymph, a person freed of gravity. It was as if she could almost leave her body, take flight. She was still Sara Stone: loser, lost cause, lonely, homely, small-breasted (Benny used to say "raisin" when she walked by), yet she was different, because something inside of her had been released from a dungeon so desperately dark, a prison of isolation so fathomless and foreboding that even she hadn't the courage to admit it to herself. She sensed more than saw, as she rounded the corner into her driveway like a winged creature from another world, a few heads turn as she flew by.

Todd's was a long, one-story, brownish-red brick building constructed against a sheer rock mountainside. It had looked dingy from the day it opened. The "M" was worn off the painted wooden sign so that it read, "Todd's otel and Diner."

Pete was the first to plow through the door, having survived his first day as a coal miner. Donny came in next, greeting Sara with, "You're a pretty sight for this sore man's eyes."

"That's good because I haven't looked in a mirror all day."

"I'm famooshed." Pete looked happy to see her.

Sara jerked her chin toward him. "So the Yankee survived. Glad to see he didn't blow you all up or anything."

"I wish he'd moved as fast in the pit as he did getting through that door."

"I kept those cables out of your way, didn't I?"

Pete smiled at Sara, but she did not look impressed. Quite the opposite. "Listen, eager beaver, if you were smart you'd catch the first train back to Massachusetts while you still can."

Eager Beaver said, "It wasn't so bad. I mean, I would've taken a job above ground, but there were none."

Donny shook his head. "You hurt my ears, Harvard, with talk about above ground. I'd say you have potential, but you had better quit that talk."

"Potential? I think I did pretty well today. Potential for what?"

"For coal fever, kid."

Not wanting to hear about coal fever, Sara took their orders and left. The tables were filling up rapidly.

"Coal fever!" He laughed. "How do I catch it?"

"You stick around." Donny leaned back and yawned. "Mining gets under your skin until you crave it." Then he jerked his head toward Sara, who was at a nearby table. "Like you crave a woman." He flicked his eyebrows at Pete, a smile on half of his face.

Sara came back with their drinks.

"Why don't you drink beer?" she asked Pete.

"Don't like the taste."

"A coal miner who doesn't drink beer." She turned on her heel. "That's a first."

Pete went over to the jukebox. When he came back, the place was packed. He mentioned to Donny that he'd overheard something at a different table of miners about some meetings.

"Now you're talking about the union? Harvard, you gotta pass your test, which you can't do for a year. After that you can join the union and sign the agreement if you like. I got no quarrel with the UMW, but I bet your grandpa will swallow his own teeth." Donny gave a hearty laugh.

The door swung open so hard it hit the wall with a bang, and there emerged a large ape of a man, filling the door frame. He wore only a yellowing T-shirt and jeans. Donny slapped the table. "Son of a bitch, if it ain't George Honeycutt himself. Heard on the CB you were up to the hospital. Pattie okay, I hope?"

George Honeycutt gave a nod to Todd, who was at the bar, found an empty chair, flipped it around backward, and joined Donny's table. He sported a mustache and his mouth had a downward curl, a kind of permanent snarl. His short hair was a mound of tight curls like the furrows in a field gone fallow. He tossed his pack of Camels onto the table and set down the can of Mountain Dew he'd brought with him.

"It's a matter of debate," he answered. "If she'd do what they tell her, she should be okay. You muckrakers run much coal today?"

"With that rheumatic crew?" Donny smirked. "We managed six cuts, only two belt splices. This is Harvard. Showed up with his steel-toed boots but no gloves." He laughed. "Darryl bought him a pair at Underwood's. Come all the way down here from Massachusetts. Guess Harvard just wasn't good enough, eh, kid?"

"Yeah, that's right. Harvard was a disappointment." Pete semi-stood to reach George's hand. "Pete Griffith. How's it going?"

"You're a long way from home."

"My grandfather lives here. You're a miner?"

"Work the tipple. Dozer operator."

"Oh, you're not underground. What's a tipple?"

They laughed. "Oh no. He's worse than I thought," Donny said, slapping the table.

George shook his head. "You were in the pit all day and no one told you where the coal goes before getting shipped?"

"It's his first day. We didn't have time to enlighten him on all the frills." Donny laughed again.

Pete shrugged, looking mildly amused.

George explained that the tipple, or prep plant, washed the coal and separated the rock and debris using pressurized water.

"We got him just in time, eh, Honeycutt? Like that guy we found who'd broken down." Donny put his beer mug down hard and laughed. "Remember him? Couldn't open the hood of his car."

George corrected him. "No, remember? He couldn't close it. Just needed a little grease. No telling how long he'd have sat there if we hadn't come along. Didn't even have the sense God gave a squirrel. Which is what I thought when that doctor told us that Pattie would have to stay in bed. I thought, man, do you know who you're talking to? Asking her to rest is like trying to get water to flow uphill. I'm telling you, if our youngin' is as stubborn as she is—"

"You mean as stubborn as you?"

George gave Sara his order and said, "You look like you could use some rest, Sara. Is that Todd working you too hard? Want me to speak to him?"

"No, George. I'm fine." Her face was red, with a sheen of perspiration. "I was up with them this morning." She pointed at Pete. "Then I went fishing." She stopped herself before she said too much.

"Where were you fishing?" Pete asked.

Ignoring him, she asked, "Do you want another Coke? I'll get you one." She hurried off. What panicked her was what Frank might say. She glanced at the door, but no sign of him. She had to catch his eye when he got there, to remind him to play it cool.

"So, what's this about a meeting?" George asked. "I damn well hope you sons-a-bitches aren't striking again."

Some other miners joined them, and Donny made the introductions. "Rino, Robert, Painter, this is Harvard, also known as Pete, our new red hat."

After Sara took their orders, George leaned over and asked, "Are you sure you're okay?" She smiled and gave him a pat on the back.

Robert said to Pete, "Heard about you. How was your first day? Ready yet to hitchhike back to wherever you come from?" His greasy hair flopped in his face.

Tipping his chair back, Pete said, "Not today."

"Anything *unusual* happen to you?" asked Rino, who was missing a front tooth.

Pete reached for his Coke, and that's when he noticed his wrists. Black between the ends of his sleeves and where the gloves had been. It hadn't come off in the shower. "Nothing that I can recall."

Pete tuned out what the miners were saying. Instead, he remembered what had happened at the "dinner hole," where they'd had their lunch. He'd been expecting something the whole day because Sara had warned him, and he'd paid particular attention to where he stepped. For safety's sake, he'd chosen a seat with his back against the wall so they couldn't come from behind, slip a rat down his jacket. He'd already seen the rats, big as small dogs. But he didn't mind them, knowing that they could feel a tremor, a rockfall about to happen. The sight of them was reassuring. He remembered Benny saying they had "feelers." Still, he didn't want one stuck down his shirt.

The dinner hole was a small space cut into the wall, better lit than most of the mine. Some of the miners had actually brought in their own folding chairs. Pete leaned back, his muscles twitching from exhaustion, and thought maybe he would get off this rite of passage easy. He'd been so busy watching every move around him that he'd almost forgotten to eat. The other miners were about done. He chased his bologna sandwich with the rest of his water from the bottom section of his dinner bucket. Someone next to him gave him an elbow and said he shouldn't finish his water.

Pete asked why. He'd been parched and his throat hurt.

Shaking his head, the miner gave Pete a long stare. "Ain't no one told you?"

"Oh, because I could get trapped and need it."

"There's another reason."

Pete waited.

"That's how we survive down here. Stick together. If you see something wrong, you pour out your water. That's our sign. If any one of us pours out our water, we all leave. It's a safety thing. You think they care one shit about us? They got numbers to make, that's all they care about."

Pete nodded. "Well, at this point I don't think I could tell if something was dangerous or not. It all feels dangerous to me."

"You'll get over that. We rely on each other. You might be the only one to see a crack, or hear a shift, or see some dust fall. And you've got to trust that. No one plays around with pouring their water out."

The miners packed up their lunches and put their wrappers and trash back in the garbage can. Everybody looked so casual to Pete that he doubted the hazing Sara had hinted at would happen. The miners weren't paying any attention to him, no sneaking looks or little smirks. Pete noticed nothing until he reached for his cap. That's when everything went dark. The place was blacker than black. He felt around with his foot for his cap, but they must have grabbed it. There was no light. He hadn't heard any click of a breaker, but obviously this was a well-coordinated trick. Every miner had shut off his cap light at the same instant.

He stood, desperate to find some spot of light, but also to be ready to run if he had to. Darkness like he'd never seen. A chasm of darkness, without gradations, no place of grayness, no hint of light. Uniform blackness. For a moment he wasn't sure if his eyes were open, so he rubbed them. Where were the miners? Why weren't they reacting? Pete felt dizzy, as if he might fall. He spread his legs wider and put his hands on his hips to ground himself.

Here it is, he thought, looking quickly around. *Thank you, Sara.* At least he was forewarned. Afraid to move, he waited. Of all the things they could have done, he told himself, if this was it, he'd be okay. Darkness wouldn't kill him. At least he could hear the noisy generator. If he had to, he could grope his way toward it. Tense as a rod, he didn't know what to expect. Would they push him, shove him? Throw their lunch scraps at his head? Jump into a buggy or a tram and desert him?

Time seemed to have disappeared along with the light. He couldn't tell how long he'd been suffering like this. He could hear the hum of the conveyor belt and the sound of the motormen somewhere far off in the mine. It was a strange sensation—total darkness. He opened his eyes wider. Then someone grabbed him.

"Get your hands offa me!"

The miners broke out in cackles and hoots. Someone shouted, "Darker than the grave!" Peals of laughter led some miners into coughing attacks.

"Not a speck of light!"

"Like no darkness on Earth!"

Still no lights. Wanting to end the prank, Pete yelled, "Turn on the goddamn lights! Sons of bitches! *Fuck off*, man!" He loaded on the expletives, but it didn't work.

"One hundred percent darkness," someone said, laughing. "No, you've never seen this before!"

Then he heard Donny say, "C'mon, boys! Let's go. Leave him here. A day or two should do the trick."

That was too much. Pete shouted every swear word he knew.

The lights came on. Donny walked by, handed him a decal. Laughing, he said, "Put it on your cap, Harvard, so you can find yourself in the dark."

For a long time after, Pete's heart had galloped like a wild stallion.

In response to Rino's question, no one said anything about it. He guessed that meant he'd passed the initiation test. He went to the jukebox and chose "Kind of a Drag" by the Buckinghams.

When the men at Donny's table got rowdy, Pete walked over to Sara and asked what they were getting all heated about. She said, "Something about Mimi, I think. Let's go see."

Robert was saying, "Mimi's got a screw loose, and everybody knows it."

"Mimi Blackstone?" Sara chimed in. "Didn't she write the governor?"

She whispered to Pete that it was about the dams. Pete looked puzzled.

She whispered, "You know, The Big Lagoon." He still looked puzzled, and she shook her head in dismay at his ignorance.

"Didn't you check it, walk on it before you drove on it? Did it look different?" George asked Painter, who also was a dozer operator.

Painter was engrossed in his tale. "Didn't look much different. Just that fissure, halfway up The Big Lagoon, oh, I'd say roughly about twelve foot by three. We'd seen that before, so I wasn't worried. Didn't think nothing about it. Then, driving on it, it felt like I was driving on cake frosting. Back tires sunk three feet down into that slop, then the front. I was gunning it to about nine thousand. Thought I'd blow a bearing. Shit, I went flying outta there, down to my wife and kids, yelling, 'Dam's gonna blow!' I yelled to all my neighbors. It about scared me to death."

"Full of shit, and that's no joke," Robert said. "That does more harm than good because you just started another round of crying wolf. How the hell will we ever know if there's a real problem?"

"You made that up," Rino said. "I think you dreamed it."

"So, who else did you tell?" George asked.

"Sweeny, but he couldn't give a rat's ass," Painter said.

"He couldn't pour piss out of a boot with both hands," Donny quipped.

"You muckmen gripe more than the prisoners I used to guard," George snarled. "I wish I'd known this before I moved here."

"Why shouldn't they complain?" Sara asked. "Complaining is how to make things better. If no one says anything, nothing will ever change."

"I agree with that," Pete said cheerfully.

George got up and headed toward the door, where he almost bumped into Frank coming in. Frank stood there looking for a table. He wore a felt fedora and London Fog trench coat, his herringbone tweed suitcoat showing underneath. The cacophony began. Controlled chaos everywhere. Chairs scraping the floor, people heading to the door. Sara hated this, but they always did it. Operator comes in, everyone clears out. She felt ashamed as she walked over to him, but before speaking she winked and hinted with a shake of her head that he'd better play it cool.

"Welcome to Otter Creek Holler," she said. "Friendliest place on the planet. In a minute, you'll have your pick of places to sit."

"What do I have to do to get a drink?" The laws still required a club membership for liquor by the drink. The dues were one dollar.

"Try the broomstick from the Wicked Witch of the West." She held out her hand. "Or just give me a dollar."

Frank gave her a dollar and ordered a martini. "Very dry, no ice or vegetables."

"You mean olives?" She gave him a menu, but he gave it right back without looking at it. "I'd like a steak, please. Very rare."

She half turned back before walking away. "No ice or vegetables?"

"Definitely no vegetables. I'll take a salad, though. With Italian."

People were leaving in droves, except Pete, who was by the jukebox.

In the kitchen, Sara wondered whether she might be able to pull off eating with Frank. For one thing, Todd had gone home. Secondly, she was starved. She hadn't eaten since lunch at about eleven that morning. And third, she'd have Todd deduct it from her paycheck. She put two steaks on the grill, dropped the basket of fries into the hot grease. Todd had done most of the dishes and asked her to clean up while he went back to the hotel.

"Good night, Pete," she said, bringing Frank his drink. Pete left, looking back over his shoulder at Frank. Frank gave him a hard stare.

On the front window, Sara turned the sign to "Closed." While the food cooked, she flew around, stacking dishes hot from the dishwasher onto open shelves, putting food into the fridge, cleaning counters, and sweeping the floor. Then, back in the dining room where Frank was the only customer, she put both plates on the table, pulled out a chair, and sat down.

"How nice that you'll join me, if it's all right with your boss. And what about your brothers, and your whole community? Won't they come in a big stampede and run me out of town on a rail?"

She laughed. "My boss has gone back to the hotel. No one else is coming in. The door is shut and locked."

It was raining, a cold winter rain, but not a pounding rain, and she figured she'd still hear the back door if Todd came in. A train horn sounded with its long, mournful tone.

"Sorry I scared off all your customers."

"Most of them leave at this time anyway. But, it's true, they don't like coal operators."

"I know. That last one gave me a scowl. Is he your boyfriend?"

"Just met him today. Maybe he doesn't like operators, like everybody else."

They ate quietly for a few minutes. Then Frank said, "That Todd, he's a character. I don't think he likes me too much, either. You'd think he'd fake it a little, seeing I'm his customer. That's what I have to do with my customers."

She chuckled. "Oh, Todd. He's a piece of work. He definitely takes getting used to. He's only a success because he's got a corner on the market. This is the only place in town to get a hot meal."

"And you work for him?"

"Most coveted job in the holler, besides mining." She shrugged.

After another quiet spell, Frank said, "I don't think you liked me at first. I kind of put you on the spot, so maybe you had good reason."

"Yes, you did." She sipped her beer. "But maybe you're easier to talk to with your ball cap on and your funny boots."

"I'll remember that."

"Are you sure you're the same man?"

Frank gave a half smile. "Oh, so you're going to run out of here like everyone else?"

"I told you, I'm not like everyone else. And—"

"And what?"

She added ketchup to her fries. "And I want to talk more about the dams."

"Okay. Shoot."

She put her fork down. "There are some in our holler who think those dams are dangerous. I don't know for sure. We have the wild young guys who drive around beeping their car horns, yelling in the middle of the night, 'The dam broke!' You can't believe them, but people are scared. Come a heavy rain, and some take their families to sleep in the school gym. One woman wrote the governor. It's not just a joke, and one thing they don't question is that the operators aren't looking after them. Why do you think they clear out when you walk in?"

He took a bite of his steak. "Writing the governor." He wiped his mouth. "Sara, what do you think that'll do?"

Another long train horn wailed in the distance, and a loud truck sped by.

Leaning back, Frank took a moment before speaking. "We've got a lot of laws." He started counting on his hand. "There's reclamation laws, the water quality laws. Now they're worried about the sulfur dioxide emissions and acid rain. We've got labor shortages and wildcat strikes, new laws and regulations every time you turn around. One way or another, we still have to get the coal out of the ground. There are risks. There are risks in a lot of occupations. I told you; I'll look into it."

Was he just filling her with a lot of details to throw her off course, to intimidate her?

"You're here. You're in charge. I just ask that you see for yourself," she said. "Those dams are right over our heads! *Our* heads. *We* live here! You live in New York."

His brow furrowed, his face grew serious. She couldn't tell if she'd gotten to him or if he was mad.

"I'm not going to repeat myself, Sara." He put his elbows on the table, hands clasped in front of his face. "My uncle, who is my boss, buys these mines without any forethought and leaves the rest to me. I'm the one who sees how we can make a profit, *if* we can make a profit."

"Profits! I'm talking about dams high above a holler full of houses, full of people!"

"Oh, Sara. I didn't create this mess. Rowan Coal didn't create this mess. But, I might add, that because Vern bought this mine, I'm here to listen to you and I *will* do what I can."

"Before you got here tonight, a guy named Painter—he is a bit of a loose cannon, but I believe him—anyway, he works at the tipple, and he talked about The Big Lagoon getting soft. He said he was skidding and almost got his truck stuck. It was no joke. He was truly terrified. I've worked here a long time and I've never heard that. Frank, it could break." She stopped to calm herself. "What if it broke?"

Frank reached across the table and gently laid his hand on hers. "Sara, I can't say very much at this point one way or another. I'll look at the engineer's report."

She had to fight back the burning tears. If she had cried, and the tears were right there, she feared he'd think she was a fanatic, a wimp who was afraid of her own shadow. But until that moment when she said those words, that it could break, she never knew that deep down within her, she really was afraid.

Twisting her gut, rising into her throat was such a stew of emotions she hardly knew how to think. This new man, so easy to talk to, so handsome. The fear of the dam, fear that she'd be caught talking to him. And then the thought that maybe this was happening because she could actually help the holler, do something about those dams. Her soaring feeling this afternoon, and now the gripping fear. It was almost too much. What gave her courage was the thought that she could make a difference, that her friendship, if that's what this was, could do something to help her holler.

"I've never known an operator to listen to me like you do. I am just someone to bring their food or take their dishes."

"You really care about your home, your community. I respect that."

They moved on to other things. She told him where she lived and a little about her brothers. He said that he was not only married, he also had three kids. "What do you think about that?"

"I guessed it."

Frank sat back and lit a cigarette. "How about some dessert? Got any cookies?"

"Nope. Just pie."

"Okay, pie." He pulled out a twenty. "I hope this will cover the tab for both of us."

She said it was more than enough, and went into the kitchen with their plates. In the kitchen she rushed around finishing everything.

With the lights off, they stood close together at the window by the front door, watching the rain turn to snow. Giant wet flakes smooshed into the glass turning to water, then giving way to rivulets taken down by gravity.

"Coming from the west," Frank observed quietly.

"I expect it'll snow all night," she said, moving closer to him.

"Nah, it'll stop around midnight."

"They'll plow before dawn. Have to, for the coal trucks."

"That's nice." He turned to her, their faces close, their eyes unmoving.

"Frank—" She tried to speak, but there were no words and the next thing she knew, they were kissing.

Later that night, she tried to remember who initiated the kiss. She remembered looking up at him for what seemed like a long time. She smiled, remembering how they both forgot about the pie.

Chapter 7

George Honeycutt left Todd's in a huff and fishtailed out of the parking lot. The night fog and wet snow were too much for the lazy wipers on his 1954 Chevy pickup, so he slowed to a crawl. His truck was a record of his life, with gray primer on the front bumper from when he'd slid on the ice into a tree, and wire holding on the rusted-off back bumper. He had no intention of getting rid of his truck because, in a way, it was like him. He had a wired-together knee and a bullet in his butt. He also had two Purple Hearts from Vietnam. He and his truck were both veterans.

He was worried about Pattie, his pregnant wife. The doctor had told her to stay off her feet as much as possible, but they might as well have asked for the moon. He rarely saw her sitting on the couch, unless they were there together. He'd felt the baby move that morning as they lay in bed. He wanted this baby so bad it hurt, and he was worried about walkouts. Every time he turned around there was another strike. What if the baby needed something? Or Pattie? The last thing he wanted was for Pattie to have to go back to work. That was his job, to take care of his family. But how could he when there was a wildcat strike every month? Shutdowns for this, shutdowns for that, once even for schoolbooks. And another time it was for tires. He felt jumpy as a stray cat.

As he turned off Otter Creek Road on to the dirt road that climbed to his home, the ruts and holes pulled and jerked at his truck. Going even more slowly, he thought back to his childhood, when he'd imagined himself as Rocky Marciano, knocking around some two-bit lightweight, two quick left jabs and a haymaker to the temple. The guy swings around, rolls off the ropes. The ref stands over him and begins the count. The crowd counts with him. The crowd ignites. They're on their feet. Papers flying. Excitement, electricity—the place is alive. Everyone is standing, cheering: "HON-EY-CUTT! HON-EY-CUTT!"

The greats. George felt like he knew them personally: Gene Tunney, Jack Dempsey, Joe Louis. And Ali. When George was little, he'd told everyone he was going to be a boxer when he grew up. He'd practiced boxing wherever he went. When he pushed his little sister on the swing, he'd take a few jabs every time she flew into the air. They couldn't afford boxing gloves, so he wore baseball mitts on both hands, forcing his right hand into the mitt as best he could. For three years he slept with the mitts, ate with them, and went to school with them. Not until he got his first crush, in fifth grade, did he lose them.

His thoughts ambled about as his truck bounced over the washboard gravel. He loosened his grip on the wheel, letting the truck work it out with the road. Tired from work, tired from the worry, tired of these strikes.

As he approached his cabin, the cabin he'd built with his own hands, he pushed in the knob on the dashboard to turn off his headlights and then put the engine in neutral. Then he turned off the ignition switch at just the right moment to coast in the dark into his parking spot, hoping not to awaken Pattie.

As a dozer operator, he hadn't thought he should have to join the United Mine Workers union. After leaving the army, he'd sworn he'd never join anything again. But they said he had to. He didn't, however, go to any of the union meetings. He was afraid he'd get pulled into something and lose it, then deck someone. Recently, miners, whether union or not—though only a few were not—had been meeting in the back of Underwood's because of the changes from the recent Coal Act: more safety regulations, more inspections. Not everyone liked these changes, even if they protected the miners, and some miners sacrificed their friends' safety by making sweetheart deals with management. George didn't trust anyone except Donny.

Leon Underwood, owner of Underwood's General Store, had taken on the coal companies in a lawsuit to protect the mineral rights to his land. Even more surprising was that he'd won. Underwood knew his rights. He was well-respected in Otter Creek, and trusted.

George Honeycutt, as a Purple Heart veteran, was second only to Underwood in terms of local stature. He had quiet courage, and that meant more than a truckload of money or degrees. Every miner knew that no matter what you had to face underground, you had to rise to the challenge and work together. One of Donny's favorite sayings was, "You don't know how to do something until you do it. Everyone has a first time." Being a jack-of-all-trades was necessary for their survival.

After 'Nam, George had moved briefly to Nashville. That was before he learned he couldn't drink alcohol. Not one drop. He'd only had a few beers the night he'd beaten two men nearly to death. He only remembered reaching for his gun. That's what he told the judge, that he'd "snapped out." Luckily, the judge was sympathetic.

Then he moved to Eddyville, Kentucky, where he'd worked as a prison guard. The only good thing that came from that job was meeting Pattie and convincing her to move back to Otter Creek, where he'd been raised. He knew that with mining he'd make more money with better benefits.

The first job he got was as a timberman in the Number 5. He set the timbers next to the rail. He was respected by his crew and made decent money. But being underground was not for him. As soon as the dozer operator job opened, he took it, happy to be outside. The others cracked jokes when he went off in the pouring rain, but he smiled and thought about how pleasant it was to be in the rain and not have to worry about bullets or land mines ripping off your legs.

Rummy, Pattie's dog, crawled out from under their small cabin, whining and pushing against his truck door. His dog, Happy, was smart enough not to get up until George actually got out of his truck.

Slowly opening the squeaky door of his truck, he whispered, "Get out, you ol' dirt bag," and pushed the dog's muzzle off his leg. He wanted to finish his cigarette. It was dangerous for Pattie to cough, so he didn't smoke in the house. A week earlier, she'd had a little bleeding, so he'd rushed her to the doctor. They'd turned them right out the door and said to go immediately to the hospital. Couldn't even go home and get her clothes. At the hospital they'd said the placenta had dropped, or slipped, or moved—he wasn't quite sure. But he was damn sure she had to stay off her feet.

They were now within a breath of their dream.

They'd been pregnant before and never even got to name the babies, the twins. That hurt him the most. Everything had been going well, no problems, until she got to six months. Then she lost them. All too late.

"I hope God's forgiven me," he said aloud, remembering what he'd almost done that day and how close he'd come to committing a crime.

Pattie's hospital roommate had delivered her baby but was cursing and crying. She wouldn't even look at her little baby when the nurse brought it in. She only said, "Look what that bastard's done to me again. How am I gonna feed them? Goddamn him."

Pattie must have asked for the strong stuff, because she slept through everything. George had to listen to the woman behind her curtain. He walked back and forth, his boots squeaking on the linoleum floor, his heart gashed open. The mother couldn't have been thirty years old, and she mentioned it was her fourth child. His nerves fraught, his thoughts tangled, he just wanted her to stop. Finally, he pulled the curtain back a little bit.

"Your baby is real pretty," he said. "If you want, I'll hold it when the nurse brings it back."

"Go ahead."

The next time the nurse brought the infant in, George stretched out his oversized, awkward hands, and the mother nodded her consent. The nurse shrugged, lay the swaddled creature close to George's chest, and left. It was the first time he'd ever held a baby. He stared at its tiny face, wispy black hair, little creases and folds of skin, little baby lips moving, eyelids fluttering. The mother turned her back and got quiet, so George assumed she'd gone to sleep.

That's when he got an idea. He stroked the newborn's back and thought, *That woman doesn't deserve to be a mother. She doesn't deserve you. We could love you, little baby. We would love you.* All of his senses were on fire. He wanted this baby. This was his chance, his and Pattie's. He could run.

The sleepy baby in his arms was supposed to be his. That's all he kept thinking. Then he went over the exit route. Getting to the staircase, past the nurses' station. That wouldn't be hard; a few nurses were no match for him. After that, down the stairs into the parking lot and to his truck, a breeze. At this time of night, the place would be empty. Only one sheriff in the holler, and it'd take him fifteen minutes to get there. George would be long gone.

But then he thought, *What will we do? Live in the woods with it?* He shifted the sleeping infant, not much bigger than a football, closer to his chest. He freed his arm to wipe the sweat dripping from his face. He didn't know how much time had passed. Was it thirty minutes? Was it five? He looked over at Pattie, his thundering heart slowed, and he got command of himself. The nurse came in and took the baby.

During his two years working as a supervisor in the prison, many good guards had gone bad. He'd never understood it, not until that moment.

I am a shell of a person, a helpless shell of a person, he thought.

Worn thin, he had sat down next to Pattie. He might be crusty and rough, and he knew he gave off that impression. But looking at his wife that night, he thought, *She's the tough one.* Pattie's eyes could disapprove yet show love at the same time. He didn't know how she did that. Those dark eyes came from some place deep and true, like the tallest trees in the mountains, the spruce trees. In the wind's blast, they barely moved. There she slept on that hospital bed, her hair spread out like a golden halo. It wasn't the thought of police or of God that had stopped him. It was Pattie.

"George! What are you doing?"

He looked up, jolted back to the present. Pattie stood at the front door, the light from their cabin glowing on her hair, the rest of her in darkness.

"I'm coming!" he answered, dragging his tired, stiff legs along with him. As he approached, she turned to go in, but he pulled her back to him for a hug. And that felt like the first true deep breath of the day. They held each other, the three of them, the embracing couple with their bump of a baby between them. Then he looked at her in the yellow light from the living room. Her hair was falling in soft waves, her skin like butterscotch. He didn't see the imperfections. He didn't see the new mole that had appeared sometime during this pregnancy, next to her eyebrow. She complained about it all the time. He knew every square inch of her body, and she was the most beautiful woman he had ever known.

They walked in together. It was a snug cabin, a main room with a small kitchen at the back, a small eating area, and then an upstairs with two bedrooms. No heating system, just a woodstove that radiated heat till the cabin was toasty.

"Are you okay, Georgie?"

He dropped his hulk onto the couch. "Did you stay off your feet today?"

"Yes. But it's so damn quiet here, George. I hate it. And you out there in your truck. I've been missing you! I need to see you. Even if I'm asleep, just wake me. I need to be with people!"

"Did you rest? What did you do?"

She went into the kitchen to wash out his dinner bucket. "I did all right."

Then she joined him on the couch, which involved a delicate maneuver of positioning her feet in a wide stance, putting one hand on the armrest of the couch, and then lowering herself.

"George, it's hard. But anyway, I did some ironing, sewed some buttons on your shirts, and stuck to dusting. Boring as hell. Listened to music, which was actually the most fun part of the day. Who was at Todd's? Wasn't there a red hat starting? Tell me everything. Start talking."

George didn't start talking. Instead he added some logs to the fire in the woodstove. "Got a good fire going. This should last all night."

Pattie knew her man. He had a funny relationship with words. He could be positively taciturn, like now, and she'd have to milk the words out of him. Or, at other times, he used way too many words when he could have cut to the chase and told her something in two sentences. Right now she was thirsting for companionship, for conversation. "Honeycutt, if I have to sit here alone all day, then you're gonna talk to me." She was smiling, but she was serious.

He sat back down, put his hand on her bulging belly. "Let's see. Donny said they were one short. And the red hat's a kid from up north. I swear he was born yesterday. I don't think he's reached puberty, barely any sign of facial hair. Didn't know what a tipple was! We got a good laugh at that. He didn't mind being laughed at, so he'll do all right."

"That's hysterical. What do you give him? A month?"

"Honestly, I think he might make it. Of course, I'm often wrong. But he's better than a lot of them. I can work with one like him because he's willing. Donny likes him; I can tell."

"Donny has good instincts," she agreed.

"His name is Pete, but they're calling him Harvard."

"Harvard? So he's from Massachusetts?"

"Yeah. But I don't know how he got through the whole day without hearing about the tipple."

They both laughed. Pattie asked George to get some sodas from the fridge. When he returned, she begged for more stories.

"Okay," he said. "You remember I told you about Hoke, the new guy from Dawson Springs?"

"Hoke? Remind me."

"Mickey Hoke. We saw him, his wife, and two youngin's at Underwood's."

"Oh yeah, that sad-looking woman. I forget her name. Wasn't it Maria? A beanpole and pale. Probably anemic. I should go talk to her, or at least give her a call."

"Well, he opens his dinner bucket, pulls out his sandwich, and all he's got between the bread is this piece of paper!" George started laughing.

"*Paper in his sandwich?*" She laughed too.

In between bursts of laughter, George went on, "Yes, paper! Donny grabbed it and read it out to the crew. 'Why don't you get your meat where you got it last night?' Whew!" George leaned back to stretch out his legs, putting his hands behind his head. "So, I'd say there's more to that beanpole than she lets on."

"I'm glad. It's not easy to move to this holler. If you're not born here, you're always an outsider. But I tell you one thing: you ever do me that way, you best not eat *any* sandwich I make. Whatever I put in it won't be good."

"Oh, I know." He tapped his upper left chest, where her name, her exact signature duplicated with a red rose, was tattooed. "This should discourage anyone."

"Only if they can read." They had another laugh.

He put his arm around her, and the couch springs moaned as she leaned over to nuzzle his neck.

"I can't wait till this baby is born," she said.

"It won't be long. You have to sit tight." George kissed her face, which was flushed from the woodstove. The snow had stopped and the wind had picked up. It shook their cabin and the walls creaked with the gusts.

She looked up at him, her expression contented, but also puzzled. "What's worrying you, George? Something else happened down at Todd's."

A log banged in the small woodstove. George tugged at the split in the fabric of their couch where the stuffing came through. "We've got to fix this."

"Oh—Oh!" Her eyes now glowed and a smile spread upward over her face. "She moved! Like a shooting star!" Pattie put his bear-sized hand on her expansive belly. "Feel here."

He waited a minute, but there was no movement under his hand. With a teasing grin, he looked back at her. "Why do you think he's a she?"

"Oh well, the little shooting star's gone back to sleep. And so should we."

Chapter 8

2019

"Do you know what a tipple is?"

"Yes," I lied, fully confident that if I saw one, it would be obvious. *How hard could it be?*

"I'll be in a burgundy Caravan by the orange pole." She told me to go nine miles after a certain intersection and to look for the tipple. "I'll be parked one mile past the tipple. Remember: by the orange pole."

Tipples, orange poles. It seemed easy enough.

I offered to give her my cell phone number, but she laughed. "Honey, there's no signal out here." That kind of freaked me out, so before I left, I bought, for ninety-nine dollars, one of those satellite devices with an SOS feature, in case I got lost.

I drove the nine miles from the intersection, and even before then I saw a lot of things that very well might be a "tipple": steel trams, jumbo-sized metal structures, obvious mining equipment, paraphernalia popping out of the sides of hills.

That's when I realized I had no clue what a tipple was. If someone had told me they lied when it would have been easier to tell the truth, I would have said, "Poor thing." I'd never realized that I did it too.

I hated that I was beginning to see myself in such stark relief. Ever since Stephen left, these things had become painfully obvious. I felt like I was at the bottom of a hole with dirt falling on me. How I'd even gotten in the car and left my home in Vernon, Connecticut, to come all the way to Kentucky, I didn't know, what with the internal winds of self-loathing pounding my ears. Any adventure can feel like relief.

The person I'd lied to on the phone was Nancy Monroe. I'd found her while doing a Google search for places to stay in Otter Creek, Kentucky. She'd offered me a room in a trailer on her property, and since it was between that and staying miles away, I'd agreed.

As the daughter of a coal executive, it seems like I'd know about tipples, but that was far from the reality. My father wore a suit and tie and went into Manhattan every day, when he wasn't traveling, which was most of the time. I knew he was in "the coal business." The running refrain of my childhood was "Turn off the lights when you leave a room." This wasn't to save electricity, I now realized. It was probably because that particular electric company probably wasn't buying his coal. Nonetheless, I thought it best to avoid revealing to anyone in the area that I was the daughter of a coal executive.

The topography I was driving through was like none other I'd ever seen. Steep, sheer rock walls right next to the edge of the road that went on for miles. Plummeting drop-offs on the other side of the road. Then giant coal trucks looming at me and taking up more than their share of the road. Miles and miles where I never saw a mailbox or any sign of human habitation. Yes, I was a tad anxious. To calm myself, I was listening to the craggy-sounding voice of an old lady with a British accent reading *Pride and Prejudice* on tape. The big dilemma of Darcy being a prick or the excitement of an upcoming ball helped distract me from the thoughts of my car pitching off the road into the ravines and coyotes tearing into my stomach and gnawing on my legs.

When the giant coal trucks barreled toward me, I instinctively leaned away, thinking of the Merritt Parkway, which I'd always thought of as hellacious, but now seemed like a ride at the fair. The closer I got to where Nancy's burgundy minivan should be, the more mining equipment I saw. At each one I set my odometer, but before I'd gone a mile there were more, and then more. No orange poles and no phone signal.

As coincidence would have it, although some would say there are no coincidences, the box containing my father's desk diaries arrived the same morning Stephen left. The pot of coffee I'd made that morning, like I'd made every morning for twenty years, sat there all day and cooked. I watched birds flutter at the feeder.

When the morning had rolled into evening, with each minute an oppressive hammer on my chest, I went into the kitchen and threw the glass carafe of coffee. Black sludge shot all over the upholstered chairs, and pieces of glass went everywhere. And for the first time in my life, I couldn't clean it. Me, the miracle woman, homemaker extraordinaire, the one who could make homemade bread in her sleep, birthday cakes in the shape of frogs, manicotti. My needlepoint pillows, some for summer and others for winter, were always carefully placed in the living room, tabletops always dusted. I smeared the black liquid while crying. Everything I'd done just made it worse. Everything I'd done for twenty years had just made it worse.

I decided to open the box my brother had sent me with no note or explanation.

Four diaries were on the floor: the 1965 book, the 1968, 1969, and the 1970 book. And that's when I saw the piece of paper with my father's chicken scratch. *Sara, Sara, Sara.*

I went up and down the road about twenty times, five miles this way and five that. With less than a quarter tank of gas, and figuring I'd better start back home, I stopped at a Miner's Mart. I could see that the road ahead dropped off into another ravine, and I didn't want to get even more lost, even more isolated. I pulled in beside a giant Budweiser truck, wondering how it rounded those mountain curves. The guy inside the Miner's Mart said they had no bathrooms. When I opened the door to leave, I saw a cheery, round-faced, gray-haired lady poking her head out of a burgundy Dodge Caravan, waving at me.

She hollered, "Are you Aleena Fitzgerald?"

"Oh my God." I trotted to her car. "Are you Nancy Monroe? I am so glad to see you!"

I've backpacked through the Canadian Rockies, and most of those trails are in better shape than the road she took me on. It was nothing more than a dirt track down the side of a mountain. Even in my Subaru, I swear I had to gun it around the curves to keep up. I kept thinking, *This should be a Dodge Caravan commercial.* We went over large boulders and down such steep drop-offs I couldn't see past the hood of my car, couldn't see the road in front of me. I eased my way through water and then zipped around, my tires spitting gravel, to keep that car in sight, because nothing would keep me from her. When we got to her home, I mentioned that she was hard to follow.

"Well, you said you had to go to the bathroom." I knew then not to underestimate the hospitality of Nancy Monroe.

We sat at her round kitchen table and she gave me a room-temperature plastic bottle of water. I could have downed twenty of them, but I sipped it.

"I guess you think it's odd, me coming here to find someone named Sara," I began.

"Not a bit," she said. "People come here for all sorts of reasons. Some are writing articles or books. I work at the Appalachian Resource Center. I teach an orientation class to the young interns every year. It's not surprising to me at all."

She introduced me to her son, who at various times while we were speaking came into the house. He looked to be in his sixties. She told me that recently some French journalists had stayed with her. They were doing a story on the miner's strike.

"I think I read something about that."

"Yes, poor things. They're camping out. Have been for weeks. But they've got a shower, sleeping tents, and a big cook tent. There was a problem with some truckers, but they're gone now. A lot of people join the strike for a time, you see. But the miners and their families, they're the ones holding it together; they have meetings, sit in a big circle, hash out the problems, and get along just fine. You should go over and see them. It's really something. A politician, I forget who, sent pizzas. Wasn't that nice?"

She changed the subject and asked about my family. I told her I was separated and had two daughters, one out of college and one a senior. I'd taken my ring off the first week after Stephen left, but after twenty years, the finger tells, with the skinny indentation, the white shadow. "Separated" is limbo, purgatory, a holding tank, the undoing not yet done. The clang of the law out there waiting, the Divorce Decree. "Separated" is like lying in the street wounded, waiting for the emergency vehicles to come and check for a pulse. I didn't yet know what last name to use, whether to go back to my maiden name or keep my married name, Fitzgerald. I didn't know who I was.

Our marriage had died from the inside out. A tree can be like that: giant, ancient, branches still holding green leaves. No one notices the leaning, the holes, the dead places. No one knows the rotten core. It falls one day with no crack, no crunch, no keeling over. No one yells "Timber!" with birds flurrying. It falls like a whacked club, a downed gavel.

Before leaving for Kentucky, I'd tortured myself with our photo albums. I'd sat with them all around me on the floor, a conflagration of memories threatening to burn me alive. All those smiles, all those laughs, all that fun, all that love. It had at one time been very, very good. In my archeological digging, I found old letters from my father. He'd worried about me. In one he'd written, "I love you." Never spoken, but once written. I'd forgotten.

"About your Sara," Nancy said. "Is she an old friend of yours?" I noticed her Bible on the shelf behind her. It had papers coming out of it and the whole thing was secured with a ribbon.

"No, not a friend of mine. My sister's friend. I found mention of her in some of my sister's things, but it didn't say the last name. I think it was from when a mutual friend and my sister visited around here. It occurred to me that Sara might not know that my sister died." I hated lying about Rose. "It's silly, isn't it? I mean, that I came here." My voice got choked and my eyes filled with genuine tears, which always happened when I talked about Rose.

"No, I don't think so. You must miss her."

"I miss her terribly. And she had so many friends everywhere. She played competitive bridge and they traveled around for the tournaments. So many friends." I loved talking about my sister. "Rose Rowan. She didn't change her name when she married, which was unusual back then. She married Luke Rowland, and she liked Rose Rowan better than Rose Rowland, so she kept her name. She died last year from cancer."

Nancy dropped her tissue. Bending down to get it, she asked, "Your maiden name is Rowan?"

I nodded assent, but couldn't believe I'd just said my maiden name. My father had severed all ties with Rowan Coal when he resigned, but it felt complicated and I was tired. I asked to see my room. She wrote down three names of people who had lived in the area a long time and might be able to help with my search. By the front door, I asked about a framed photo. It was obviously a wedding photo.

She took it off the wall and pressed it to her. "We were childhood sweethearts. I lived across the street from him and would wait for him to come home from the mine. In the winter he'd blink the light and I'd know he was home. We would meet outside no matter what the weather. We had to wait to marry until I was eighteen."

Her eyes got glassy. I told her it was a beautiful photo.

"Eighty percent of his lungs got damaged from black lung. You only need sixty-five to get checks. But he got along all right. Could still mow the lawn, set out there afterwards. What he liked best was setting on that lawn with friends stopping by." She wiped her face with a tissue from her sleeve. "But then he caught that pneumonia from the rescue work."

"Wow, he was a rescue worker also?"

"No, he got that walking pneumonia from helping with the clean-up." She hesitated, probably because of my blank stare. Then she clarified, "The clean up after the flood."

"Oh?" I gathered this was something else that I should know about. She said it so definitively that I didn't dare ask for more information.

"Course his name isn't with those who died, but he died from that flood, sure enough."

I blurted out, "Flood? What flood?"

"The disaster. November 26, 1970. When the dams broke."

I didn't know anything about it. "Oh, yes, right."

It didn't seem that my stupidity, or lack of awareness of local history, had much effect on her. Matter of fact, in a contemplative tone, she said, "We'd had a little—well, we had words that early morning before he left for the mine. I hated how he always took on extra shifts, and there he was taking on an extra shift. Of course, if he hadn't taken on that extra shift and been safe down in that mine, he might surely have died in the flood. But, as God is my witness, it was the only morning that I didn't kiss him goodbye. The only morning. You see, you always kiss a miner goodbye. And when I saw him walk through that door that next morning, I was at my mother-in-law's and my boys were with me, I stood but my legs gave out from under me. I sunk to the floor just a'bawling my eyes out. And I couldn't stop. He held me and I just shook and cried. All day long, every time I saw him, I cried."

"I'm so sorry," was all I could say. Such a fresh wound, such ready tears, such pain. She wiped the glass frame on her shirt and reverently put it back on the wall.

When I got settled, I did an internet search on the flood. It happened in November of 1970, and then I read that the responsible coal company was Rowan Coal. That was the year my father resigned. I always remembered that because that was when my mother went to Winstead Hospital.

I read on. Rowan Coal had acquired Otter Creek Mining in December of 1969, eleven months before the disaster. It said the dam had been built years earlier. The company claimed it was an "act of God" because of heavier-than-normal rains. The dam stood sixty feet high, was four hundred feet thick, and spanned the valley from left to right at around 550 feet. When it broke, the gushing liquid hit a slag pile. The liquid and the "smoldering mass of rock" formed a thirty-foot tidal wave that wiped out ten miles of villages.

One hundred twenty-five people dead.

Chapter 9

I had one of those nights where you wake and think it's morning, and you've been asleep only an hour. It kept happening all night till I just wanted the night to be over. The next morning, I had instant oatmeal and a cup of hot tea that I made with Nancy's electric kettle, and then I headed out to find the first person on the list she'd given me. She had checked with them—there were only three—and they'd agreed to speak with me.

As none of the roads had signs, I got turned around, and I'd almost given up when I saw a sheriff pumping gas. I pulled in and asked him if he knew where Thelma Owens lived. His directions came in a series of questions: "Do you know where the old high school is?" "How about where the hospital used to be?" I flunked his short quiz. He suggested I wait there, as he was going to buy a pack of cigarettes to bring to his wife, and then he'd let me follow him.

He came back as promised and led me to the first address. I popped out to thank him but also to ask my own question, my one question, about the Sara—any Sara—who had lived there before the flood. He was young, but I thought it worth a shot. He pondered but then suggested the same people already on Nancy's list.

The friendliness of the area was what struck me. Where I live, if you slow to ask directions, you'll get a pile of cars blasting their horns and drivers leaning out their windows cursing.

I knocked on Thelma's door. She was warm and welcoming and before long she was talking in detail about her life as if we had known each other for decades. She talked of her husband, who had had a stroke. She said, "The stroke left him with brain damage, but he could still dance." But it wasn't said with regret or remorse; it was almost with pride, a savoring. They went to dances, and they danced at home. I couldn't tell what else, if anything, he could do. The way she talked of their dancing, though, it was like the magic had never left her. She said his seizures led to more damage, and then he needed full-time care. She never divorced him because her job provided the insurance needed to keep him in the nursing home.

About my search, she said that no Sara came to mind. I thanked her for the tea.

I met the next person, Colleen Bickford, who worked at the local library. The first thing she wanted me to know was that she had married into the area. "I'm not from here."

"Where are you from?"

"Two counties north of here. Now, my husband, he grew up in Otter Creek, and his people are all from here. He lost four family members in the flood." She said she had moved here three years after the flood. That was good enough for me.

She couldn't recall any Sara without an *h*, although she joked that she wasn't in the habit of asking people how they spelled their names. When she discovered that I knew almost nothing about the flood, she straightened and froze for a second. I wasn't sure what she'd do—maybe throw me out of the library. She looked at me like I was a species she'd never before encountered. However, she quickly regained her composure and got up, stating that she'd get out the newspapers. I raised my arm to signal it wasn't necessary, but she told me it would only take her about fifteen minutes. She went into the office.

Needing a coffee, and because there weren't many options, I settled on Wendy's. When I returned, the large table was covered with newspaper articles. She was on the phone in the office. I walked around the table, looking at the photos and reading captions:

"The wave was like a living thing, undulating from one side of the hollow to the other." It said that people watched helplessly while their neighbors were swallowed up by the black wave.

"My little girl, she had a wisdom beyond her years. She could talk to anyone, made friends with everyone. Almost as if something inside her knew she didn't have long."

And this one from a resident named Darryl Stone:

"The noise was like war planes everywhere. I didn't know what to do. The black waters lifted our house. It was like I was frozen, but there was nothing I could do."

The photos were shocking. People wrapped in blankets in a building for survivors. Children with terror in their eyes as they watched their parents crying. It said a thousand were injured and four thousand left homeless.

I couldn't read anymore. I could barely swallow. My knees were jittery, I felt nauseated, and I needed fresh air. Out the door, I stood in the almost empty parking lot under a brilliant blue sky with small clouds that looked like a parade of tugboats. The bucolic scene seemed flagrantly out of place. This whole trip seemed frivolous in light of what the photos had so graphically displayed, in light of the suffering these people had endured, the tragic untimely deaths, albeit fifty years ago. How was it I'd never heard of this disaster? Never learned about it in school, never even heard about it at home or from my father? Of course, he never talked to us much anyhow. Could I have lived the rest of my life and never known about it?

Frank Rowan had been a man of contradictions, like a jigsaw puzzle where the pieces were related but none matched. How could all those pieces be from one man? The man who came home from the city and, about six months out of the year, in fair weather and foul (because we had an awning), cooked his dinner on the grill? He came home from work after we kids had eaten. I had more memories of him outside than inside the house. When I was in college, we talked trees and birds. It was nice to have an interest in common. I explained that paper birches have black mustaches and gray birches have dark triangles; he knew about the black birch smelling like wintergreen when you run your nail through the thin bark on a twig. He pointed out to me the difference between the summer tanager and the scarlet tanager. The scarlet says *chick-burr*, the summer says *piti-kuk*. Once, as we walked in the woods together, up near Pawling where he hunted, he took a branch and rubbed it at various heights on the trunk of a tree. I followed his gaze to a hole in the upper third of the tree. He said he'd often seen a great horned owl in around there and thought that if he rubbed the stick on the tree, it might wake the owl. He'd seen that trick on his favorite TV show, *Mutual of Omaha's Wild Kingdom*. I'd always thought his tendency to be alone outside was to avoid Mom, and I'd judged him for it. But the fuller picture, with more pieces, showed a man who was deeply connected to nature.

Here was a man who, from looking at his desk diaries, could schmooze with politicians and owners of large conglomerates, who flew all over the place and dined at the most fashionable hotels and restaurants. Yet how did he spend his free time? In the backyard mowing or planting trees, hunting or fishing. I had photos of him climbing out of tents in Montana, getting out of small propeller planes. A million shots of his smiling face as he held up some dead fish. Tahiti, Barbados, Vegas—they weren't for him. He'd pack his fly rod, drive to some river in New Brunswick, and stay in a fishing lodge for a month.

I wondered what Sara was like. If there even was a Sara.

Jo Jo, the woman he married a year after Mom died, never went fishing or hunting with him. She preferred to get her hair and nails done and to sleep till noon. She was never a mother to us; she was just the woman Dad had married. I don't think Dad cared what she did during the day, as long as she was by his side at night. The house held memories of Mom. It was the house where she died. I was too young to think of it then, but I thought of it now—Mom died in her bedroom, the bedroom he later shared with Jo Jo. No wonder he was gone a lot. No wonder he was always in a bad mood. I realized that we don't really know our parents. And maybe our parents don't really know us.

Most of his business trips in the 1970 book, a cluster of them, were to Otter Creek, Kentucky. He traveled less after starting his own company, Hudson Valley Coal Company. I never saw mention of Otter Creek in the other books. He wrote down everything, in case of an audit, I suspect, and also because he was obsessed with saving money. Dad would drive ten miles out of his way to dodge a ten-cent toll. I was only seven years old in 1970, but I can say for a fact that I never saw him go through a toll and not ask for a receipt. He kept meticulous records. On October 24, 1970, it said, "Submitted letter of resignation." The dam broke November 26.

Leandra Blackstone lived off Otter Creek Road, up a steep hill, on Pitkin Mountain Road. There were no more houses above her house; in other words, the only way out was down. She was welcoming despite the sign next to her door that read, "The Witch Is In." She was tall, and while thin, she was lithe and fit, moving around easily. I was shocked when she announced she was eighty-five. Her house smelled fresh and clean, and I could hear the kettle whistling. I stood in the middle of her living room, captivated. All along the walls and on every table were plants and dried herbs and flowers. I went over to one, and felt the leaves. It reminded me of marijuana. "What's this?"

"Goldenseal. Do you have trouble with digestion?" She was walking into her kitchen, so I followed.

"No. No trouble." The counters were lined with large glass jars filled with what looked like grass cuttings.

She gave me a sideways glance, then said, "You're thin."

"Excuse me?" I braced myself for what might come next.

"Ever had your thyroid checked?"

"Not that I recall."

"Trouble sleeping?"

"Sometimes."

"I'd say," she said with her hand on her hip, examining me under her furrowed brow, "you could use some of my 'serene system' tea." She turned back to her jars and began spooning out little bits of the herbs. She put the tea strainer, filled with green herbs, over the mug and poured from her kettle.

"The water shouldn't be too hot. Here ya go. Let it steep for a few minutes."

"What's in it? I hope it won't get me high."

She laughed. "Of course it won't make you high, but it might calm you down a bit. It's got nettle, lemon balm, bunchberry, and some spearmint. That's the special ingredient, spearmint, but you gotta climb real high for it. It's mixed in with moss, and under the wandering cedar, usually at the base of large spruces. It likes the shade and high altitudes. I use it judiciously."

I smelled the tea. It brought to mind a playground. It smelled light and summery.

"Thank you." I sipped. I was prepared for it to bite, or at least to taste like a shag carpet, but it was smooth and soothing. "Oh, my gosh, it's delicious." I was tempted to chug it.

We sat in her living room. She was in her well-worn recliner, and I took a small side chair. She began, "So, you're staying down with Nancy?"

I said yes and asked where I might get some dinner.

"Todd's. Down-home food, but sufficient and plentiful."

The name "Todd's" rang a bell from my father's books.

"And you're from Connecticut?" she asked.

"Yes."

"You have family there?"

Here we go. "My two daughters."

"That's nice. I never married or had children. Went to medical school and practiced medicine in North Carolina. My mother lived here, though. Mimi Blackstone. She died in the flood. I moved back shortly after."

"I'm very sorry."

"So, you're looking for someone?" Leandra pulled the lever on her recliner and her feet popped up. She had a hole in the big toe of one of her socks. "You're sure she didn't die in the flood, this person you're looking for?"

I burnt my mouth slurping my tea. "No. Well, I don't know. I just learned about the flood from Nancy."

"I didn't think anyone came to this holler not knowing or hearing of the disaster. You never read about the Otter Creek disaster?"

"Well, I was pretty young then."

"Of course. Just thought you might have looked into—I mean, you surfed the net before coming here, right?"

I heard a *you dummy* in her tone and was shrinking in my chair. "Actually, I only searched places to stay."

I was getting more ideas since being here: for instance, I figured I could look into death records and birth records too. Marriage licenses. These interviews were not proving helpful. But I might as well push on. "I don't suppose you recall someone named Sara? Spelled without an *h*?"

"Honey, at my age I can't tell you what I had for breakfast. Now, this drug crisis, they'll steal the catalytic converters off your car. In case Nancy didn't tell you, don't go walking after dark. They'll steal anything to get dope. Boy, that's a terrible addiction, and I've seen more than my share of addicts. I practiced general medicine for forty years. Believe me, I've seen a lot of things."

I needed her to get off this topic. "When did you leave this area?"

"I did my undergrad at the University of Louisville, and my MD in Charleston, South Carolina. Did my residency at UNC, and that's how I ended up practicing medicine in Chapel Hill."

She wasn't giving me years but I did enough rough estimates and calculations to figure she was probably ten to fifteen years older than Sara would be if she was still living.

I thought I'd better wrap things up.

"I'm sorry to hear how your mother died." I couldn't get those newspaper images out of my mind.

"They broke the mold when they made my mama. This was her house, and she would have been safe here from the flood. The flood didn't come this high. Funny that I became a doctor, because she also practiced medicine, in her own way. She practiced mountain medicine, made all sorts of herbal remedies. They won't admit it, but she had quite a few regulars. From asthma to rheumatoid arthritis, skin ailments, fevers, sores, sleep problems, and headaches. And she delivered half the babies in this county. They couldn't always find a doctor who could get here quick enough. I can show you her office where she saw patients. I keep it up real nice; it's out back, just a one-room deal.

"She left notebooks of plant drawings, where she found them, the particular day when she'd picked them. With no formal education at all, she knew about foxglove for cardiac regulation, lobelia, mullein, and comfrey root for lung ailments. She used echinacea for infections, and St. John's wort for depression. Elderberries to boost the immune system, raspberries for uterine complaints and to stimulate labor. I'm writing a book about her."

"Where was she when the flood hit?"

She shook her head and looked out the window where the birds were flocking to her feeder. The color drained from her cheeks, and her face had a mournful expression. "Mama loved this holler. About that dam, they didn't listen. She tried to warn them with her last breath."

At that moment she did look frail, or I saw the frail woman she really was, and I wondered who helped her with cleaning, laundry, cooking, shopping.

"Do you have family in the area?"

"No, but I get about just fine. I have a car, but I walk every day, and my neighbors are all the time bringing me something. I know everyone in this holler and I have everything I need."

"That sign on your door—" I began, but she cut me off.

"Oh, that was Mama's." She leaned back again and looked out her window. There were half a dozen squirrels rustling on the ground below for the windfall. Lined up along her window ledge was an array of those small animals with bobbing heads. I had such an urge to tap them all, get them all bobbing. "She was so proud of her letter from the governor, that bastard. She wrote him about the dam a full year before it broke. Didn't she know he was deep in their pockets?" The question hung in the air in a cloud of pain. "Mama," she said, looking at me with a smile of regret, "she wasn't like me. She believed in people, that you could appeal to their better nature. I don't expect a better nature until I see one.

"About this woman you're looking for. I think I can guess why. Perhaps you suspect that your father had an affair with her?"

Throughout most of my life I'd been such a people pleaser, always trying too hard, which I'm sure contributed to my failed marriage and pathetic friendships. But I'd felt something changing since being in Otter Creek, maybe from the couple of people I'd met, from their stories, from their openness.

For once I didn't want to hide. I said, "I bet you were a good doctor."

She scratched her head, then stretched and yawned. "Yes, I like to think so. In all my clinical years, I was rarely surprised. Once or twice, maybe. I might have been wrong sometimes, but I was usually on the right path." She brought her hand down and pointed at me. "But I find it puzzling that you'd care about your father's philandering. The swinging '70s? Open marriages? How could it have any bearing on your life now? It's usually best, as they say, to let sleeping dogs lie." Her eyebrows went up, with a slight smile.

I hesitated. I needed to think. I wasn't sure of the answer myself, so how could I explain it? I was in such foreign territory that my impulse to placate or hide had no appeal, probably because I wanted the true answer, for a change. And, in a bizarre way, maybe from the tea, I felt calmer. The calmness was a strange and new feeling, more grounded, more solid.

With a compassionate tone, she offered, "There must be something going on in your life that brings you on this quest."

"Like I said, I bet you made one hell of a doctor." Then I began, starting with my marriage. I talked for some time, and she listened without interruption.

"There was deep affection at first, maybe love," I told her. "I suppose this sounds clichéd, but something left or changed, or died, at some point. I was contented, though, and we had the girls to raise. It's like I just looked up and there was no marriage, but I never would have had the guts to do anything about it, so he did."

Then I talked about Rose. "She was my rock. My mother-in-a-sister. She died last year. I write her a letter every day."

She asked about Rose's type of cancer.

"Head and neck. Only five percent of all cancers, which I guess you know, and her tumor was the size of a fist and inoperable because it was wrapped around her carotid. She went to the best, New York Presbyterian, where that movie star went. I always forget his name. With two first names?"

"Michael Douglas."

"Right." She really was a good listener. "Rose got into hospice, but they were still talking weeks, maybe months to live. I mean, she was even able to get on that jump-seat toilet thing the night before she died. The next morning, I got there before seven, and I knew from her breathing. We got in touch with everyone to get there fast. I sat by her and whispered in her ear, but around ten the nurses said they needed to wash her. I wish now I hadn't let them, but maybe things happen as they should.

"I went out for a walk, and I distinctly heard or felt Rose next to me saying, *Hurry up, walk faster.* It was like she was pulling me. I had no energy, my legs were dragging, but she wanted me to walk fast. Rose was a power walker until the cancer. When I got back to her room, she was gone. She'd died in the nurses' arms. This one nurse, she turned and met me with outstretched arms. I just fell into them. She held me while I heaved and sobbed. Such wonderful people." My face was wet with tears, and in trying to say the next thing I had to wait and calm myself, but then I said, "I hadn't packed a black dress. Had to go to Marshall's to get one. I *never* wanted to give up hope."

"And now your husband has left you. That's hard."

We were quiet for a minute. I stood to leave and thanked her.

"Before you go, would you like to see the memorial?"

"What memorial?"

"For the flood victims."

"Yes, of course."

I helped her with her coat and cane and we proceeded down the steep hill. She told me she'd bought the land for the structure herself. It was like a large tombstone with the names of the dead engraved on the front. The stone was about three or four feet wide, with a rounded top, set in a kind of pebble garden. There was a small pavilion next to it. I found Mimi Blackstone's name and gently passed my fingers over it. There were no Saras, with or without the *h*.

She invited me to sign the guest book, in the pavilion, the binder pages wet and curling with humidity. I signed my name and took a moment to be still.

"Leandra, where was your mother when the flood hit?"

"No telling, but they did recover her body. They said she'd been down to Underwood's getting them to call the National Guard, which never happened. She never did learn to drive, so after that she went on foot trying to warn people. More than one told me she came to their door and because of her warning, they survived. That's how she died, trying to save her holler."

Chapter 10

1970

It was Valentine's Day, and Frank walked in the door at four thirty to surprise Allicia with a bouquet of flowers, but the surprise was on him. Allicia was out. He found the kids in front of the TV, which was a relief, but his jaw was clamped at the reality of them alone in the house.

He asked Rose, who was nine, when their mother had gone out. She thought it was when their show had started. It was a thirty-minute show, almost over. Aleena, who was seven, got up to give him a hug, and he tried to get a response from Ray, who was five, but Ray made no answer.

"Ray? Ray!" Finally, Ray turned as if waking up and dutifully said, "Oh, hi Dad." And disappeared back into his show.

Frank went downstairs to the basement to lift weights. He had extra clothes, a nice mat, weights, the whole setup. Lifting fifty pounds should hold back most of the troubling thoughts that were piling up at the door of his brain. He growled through clenched teeth and added ten more on each side. Squatting down, he banged the bar to the floor then dropped on the mat without resting to do fifty push-ups. He was not going to allow himself to sink into worry. His usual response to trouble was to get busy.

At five he heard Loretta, the babysitter, arrive. He and Allicia had dinner reservations with his parents in Manhattan. He cleaned up, splashed on some cologne, dressed, and went upstairs. If they left by five thirty, and if there were no backups, they wouldn't be late. But there were always backups. Loretta was already busy settling squabbles about what to make the kids for dinner. Aleena and Ray were shouting for SpaghettiOs, and Rose wanted a turkey TV dinner.

At 5:10, in walked Allicia. She made no apologies, just went straight upstairs to get dressed for dinner.

At exactly five thirty, she came into the kitchen in her black sequined halter gown and diamond earrings. Her hair was perfect, her makeup on. Dazzled by what she could do in twenty minutes, he helped her into her full-length mink coat. Fawning around her, the kids were also spellbound by the transformation of their mother into a glamorous woman. She bent down to hug them, and Aleena reached for her earrings. "They look like spiders," the child said.

"No, no, don't pull." Allicia stood. "Be good for Loretta, kids. I love you."

Navigating the back roads to miss the traffic, Frank made his way to the Hutch in Harrison. Allicia broke the silence. "I don't know why you're upset with me."

Frank lit a cigarette and rolled the window down a bit. "I'm upset because you left the children home alone."

Pulling her mink tighter around her neck, she said, "Frank, I'm cold." Then she looked down next to her on the seat. "Oh no. I don't see my gloves."

Frank turned on the dome light. "Did you bring them? Maybe they're in your purse."

She spilled the contents of her evening bag. "No, they're not here. Can we go back?"

Frank glanced at her, shook his head. "Are you out of your mind? And speaking of that, why did you leave the children alone?"

"I just had coffee with Flo. Is that such a crime? She's my only friend."

"It's not about your friendships, and you have a lot of friends. It's about *leaving the children alone*. What could you have been thinking? If you needed to go have coffee so desperately, you could have asked Loretta to come early."

"She works. You know she comes straight from work."

"Rose is only nine years old. I know you weren't gone long, but we've never talked about leaving Rose in charge. There couldn't be a more trustworthy child, but I just don't think she's ready. What if there was a fire? What if Ray was choking on something? Wasn't it just a month ago that he pulled all the books off the bookshelves to build a fort? The whole bookcase could have fallen on him."

Allicia put her hand to her mouth to stifle a snicker. "Frank, at ten years old, I could drive a tractor and round up cattle bareback on a quarter horse. At twelve—"

"I've heard all your stories before. How you drove a car at fourteen. Times have changed. These kids aren't growing up on a ranch in New Mexico."

Allicia checked her lipstick in her compact mirror, then dropped it into her purse. She patted her rich brunette hair that fell in soft, obedient waves. "Well, you could do worse."

"My mother will forgive the lack of gloves, if you'll lay off the booze."

"Frank," she said with a high-pitched giggle, "don't be ridiculous."

At the restaurant, the maître d' led them to the table where Frank's parents were seated. Allicia walked extra slowly to take it all in: the giant chandelier in the center of the room, the wall of windows with the twinkling lights of the city sixty-five floors below, tables crowded with crystal and small candles and little purple flowers. The noise, the laughter, the excitement, sent a shiver across her bare shoulders. This was what she was born for, destined for. Without forethought, she grabbed the sleeve of a passing waiter and requested a Bloody Mary, "extra strong." He looked momentarily miffed, then mumbled an affirmative.

Frank's parents were nursing their first drinks and didn't seem bothered at having had to wait. Francis Sr. wore a tux. He had a generous belly and a warm smile. He got up to hold her chair. "Allicia, you look ravishing tonight."

"Oh, Francis," she demurred, "flattery will get you everywhere."

She hadn't fully sat down when Frank's mother, Lauren, a petite woman with short gray hair and thin lips, said, while stirring her drink, "Allicia, those heels make you look too tall."

For an instant, Allicia's shoulders caved and a flash of discouragement swept across her face. She stared a moment at her mother-in-law. Her head tilted a bit and one eyebrow went up, and the discouragement dissolved as quickly as it had appeared, leaving a grown woman who could shoot daggers with one look.

Allicia had felt insecure about many things since marrying Frank. She'd never touched a golf club, didn't know how to swim, and hadn't gone to college. "Saltimbocca" and "escargot" required translations. And once, in a circle of Frank's important customers and their wives, she'd embarrassed herself because she'd thought Toulouse-Lautrec was something on the menu.

But Allicia knew about hard work. Her mother had died when she was fifteen, and her father couldn't bring up a teenage girl, so he'd arranged for her to live with the minister's family. The minister's wife made her work from sunup till sundown, and sometimes in the middle of the night she was called on to help with a kid's accident in bed, or if one of them was sick. Not only was she made to cook, clean, and take care of the children, but she often had to wait on the minister's wife, such as cleaning her bathroom, which was particularly galling.

After her blunder about the painter, Allicia had vowed it'd never happen again. To get up to speed with this new country club set, she poured over art books, kept them open on tables and in the bathroom. She now had two prints framed and hanging in her house: *Jane Avril* and *Marcelle Lender Dancing*. Her favorite artist was Van Gogh, and she'd read *Lust for Life* and *The Agony and the Ecstasy* by Irving Stone. She'd learned about lesser-known impressionists, such as Bertha Morisot, who'd been married to Édouard Manet's brother, Eugène, also a painter. She loved the Manets, Monet, and Matisse, and many of the Dutch masters, whether the work was a still life or a pastoral theme. They spoke to her loneliness. At the club, she'd try to strike up conversations about art, but her attempts failed. Those ladies preferred to gossip.

Allicia took pride in her New Mexico roots. If she had a knife and a match, she knew she could survive in the wild, where those women wouldn't last a day. Allicia had come to New York City as a John Robert Powers model and quickly became a cover girl, making one hundred dollars an hour. She was the epitome of success in her siblings' eyes, and she was pretty damn proud of herself. If she knew one thing, it was to make the most out of what you had, to "accentuate the positive," as the song went.

Comfortably taking her seat and opening her napkin, Allicia turned to Lauren and, with a tiny smile hovering around her lips, she said, "A woman, Lauren, can never look too tall."

Frank was talking to his father, so Allicia was forced to listen to her mother-in-law, but as long as she had a drink in hand—and she told the waiter not to let her see the bottom of her glass—she could survive. Lauren launched into why Allicia and Frank should live in Manhattan instead of Connecticut. Allicia drummed her manicured nails on the table, chin resting in the other hand as she scoured the room.

Lauren rarely required a response; she was like an AM radio station. Allicia would meet her eyes every five minutes or so, nod occasionally, and give a half smile, and that was enough to keep her going. Lonely people were like that, Allicia had observed. Lonely people would talk your ear off, like they needed to make up for all those quiet hours and all those thoughts that piled up with no outlet.

Lauren continued, "You can skate and sled in the city. You have the best in the world to choose from, masters of the arts and music."

"Lauren." Allicia refused to refer to Frank's mother with a term related to anything maternal. It was one of those things she would not compromise on. "You know your son hates the city. Every day when he gets home, the first thing he does is go out on the patio." Allicia smiled demurely. "Frank would never leave his two acres of peace and quiet. And he loves the weekend chores."

This was one of the few times Lauren was unable to offer a counterargument, so she simply smiled politely.

Their food arrived. Allicia heard Frank say something about someone not listening to him, and as she was desperate to escape her mother-in-law, she asked, "Who won't listen to you, darling?"

Frank cut into his steak. "It's business, Allicia. It wouldn't interest you."

Wearing his restaurant-proffered bib and breaking his steamed lobster in half, Francis Sr. sprayed his face and Allicia's. He gave Allicia a friendly wink. "I'm sorry, Allicia, did I spray you?"

"You did, Francis." She made a show of patting her face. "I didn't know I should bring an umbrella." They laughed. "Pass it here and I'll show you how to get the lobster out."

She showed Francis Sr. how to get the meat from the legs, then the tail, her laughter ringing out loudly. Then they talked about the kids, but he also asked her about her two sisters out west. Her sisters hadn't been able to come to the wedding because it was in the Notre Dame cathedral in Paris. Her sister Rosemary had married and moved from their home in Clovis to Santa Fe. Ida had married and moved to Los Angeles. Late at night, Allicia called them long distance and talked for hours.

Lauren tried to get Frank's attention, saying his name a few times. Frustrated, she dropped her fork on her plate. "Frank, are you quite well?"

"Pardon me, Mother; lost in thought. What were you saying?"

"What's worn you out? You're traveling too much, aren't you? I was telling Allicia, and I'll mention it to you, just think how easy it would be if you moved into the city. No long commute, no catching or sitting on a crowded train. Everything at your fingertips. No need to drive."

"Oh, some things that look like trouble are worth it." He tried to spread a pat of butter on a round piece of baguette, but the bread ripped apart and the butter fell through. "But how have you been doing, Mother? Have you been walking? It's so good for you to get your exercise." He popped the whole piece of bread into his mouth.

"It's cold and too hard on my joints."

"Yes, of course. But you can call Theresa. The two of you could go to lunch. You're looking pale. Get some fresh air. It'd do you good."

She put her hands on her cheeks. "You're right, Frank, as always. I would love to have lunch with you."

"How about this, Mother: If I take you to lunch this week, you'll agree to make a date with Theresa?"

She readily agreed.

Allicia stood. "Darling, look. The photographer's here." She bent down to get her purse. "He's coming our way."

"How nice," Lauren said, turning to her husband. "We do need to get our picture on Valentine's Day, dear."

"I'm going to powder my nose. Back in a sec." Allicia took off.

Francis Sr. picked up the conversation he'd been having with Frank. "Why not speak to Vern yourself? We have the board meeting this week, the first one of the year, and some new members will be there."

The waiter started clearing the table. "Dad, I wish I didn't have to bother you with this, but couldn't you try speaking to Vern about taking on these truck mines? I hate running all over the East Coast trying to figure out how to make them productive. My job is to sell coal."

"Aren't most of them productive?"

"Poorly managed, at best. And some have significant problems."

"Frank, you know Vern doesn't listen to me."

Frank polished off his wine. "Well, that may be the case, but someone has to talk to him, and I think he'd hear it better from you than from me."

"Now, now, gentlemen," Lauren interrupted. "I feel quite left out when you talk business."

"Sorry, Mother."

Allicia found herself walking by the wall of windows. She longed to merge with the dazzling lights, saunter along Fifth Avenue, and window shop. This is what she'd dreamed that she would do when she married Frank, but it rarely happened. He worked all the time, was always away on business trips, leaving her stuck at home with the kids.

The road down below was choked with cars. There was a long line of red brake lights going one way, and a line of white headlights going the other way. She stepped back a little until the window became a mirror and her reflection along with the cars merged to where she saw, or imagined, the car lights as a string of pearls and rubies slung across her neck. "My ruby and pearl necklace," she whispered.

Her hand went to the empty place.

Chapter 11

There was never a question who'd be at the office first. Frank was. But this morning his secretary arrived just after him, at five minutes to seven.

"You're here early, Mrs. Dominici." Frank put his coat on the rack.

"The garbage strike, sir. I was afraid I'd be late. I'll have your coffee in a minute."

"No hurry. It's awful out there, and what a mess someone will have to clean up." He took out his handkerchief and blew his nose. "I think I can still smell it in here."

"I don't know how anyone can walk. The trash is blowing all over the sidewalks and into the streets."

"Yes, well." He went to his desk. "Any excuse not to work."

She brought his coffee and the xeroxes of his report. "Don't forget, you have the board meeting at noon."

"Looks like we'd better do dictation at eleven. Thank you." Tapping his pencil on his desk, he pondered the meeting, the new members with excellent financial portfolios, and Warren, their new engineer. He wondered if Warren had visited Otter Creek yet.

Frank was the last to take his seat in the boardroom. He knew it pissed Vern off, but he had no interest in listening to Vern's self-aggrandizing bullshit. He'd timed it perfectly, because Vern was about to start his introductions. Vern sat with his body at an angle to the table. Frank wondered if it was to give the impression he might dash off at any moment, to keep people on edge. Vern launched into a long introduction of the new board members.

Frank pictured Sara, her hair glistening in the sunlight at the water's edge, the way she walked back and forth, so passionate. She could carefully choose her words in one moment and the next be blunt and unrehearsed. Impetuous and ethereal. No cunning or guile with her, yet she was beguiling. She had something perennially childlike that he hoped she'd never lose, something that didn't at all depend on age.

He looked up. All eyes were on him. "What?"

"Frank, snap out of it." Vern laughed and the other men followed suit. "Frank, as I said, gentlemen, is our newly appointed president. So he can fill us in on our other subsidiaries."

"Yes." Frank pushed his planner aside and opened the report. "If you'd please turn to your reports, gentlemen."

Frank reviewed the stock dividends and cash payments. Their cash flow had increased, and they'd been able to prepay seven million dollars of their bank loans in the last fiscal year. He briefly reviewed their oil, trucking, and warehousing interests, including the recent acquisition of Fortus, a security transport company.

He needed to influence these new members. He knew from hunting to anticipate the target when shooting a bird, to shoot in the direction it was flying. He'd put pressure on Vern by influencing the board members, hit him from the flank.

"Gentlemen, in light of the new members, I will give a bit of history. Coal has, in recent years, been doing well, arguably better than ever. As you know, the war was good for coal. In spite of some fluctuation, so were the '50s and '60s. But this is a new era."

Vern, who was holding but not smoking a cigar, said, "Frank, we're not on the lecture circuit."

"It bears mentioning that the political atmosphere now and for the foreseeable future"—Frank slowed down and tried to modulate his voice and word choice—"has changed considerably. New laws, new regulations, and, I might add, a whole federal department for inspections will cut into our profits. It's going to lead to an increase in costly improvements or burdensome fines. Given this change and this new climate, gentlemen, there's little need, in my opinion, for the continued policy of purchasing new mines."

Vern lit his cigar and puffed at it until the smoke framed him in a gray fog. "Frank, the record shows that recent years have been our highest production years since 1948. Six hundred million tons on average. Long before I gave you a job here, I built this company from nothing. Our record stands for itself. We are the third largest coal company in the nation."

"The fourth." Frank glanced at his father, who shook his head disapprovingly. "Many of our latest acquisitions are overgrown truck mines. They're decrepit, out of date, and a huge liability."

"Frank"—Vern puffed his cigar—"we need not"—*puff puff*—"burden these gentlemen with trivialities." A long exhale of smoke. "Diversification has been our ticket to success. I see no reason to give it up now. You don't change your tactics when you're on a winning streak, now, do you?" He gave a gratuitously toothy smile to the group. "If it ain't broke, don't fix it."

There were other reports. Frank took notes in his planner. He scribbled calculations on costs of freight, labor, tipple, wheelage, and benefits. Then his mind wandered. He thought of going to confession after work, but he didn't think heaven would lay out the welcome mat. It was safer to bet on Earth, on what was right before him. And that reminded him of his favorite quote, but he never could remember where he'd read it. In his planner, he wrote: "Relegating happiness to heaven is too much of a gamble. I'm going to find it on Earth."

Frank's attention piqued at the introduction of Bill Emery, their chief corporate counsel. He stood, took a moment to quietly look at his open notebook, then began. "It's a changing tide in the coal industry, and I'm referring to the Coal Act. Frank is correct in saying that this piece of legislation is different; it has teeth. It requires periodic inspections and provides for adequate enforcement. In the past sixteen years, 5,500 miners have lost their lives. Previous laws only covered five causes of disasters: explosions, mantrip accidents, hoist accidents, fire, and—" He glanced at his notes. "I seem to have lost my place."

"Inundation," Frank said.

"Yes, inundation. Thank you, Frank. Drownings from water bursting into a shaft. But these accidents only accounted for ten percent of the fatalities." He closed his notebook. "We don't drive our cars without following the rules of the road. Regulations and safety policies are important and needed. Gentlemen, we are looking at a changed ballgame." He sat down.

Vern interjected, "Every business has its share of risks."

Emery looked at Frank "It's my professional opinion that taking on problem mines may indeed jeopardize our bottom line. There's no doubt it'll increase our potential liability and likely involve costly improvements."

"Well, gentlemen," Vern said, putting his cigar down on the ashtray, "that gives us a lot to think about. We've got production up. Utilities have increased their coal use by ten percent. Exports are up. We're making progress with the Japanese market. I don't see any cause for worry. We have yet to hear from our new head engineer, Stan Warren. Bring us up to speed, Stan."

Warren's hair was combed straight back with a heavy dose of something, such that not a single hair separated from the mass. Under his bushy eyebrows he wore wire-rimmed glasses, held firmly in place by his large nose. His report was a load of obsequious bullshit, and Frank tuned him out.

Frank looked at his watch, and when four minutes had gone by, he'd had enough. He interrupted Warren to ask if he'd been to Otter Creek. Warren said he hadn't, and Vern quickly added, "Strip mine bonanza. I'd like to start as soon as possible."

While walking out, Frank caught up to Warren and asked for a minute of his time. Frank followed him into his office. Warren's side table was filled with framed photographs; his wife and children, Frank presumed.

Leaning back in the leather armchair opposite Warren's desk, Frank asked, "Have you had a chance to look at that new acquisition, Otter Creek, in Kentucky? You heard what Emery had to say. I'm not sure what it'll cost to keep the Feds off our back. And I'm gonna need you to help Vern see the light of day."

At his desk, with his fingers making a tent that partially blocked his face, Warren replied, "There were so many others. What's the hurry? What did my predecessor say?"

"Maybe you should check the file."

Warren opened his desk drawer and searched, at last saying, "I see no record of Otter Creek Mining at all. Could it be under a different name?"

"We don't change the names of our subsidiaries, for legal reasons."

"There's no report." He closed the drawer. Now he leaned back. "It doesn't look like Gould ever went there."

Frank lit a cigarette and thought for a moment. "If my memory serves me, you were with Hinkley's outfit, Wilson Coke and Coal, in Colorado, right?"

"Yes. Their office is in Denver. I lived in Loveland. Denver is still a cowboy town." He looked out his window. "It's nothing to this grand city."

"Mining in the Appalachians is a bit different from the Rockies."

Warren choked out a laugh. "I know that."

"The Colorado coalfields are plateaus and barren regions."

The muscles in Warren's jaw flashed. "I wouldn't say—"

"There's no argument here. Facts are facts. In the Appalachians we're dealing with heavily populated areas because much of the land is too steep for habitation. Homes get penned in by rugged terrain. Our miners live next to the mines."

Warren's beady eyes bore into Frank. "What are you getting at?"

"You look at everything Vern's bought, and Otter Creek is the worst. The Bureau of Mines has thirteen hundred inspectors, and that's just for underground. The former owners of Otter Creek Mining were in over their heads and bailed into Vern's willing hands. The slurry ponds are overtopping now. You start strip mining, and it'll all come rolling down. What's your experience with impoundments for refuse water?"

"In the west they don't use impoundments. They use a system of back stowing into old mine shafts. That's—"

"I know what back stowing is. There's no back stowing in this region. Shafts fill up with water. That's what we were talking about in the meeting. Inundation. They're mining too close to old shafts. The maps are unreliable."

"You're concerned about a possible breach?"

"Very concerned, yes. The Kentucky Water Resource Commission and the DNR won't issue a strip permit with the present setup. You're our engineer. I need you to review those inspection reports and the violations and issue your own report."

Taking his calendar in hand, Warren sucked saliva through his teeth. "I'm not quite sure when I could."

"Your title here is?"

He chuckled. "As you know, having hired me, I'm the director of engineering, Rowan Coal Group."

Frank knew his type. Probably sat with his feet on his desk, planning his vacations. Seemingly docile but could turn on you like a weasel. "Warren, as you know, Vern is chairman of the board. But I am president, and I run the day-to-day operations. I know everything that goes on here. Without me, this company would grind to a halt in a matter of days."

"For cryin' out loud, Frank, I've only been here two months."

"And your job is to oversee engineering plans, calculations, and specifications at all Rowan mines."

"I've been busting my chops. I've already looked at twenty-three mines and prepared reports on each one."

"If you need more staff, you let us know. Let's get one thing very clear. I recommended you for hire, Warren, but I don't need a recommendation to fire you." Frank stood. "Next month you'll be joining me on a site visit to Otter Creek. We'll fly into Lexington, then it's a couple hour drive. You'll need your own rental car; I may have other appointments. You have a month to get ready. That should be plenty of time."

Warren stood and looked like he was going to say something. Frank looked straight through his eyes. Warren simply tugged on his vest, and Frank turned on his heel and walked out.

Chapter 12

The winds of March whipped clumps of pine needles from the trees, and they tumbled down streets like small animals. Purple clouds clung to the mountain ridge, blocking the white winter sun and sending dustings of snow that flew with puffs of chimney smoke. The long talons of winter still held Otter Creek Hollow in their grasp.

Sara's brothers left for the Number 5, and the house was preternaturally quiet. Sometimes she sat wherever the sun shone, like a cat, in the pockets of warmth, but today was gray. She sat at the table, picking at her split ends and thinking of Frank and things she couldn't talk about with anyone.

It wasn't that Sara had felt hopeless. She never knew it as such. But something new had come about and she was only able to recognize it because of the contrast. Before, she'd felt helpless to make her dreams happen. And then meeting Frank, that unlikely event, and their surprising conversations, seemed to have put a tiny hole in that feeling, a chink allowing one shaft of light. And where there is a weak point, if you begin to push on it, lean into it, worry it, other parts loosen and weaken. Crumbling happens. More spots of light appear.

Over the years, Aunt Betts had given Sara makeup, and Sara had put it all away in a box. But today, she took it out. In it was a little gold-colored tube of lipstick. It was pink, had an odd smell, and felt sticky on her lips. She applied the mascara and a little blush. Then she decided to put on a black skirt and a button-down purple blouse. She'd worn the skirt to her father's funeral and then stuck it in the back of her closet. The blouse she'd bought when she and Aunt Betts went shopping in Louisville. Then she put on earrings that Linda Lee had given her for her twenty-first birthday. With her hair loose around her shoulders, she turned to each side in the mirror and thought, *Who is that woman?*

Someone was calling her from the front door. Or they might be in the house. No time to change or wipe her face. She went into the living room, where she found Linda Lee holding Baby Jake.

"Cripes, Linda Lee. It's only eight fifteen. Did you blow a tire or run out of bacon? You're never here this early."

"Ha, ha. I guess it is early, but I knew you'd be up." She put the baby down on the floor, and when she looked at Sara, she exclaimed, "My goodness, Sara. Don't you look just beautiful! Where are you off to, a hot date?"

"Yes, at eight in the morning I'm off on a hot date. Just trying on stuff from Aunt Betts. Oh, and these nice earrings from you."

"They're so nice on you. I brought you some cookies." She put the plate of cookies on the counter.

Baby Jake squeaked on the floor and tried to crawl, rocking back and forth on all fours. Sara's dog began licking the infant's face. Sara scooped the baby up, rescuing him from the slobber.

"Here you go, Baby Jake. I'll wipe your face dry."

She wondered if the connection between her makeup and the new operator in town would occur to Linda Lee. But that was a long shot. On the spot she made up something, which wasn't that far from the truth.

"I'm tired of that uniform," she said. "Might as well start dressing up for work. Want some coffee?"

Over coffee, sitting at the round kitchen table, Linda Lee said she was going to Pattie's. "It's St. Paddy's Day, and I made cookies for her."

"I thought they were for me."

"For you too. But I'm sure she's a bit nervous, what with losing the twins before. And stuck at home so long, poor thing."

"I'm alone a lot. It is hard sometimes."

Linda Lee looked sympathetic. "Weren't you going to volunteer at the library?"

"I did for a while, but they needed me on Saturdays and that's when my brothers are home, and I kind of like to hang out with them. Mostly Darryl, not Benny. Benny doesn't usually roll in till noon. I guess I just like the feeling of people in the house. Pete shows up a lot and I cook for them. I seem to crave pancakes when I'm alone, and you can't make pancakes for one. I love a full house."

"I hear Pete's pretty cute."

Sara's eyes grew big. "Please, Linda Lee. Don't." She sipped her coffee.

Linda Lee rested her chin in her hands and took a long minute, looking at Sara. Sara's purple blouse showed off her long, elegant neckline. The small, gold earrings, in their simplicity, gave a sparkle to her face and accentuated her almond-shaped eyes.

"I think it's a good idea, you wearing makeup and getting dressed up. It makes you feel a little better, don't you think? I get dressed up every day. If I have to clean and cook, the least I can do is look nice."

"You do a lot more than cleaning and cooking."

"Why don't you come with me to see Pattie? The more the merrier."

They tucked Jake into his carrier and Linda Lee rode shotgun so that she could keep the pacifier in his mouth.

"Maybe there's something else you could do with your days," Linda Lee suggested as Sara drove.

Talking about her days made Sara nervous. She didn't want people questioning her or looking in on her. She hoped she'd see Frank again sometime. She changed the subject. "How's Clay?"

"He loves his new position. He knows his stuff because he's worked with Robert Hawkins for years. You know him, right? He just retired, but his big thing was: "Never pin a top if you have doubts." She rambled on about that as they rounded the last curve and approached Pattie's house. That's when Sara saw something under the clothesline. At first she thought it was a pile of clothes, but the basket was there, overflowing with clothes, and there were no clothes on the line.

Then she realized what it was. Under the clothesline, next to the full basket of wet clothes, lay Pattie, her body in a heap.

Chapter 13

In the wee hours of the morning, Pattie had awakened with what she figured were Braxton-Hicks contractions. The cramps were too strong to let her doze, and George was snoring, so she tiptoed downstairs. She wasn't sure what to expect, but she didn't want to get her hopes up. Starting a fire in the woodstove gave her something to do to keep her mind off the cramps.

She was thinking of how George had proposed, or sort of proposed. What a chicken he'd been. He'd said, "Do you want to get engaged?"

"George," she'd said, "are you asking me to marry you?"

The heat of their love had almost set that couch on fire.

She started a load of wash and then had a snack: some leftover biscuits, blackberry jam, and two hard boiled eggs. She kept boiled eggs in the fridge because as soon as she finished eating any meal, she was hungry again. Another snack, which held her over between meals, was baked beans and hotdogs. She wondered if this child would have a love of these foods because she ate them so much. Eventually, she heard George moving about upstairs, so she slowly lowered herself onto the couch and pulled an afghan over her to hide the contractions when he came down.

After breakfast George said, "You stay quiet on the couch. Don't you have some knitting or something? What can I get you? I want you to have everything you'll need."

He kissed her in that slow, soft way she thought of as his Clark Gable kiss, coming in slowly, taking her face in his big, calloused hands. It never failed to stir her. She felt a contraction starting.

"Go. Shoo."

"Now, call if anything happens."

"You'll be late."

As soon as the door shut she held on, tried to do her controlled breathing, inhale for four, exhale for eight, but she could only inhale two, exhale three. It helped to count her breaths. After a while the contractions stopped, so she figured they'd been fake. When the day warmed up, she got the wet clothes into a basket and went out to the clothesline. She put the basket down, then walked to a cleared place, not far away, on the edge of the property, where there was a circle of small white rocks. Green shoots, bulbs she'd planted, poked through the soil within the circle even though the ground was frosty. She didn't dare sit down for fear she wouldn't be able to get up.

She spoke out loud to her lost twins, asking their blessings and their help. Then another contraction came, and this one was the biggest. It hurt, and hurt bad. Doubled over in pain, she headed quickly back to the clothesline so she could hang on to the pole. She was almost there when warm water rushed between her legs, and then everything went black.

* * *

Sara jerked the car into park, then ran toward Pattie. "Holy shit!"

Linda Lee picked up the baby carrier, set it outside the car, and screamed, "Oh my God!" as she took off running right behind Sara.

Sara felt a pulse. "She's alive!" They turned Pattie over. There was a pool of liquid between her legs, tinged pinkish, like blood.

Linda Lee's eyes filled with tears. "Please, God, save her!"

No time to wait for an ambulance. They carried her to the backseat. Linda Lee squeezed in beside Pattie with Baby Jake at her feet, saying, "Wake up, Pattie. Please, dear God, stay with us. Hang on." Sara drove as fast and as safely as she could.

Sara ran into the hospital, hardly able to speak. "Pattie Honeycutt. Bleeding. Unconscious, nine months pregnant." Everything after that was a whirlwind of white coats appearing out of every corner, running, then Pattie on a gurney, whisked through the double doors. Sara watched it all in amazement with tears running down her cheeks. They must have gotten Pattie through those doors in less than a minute. Teamwork so well orchestrated it would put any army to shame.

Linda Lee stayed outside trying to quiet Baby Jake, who'd screamed for the whole drive to the hospital. It wasn't long before George barreled into the lobby.

"Where is she?" he yelled.

Someone at the hospital had had the good sense to reach him at the mine office, and Sara chided herself for not thinking of it. A couple of nurses raced over to speak to him. They asked him to sit down, pleaded with him, but he got louder.

"Pattie Honeycutt! Where is she?" He didn't wait for an answer, just barreled through the double doors with them scurrying behind him.

"Mr. Honeycutt! Please! Mr. Honeycutt, you must stop!"

Sara smiled to herself, smiled through her tears. They looked so funny, falling over themselves trying to stop him. They should know better than to go up against George Honeycutt.

A couple of hours later, the nurses came back and said that everything had gone well. They'd performed an emergency cesarean. Mother and baby daughter were fine. Sara hurried out to Linda Lee, who'd finally nursed Jake to sleep and hadn't dared to move him. They grabbed each other, now with tears of relief. Then Linda Lee left to get Jake home.

When Sara went back in, George was coming out to find her. She'd never seen him like this, a big burly man as giddy as a kid. His face was radiant with joy, bubbling over with news of his baby girl, seven and a half pounds, twenty-one inches. He took hold of Sara's hands and thanked her profusely.

"But I only did what anyone would do," she said.

"Believe me, I know what you did. It took a lot of strength and courage. You saved Pattie's life. You saved my little baby's life, my family." He gave her a big hug. "How could I ever thank you enough?"

"Please, George, just show me the baby." They went to the nursery window, and she saw the delicate thing, swaddled and sleeping in a clear plastic bassinet with a pink name card: Baby Honeycutt.

Sara said, "Born March 17, on St. Paddy's Day. What will you name her? Pattie, like her mama?"

Without looking away from the infant whose little lips were puckering, he replied in a whisper, as if afraid he'd wake her, "We talked about naming her Amanda. Pattie loves the nickname Mandy. She looks like a Mandy, doesn't she?"

Sara chuckled at the gushing dad, and agreed, of course. She asked if she could see Pattie. George said she was sleeping, but he opened the door a few inches and Sara stared. She saw Pattie's still-protruding belly going up and down, and instant relief flooded her. The terror of the whole event needed that confirmation of life. Seeing the baby and seeing Pattie produced more tears, tears of joy, tears of relief. They closed the door without a sound.

"You're a lucky man, George Honeycutt."

"The luckiest." He put his arm around her. "C'mon, I'll take you home."

Chapter 14

Frank landed ninety percent of the deals for Rowan Coal, yet Vern still treated him like it was his first day. Vern treated everyone like that, including his own brother, Frank's father. Francis Sr. was in charge of exports, and that suited him fine. Frank often thought that his father should have been a priest, he was such a kindly soul. He admired him, but didn't aspire to be like him. Every fiber in Frank's being resonated with ambition. Whether in business or hunting, fishing, or playing golf, Frank wanted to do his best, maybe even beat his best.

Because of various scheduling conflicts and delays, he wasn't able to get Warren to Otter Creek until March 17. Frank had spoken with Vern about Otter Creek, trying to get the point across that they needed a budget for improvements, but Vern laughed in his face.

He'd also found a new doctor for Allicia. They'd gone together, but as soon as the doctor had mentioned her drinking, she'd picked up her coat and walked out.

Try as he might not to think about her, his thoughts went to the woman by the river, her sparky personality and whip-sharp intellect. Sara had tucked herself into his brain. She was the bright spot and he could hear her warning. "Those dams are right over our heads." Could he turn tail, resign, and for all intents and purposes abandon Sara? No, he couldn't. Much like he couldn't leave his wife, who'd put herself deeper and deeper into a childlike state. He felt like he was being sucked into a vortex, with no handholds, no solutions.

He pulled into the Otter Creek Mining office shortly after noon. Stan Warren was already there, talking to Sweeny and some other men Frank didn't recognize, probably foremen. Apparently there had been some commotion, and Frank asked if there'd been a problem with the dam. Sweeny explained that Honeycutt, the dozer operator, was at the hospital. He'd raced there because his pregnant wife had been found unconscious. Others chimed in about how "Sara Stone drove like Mario Andretti."

"Radio down to Painter to work the dozer," Sweeny told one of the miners.

Frank wanted to ask if Sara was okay, but refrained. "Well, I hope she got there safely," he said instead. They said she was fine and made it to the hospital in time.

"Might as well see those dams, then," he said.

Frank climbed into the back of Sweeny's car, saying to Warren, "You sit in front. You're the engineer."

As they drove, Sweeny described everything they passed. As if it wasn't bad enough that Frank had to sit crammed into the backseat, now he had to listen to this guy give a blow-by-blow about every house in the neighborhood.

"Right there, that yellow house, is where I lived when I first got married. And the one next to it, with the blue wheelchair ramp, that's where my mother-in-law lives. I built her that ramp. Over there, well, it's a field now, but that's where the house was that I grew up in."

Frank wanted to throttle the guy. Maybe he should quit and convince Sara to leave too.

Warren said over his shoulder, "You never told me how entertaining Sweeny was."

Frank rolled down his window. "How long is this drive?"

"The holler is ten miles long, and the office is just a half a mile in, so we've nine to go." They were going about twenty miles per hour. "We've passed Kent and Deer Run; those are little towns. Now we're getting to Baden. Then there's Larabee, Chittendale, and the last town before the Number 5 is Elliston. The dams are up beyond there."

Frank yawned a loud, long yawn.

"All of this is Otter Creek Hollow?" Warren asked.

"Yes." He rattled on about the refurbished houses, most of which had started out as coal camps. Now they had indoor plumbing and two-car garages."

Up on a hill, Frank noticed a woman sweeping her front porch. She was tall and thin, with what looked to be layers of clothing on, pants with a skirt over them and a shawl wrapped around her shoulders. Sweeny was driving so slowly that she met Frank's eyes with a hard stare. Sweeny worked her into his monologue. "That woman up there's Mimi Blackstone. Biggest nuisance in the holler."

The name jogged Frank's memory. He recalled Sara mentioning it. "Why is she a nuisance?" he asked.

"Besides crying wolf every other day and stirring up trouble, she wrote our governor."

"About the dams?" Frank asked.

"Yes. Crazier than a March hare. Makes some sort of potions up in the hills." Sweeny tooted his horn and waved at an old man walking along the road. "That's Matt Peterson. Retired miner."

"I heard that there was a flood," Frank said. "Can you show us how far the water went?"

"Where'd you hear about that? Underwood's or Todd's? Just a little slump." Sweeny coughed. "I think it got the church and a couple of houses in Elliston. I'll point it out when we get there."

"Christ! What's that smell?" Frank asked, rolling up his window. They were driving by what looked to be a smoking mountain of mud.

"That's the biggest gob pile I've ever seen," Warren said.

Sweeny mumbled, "Yeah."

"It's not supposed to be burning like that, you know," Warren said. "I expect you've been cited for it."

"Is that another problem?" Frank asked, with his handkerchief over his nose.

Warren turned to Frank. "It's supposed to be aerated, vented, and layered with ash so it doesn't ignite."

Sweeny cleared his throat. "It's gotten a little big. Been there as long as I can remember, and my family moved here when I was three."

Frank tapped Warren's shoulder. "Make notes, would ya?"

Warren scribbled on a small pad. He asked for the dimensions.

"It's a thousand feet long and four hundred feet across," Sweeny said. Then he turned onto a rough gravel road with a steep incline, the Haul Road, carved into the edge of the mountain. "Here's what we call Hanson's Fork, runs into Otter Creek. Up here's the dam, well, what's left of the first one, and the second." They parked and got out.

The first pond looked fairly average to Frank, roughly the size of a backyard swimming pool. He'd seen many similar to it. The problem he could see without having to go any farther was that these impoundments were sandwiched between two steep mountains high above Otter Creek. If there were a breach, the water would travel directly into the path of the towns. He needed to see no more, but Warren did. It would be Warren's report that Frank would use for any construction costs or retrofitting work that might be needed. And the RFE, the money, would have to have Vern's approval.

They walked farther up the dirt track. The ravine narrowed. Sweeny babbled on about strip plans. "Winifred Seam is farther up this road," he said. "That's where we'll do the strip when we get the permit. Draglines and buckets are up there, see?" Frank thought he saw something glimmering in the sunlight.

Warren pointed to the two steep mountains on either side of the ravine. "So, Otter Creek is the main watershed for these two mountains?"

"Yes, I suppose that's right."

To Frank it sounded as if Sweeny had never thought about it before.

"And how much refuse liquid is added daily?"

"Oh, between four and five hundred thousand gallons."

"And how much solids?"

"Running about a thousand tons."

Warren whistled. "Well, let's see this next dam."

They walked at a quick pace for at least a quarter of a mile. Sweeny, in front, said it was just over the next knoll. Then they saw it. A gigantic lake of inky black water. The sun shone on it, and it had small waves from the wind, yet it absorbed all light. No reflections. No shimmering.

Warren was shaking his head. Frank was speechless. The dam stretched the whole way across the ravine to the other mountain, and it looked to be fifty or sixty feet to the valley floor. The width from front to back, where they drove bulldozers back and forth, looked like it matched the length. It literally formed a massive wedge between the two mountains. All comprised of crushed rock.

Warren started talking about measurements and regulations, but Frank wasn't listening. The god-awful truth was, this was so much worse than anything he'd imagined, so much worse than anything even remotely connected to what Sara had described. He'd seen enough impoundments in his day to know that this was the most outrageous, egregious display of idiocy imaginable.

To Sweeny, Warren exclaimed, "Holy shit! What have you done here? This thing looks bigger than a football field."

"You're right. It's roughly five hundred feet across the hollow—of course, it varies depending on where you're measuring—and the thickness is roughly about the same. And it's about sixty feet high."

Frank lit a cigarette. Twice he started to say something and then stopped himself. At last, he said, "I take it, Warren, you'd call this unprecedented?"

Warren took off his sunglasses and looked straight at Frank. "There are just no words."

Sweeny said, "Well, the lake is about a half a mile long and some say around forty foot deep in some parts. Summer, they take boats out on it. Course, it's trespassing, but they're miners, so we look the other way. Believe me, we keep a watch on these dams."

Pacing now, holding his hat in his hand and looking down, Frank looked like someone waiting at a cemetery for the hearse to arrive. "You mean to tell me that all this water is held back by tipple waste, by tailings?"

"Bulldozed twice a day every day, adding crushed rock, shale, and solids. Probably an old truck or two, to be honest. Tree stumps. You name it." He laughed.

Warren rubbed his forehead.

Frank said, "Well, Warren, what do you have to say?"

Warren said, "What's the foundation?"

Sweeny kicked a stone. "Slurry, mostly."

"Slurry!" Warren exclaimed, as if jolted back to life. "Now I've heard it all. *Please* tell me you're joking." Warren turned to Frank and for a moment had his hand over his mouth. Then he spoke. "For a hundred years, it's been standard practice when impeding a waterway with any structure to build it on a solid rock foundation. Any moro—" He stopped himself and changed his words. "Any simpleton knows this."

Sweeny piped up confidently, "I assure you, it is solid. Compacted twice a day. George Honeycutt would normally be here, except he's—"

Frank mumbled, "So this is the 'The Big Lagoon'?"

"Where'd you hear that name? Down at Todd's?"

He wasn't sure where he'd heard it—possibly from Sara—so he didn't answer.

Walking back to Sweeny's car, Warren asked about the population of Otter Creek.

"Four thousand in Otter Creek Holler. In all of Whitfield County, there's thirty-five thousand."

Warren interrupted him. "There are *four thousand people* in this hollow?"

Frank asked Sweeny to tell Warren about the recent inspection reports.

"The usual bullroar," Sweeny began. "Dams are too close to the road. They want an overflow spillway."

"Anything else?" Warren asked.

"They want us to raise the road six to eight feet and put in new pipes down in that culvert. We'd have to get it surveyed, get a permit. That would be a major operation. Close us down for months. We couldn't do that. We did install a couple of thirty-six-inch pipes."

"Where does the prep plant bleed empty?"

"Above." He pointed. "The pipe goes from the inby under the mine track. Well, I should say pipes, because there are a few welded together."

"Last question." Warren chose his words carefully. "What exactly happened to the dam when you had that small flood, as you called it?"

"There was a slump."

"A slump. Where and how much of a slump?"

"The corner. Very little."

Sweeny's car was now in view, and he hurried ahead to catch his CB radio.

Frank took advantage of having Warren alone. "I know it's bad. But just tell me how bad."

"Scary. Impossible to even put words to."

Lighting a cigarette, Frank said, "What are we talking here? Give it to me in dollars. It's fixable, right?"

Warren said, "Frank, this looks like some sort of Stone Age monstrosity."

Frank noticed the change in Warren. There wasn't a trace of the cavalier, lackluster guy in his office. Frank saw in Warren a man with sober, calculating discernment. Yet it also was apparent that Warren was as shocked as he was—and Warren was the expert.

After a pause, Warren continued, "First of all, for an earthen dam to work, it must have no seepage at all. This dam was built with the opposite purpose: filtering the liquid. Seepage will eventually erode the structure. Not only that, but it's going to stop working because it'll get clogged with silt, which is what happened with the first dam. The second flaw is that it isn't on a solid foundation. It's on a slurry foundation. And it impedes a waterway. I would say this is basically a *Titanic*. It's not *if* it fails, it's *when* it fails. It will fail."

Frank exhaled, a long exhale through pursed lips. "That's what I thought. What do we do?"

While Sweeny was talking on his CB, Warren looked back at the dams. "I think we'll need a third dam."

"A third dam! Christ, Warren. Is that the best you can come up with? Sounds like lunacy."

"For solids, just solids, no liquids. We won't need a permit because it won't exceed the fifteen-foot limit on height. We'll build it on a concrete foundation, the way they're supposed to be built. It'll speed up the filtration so we can empty more liquid from this giant dam."

"Oh, I see. Anything else?"
"I'll need time. But I'll work on it."
"You'd better."

Chapter 15

The mood at Todd's that night was festive. Everyone kept calling Sara "Mario." Her thoughts were on Frank, who she'd heard was in town. She kept making mistakes, overfilling the beers from the tap, confusing root beers and Cokes, burning the fries. Things she'd never done before. When she broke a glass, Todd smirked, "Those fancy clothes getting in the way of your thinking?"

"Very funny." She'd touched up her makeup at home before leaving for work, and had even put on pantyhose.

Thirty minutes before closing, Frank walked in. She motioned for him to have a seat. People simultaneously started clearing out. She took his order, then in the kitchen she started his steak and fixed his drink.

Saying good night to her customers, trying to act as normal as possible, she put his drink down in front of him and asked, "Do any fishing lately?"

"Not today. But everyone seems quite pleased with you. Apparently you're a local hero. I gather you raced that woman to the hospital and saved her life and the life of her baby."

"Yes, well, we were lucky to get her there in time."

"Sounds like it. The way they talk, you might have a career as a race car driver."

"More like a stunt car driver. It wasn't so much smooth handling, as desperate handling, and a lot of luck. People pulled off the road to let us by; of course, I was blasting the horn." She started clearing tables. "But it looks like I'm going to have to give up on a lot of good careers because I just love clearing tables."

"Sarcasm doesn't sound right coming from you."

She stopped, looking at him as if just seeing him for the first time. "That's a nice thing to say. Thank you." It was surprising that he'd say that, that he'd know her, or know what was uncharacteristic of her. She thought: *there are people who've known you your whole life, who don't know you as well as someone who just met you. How could that be?*

In the kitchen, Todd said, "I'm sorry I jumped on you like that.

You must be worn thin. Let me take care of that operator and close up. You need to get on out of here. You've already had quite a day, make no mistake. You were up at the hospital all day, weren't you?"

"Uh-huh," she mumbled while unloading piping-hot clean dishes and keeping her back to him, so he couldn't see that leaving was the last thing she wanted. Then she turned and, as cheerfully as possible, said, "No, Todd, I'm really not that tired. And I'm sure Sally's waiting dinner on you." Sally was his wife, a delicate blond thing who probably didn't weigh one hundred pounds soaking wet. Not the kind of person Sara would've thought Todd would go for, and not the type she'd have thought would go for him. So much for types. "I can fix her a plate."

"Nah, she's grilling out. It's Eliza's tenth birthday. We let her invite ten friends for the night. *Please* don't make me go home."

"A birthday! You get on out of here."

"Okay." He got his coat and left.

The place was cleared out except for a few stragglers and Pete at the jukebox. She gave Frank his steak with fries. "Want salad?"

"Not tonight, thanks. I hope they remembered to give you a tip before flying out of here."

"Most of them had finished eating anyway, but they do fine."

"I thought I might go fishing in the morning."

"Is that right? Don't forget your funny boots."

On her way back to the kitchen, Pete met her at the swinging door. "Who is that guy?"

"What do you mean? An operator, of course."

"Why's he so smiley?"

That's all she needed, another male supervisor—as if her brothers weren't enough. "Can I help it if he's smiley? What do I care? I work for tips, Pete. If he's smiley, I smile back; that's how it works until I make enough money to get the hell out of here. Don't you have better things to do than hang around an empty restaurant?"

Stepping closer to Sara, he asked, "Poker later on?"

"Oh, now you're inviting me to my own house?" Pete had been spending a lot of time at her house, playing cards with her brothers.

"Man, you're touchy tonight."

"I'm exhausted."

"That makes sense given your day." Pete had his coat hooked on his thumb over his shoulder, which Sara thought looked sexy. He said, "I'll be there. So maybe I'll see you. It'd be nice if you want to join in. I mean, if you're up to it."

She started to say that she'd probably be there, but then another idea occurred to her, to give her an out. "I heard my friend Becky's in town, visiting Maria. I may go over there. I think I will go over there because I hardly ever get to see her."

She'd made up Becky. Maria was a high school friend who'd never left Otter Creek and worked for her family at their laundry business. Her brothers wouldn't ask about details. Pete was the only one who cared.

Sara was wiping tables when Pete left. He glanced at Frank, giving him a dirty look, and then bumped into the door. Amused, she thought he was such a Gumby. Kind of cute—too bad he was a coal miner. And such a kid compared to Frank.

The kitchen was about done. She'd cleared Frank's plate and finished the dishes and the floor.

Frank said, "So, where's your boss this evening?"

"Gone home."

Frank was the only customer left. The brick building was a dark space in the light of day; at night it was like a cave, the night magnified by the cinderblock walls and dark wood floor. Sara pulled the window blinds down.

"Sara, why not sit down a minute? You've been working hard. This place looks spotless."

She joined him at the table. A train horn sounded, followed by its resonant percussion, puffing, puffing, puffing, like the breath of a monster. Her nerves were frayed from the events of the day, the fright at finding Pattie on the ground, and the elation of a new and healthy baby. And then there was this man who, for whatever reason, Sara liked. The fact that he was married should, of course, been an insurmountable obstacle. The fact that he was an operator should have made it ridiculous to consider him.

She asked herself, while looking at him, what it was she wanted. Was it the forbidden? Not at all. He was a bit like the train horn that had just faded. He was possibly a step in the direction of breaking free from her suffocating life. Would he have the key, would he have the answer? She doubted it. There was one thing she could do. She could influence him to do something about the dams. Doing something toward saving her holler could help to make it easier to one day leave the holler. And there was something else. His kiss.

Frank was the first to speak. "Did you get dinner?"

"Nibbled."

"You must be exhausted. You should get home and get some rest." Frank stood and got his coat.

At the door, Sara took his hand. "Frank, they're wrong about operators. I wish I could tell everybody in this holler how wrong they are."

They kissed and then held each other. She'd never experienced a man who knew what a hug was. Frank didn't let go until she did.

She watched him go; then she left, locking the door behind her.

Low clouds were swiftly passing in front of the moon, which was high above the mountains, lighting the world in its milky glow. Sara simply wanted to be outside and under its soft light. She walked into the woods behind Todd's and sat on a downed tree trunk. For some reason, thoughts of her mother emerged. Sara rarely thought of her mother, beyond thinking that she didn't want to be like her. But for the first time she began thinking of her more dispassionately, more objectively.

Had her mom felt trapped? She had never complained to Sara about the mine, but Sara saw the fear in her eyes every morning when she kissed her husband and sons goodbye. For the first time, Sara had an inkling of compassion for her mother. After all, she was just a woman, a woman like herself, vulnerable, doubting, confused, lonely.

Sara realized she'd never seen it from her mother's viewpoint. She'd been too consumed with her own pain, the pain of rejection. But how tragic for her mother. To think that her mother was so alone with her troubles that the only solution she could come up with was to abandon her family. How very tragic.

Sara's diaphragm was in her purse; she'd put it there when she'd heard that Frank was in town. She walked back to Todd's. Frank, she knew, always took the room on the end, and that's where his car was parked. There were very few customers this time of year, and his was the only light on. She tapped on the window. He opened the door a crack and she slipped through and into his arms.

Frank sat in the armchair; Sara stretched out on the bed.

They talked for a long time. They talked of their families, their goals, careers they'd each dreamed of. Frank's was woodworking and furniture-making.

"Woodworking!" said Sara. "I never would have guessed that. I've often thought about journalism, or some sort of writing job. I think people are so interesting. I'd love to just go around and interview people. At Todd's I hear the most unusual things. I've often thought that if I had to take a test, about who would be most likely to have done this or that, I'd flunk. There's so much behind people that you just can't tell from the outside."

"I wonder if people in Otter Creek know what a gem you are."

Sara stood, and reached out her hand to Frank. "Were you surprised I came here?"

"A little. And pleased."

"Before I came here, I sat in my favorite spot in the woods, and thought, mostly about my mother. She up and left us, and two years later my father died. I guess she just couldn't handle it. Couldn't handle my father's noisy lungs, which you could hear in the next room. But more than that, I think the fact that her three sons were working in the mine—Benny had been there for a year—was just too much. It wasn't until tonight that I had the thought that she was impulsive, that she might have so much guilt and regret that even if she wanted to come home, she couldn't. She left because she was afraid: afraid to watch her husband die, afraid her sons might have the same fate, and she can't come back because she's afraid. Her whole life, if she's even alive, is a sad, tragic life."

Frank had taken her hands, his warm, dark eyes focused on her.

At last, she said, "I've not wanted to be like her. All my life I didn't want to be like her. But I now realize I've been frozen. Too scared to do anything, to take any chances. Too afraid to make a mistake."

He pulled back and smiled. "I hope that's not what you think I am."

"How would I know? How does anyone know? I know I've never met anyone quite like you."

"I've never met anyone like you."

Sara led him to the bed. There, with their bodies close, Frank said, "I've made some mistakes in my life. I didn't know it at the time. You know how you said you can't predict what a person is like. Well, all I can say is, I know exactly what you mean."

"Your wife?"

"She drinks too much. But running away is no way to solve your problems. And I could never leave my children, not...not the way she is."

"I am here with you."

"And I, sweet Sara, who needs no *h*, am here with you."

Chapter 16

2019

Standing at Nancy Monroe's front door, having paid her for the accommodations, I was saying goodbye before heading back to Connecticut. I was anxious to get on the road. Just then, two men came in. One was her son, Walter, whom I'd met, and the other was his friend, Benny Stone. Both looked to be about the same age.

"This is Aleena Fitzgerald," Nancy said to Benny.

"Is that your car out front with Connecticut plates?" Benny asked, with no other preliminaries. He was tall and thin. I said it was, and he asked if I was there to help with the strike.

"No. She's looking for someone named Sara who was living here back in the 1970s."

"That so?" Benny said, "Someone named Sara, huh? Are you from the State Department, or the FBI?"

I wasn't sure if he was joking or not, so I didn't answer. Nancy, who'd gone into the kitchen, shouted, "A friend of her sister's." She came back with four glasses of iced tea. Benny helped her with the glasses and set them on the table. Taking a seat and sipping one, he said, "An old friend? What's the last name? Probably need a last name."

I was closing up my bags and organizing my things by the front door. I tend to be kind of a bag lady when traveling, using multiple totes instead of a suitcase, with the premise that I can find things more easily, but I never can. I said, "She was a friend of my sister, who passed."

"My condolences. Have some tea before your long drive." The three of them were sitting at the table. "Maybe we could convince you to help with the strike, since you haven't found your sister's friend."

I walked over to the table. "I really should get going. What kind of help do they need?"

Walter said, "I guess you don't know very much about these things. They're camping out on the tracks, with families. They need just about everything. Why not stay a few more days? You have room, don't you, Mom?"

Benny stood and handed me a glass, then held the chair for me. I sat on the edge.

Nancy said, in her cheerful voice, "Now, you know I do. Unless it's the Hatfield convention; when those people are in town, phew! They run me ragged."

I took a teeny sip, not wanting tea before heading out on a long drive, because I'd need a pit stop in an hour.

Nancy asked, "You know what I'm talking about, don't you, Aleena?"

"Uh, yeah, the famous Hatfields and McCoys. I think everyone's heard of them."

"Yes, and for a week they drive their four-wheelers all over this county. You're very welcome to stay. I'd be glad to have you."

"I've taxed your kindness quite enough."

"Not a bit. You've been no trouble at all."

"See? She wants you to stay," Benny said with inviting eyebrows.

"But I've got to get on the road, and I'm not good with directions."

"Your GPS won't do you much good out here," Benny agreed.

We discussed my directions, and Nancy was walking me to the front door when another person arrived. This time it was a young guy. He had dark hair, a beard and mustache, but his face was uniformly covered with black coal dust, except the tip of his nose and his lips. The black was very dark on the top of his nose and under his eyes. My immediate thought was to wonder how could anyone in 2019 come out of a coal mine with this much black coal dust all over their face. Could the air they're breathing be *that* bad?

"Hey, Grandma." He reached around to hug Nancy. That's when I noticed his hands, which had a thin layer of dust. But the thing that shocked me was that they were red, and looked puffy and swollen.

Nancy introduced him. "This is Robbie, my great-grandson."

He nodded toward me, then disappeared into the house.

Despite the shock of this young man and what he had to go through for his daily bread, I was so impressed with the warmth and closeness between generations. Nancy was one lucky woman. I said my goodbyes.

As careful as I was with the directions, reversing them was hard. There were four million turns on these long country roads with nothing but fields or woods, and therefore four million ways for me to get lost. And get lost I did. I think I was on my way to Tennessee instead of Connecticut. I finally pulled off the road to study my notes, saying out loud, "If I turned right then it's a left," and so on. However, only a minute or two had gone by when a car pulled up next to me with a friendly woman offering to help. She gave me directions, I wrote them down, and she even gave me her son's cell phone number in case I still needed help before reaching the highway.

I felt blown away by the kindnesses I'd been shown. I don't know what I'd expected, but it wasn't this. Multiple generations living together or close by, helping one another. Strangers offering to help direct me. I thought I'd come here to find out something about my father, but I was finding something quite different. I hadn't known how lonely I was until I felt this warmth and openness, until I experienced these kindnesses. I went home feeling very full.

I didn't mind the long drive ahead of me because my mind was peaceful. The ache I'd been feeling since Stephen left had vanished. Maybe I'd find Sara and maybe I wouldn't. I was certain that, if there was a Sara, she didn't die in the flood. It occurred to me that there was plenty I could do from home. Plenty of things could be found because of the Freedom of Information Act. I wasn't ready to give up.

Chapter 17

1970

Frank went to Warren's office, but he was out. Frank stepped in far enough to notice a brochure on the table near the door. He picked it up, thinking maybe Warren was headed on vacation, but it was from the National Coal Board, the British outfit, concerning the 1966 disaster in Aberfan, Wales. Frank read the caption under the photo: "Over a hundred schoolchildren were buried alive."

"Is that off my desk?" Warren asked from the doorway.

"It was on this table."

Warren motioned for Frank to take a seat. "Junk mail. I put it there for my secretary to take."

"Junk mail? Is that right? Seeing they sent it to the head of engineering at a large coal company, I'd say it was fairly well-directed mail." Frank took the brochure and sat in the chair opposite Warren's desk.

"I know why you're here. Otter Creek."

"Yes, I am here to discuss your recommendations for Otter Creek, and this pamphlet"—Frank shook it in Warren's direction—"is relevant. Do you know what happened in Aberfan?"

"The slurry tip crushed the school."

"'Crushed the school,'" Frank repeated. He stood and lit a cigarette, giving a long exhale before asking, "Mind if I smoke?" Warren shrugged.

Frank walked in a small circle. Then, turning to Warren, he said, "It's easy to say, or easier to say, that it crushed a school, isn't it? But the caption right here"—he pointed to the brochure—"reads 'buried alive.' Over a hundred children were suffocated, Warren, suffocated because a gob pile slid." Frank sat back down. "Didn't you see, on TV, the pictures of the parents digging in the waste pile for their children?"

Warren took off his glasses and wiped them with a tissue. Then he said, "Frank, I have a lot to do today. Could you get to your point?"

"I'd like to see your report on Otter Creek."

"I have been up to my eyeballs."

Frank leaned toward him. "Warren, you've had a month."

"I'm not shirking my responsibilities here, and I am not knocking your authority."

Frank snorted. "Shirking your responsibilities?"

"It's just that I got word from above you, that's all."

"Vern?"

"He invited me to lunch—let's see—two weeks ago. Otter Creek came up and he didn't let me have a word in edgewise. He said I was not to make any improvement recommendations or plans. I said it'd be hard to get a strip permit with the way it is now. You know, I didn't like what he said next. And considering what happened to Yablonski . . ." His voice trailed off.

"Yablonski! Those drunken hoodlums! Come on, is that what you think of Vern? Of me?" Frank looked incredulous. "Warren, pull yourself together."

"He told me he had ways of getting the permits. That was his exact word, 'ways.' I didn't want to question him. I'm a family man; I do my work and do what I am told. This is just a job. I've got kids, for Christ's sakes!"

"Warren, Warren, listen to me. He meant perks, comps." He leaned over to put his cigarette out in the ashtray on Warren's desk. "Like offering the use of a nice apartment in Palm Beach. And, if you play your cards right"—Frank leaned back—"I might be able to arrange for you and your lovely wife to spend a week there sometime. It's true that 409 is better than 407, but both are nice and right on the beach. Does your wife like blue? The décor in 407 is blue, but 409 is a bit bigger, if you think you might entertain. If my memory serves, it's a bit more on the soft green side."

Warren wiggled in his seat, getting more upright. "My wife likes both, but I do think more space is always preferable."

"Send me your preferred dates and I'll see what I can do. It's not a place for children; I hope you understand."

"No, no. We won't bring our kids. Of course."

Frank nodded agreement. "Parents deserve a getaway on their own, don't you think? Now, please show me your notes on Otter Creek."

Warren opened a manila folder. "To start with," he began, but then he dropped the file on the desk and stared at Frank a moment. He began again, "Frank, I've just never seen any impoundment built to this magnitude. I can't help but say as an engineer—and, quite frankly, as a human being with common sense—that I really think you should sell. Get out."

"I'm not a betting man, Warren, never have been. I know the wager of getting that dam to a safe level is a long shot, but I know too well how stubborn and intractable Vern can be. He won't sell. So let's carry on, shall we?"

Warren read from his notes. "Installing overflow pipes along the outby. Then installing a spillway. Raising the road certainly would be a good idea, but that's not enough. The dams impede a waterway that drains the sides of two mountains, and they've been built on a silt foundation. To conclude, there's no way to eliminate the perilous nature that already exists." He put his hands up in a surrender gesture.

The commercial for Tareyton cigarettes was "I'd rather fight than switch." Frank liked that. He could be a bulldog, and this was one of those times. He was too far in to go back. As a salesman, he knew how to overcome objections, or at least move the discussion forward against them.

"What do we do first?"

Warren gave a short laugh. "You're good."

"I know I'm good."

"All right. The third dam, for solids."

"I've got them started on that. That should lower the solids and speed up the filtration rate. We can then empty more water and lower the level. We'll do the pipes, which also will lower the water. Give me the specs on that. But what else can we do?"

Warren was wringing his hands. He shook his head. "Frank, you've got a body of water forty feet deep."

Frank picked up one of Warren's framed photos. "I've been admiring your lovely family. Is this your wife and son? He plays soccer; good for him. Nice-looking boy." He put the picture down and looked thoughtful for a minute. Then he said, "Warren, I have one last question for you. If your family lived along that ten-mile stretch of Otter Creek, what would you do?"

"Move." Warren didn't have to think, didn't hesitate.

"That's what I thought."

"Okay," began Warren, "about reducing the solids, there's limits to what that'll do, with the water as high as it is. We'll have to release black water, which is what got them into this mess in the first place. Go ahead and have them do that to reduce the pressure. When we get cited from the DNR or the Water Resource Council or from Batman himself, we'll call it an accident that we're rectifying. This will get us a deferment and buy us some time. There's only one other thing, but it's a long shot."

Frank leaned forward. "I knew you'd have something."

"A chemical thing called froth flotation. It's not really new, but it's hardly been tried. You add these chemicals designed to adhere to the tiny coal particles, which will increase the separation of filtrate. The solids precipitate out faster."

"I see, so there's more clear water that we can drain. Good. That's good. Couldn't we also dredge it? Wouldn't that also get the level lower?"

Warren thought for a minute. "Might be a good idea. I'd have to look into it. I don't think they usually dredge, and with that steep topography there, it might be impossible to get the equipment close enough. Releasing water will be our best bet. They're using this new chemical system at Hickman Coal."

"Perfect. Call over there and find out everything you can. Run some numbers on all of these ideas ASAP. Get estimates if you have to. I need hard numbers. Then we'll plan another trip down there." Frank stood, still holding the pamphlet. "By the way, can I have this?"

"Be my guest. But, Frank, I hope this doesn't get me fired."

"What an old lady you are, Warren. It won't get you fired."

Frank was halfway through the door when Sara's words came to him: "Those dams are right over our heads." He turned around and said, "It might get you rewards in heaven, though."

With that he left.

Chapter 18

Back at his office, Mrs. Dominici gave Frank a pile of phone messages. Ignoring them, he focused on the pamphlet, titled "Summary of the Report of the Tribunal." The first paragraph began: "The Aberfan disaster is a terrifying tale of bungling ineptitude by many men charged with a task for which they were totally unfit . . ."

He slammed the brochure down. "Bungling ineptitude," he said loudly, and marched out of his office, gruffly saying to his secretary that he'd be back shortly. He had no idea where he was going. He just needed to move.

Jackhammers, fumes from buses, throngs of people on Madison Avenue. Smells of pretzels and burgers and warm exhaust coming up through manholes. The city provided little comfort. Still, he walked.

He was thinking of Sara saying "right over our heads" when a cop yelled at him—he'd almost walked into the path of a truck. Maybe Vern kept his head in the sand to ease his conscience, if he had one. Maybe Vern deliberately remained callous to the world around him, but Frank couldn't, and Sara had been—no, Sara was—a part of that.

Hadn't Warren said that Vern cut him off? Wouldn't let him report on Otter Creek? Frank couldn't sit by and do nothing. *When something's wrong, and you know it's wrong, you've got to try to make it right,* he thought. An elderly woman with a cane was having trouble stepping down off the curb, and he offered his arm. She reminded him of his own mother, who might at that very moment, somewhere in the city, need someone's arm herself. He couldn't recall giving assistance to anyone in New York before. He'd always been in too much of a hurry.

Frank felt as if he were waking up. Even the city seemed like a different place. It was hard to look at who he had been, but something was forever different and he would never go back. He didn't want to go back.

He became aware of his hunger; in fact, he was famished. It was going on two o'clock and he'd skipped breakfast. He stepped into Neil's Coffee Shop on East 70th and Lex. The place was crammed, smoky, and loud. More people were pushing him from behind into the hot space. Waiters yelled to the cooks at the grill and carried plates of food high above their heads. Frank turned around and forced his way back through the crowd and out the door. The street was peaceful compared to that mayhem. The Palm would be a safer bet and had the best steaks in the city. There he could hear himself think.

In the dark booth, the waiter brought his steak, and Frank thanked him absently, still puzzling over the situation with Vern. To Vern, Frank was still the little guy, the nephew. Vern had no kids, but he'd never shown Frank any preference or respect. Vern had made him president but never treated him like a president. It was fear. Vern was afraid to lose his power, to lose control. He lived under the Sword of Damocles. Either way, Frank knew there wouldn't be that many years till Vern would kick the bucket and he'd be next in line. Then he could fix and throw money at whatever he wanted, if he could hang in there that long. And the bigger "if": if that dam could last that long.

Frank went to church every Sunday, when he was in town, but he struggled with prayer. He hoped that being quiet in the woods, or while fishing, would serve as sufficient prayers, because at those times, no words ever came to him. In the woods, it seemed no words could come close to what he was feeling, and what he was feeling was the closest he ever got to prayer. Before he left the restaurant, like a prayer, or perhaps an incantation, he wrote her name three times on the paper placemat. *Sara, Sara, Sara.* He tore it off and tucked it in his inner suitcoat pocket.

Back at his desk, he shuffled papers aimlessly and stared out the window. It was April 19. He'd always loved that poem by Emerson:

By the old rude bridge that arched the flood,
Their flag to April's breeze unfurled,
Here once the embattled farmers stood
And fired the shot heard round the world.

He looked out at the bustling city of New York, the grand skyscrapers, the throngs of people, and said out loud, "They weren't even soldiers. They won the war and they weren't even soldiers. They were farmers."

He put the piece of torn placemat into his daily planner.

The next week, Frank went to meet Vern for lunch. When he stepped into the dining room, Vern was waiting for him, puffing his cigar.

Frank knew from photographs that his uncle had once been a

handsome man. Now he was a withering marshmallow. At one time Frank had held him in high regard, even looked up to him. Those days were gone. Vern's success had made him smug, and his greed made him brittle and inflexible.

The waiter brought their drinks. Vern got a martini, Frank a bourbon and water.

It was actually Vern who brought up Otter Creek.

"Warren had his panties in a twist over the new mine in Whitfield County, Kentucky," Vern said. "What's it called, Fox Hollow?"

"It's called Otter Creek Mining."

"I knew it was an animal of some sort."

"Look, Vern, why do we need to buy these small mines that have been mismanaged for years? Now they're our problem. And believe me, there are things I'd rather be doing than going down there to straighten out the mess."

Vern sipped his drink. "What's the big deal? You've gone once, right? What possibly could you have to go back for? Here's how it works. There's a mine. Filled with coal. They get the coal out; we sell it and even deliver it." He glanced around the room looking bored. Then he looked back at Frank. "Warren's just getting his feet wet here. What do you want him to do down there?"

"Inspecting our mines *is* his job. I want him to inspect the mine. Rather important, I'd say, seeing you're buying these mines sight unseen."

"Listen, a few years back when we moved into oil distribution, warehousing, and the armored cars division—"

Frank interrupted, "Which was my idea."

"I know it was," Vern snapped. Softening a little, he went on. "I'm glad we did. But coal is profitable. I've got ten million for capital expenditures. Our new acquisitions are good producers: Parker Ridge, Sutton, Longhorn. Our biggest gains are from coal."

"Do you think I want to downgrade coal? That's not at all the case. All three markets are good right now. Dad is busier than ever with the export side, and demand from utilities is increasing along with metallurgy."

"That's exactly right."

Their lunches arrived and they began eating. Frank was at a crossroads. He didn't want to convince Vern to sell Otter Creek, which could lead to a catastrophic outcome. He needed to convince Vern to give him money. "With a little monetary outlay, an RFE, we can be on track to get the strip permits sooner rather than later. Otter Creek has a grossly out-of-date tipple and impoundment situation."

Vern smiled. "Of course we'll get the permit." Peering at Frank with narrowed eyes, a slight curl to his lips, he said. "A week in Palm Beach usually does the trick."

"Normally, I'd have no objections. But not this time."

"What do you want me to do, rebuild the entire mine? Come on, be reasonable." The old man washed down each bite with a slurp of his martini.

"I'll tell you what's reasonable. We have to get those lagoons down to a reasonable size. They're threatening to overtop now, and we haven't even started the strip."

Vern scoffed. "It's a subsidiary. Any legal tangle will be handled locally." He leaned back. "We don't have anything to worry about."

"Did Warren mention the notices to comply?"

"From?"

"Water Resource Commission, as I recall."

"The Water Resource folks." Vern repeated it slowly, with disdain. "Bunch of do-gooders. Waste of good taxpayer money." He cleared his throat. "That's where Palm Beach comes in handy. They fall for it every time."

Frank realized he'd better take a different approach.

"Vern, you've given me the reins, and you know my track record. As you know, I've made roughly eighty percent of our sales these past ten years. Emery talked about this new omnibus bill, the Coal Act, and it's got teeth. Did you see today's paper? Now the mayor has made it illegal to burn coal in Manhattan."

Vern laughed. "Your point?"

"Vern, if those dams break, it could mean not only property damage but human casualties. The way this tipple is situated, directly above this narrow valley, population of almost five thousand, it could be devastating. I don't need to remind you of what happened in Aberfan. I'm telling you, we need to put some money into getting these lagoons straightened out. It's just all there is to it."

Vern dropped his fork. "Oh, for cryin' out loud, Frank. That's what we pay lawyers for. They'll worry for us."

The restaurant was emptying out. Frank put his napkin on the table and pushed his chair out. "Vern, I want an RFE."

"What the hell for?"

Trying to strike a note of optimism, Frank said, "Improvements.

You're just gonna have to trust me on this one. Unless, of course, you want to come down and see for yourself."

"How much?"

"Two hundred thousand."

Vern slapped the table. "Good God." The waiter approached, but Vern waved him off. In a lowered voice, he said, "Frank, if something happens, it's the cost of doing business. You know that. What's happening to you? You're going soft. Maybe you need a vacation. I mean, if we stopped at every potential hazard we wouldn't get out of bed in the morning."

Frank lit a cigarette. "I don't need a vacation, and might I remind you that I get other offers every day."

Vern signed the tab. Through clenched teeth he said, "You're a lousy pain in my neck. I should never have taken you on. You'd be selling shirts at Gimbels if I didn't hand you a job."

"I'd own Gimbels by now."

"All right." His uncle smiled. "What'll it take to shut you up?"

"Two hundred thousand and six months with absolutely no strip."

"You could buy the whole damn state for that much money." Frank figured he'd reeled Vern in, so he didn't dare say anything. "All right. It's pissing in the wind, but fine."

They both stood, and Frank said, "Today is April 25." He counted on his fingers. "May, June, July, August, September, and October. Absolutely no strip at Otter Creek until October 25. We'll meet then to discuss."

"All right, all right."

"You need to shake on it and give me your word."

They shook, and through clenched teeth Vern mumbled, "You have my word."

Chapter 19

It was early May, the air had a velvety warmth, and the grass emerged in green lushness, sprinkled with yellow petals from the forsythias. Sara was walking home from her shift at Todd's. The sidewalk was a carpet of pink petals fallen from cherry trees. At home, Benny, Darryl, and Pete were playing cards. The Sgt. Pepper album was on the turntable, playing "Fixing a Hole."

She dropped her purse by the door, put her coat on the rack, and bent down to pet Bonnie, nuzzling around her legs. "Deal me in, boys. Except switch to matchsticks. You're not getting my hard-earned money."

"We know," said Pete, who was dealing. "How was work?"

"Boring and long." She scanned her cards, slapped two down. "Hit me two."

Benny won the hand. "Full house, kids. Oh, the gods are smiling on me."

Pete asked who was at Todd's.

"Small crowd. Cleared out early. Skimpy tips." Sara went to the kitchen for more drinks. She came back with three beers and a Coke for Pete. She asked Darryl where his girlfriend, Sherry, was.

"Coming over later."

Pete asked if she'd had dinner, and she said she'd eaten on the go. He handed her the bowl of chips.

"Stealing food from Todd. Tsk-tsk," Benny said.

"I eat right in front of him." She pulled the pop-top on her PBR and dropped it into the can, studying her cards. "There's not a squirt of ketchup that Todd doesn't know about."

Benny tapped his nails on the table. "C'mon, Sara."

"I'm thinking."

Sherry arrived and Darryl threw his cards in so he could join her in his room, their usual routine. At least they were quiet. Sara never, ever heard a peep. Benny folded after that hand, saying that if the gods were smiling on him, he'd better go. "I might get lucky with Maggie."

Sara gathered the cards. "Maggie, is it?" To Pete she said, "He keeps those cards very close to his chest. We never hear him mention a name."

"I've heard the name Maggie mentioned."

"This must be serious."

"I doubt there's too much that's serious with Benny."

Sara shuffled the cards as if they were held by centrifugal force. "Want to keep playing?"

"Sure. Gin."

"Ten card and you hold the cards in your hand. I don't like that game where you lay the cards out." She dealt.

"Fine with me."

The song, "Getting Better," came on and Pete sang along. "It's getting better all the time." He drew from the deck. "Oh, I just remembered, I've been wanting to ask you a favor." He told her he had to go to a revival with his grandfather and he couldn't face it alone. "I'm worried. They might make me eat a raw chicken."

She laughed. "Might do ya some good, Harvard."

"Thanks, Frisky." Examining his cards before discarding, he said, "Don't they, like, handle snakes?"

"No snakes," She picked up his card, then looked at him and smiled. "But I'm not going."

He drew from the pile, then rearranged every card in his hand. "Oh, c'mon. Grandpa said the food's good."

She put her feet up on the chair next to her and leaned her head back, looking at the ceiling.

"Pah-leeze." Then, swinging her feet back under the table, she blurted, "Wait. I have an idea. I might go, on one condition."

"What's that?"

"You have to check out The Big Lagoon with me. There's so much hype. I want to see it for myself."

"No hype and no go." He discarded.

"C'mon, Pete."

"I'm not going to risk my job. And then get arrested. That would be my luck. My grandfather would kick me out," he said, looking up at her with that boyish grin. "Anyway, I kind of like it here."

"For cripes sake. It's 1970. No one would throw you in jail for trespassing." She drew a card.

"Puh. No, nein, nada. Not happening. Nope." He spoke each word with knife-edge precision. In fact, Sara didn't realize he could be so definitive.

Pulling a card from her hand as if it had toxic waste, she added it to the discard pile. "When's this *torturous* revival?"

"Next weekend. Memorial Day. I guess they figure a lot of people are off, so they don't mind giving up part of a Saturday. We don't go till noon, so you can sleep late, and you'll have plenty of time to get to work at five."

"You know they're gonna grill me about whether I've accepted Jesus as my Lord and savior."

"It can't be that bad."

"Gin." She laid down her cards. "Of course, seeing the dam is for the holler."

"How do you make that out?"

They moved into the living room, both sitting on the couch, leaning back and facing each other. Sara had her arms around her knees. "You've heard the rumors, Pete. They think it'll break. There's already been one flood."

"From what I heard it only reached a couple of houses."

"You hear everything from the miners. They're the last ones who'd think there was a problem. They're on it every day. Even if they truly had worries, which one of them would speak out about it? Possibly George, but anyway. C'mon. What does your grandfather say?"

He shrugged. "Grandpa doesn't like it. He calls it 'that lake' and blames it on the environmentalists. He goes, 'All they care about is them trout. Don't give nothing for us humans.'"

"That's my point exactly." Growing more emphatic, she said, "We need to go see them for ourselves."

"I can't risk my job."

"Okay." She was twirling a lock of her hair. "I don't need you to go. I only thought it might be nice because you have a car. I can get there. No problem. I'll do it by myself."

Pete explained that he'd already been in legal trouble in high school. He and a girl were stupidly smoking in someone's barn. When he struck the match, the whole pack of matches burst into flames. They were sitting on a huge mound of straw, which ignited immediately, and they'd barely gotten out alive. It was in all the papers, and they'd almost gotten kicked out of school. Somehow his mother found a good lawyer. "I still feel really guilty about the whole thing and the trouble I put my mother through."

"Of course. I understand. No problem."

Pete got up to leave and offered to help clean up, but Sara said she'd do it. She walked him to the door, which was out of character for her.

In a cheery voice, she said, "So, have fun at that revival."

He took a couple of steps out the door, then turned around. "All right, all right. I'll go with you. But we have to be incredibly careful."

"Oh my God, that's great! You'll go see the dams?"

"I said I would, didn't I?"

"We'll go Memorial Day weekend. We won't get caught. I promise. We'll go after dark."

"Like that movie, *Wait Until Dark*."

"Didn't see it."

"You're kidding! With Audrey Hepburn? Best movie ever."

"I don't go to a lot of movies. Good night!" She shoved him out the door.

Chapter 20

Before marrying George, Pattie, born Patricia Capellini Danforth, lived in Cincinnati, the daughter of a civil engineer father and an Italian immigrant mother. Her mother, Sofia Capellini, was resolute that her two daughters, Pattie and her younger sister, Madonna, would have all the advantages possible, no matter the cost. The two girls went to the best schools, took classical piano lessons, went to Sunday school, and attended summer camps. She took them on trips to Colonial Williamsburg and Washington, DC, force-marching them through all the museums, monuments, and cemeteries. Trips to Europe were planned, but always, at the last minute, Alfred Danforth made up an excuse not to get on a plane, and Sofia, who didn't have the fortitude to go on her own with the girls, had to return the tickets and unpack the bags.

Pattie had already been accepted to Oberlin when she met George, through a friend of hers who was dating a former Army buddy of George's. It was an exception to the rule of blind dates. Occasionally, they work.

The college, the culture, the accomplishments, the piano, flew to the wind. Pattie was snowed. There was no comparison between George and anyone she'd ever met.

What got her hooked was the night his car broke down. They'd been to a concert in Columbus. Because of construction on Interstate 71, there was a detour. They were on some rural road and their car headlights were flashing on and off, and then the car died. They started walking in the rain. George said it was the alternator, but they were far from any gas station. As they walked, Pattie was frightened, imagining a car running them off the side of the mountain. There was no shoulder and no visibility because of the weather.

A dim light led to a small house, where a family welcomed them. It was cold outside but also cold inside. The family, mother and father and two kids, were huddled by the woodstove. George, after going outside in the dark and returning with overflowing armloads of wood, acted like it was a party. He helped cook up some vegetables, added a couple of eggs and some sort of magic sauce he made with vinegar, sugar, and corn starch, and called it "egg foo young." Pattie didn't even know he knew how to cook. He played on the floor with the kids, his knees awkward as he tried to sit cross-legged, playing board games. The whole mood changed from when they'd arrived to when they'd left. George had, in essence, brought the party, in his big ol' self, and everyone had fallen under his spell.

Later she asked him how he could have been in such a good mood after the car breaking down, the cold rain, the treacherous road, and the family who were so poor.

He replied with one sentence. "I've been to Vietnam."

She never looked back. This was the man for her. Living back in the woods on ten acres in a small cabin that he'd built with just a woodstove for heat was a monumental change from the comforts of upper-middle-class living. She learned to split firewood and how to turn, plant, and weed a garden. She learned when to pick the vegetables—overgrown okra is tough—and how to tie up tomato plants. The cabin was a cinch to clean: just sweep the upstairs, then the downstairs—although she did have to give it a thorough cleaning when she'd moved in, including washing the curtains and windows and spending half a day scrubbing the rust stains from the hard water in the shower. George was amazed when she turned the brown shower stall back to white. They had a clothes washer, but no dryer. A lot of problems were solved by ingenuity, wit, and perseverance, of which she had plenty.

After about six months, she gained weight and her hands became splotched from sunburn, rough from splitting and carrying wood, cracked and sometimes bloody around the cuticles. She stopped thinking about her hair and forgot on most days to even look in the mirror.

That's when the fights with George started. "You don't look at me, you don't do things with me, you don't even want me here," she'd say to him. What could George do? He worked all day and came home ready to collapse, just when Pattie was ready to do something. It was actually George who mentioned that he saw a sign that they were hiring at the local hospital.

She marched down there, filled out an application, lied on every question. *Have you taken vitals, have you assisted with this, emptied that, administered this? Do you know how to transfer a patient?* She answered yes to everything and got the job, which luckily was day shift so that she could bring George to the mine, go to work, and pick him up on the way home. And the entire first week was an orientation and staff training where they taught her every single thing that was on that application. It wasn't long before she was helping coworkers who'd been doing the job for years.

The job changed everything. Their fights stopped. She felt fulfilled and productive. She fell back in love with George and their life together. One night they'd been sound asleep and she heard something outside that woke her. It was like no sound she'd ever heard, sort of an eerie high-pitched screaming. She woke George, who groggily said it was the screech owl, then turned over and went to sleep. She went to the window to listen. She loved dancing barefoot without a top on in the sun-filled garden, twirling, twirling, twirling with her arms open wide. She loved the smell of woodsmoke in her hair, snuggling up to George in her flannel nightgown with the wind howling outside their snug cabin.

Life with George got even better when their longing for a child, after the heartbreaking loss of the twins, was finally answered. At first, Pattie was in heaven. She at last had her baby, her live, healthy baby girl. None of the bothersome parts of new motherhood, like lack of sleep or sore nipples, were an issue for her. She'd loved every minute. Every nuisance paled next to the miracle of her angelic baby falling asleep in her arms.

But, as the weeks passed, a dark cloud emerged on the horizon. Mandy was growing and flourishing. Pattie didn't pay attention to it at first, thinking nothing could dampen her dreamy state of motherhood. But she'd be singing to her happy baby, "Mares eat oats and does eat oats, and little lambs eat ivy," when the tears would fall. Some days she cried all day. This was much worse than the way she'd felt when she'd first moved in with George, before starting work at the hospital. And it was getting to the point where eating and even thinking were too much effort.

She was terrified, terrified that this would be like the other depression, terrified that it would get worse. In the night, her thoughts were like wild animals set loose that she couldn't catch or contain. *What if I lose it? What if I can't care for Mandy?* She'd hurry to check on her baby, sometimes two or three times in the night, watching the tiny chest move up and down. The baby was safe, and snug, and swaddled. She'd stare at the sweet chubby face, the teeny puckered lips moving, eye lashes fluttering. She'd lean on the door in relief, tears running down her cheeks.

One morning, while making breakfast, she got up the courage to say, "George, I'm feeling low."

"I've noticed." She hadn't been interested in touching him or being touched for a while.

"At least I'm not fighting with you like I was the other time, before I went to work."

"I almost like the fighting better." He tried to hug her, but she pulled away. "What's brought this on? Did your mother write you another one of her letters?"

"No, they're okay. I think they've even accepted you. I don't know what it is." Tears fell, and this time she let him see. She wanted him to see.

That evening when George came home, she said nothing, but an idea had occurred to her that day, and with it came a bit of relief.

The next morning, George was leaning over the porch railing, smoking. She'd made up her mind, but she knew it wouldn't be easy. She opened the screen door, releasing the scent of the sausage and biscuits that she was cooking, his favorite. In as normal a voice as she could manage, she asked, "Can I bring you to work?"

He still had his back to her. "What for?"

"Because, George, I think I'm cracking up."

He flashed around and stared at her, frowning. "What are you talking about?"

"I'll tell you what I'm talking about. I'm crying all the time and I don't know why. It must be that I need adult companionship. I need it or I'll die. I'm just not cut out for being alone at home day after day. It's like the loneliness is corroding my soul."

"But Mandy. I thought you loved being a mother. You're the best mother. I've never imagined a more devoted one. You're so loving."

"Of course I am. But this loneliness is like choking the life out of me. And my worst fear, and it's been haunting me and waking me up at night, is that I won't be able to take care of Mandy."

Pattie saw fear in George's face. Maybe for the first time. He had stepped on his cigarette, and he was grasping his hands, and his face was drained of color. For a minute he said nothing, just stared at her. Then, a series of questions shot out like bullets. "What should we do? Do you need help here? We could ask around. It's a lot of work around here. Do you want a dryer? I'll get a dryer. Or a piano. We'll get you a piano."

"George, I don't know where we'd even fit a piano in this house."

"I see you tapping your fingers on the table."

"Do you? I hadn't realized. I think a piano would be good, but not enough. I need people!"

"Okay. What about Sara? She's free in the day. And Linda Lee."

"No, George, I can't burden them. I'm alone sixteen hours a day."

"Not sixteen."

"All right, but when you go to Todd's, I'm alone from sunup to sundown. I can't go on like this."

She knew that just having transportation wouldn't be enough. She needed to move him along slowly.

"I have it all planned out. Mandy is two months old, and the doctor said her weight is fine and she's perfectly able to maintain her body heat outdoors." She told him she'd drive him to work, then get him either at work or at Todd's. "Please?"

He lit a cigarette. "But, Pattie-Cap"—his nickname for her—"what if she starts wailing while you're driving? I could hear that youngin' crying over my bulldozer." He attempted a laugh.

Pattie nuzzled up to him. "I'll pull over if she cries." Pattie figured she had two approaches, but desperation never worked with George. The more you pushed him, the calmer he got. She figured that's how he'd survived the war. She went the other way. Besides the sausage and biscuits, she was wearing one of his long button-down shirts, a few buttons opened in front, and nothing else. She slid her arms around him, leaning in with her engorged breasts. "Your favorite breakfast is ready."

He moved the soft waves of her golden hair from her face. "There's my girl."

"I'm not perfect."

He kissed her. "And I like you the more for it."

"I'm weak, George. I know you think I'm tough; everybody thinks I'm tough. But I'm not. I'm weak. I can't help it."

Mandy was in the early stages of cranking up in the living room. George's hands went up under Pattie's shirt, over her naked buttocks. He began kissing her face, then her neck, then her mouth. He broke away. "What time is it? When do you feed Mandy? Do we have time—"

"I'd like to," she said, moving in on his hardness. "But no, we don't have time."

Mandy broke out in a scream. She seemed to have two drives: idle and full blast. Pattie went in and got her and began nursing her on the couch. George got his keys, set them on the table beside Pattie, and flopped down on the couch next to her.

"We have to leave in fifteen minutes."

"I'll be ready." She leaned over and kissed him.

It was May 20, and Patricia Capellini Danforth Honeycutt felt hope. Hope and desire.

Chapter 21

Sara went to the revival, her part of the bargain, and was now on her porch waiting for Pete to pick her up. Dark clouds crept over thin streaks of pink and purple as the shadow of night enclosed Otter Creek Hollow. Sara and Pete had decided that Sunday night would be best for seeing the dams.

She sipped her coffee, reliving the unpleasant experience of the revival. About three-fourths of the way through the afternoon, the preacher started to call her by name. Pete denied telling the preacher her name, so it must have been his grandfather. She had no idea why the guy would pick on her. She had even dressed up for the occasion in a floral blouse, black slacks, and nice sandals. She'd put on makeup and earrings, and put her hair in a French twist.

"Sister Sara, come to the fountain." He repeated it over and over, all while staring at her. She knew it was probably only because she was unfamiliar to him, a new face, a lost sheep, an addition to the contribution basket. But her anxieties said much more. She looked around, afraid all the faces would be focused on her. Did the whole congregation know about Frank? She wanted to crawl under her chair.

Then the preacher, fervent and looking possessed, came down the center aisle and stopped next to her row, staring at her.

"Pete, help!" she whispered. He shrugged; he didn't know what to do.

There was no way she'd go up there to repent. The preacher would have to die trying. She kept her eyes staring straight ahead.

"Sister Sara," he went on and on. "Come to the fountain." *Oh, when would he give up?*

At last, he turned and went back to the pulpit, his shirt sopping wet. She wondered if he'd collapse with a heart attack and it'd be her fault. One more thing to feel guilty about.

Later, that goofy Pete had sung along with the music, clapping his hands. He was a strange one, she remembered with a smile, just as he pulled up in his little blue 1960 Toyota truck.

"You should know better than to drive a foreign car around here," she said as he approached the porch. "Benny told me you won't find anyone to work on it."

"Benny has apprised me of that and every other opinion that's ever run through his head, about fourteen hundred times. I can do my own repairs."

"Let's hope it doesn't break today. You want coffee?" He shook his head, and they got on their way.

"The guy I bought it from said he works on them all the time, and knows how to get parts."

"Well, I know nothing about fixing cars and I don't want to learn. When the pump goes out, I hit it with a hammer. By the way, I thought that preacher was going to drag me up there by my hair. Seeing the dam isn't going to halfway make up for that revival. You still owe me, but big!"

"The food was good."

"Which food are you talking about? The green Jell-O with marshmallows in it? Or green beans floating in cream slop?"

"I meant the fried chicken, the mashed potatoes with gravy, and the apple cobbler."

"I guess."

"And those brownies were great. Did you try them?"

"I missed out on that particular pleasure."

They were heading up Otter Creek Road. Pete said, "The tricky part is not being noticed, because there's not much traffic toward the top of the holler. But being that it's Sunday night, maybe they'll be out back having barbecues. In my hometown we had a Memorial Day parade. They'd wheel out these veterans. I swear, they looked like they'd been preserved in stone the rest of the year. Like maybe they just poured water on them and they came to life. They were really old."

She looked behind them. "Keep an eye out behind you, okay? If a car comes up, I say we take the first turn. And if someone asks what we're doing, just say we're looking for night crawlers."

"Hey, that's good. I could have used a friend like you in high school."

"Apparently I missed my calling. In high school I was busy taking care of my father."

"What was wrong?"

"Black lung."

Pete looked over at her and said, "That's right. I think I did hear that from Benny. Sorry."

There were few cars on the road, and most had turned off to go home. After a while they came to the gob pile. They could smell it and see the glowing embers.

"Man, can you imagine if the water hits that smoking gob pile?" Pete said.

"I know. Like pouring water on a dying campfire. Ka-boom!"

They parked in a pull-off area and stood next to the car in the dark, not turning on their flashlights, just to be sure everything was quiet. A barred owl called, *Who-Awww, Who cooks-for-you -all,* and a slumbering bird skedaddled from a nearby bush with a thudding of wings. Pete asked if she was nervous.

"What's there to be nervous about?"

"Are you kidding? They might have plainclothes police officers hiding out."

"Plainclothes police officers!" She laughed. "You crack me up. You really are a city boy, Pete, and that is for sure."

"Well, they might have deputized thugs."

"Where do you come up with this stuff? We only have one sheriff, and right now he's probably a couple of six-packs in and knee-deep in barbecue. Anyway, everyone knows I fish. We have our worm excuse. Let's go."

"Night crawlers. That's right. I forgot." Pete hurried to keep up with her.

It was a fairly steep climb. Using their flashlights sparingly, they passed the first dam, which looked normal enough. They kept walking until they saw what they thought was a road across the ravine. They weren't sure if they should turn around when Sara whispered in disbelief, "It's not a road, Pete. It's The Big Lagoon."

Using their flashlights, beyond what they thought was a road, they illuminated the inky water.

Pete stammered, "Ho-ly fuck! It's gigantic."

"Cripes!"

They walked along the edge, the water lapping about two feet from the top. The clouds gave way to a rising moon that left a white smear across the black water.

"I can't believe what I'm seeing." Pete stopped to stare. "The water seems endless."

"It's so much bigger than anything I'd imagined."

"It's a lake," Pete said, "and that tailings thing is no dam. I studied dams in high school, and that's not a dam. Nothing like. All held back with crushed rock? How long's it been here?"

"I don't know. It is huge. I went to Kentucky Lake once with my Aunt Betts. The dam was also a road. Miles of concrete." After a minute of staring, she said, "What should we do? Do you think this is like, against the law?"

Pete kicked a stone and threw another. He looked at her and shook his head in disbelief. "Against the law? Ha! That's a joke. These mining companies, they control everything. All their pawn politicians and judges have bought into the establishment. And how could they not when they get briefcases of money? I might not know a lot about mining, but I know that any laws out there are protecting the greedy corporate shareholders of these massive companies."

She thought then about Frank. "Companies are made up of people. Human beings like you and me. Flesh and blood."

"No, Sara, they're not people. They're mammoth money-making machines with no human element." He raised his voice. "They're people who lost their moral obligation to do right. They only look at their wallets."

She sneered. "Well, *you* didn't want to come up here for fear of losing *your* job." Sara resented him for acting so high and mighty. She knew that Frank was doing what he could. She had so much she wanted to say, and most of it she couldn't say.

They walked back to Pete's car in silence. When they pulled into Sara's driveway, she said, "You know at that revival when the preacher went on about Jonah in the whale? I didn't ever hear him say how Jonah got out of the whale."

"He prayed."

"Funny." She looked at him. "Sometimes I feel like I'm Jonah. I'm in a whale with no way out. I mean, that's why I couldn't believe you moved here, and I wanted to warn you—there's no way out."

"I could leave any time. This is me getting out of my whale."

"You think so. But you could die in that mine. My father had eighty-five percent of his lungs damaged from mining."

"I won't stay anywhere near that long."

"How do you know?"

"This is just a phase. Something I'm doing for the experience and for the money and to see a new area of the world. It's kind of a holding pattern until I figure out my next step, what I want to do with my life."

"I've never heard you talk like this. You always seemed kind of—"

"Kind of what?"

"Well, you're lighthearted and easygoing. I guess you've struck me as the type that good things come to naturally. Of course, taking a job in the pit couldn't be the brightest thing you've ever done."

"You're a cynic."

"A skeptic, maybe, but not a cynic."

"I'm not sure I know the difference. But I have a serious side. I suppose I don't show it that much."

"To be honest, Pete, I admire you for coming here. And I'm a little jealous. I mean, I'm still stuck in the whale."

"What's your whale?"

"Everything. Money. I don't know. Fear, maybe. You're doing exactly what I'm afraid of doing. You've gone to a new place and started a new life. I'd like to go someplace, get work, and go to college. That's my dream. That's what's outside my whale."

"I don't think prayer will get you out."

She chuckled. "Neither do I." Then she put her hand on his arm. "Thank you for coming with me tonight."

"Sara, whether cynic or skeptic, I don't know. But I see something very positive in you. I think you're the most positive person I've ever met. Look how you are at Todd's. You're loving to everybody." He put his hand on hers. After a moment she moved hers away.

"I'm scared for you, Pete."

"Why?"

"You could get hurt in the pit. People die in there."

"They die walking across the street."

"I hate that stupid argument. I've seen bodies get pulled out. Or they get trapped and suffocate."

A few moments of silence passed. Then Pete said, "Life's weird. I mean, one minute I'm pumping gas in Lowell, and the next I'm here, a coal miner. In some ways, I'm surprised to see myself here; it all happened so quickly."

"What's outside your whale? I mean, besides coming here."

"I'm kind of interested in civil engineering, or architecture. Maybe both? You mentioned college; what would you study?"

"Writing. Maybe journalism, except newspapers are boring. I might like teaching. Something with people. Honestly, I think there's a lot of things I would be interested in doing."

"Sounds good."

"It's actually very fun to talk to you about this. I do not talk to my brothers about it. To tell you the truth, I'm not sure why. I may be afraid they'd laugh." They were quiet. Then Sara said, "I'm glad I can trust you, Pete."

His arm had been across the back of the bench seat. He dropped it around her shoulder. "People who trust are usually trustworthy. That's what I've found."

"Thanks, Pete." She kissed him on the cheek and climbed out of the truck without turning back.

Chapter 22

They were circling over the airport because of fog. It had been almost an hour, and if the situation didn't improve soon, they'd be diverted to Louisville. As it turned out, the pilot landed. It was a hard landing, one of the roughest Frank had experienced. The man next to Frank grabbed Frank's arm in terror.

"Not used to flying."

Frank smooshed his cigarette out in the tiny well of an ashtray in the arm rest. "Relax. This pilot probably trained in the Air Force. It's a piece of cake to him."

This trip was to see the improvements to the dam, if there were any. Frank started on his way, but after just a few miles he had to slow to a crawl. The fog was a gray pudding. If there was one thing Frank hated, it was fog. Nothing in front of you and nothing behind. No way to protect yourself. By the time he got to the Otter Creek office, he was four hours late.

Sweeny handed him a mug of coffee. Frank noticed his spotless boots. They both sat down and Sweeny began. "Pea soup. Some of our trucks haven't shown up. Haul road's a tricky drive in this. Can't make it up to the dams today, and you wouldn't be able to see past the end of your arm." He checked out the window. "It'll be dark soon, anyway."

Frank took a pad of paper from his briefcase. "I wish Warren could have been here. Well, let's get started." He pointed his pencil at Sweeny. "I want all the details, all the improvements, everything we've done since the last time I was here."

"I talked with Warren yesterday and gave him a full update."

"I'm here. So just go ahead and say it all again."

Sweeny started with the new dam just for solids. "It's been a big help, and we're releasing more black water. We've installed four new overflow pipes. Work's underway on the spillway, but with the rain, it's been slow."

Frank asked about the haul road.

"I can't see doing that while running the Number 5. We need access for the trucks. I'm not sure it would make much of a difference anyway, in terms of a breach. Seems to me that an overtop would most likely be on the lower side. Oh, and that froth flotation thing should start later in the week."

"What do you mean, the froth filtration thing? It's chemicals; you put them in the water. It's the middle of June, for chrissakes. You've had over two months."

"You wouldn't believe what it took. Those guys are backlogged. They only recently made the site visit. Had to take measurements. Next, they had to install the panels."

"Panels?" Frank downed his luke warm coffee.

"Yes. Panels."

"Well, from the pipes, and the dam for solids, has the water in the dam gone down?"

"Oh, yes. Absolutely. Maybe a foot."

Frank shook his head. "How long will the spillway take?"

Sweeny's face drained of color; his shoulders hunched, and he was looking up from under his eyes like an animal wanting to flee. "A month, maybe."

Frank said, "Look, Sweeny. We own this mine now. We are responsible if anything should happen."

"We're doing all the things you wanted."

Frank didn't want to argue it. "When are those inspectors due?"

Sweeny opened his desk drawer and hunted for the file. Finding it, he said, "Let's see. The state boys are due the end of August. The Feds usually sometime after that; they don't tell us. To get the permit, though, we have to have the state's approval." Leaning back and sipping his coffee, he added, "And unless things have changed, the Feds go along with whatever the state say. Those state boys are running around with their asses on fire, and the Feds are worse. They have more work than they could ever do and many of their new hires are still getting up to speed. It'll be a long time before they get caught up."

As far as Frank was concerned, the sooner they came the better, because he didn't want the permit. Still, he knew he'd better run the riot act on this guy to make an impression.

"Were you there today? How recently did you check on it?"

"I, um. Not really recently. There's been a lot going on here." He began to shuffle some papers.

"Listen, next time I'm down here, the chemicals should have made a difference." Frank stood and walked toward the door. Sweeny followed.

"I want to know exactly how much progress has been made. I want it in inches. Is that clear?" Before he left Frank turned and stared at Sweeny's boots.

"By the way, nice clean boots."

Chapter 23

Pattie was taking a hot bath. Mandy was three months old, and her naps had gotten regular. The morning was Mandy's best nap of the day, beginning at around nine and sometimes lasting until noon. At one thirty, with extra diapers, extra clothes, and a bottle of formula, Pattie got into the truck, with Mandy tucked in her carrier on the floor in front of the passenger's seat. Pattie let her hair fly with the wind and sang along as loud as she could with the mushy country tunes she knew by heart.

Her first stop was the army and navy store, where she bought some blouses, then on to Underwood's for groceries. But her main reason for going out was to feel like a normal part of the human race, to talk to other adults. The problem wasn't Mandy, because Pattie loved being a mother; it wasn't the housework, she could do it in a flash; it was being alone. She just knew that, if it continued, something inside her would crumble, and, as with Humpty-Dumpty, she wasn't sure if the pieces would ever go back together again.

She decided to stop in at Sara's, maybe offer her a ride to work. Sara answered the door and seemed pleased. The radio was playing, the house smelled clean, and the couch had a sheet covering it, for a change.

"Hope you don't mind some uninvited guests," Pattie whispered, and put a finger to her lips. Mandy was asleep in the carrier.

Sara whispered. "You're always welcome. Want some tea?" Sara went into the kitchen.

Pattie put Mandy in the living room and joined Sara in the kitchen. "Looks like you've been cleaning around here."

"Yeah, so it doesn't feel like we live in a barn. I washed the couch pillows; never did that before. Colleen Bickford told me to put the covers back on while they're still wet, so they don't draw up as they dry. Good tip, huh? But it probably won't last long, never does. Benny will have this place like a pigsty in no time. He comes home from the pit and passes out on the couch. His jeans are full of grease from working under cars. All I can say in his favor is that at least he takes his boots off and leaves them on the porch."

"I never thought about it, but maybe cleaning up after two grown men is harder than taking care of a baby."

"You bet it is. I'd take Mandy over these brutes any day."

"I heard you'd gone up in the world as far as your wardrobe. No more waitress uniform for you. I think it's great. You look real good."

"Thanks. At my age, I think I've outgrown that pathetic uniform. I already had a stash of makeup collected over the years from Aunt Betts. I guess I hung on to that tomboy thing long enough."

"Makeup and nails and getting dressed up never seemed particularly grown up to me," Pattie said. "We played around with those things in elementary school, and I had to get dressed up from age three. Prim and proper and puffy-sleeved dresses, and my mother always put my long hair in curlers at night and in a ponytail with a ribbon every day. In a way, it was hard leaving my home and my friends to marry George, and they all tried to talk me out of it. But there was nothing that would hold me back. It's been the best decision of my life."

"If I were really independent, I'd pack up and leave this holler."

"Would you? You seem so much a part of it. Unlike me. 'She's not from around here,' that's what they say about me."

"Oh, it's not that bad." But Sara knew the peculiar attitudes of some of the older residents. "But that might be what I'm afraid of. What if I go somewhere and I'm not accepted there? Then, if I come back, maybe they won't want me back here either."

"You are talking silly, girl. You could leave for fifty years and they'd put on a parade for your return, and you know it!"

"I can't picture myself anywhere but here, I guess."

"Maybe take baby steps. Start small."

Sara thought of Pete and how easy he made it seem. Some people could slip into new roles, new jobs, new locations. What was it they had? Maybe confidence. Then she thought of Frank in New York, but it was hard to picture. "Maybe, yeah."

"Since George said I could use the truck, I can't tell you how wonderful it is to get out of the house. To wear pants with a zipper!"

"You look good, Pattie."

"Thanks. Well, it's not as if I sit around all day. I do sit to nurse, which is an extraordinary amount of time. After a while, Sara, the four walls start to close in."

"Tell me about it. Sometimes I'm alone so much I think I'll scream."

She hadn't seen Frank in three months, but he was never far from her thoughts: his smell, his rough skin on her face, their long talks, the way he laughed at all her jokes. Their lovemaking, it left her dazed. She could be so silly with him.

Pattie showed Sara her new shirts, and they chatted in the kitchen until it was time to leave. They had run a tad late, so they hurried out for the short drive to Todd's. When Pattie pulled into the parking lot, her truck was right next to Frank's rental car. Sara had been bending over to give Mandy a kiss, and when she turned to open the door, Frank was standing next to his car. He gave Sara an almost imperceptible wink.

Sara tried to get out quickly.

"Wait a minute." Pattie grabbed her sleeve. "What's with that guy?"

Alarms went off in Sara's head, and it felt like there was a splinter of wood in her throat. "Let go of my arm!" She yanked her arm back.

Pattie had a serious look that Sara had never seen. Her lips were kind of crooked. "You're gonna stay here and talk to me."

"I'll be late." Sara once again tried for the door, but Pattie pulled her back.

"That's the new operator, isn't it? What's it called, Rowan Coal?"

"I think so. Yeah. What does it have to do with me?"

"Sara, I saw him wink at you. Plus, your face is purple and splotchy."

"So what? Is that my fault? I get winked at and whistled at regularly. What else is new?"

"So this guy is why you're dressing up."

She watched Frank go into the hotel office. "Get off it. Why are you questioning me? I get better tips dressing up. I'm no flirt and I'm no slut!"

"Of course you're not. But that's what I'm worried about. That's exactly what I'm worried about."

"Cripes, Pattie. I'm twenty-one. What is this? Now that you're a mother, you're some sort of worrywart. I have enough of that shit from my brothers. I thought you were my friend."

"I am your friend. But he's an older guy. I'm not sure what you know about older men, and—"

"And what! You're going to help me grow up? Is that what you're saying?"

"Sara, you're sounding a little defensive."

"I have to get to work."

Pattie opened her mouth but then stopped and swallowed. Then she said, "Sweetie, I'm only thinking of you because I care about you."

Sara got out, but before closing the door, in a softer voice, she said, "I'm sorry, Pattie. I guess I reacted that way because of my brothers. But I promise you, I'm fine."

* * *

When Frank walked into Todd's, the diners popped up like corks from champagne bottles. Frank took a seat quickly to get out of the way of the rush, and Sara gave him a compassionate smile. Sweeny was there eating with his family, and Frank gave a nod in their general direction, then looked away. Sara circled around with his drink.

"I wasn't going to drink tonight, but thanks," Frank said. "Why don't you have it?"

"No. I go for the tips, not the tipsy. I couldn't imagine doing this job with a buzz. I might not love my job, but I don't want to get fired. I'm perfectly capable of quitting on my own when the time is right." She went on to take cash and pat the heads of little children as patrons plowed out the door.

Pete was still there, and after most of the patrons left, he caught up to her and asked, "Gonna join us for poker tonight?"

"You're always leaving your poor grandpa alone at the house."

"Yeah, like he was for thirty years before I moved here."

"It's easy to be alone when no one else is there. It's when someone else could be there and is choosing not to be there that it's hard."

Pete frowned. He knew about her mother.

"Grandpa falls asleep in his chair right after dinner," he said.

She was holding a stack of dishes. "I'm too tired to play. Let me get these dishes in there before I drop them."

When Sara brought Frank his soda, Todd was behind the bar so she couldn't talk to him, but she stalled long enough to breathe deeply, trying to inhale his scent. His shirt was unbuttoned at the top and his tie was loose. She wanted to bury her nose in his neck, but turned to gather dirty plates.

While taking out the trash, she bumped into Todd, his stubbly cheek bulging with Red Man.

"You about scared me to death," she said.

"Why are you blushing?"

"I happen to be working. Isn't that what you pay me for?" She left before he could reply.

Back in the dining room, Frank asked if Todd was gone. In a

hushed voice, she said no. He whispered with his head down, "I'd like to see you later."

"I'll be there, but late."

By the time Sara finished in the kitchen, Frank was done with his dinner. He dropped some bills on the table. She was sweeping up, and Todd was still in the dining room. Frank didn't look around before he left.

The house was quiet when she got home, a welcome change, because she wanted to treasure her good mood. She felt sparkly, like carbonation was running through her veins. After showering, she threw on one of her brothers' sports jerseys, white with black sleeves, and her black Levi's. Her hair was down and she'd only freshened up her lipstick. She left at eleven; the streets were dark and empty. Soon she tapped on Frank's window and he let her in. They fell onto the bed in each other's arms.

"It feels ridiculous to have to sneak around like this," Sara said, putting her clothes back on. "I mean, what's their problem—what have you done? Because you're an operator? It's infuriating!"

"I'm the enemy around here."

"You give them their jobs."

"Running a business doesn't always make you chummy. Are you chummy with Todd?"

"Don't even talk about Todd."

"You can't run a business and run a popularity contest—it just doesn't work. And right now, the unions are powerful."

"Yeah. After the Farmington disaster, even my brothers protested."

"And that was surprising?"

"Yeah. They usually don't show any interest in anything besides fixing cars and playing Poker."

"Farmington was a horrible tragedy. Now Congress and the Bureau of Mines are tightening things, which is good. Mining companies are having to change, and some are doing it better than others. The problem is my boss is an old bastard. Excuse my French."

"That's okay."

"Getting money from him is like getting water from a rock. I strong-armed him into delaying the strip and got money for improvements. You probably caught wind of that at Todd's."

"Yeah, they've been talking about some stuff, so I knew something was happening. How long is the delay for?"

"Six months, when we made the agreement. Until October 25."

"So, it's June 17 today. That's a little more than four months."

They were sitting close together on the side of the bed. The only light in the room came from the bathroom. After a while, Sara said, "Frank, why didn't you want to drink tonight?"

"A couple of weeks back I was sitting down to have my usual evening cocktail and I suddenly felt nauseated. I couldn't take a sip."

"It has to do with your wife."

Shaking out the match from his smoke, he said, "I suppose you're right. Her friends, I'd imagine, wouldn't even suspect she has a drinking problem. She can really hide it. But every night at home, she's three sheets to the wind: glassy eyes, incoherent speech, nonsense talk. It's like she's gone. I raised the issue with one of her sisters recently. To put it mildly, it didn't go well."

"What happened?"

"Just backfired. She implied that I didn't love Allicia enough, or the right way." After a minute, he asked, "Do you know anyone who has a drinking problem?"

"No, I don't. Well, some people in my holler have that reputation, but personally, no. My brothers drink most nights, but not every night. And"—she shrugged—"it's not a problem."

"I'm all for moderation, in all things." Frank stood. "Listen, let's get off this, shall we? How about some cookies? I picked them up at that gas station grocery store place. I've got Tab, too," He took some cookies, then handed her the bag.

"Pecan Sandies! Sure. And a Tab, but next time please get me a Coke. You eat that many cookies? How many did you get, five?"

"Yup," he said with his dimpled smile. "But I don't eat breakfast or lunch." They were quiet for a minute and then Frank said, "Are you sure no one saw you coming here? I worry about this for you."

"Todd is at his house. Everyone's asleep. I'm fine. Let them find me, for God's sake, and get over themselves."

"If only it were that simple. It would be in New York, of course."

"Have you? Done this? I mean—"

"No. The answer is no." He shrugged.

"I went to see the dam, The Big Lagoon. We went at night, Pete and I. We couldn't believe it. How did they ever get away with it?"

Frank said, "The majority of it was in place when we came onboard." Under his breath he said, "Bungling ineptitude."

"What?"

"I'm just so disgusted."

"Frank, I'd really appreciate it if you'd be honest with me."

"I am honest with you."

"Then what are you disgusted with?"

"With this whole situation. Somehow we need to make faster progress. Maybe when we get this chemical thing going." His voice trailed off. "I didn't see the dams today because of the fog. I'll get a look tomorrow."

"Did you stay over for the dam?"

"Sara, had it not been for you—" He shook his head. "I don't know."

Leaning on him, she said, "You're trying. I'm grateful for that."

"And I never want you to feel any pressure or any expectation from me. We're adults, we can make up our minds about what we want to do. But I want what's best for you, and God knows I don't want to put you in any jeopardy."

They stood for a last hug.

Chapter 24

He'd said it in his sleep, quick, muffled, when he'd turned over. It wasn't something she'd imagined or hallucinated. Allicia had heard it.

She'd argued with herself for days. No, no, it couldn't be. She'd tried to convince herself she'd dreamed it, but she knew better. And every night since, she stayed awake, listening.

Try as she might to excuse it or explain it away, she knew he'd said the name of another woman, and her tears burned but didn't fall. Had things really gotten that bad? Was it her drinking? No, it couldn't be. Everybody drank. He'd said it in his sleep, and she couldn't get it out of her head: *Sara.*

Allicia was no quitter. Her father had taught her that. He'd been a champion team roper at rodeos. She had a box of the belt buckles he'd won. He occasionally won money, but not much. In all honesty, he'd never made much money, so the rodeo earnings helped in lean times. Once their family went for a few days with nothing to eat but coffee and popcorn. As a young man, Troy Caldwell had been a cowboy, but when those jobs dried up he had to make money however he could.

When facing something hard, her daddy would give her the advice of a rodeo champ. "Allicia," he'd say, "take a deep seat and a long rein and come out spurring."

It was mid-July in Connecticut. The smell of rich black soil mixed with fresh cut grass wafted into her window. Their yard had willows, copper beeches, and a majestic American elm the kids called the Frankenstein tree, where Frank had hung a swing from a tall branch so the kids could kick their feet in the air for the long and lovely ride.

The air rang with mourning doves, robins, and busy woodpeckers, mixed with the rise and crescendo of cicadas. And in the garden, hydrangeas, hollyhocks, and hostas were offset by the petunias and impatiens with their splashes of color. Limbs from the gangly apple trees dipped low for the kids to swing from.

But Allicia's curtains were closed to these wonders. The kids were on summer vacation, and she had to think of something for them to do. Nothing worse than being stuck at home all day with bickering children.

"Mommy! Mommy!" Rose was knocking on her door. "They're fighting again. They're behind the piano." Allicia splashed water on her face, put on some powder and mascara, threw on a summer shift, and went downstairs.

Marching toward the piano, in a loud voice, she said, "Fighting children? Oh well, I guess they'll have to miss a fun day. Let's you and me go to the beach, Rose. They can stay here and fight all day. Too bad for them."

There was bumping, banging, and shoving as the two piano-hiding rascals instantly transformed into cheerful and compliant kids, raring to go to the beach.

After a mad dash for suits and towels, sand buckets and Styrofoam bubbles for flotation, flip-flops and Coppertone, carried out mostly by Rose, the three kids were ready and waiting by the back door. Allicia was filling her flask, but before going out the door, something occurred to her. She knew what it felt like to be the youngest, so she asked Ray if he'd like a friend to come along. He immediately said, "Glenn Friday."

That name rang a bell. "What is it about Glenn Friday? Isn't there—"

"Polio," Ray said.

"Polio? I'm not sure we should ask him. How about another friend?"

He didn't want another friend, so she called Mrs. Friday, who said Glenn would be happy to join them. Allicia put the receiver down. "Well, he's coming. His mother said he could swim."

"Does he use his crutches in the water?"

"No, darling," she said, suddenly realizing she'd need backup. She decided to ask her best friend, Flo, to join them. Thankfully Flo said yes.

"Everyone in the car and no fussing and fighting."

She dreaded the car ride; the kids fought like cats and dogs, and driving hurt her back. The doctor had told her that her muscles were strained from her three pregnancies and from lifting and carrying her children. It was the reason she had to drink. Her liquid medicine was better than those pills he gave her. Her flask was tucked under her seat.

She pumped the gas, making the engine cough and sputter, then floored it. The car started with a roar, drowning the noise of the younger kids in the backseat, who'd already begun slapping each other. You're taking up the whole seat! You're pinching me! I had my foot there first! Stop spitting! You're pulling my hair!

"We're going to the beach. You get to have a friend. Aren't you kids ever satisfied?" she said. She always said this to them, and they always fought. It never sunk in. "Aleena, sing that Beatles song that I love."

The tender voice emerged from the backseat, and as if by magic, a calm came over the car. "Close your eyes and I'll kiss you." She knew every word. The tension eased from Allicia's shoulders. "I'll send all my lovin' to you."

Glenn Friday was leaning on his two half-size crutches when Allicia got there. "Just make sure he wears his bubble," Mrs. Friday said, her arms encircling her son.

"All my kids wear their bubbles. And I'll have them swim right in front of the lifeguard."

Driving away, she had a moment of panic. *What have I gotten myself into now?* she wondered. But it was too late. The kid was in the backseat; the mother had trusted her. She said he could swim, and he had a bubble.

The Greenwich Beach parking lot was packed, the pavement stinging hot. Flip-flops and bubbles on, Allicia's three kids took off running. She yelled, "Stay near the lifeguard, you kids!" Glenn leaned on his crutches while Allicia snapped on his bubble, grabbed the beach bags, and threw her own towel over her shoulder.

"I like your sandals, Glenn. Are you all set?"

"Yes, Mrs. Rowan." He kept up with her down the sidewalk.

"Can you kick in the water, Glenn?"

"Sure, I can swim. The water is where I can float and be like all the other kids. There's nothing I like to do better than swimming."

Allicia couldn't think of anything more terrifying than being in the water. She'd grown up where there were dry riverbeds most of the year, unless they were gushing with torrents from a downpour. There were no swimming pools and no lakes.

She began walking on the hot sand. The blue sky carried some wispy clouds; gulls swerved under kites and over beach balls. The beach was broken up by sandcastles and bodies on towels under giant umbrellas. She pointed and said, "The bathrooms are over there, by the snack bar. We'll get our lunch there and eat on our towels. They have popsicles." Allicia spotted Rose and the little ones in the shallow water in front of the lifeguard. "There they are, right by the lifeguard, where they're supposed to be." She waved to them and they waved back. "I make the kids stay out of the water for thirty minutes after lunch. I bet your mommy does that too, doesn't she, Glenn? Glenn?"

She looked down. Glenn was gone. For a minute she was in disbelief. She looked around her, dropping her towel and bag, turning in circles. How could a little boy on crutches disappear? But he had. There was no Glenn anywhere.

"Glenn! Glenn! Glenn!"

No sign of him, and there were people everywhere. She jerked her head and began darting around the crowds to find the little boy. A surge of panic rose up in her. This couldn't be! Her heart thudded in her throat. She waved both arms to the lifeguard and screamed, "I've lost a boy! I've lost someone else's child! Oh, my GOD! Glenn! Glenn!"

The lifeguard came running, and breathlessly, she said, "I've lost a boy! Glenn. A little boy on crutches! He's not my child. He can't even walk! How could I lose a boy who can't even walk?"

The lifeguard sprinted toward the water, yelling, "Glenn! Glenn!"

The next few minutes were excruciating. She imagined what she'd say to Glenn's mother. In a panic, she ran toward the parking lot, and that's when she saw a figure on the sand very close to the sidewalk. Spraying sand in all directions as she ran toward it, she soon saw it was Glenn. He was lying face-down on the sand, where he had apparently been crawling. She collapsed next to him, gasping and grabbing him into her arms.

"Oh my God, Glenn! What happened? Are you okay? Have you been hurt? Oh my God!" He was covered in hot sand, yet he said he was fine.

"Fine! You poor little boy. What happened? Were you pushed? Where are your crutches?" She wiped the sand off his face and hands. His face was sweating, and the sand was sticking. "Oh, my dear boy, I'm so glad you're okay!" She cradled him in her arms, apparently a bit too tightly.

"Ouch, Mrs. Rowan." He tried to get free from her zealous embrace. "I can't use my crutches on the sand. They don't work. I left them over there." He pointed back in the direction of the car.

She retrieved the crutches and waved to the lifeguard, who came over to check on the boy. Glenn said that he always crawled on the sand. The lifeguard offered to carry him, but he said he didn't want to be carried.

"It's nothing," he said.

Allicia had an idea. She shouted for her son. "Raymond! Raymond! Raaaymond!"

Dripping wet when he reached them, Ray skidded to a stop. "What, Mommy?" Just then he noticed his friend on the sand below him.

Allicia pointed to Glenn. "Get down there and crawl with your friend."

Young Ray looked down at his friend, prostrate on the sand, then looked up at his mother, puzzled. He began to object. His mother said, "If your friend has to crawl, you're going to crawl with him."

Raymond took another moment, saying nothing, his brain working. Then, with no further argument or hesitation, he got down next to his friend, stretched his legs out behind him on the hot sand, and they both started army crawling toward the water.

Allicia thought, *There are times when, through the little bodies of these children, I can see their souls.*

About twenty minutes later, Florence arrived, wearing her large sun hat and holding the hand of her daughter, Nina. Flo had golden hair and butterscotch skin, and a calm demeanor. Speaking to Nina, Allicia pointed toward the water. "The kids are over there, sweetie." The little girl took off at a full run, spraying sand behind her.

Flo spread out her towel, took off her sandals, and stretched out in the sun. "Fabulous idea, Allicia!"

"I'm so glad you could come, and on such short notice."

Propped up on her elbows to watch the kids, Flo said, "Short notice is the way I work. Nina nags me all day. 'Let's do this, let's do that.' So it's not hard to talk me into a day at the beach. If I have fun, everyone's happy."

"Everyone's happy now, but that was not the case twenty minutes ago. I nearly lost my mind." Allicia explained to her friend the scare she'd had with Glenn. She pointed at him in the water with the other kids. "But look at him now. Swimming like the other kids, having fun. He refused to be carried. What a kid!"

"Allicia, you're remarkable. Very few people that I know of would have taken on that kind of responsibility."

Covered in Coppertone, they chatted while watching the kids. Flo said, "I'm getting Nina into ballet. She's double-jointed, and the doctor recommended it for strengthening. He said either ballet or gymnastics, and I figure ballet has less chance of a broken limb. It would scare me to death to watch her balance on some high beam. That girl crawls on and jumps from everything as it is. Did I tell you that we were in the Met, and she ran over and sat on an empty block? One of those blocks that held a statue. I can't look away from her for a second. Is Aleena that way?"

Allicia mumbled agreement.

"Maybe Aleena would like ballet."

Allicia was lost in thought. "Huh?"

"Or gymnastics."

"Oh, yes, that sounds good. Nina would love that. Where will you take her?"

"I haven't decided; probably Mrs. Livingston's." Flo paused and then said, "Allicia, you seem to be in a dreamy state. Is something bothering you?"

Allicia had been thinking of Frank. Each night, she was rigid, listening, waiting to see if he'd say anything else.

Seagulls circled, and a cooling breeze passed over their hot bodies. Flo looked at her friend.

"Sometimes, Flo, life can flip everything upside down."

"You're not at all yourself today. What is it? Is it your health?"

"No. It's not me. Well, I'm not myself, but it's not me that's the problem." Allicia turned to Flo, wondering if she should say it. Yet, Flo had been through a divorce; maybe she would understand. "It's Frank."

"Is he sick?"

"Not unless talking in your sleep is a terminal illness. Listening to him talk in his sleep and say another woman's name has made me sick. I don't sleep anymore. I don't sleep when he's gone, wondering what he's doing and with whom. I don't sleep when he's there, waiting to hear what he might say in his sleep."

Flo shook her head. "It might not mean anything."

"He said a woman's name."

Flo asked, "Does he talk a lot in his sleep?"

"Never. I never heard him talk in his sleep before this."

"Just a dream, perhaps. Anyone can dream. I wouldn't want my dreams opened to the public. Has there been anything else? Are you sure you have reason to be suspicious?"

"He's traveling all the time. I call his secretary and I can never get a straight word out of her. Every damn week, off to Chicago, to Bethlehem, to Kentucky. Even his damn secretary doesn't always know, or she's vague about it."

"My first husband, Edgar, was screwing just about every woman in town." Flo gave a crisp laugh. "I was the last to know."

Allicia touched her friend's arm. "What a horrible thing."

"I was so stupid. The town doctor! Of course everyone loved him, and called on him at odd hours. He was the town doctor, and I was the town fool. It wasn't until that woman, and believe me I know her name, and this was in Mystic so you'd never in a million years know of her, but still I won't say her name. Anyway, she came to our front door on Thanksgiving Day, asking to see him."

"On Thanksgiving?"

"During our dinner! I marched out there and confronted her. She didn't say a thing. Just scowled at me. That was the end."

"I'm so sorry, Flo." They were quiet, listening to the squeals of joy, and the thud of waves, and screech of gulls. After a few minutes, Allicia said, "He never takes me out anymore, except when there are customers."

"Go to his office unannounced. Usually the culprit isn't too far off."

"Oh, Frank would be furious."

"Allicia, you're the president's wife. You can go to his office."

"Well, he was just recently promoted. He works all the time. I'd be disturbing him. He doesn't even like me calling him there, but I do anyway. I can't imagine what he'd do if I were to appear at his office."

"Has he said, 'Don't come to my office'?"

"Not in so many words."

"Allicia, this is your marriage we're talking about. And you have three children. I just had one. It was hard enough to find someone to take on one kid, but three? In my opinion, you're far too well-behaved."

"Flo, divorce is out of the question." Allicia protested. "I love Frank. More than anything."

"Well, sometimes you have to fight for the things you love."

The kids had come back for a rest. Ray was crawling with Glenn. When he got to his towel he was exhausted but happy. His verve, his chutzpah, his courage, impressed her. Allicia heard her daddy's words: *You're no quitter. Take a deep seat and a long rein and come out spurring.*

"Flo, you're right," she whispered to her friend. "I'm far too well-behaved."

Chapter 25

Pattie thought that having the truck most days was fine, a big improvement, but the day George surprised her with her own car, she thought she'd gone to heaven. Two cars had pulled in that afternoon when she was at the clothesline. At first she thought nothing of it, just a friend of George's, probably Donny. She picked up the baby in her carrier and walked over. She noticed that it was Donny, but he was driving George's truck, and there was no one else in the truck with him. Where was George? He never let anyone drive his truck. There was another car behind Donny that she didn't recognize.

A frozen panic came over her. It was one of those times when everything slows to a supernatural crawl. Her throat tightened, and her heart took off pounding. Too afraid to scream, she ran over. "Where's George?"

Then George popped out of the other car. "Surprise!" he said, tossing the keys to her. "It's your new car! It's a Nova, not new, but it runs good. And I've ordered you a piano."

That night she went for him like never before. Lying back and out of breath, he said, "Wow, woman, I don't know if it was the car or the piano, but I should have gotten them a long time ago."

She made two phone calls: one to Sara, who said she'd be happy to babysit, and the other to Otter Creek Memorial Hospital. She asked for her old job back, and they told her she could start in two weeks. When he'd bought the car, George probably hadn't realized that the inevitable would happen. It was like opening the door to a caged bird, then saying, *Don't go out, don't fly away.*

When she told him she was going back to work, she said, "I like it, I'm good at it, and it's good for me." He didn't say a single thing. He had no argument. She was curious, though, about what had prompted him to get her the car. Was he worried about her? He never asked about her moods, and yet he went out and bought her a car, without mentioning anything about it, not even a hint. There was a lot going on in that man that she had no idea about, and under that gruff exterior there was a pussycat.

When she told her mother about her sadness, her mother had said, "I told you not to marry him. Come home, darling."

"Mom, you don't understand. It's not George. I love George. It happens even when I'm out with Mandy in the truck. I'm sad all the time. I don't know why. I hate it!"

"Don't stay another minute. Come home. Your sister is seeing Don Rodman, remember him? He has lots of nice friends."

Pattie had gotten off the phone and the dark cloud, like a blanket, was more unbearable. She'd confessed to her own mother, and her mother had denied the problem entirely. It had made her feel so much more alone and even more hopeless.

On her first day back at work, she arrived at Sara's at 5:40 a.m. even though she didn't have to be at work until seven. She'd dressed Mandy in a pink outfit with matching bonnet and little pink crocheted booties, handmade by Pattie's mom. Sleepy-eyed and in her nightgown, Sara opened the door. "Cripes, I didn't expect you until six thirty. Where are you going to go at this hour?"

"I wanted to get oriented."

"Pattie, I've taken care of a baby before. I take care of Baby Jake all the time."

"Not to orient you, silly. Me! I guess I'm a bit anxious, but they've probably changed things, and I might not know where things are now. I can't ask them questions all day, or they'll be sorry they hired me back."

Sara took Mandy from Pattie's arms. "Golly, she's pretty enough for church. I hope you brought a change of clothes; I wouldn't want to spill on these nice handmade things." She noticed the three large tote bags on the porch. "I guess you brought a change of clothes. Looks like you brought the whole store!"

"Better safe than sorry." Pattie brought the bags in and began checking things off on her notepad, counting on her fingers and talking to herself. She'd brought bottles and a bottle warmer, nipples, formula, diapers, ointment, three outfits and three onesies, receiving blankets, an umbrella stroller, even a bottle brush. She kept saying that she hoped she hadn't forgotten anything.

"I never pictured you as such a worrywart."

"I'm efficient. Anyway, wait till you have kids. Now, call me at the hospital if anything comes up. I'll probably be tied up when you call, but I'll get back to you. Don't hesitate to call."

"Pattie, she'll be fine. If anything comes up, I'll call you. Plus, Linda Lee is around. As a matter of fact, she said she might come by with her famous buttermilk biscuits."

Pattie backed out the door, reluctantly, giving more last-minute reminders. She kissed Mandy, saying goodbye sixteen times in a singsong voice.

"You should try out for the opera," Sara joked. "Now go."

At the hospital, Pattie didn't know if they were happy to see her or just desperate for the help. They greeted her with shouts, hugs, and pats on the back. Her friend Lynn, another aide, had even brought Pattie lunch, homemade potato soup and a roast beef sandwich.

At the nurse's station, Sheila, the charge nurse, said, "Before I go into the day, tell me about your baby. How old is Mandy?"

"She's five months, just about. Born on St. Paddy's Day. You probably remember."

"That's right! I remember, just forgot the date. You gave us all such a fright. But how wonderful that the baby is doing well. I'm so happy for you."

Dr. Bradley Randall stopped in and added his pleasantries, but quickly changed to the work of the day. "Good thing you know your way around. We're short-staffed, as usual, but I know you can handle it. Dr. Shepherd's in with a renal tumor the size of a tennis ball. We're waiting on transport. I've got an appendicitis, spiking a fever. He's first for the OR. Be ready." He picked up a stack of charts and gave them to Sheila. "Get her going." While rushing off, he asked, "Oh, how's the baby?" but he'd turned the corner before Pattie could answer.

Pattie looked through the charts. First a bleeding ulcer, then a pneumothorax in a twenty-two-year-old male. She looked at Sheila. "This pneumothorax in 36-A. He's a miner, right?"

"Need you ask? Sorry we can't break you in easier. Are you ready?"

"I am. I have missed being here."

"Great. Don't worry. I'm here if you need me."

"I know. Thanks."

Soon she was finished with her first two patients, helping them up, getting them what they needed, helping them walk and get back to bed without incident. She was on to her third patient, an eighty-two-year-old male with black lung and an enlarged prostate. She pushed open the large door. "Hello, Mr. Nichols. How are you feeling this morning?"

He grunted a reply. She went over and stood next to him. His face looked ashen, plus his cath bag was empty. Her training and experience kicked in. She had to fake her reaction, because she didn't want to upset him. It was like jumping into cold water and pretending to onlookers that it's just fine and you like it. While taking his vitals, she chatted on about her new car, and how George had surprised her.

"It drives so smooth," she said while checking his chart, which said it had been four hours since the cath bag was last emptied. "Now I'm going to check your cath."

It was inserted properly, so she needed to get the doctor. "I'm gonna have someone look at your cath bag, Mr. Nichols. I'll be right back." She moved his overbed tray where he could reach the nurse's call button. "Here's your call button." He grunted a reply. It often happened that the patients she thought would be easiest were hard. They weren't breaking her in slowly, that was for sure.

Friday rolled around, and her first week was over and it had gone well. She and Sheila were at the nurses' station writing last-minute notes.

"Hope we didn't wear you out too much on your first week," Sheila said.

Pattie was worn out, but mostly she dreaded the weekend, dreaded the thought of the sadness hitting her again.

"No, it was—it was good. A little hard, but good." She put away the last file. "I love being busy. I'd better check the med closet, though. I think I was a little rushed. Just want to make sure I put things where they go. Triple checks—that's how you trained me." She gave Sheila a smile and left.

A wave of relief wafted over her before she even opened the medicine closet door. She locked it behind her; that way she'd have a second of warning if someone came in. The next shift was there and would be getting the report, so Sheila would be busy.

She had eyed the bottle earlier in the week, so she knew exactly where to find it. Quickly, the cap was off, the white pills in her pocket, the cap back on, and the bottle back on the shelf. Furtively, she secured the door behind her. Not a soul was in sight.

At Sara's, she tucked Mandy into the backseat, then drove off while swallowing a little white pill, phenobarbital, hard and dry. She drove slowly and carefully going home. In the living room, she put Mandy in her playpen, then stretched out next to her on the couch. The happy baby lay on her back, whacking at the mobile and kicking her little feet in the air. Pattie leaned back, waiting for the delicious fog.

Chapter 26

The news said it was hot enough to fry an egg on the sidewalks of New York. Limp laundry hung on lines and open fire hydrants unleashed torrents of cold water, to the delight of neighborhood kids. Allicia's dress stuck to her sides. *How could a plant be so heavy?* she thought, as she mounted the steps of the Manhattan-bound train.

The philodendron was her excuse to visit Frank's office. She had decided on her black dress mostly because it wouldn't show underarm wetness. Loretta had said she'd give the kids dinner and put them to bed if Allicia wanted to stay late. She had imagined Frank showing her around the office, proudly introducing her, then on a whim, grabbing his jacket and flying out the door with her to blow off the day. They'd dine, and walk, and window shop. On the other hand, a smaller inner voice hinted that he very likely would not be happy about this, but she tried not to think about that. Either way, she'd act as if the visit was long overdue because, of course, he needed her decorating expertise.

"Pohhhhrrrrt Chester, Port Chester next." *Why did the conductor have to yell like that?* Out the window, scenes of houses, empty spaces, parking lots, apartment buildings, and storefronts were each eclipsed by the next and the next: zip, zip, zip, pulled away and replaced faster than you could focus. The rhythmic beat of the train was comforting, and after a while Allicia closed her eyes.

She wished she could pull back the layers of her life, the veils, the scars, the mistakes, the dullness, the staleness. She wanted so much for those days to return again, the days when Frank had responded to her. He'd made her breakfast, bringing the steaming scrambled eggs to her when she was in bed. They'd stayed in bed until the afternoon. But those days were a faint memory.

In Grand Central Station, she made her way to the ladies' room to rest on the red velvet bench. It was too early to see Frank, so she went back into the main terminal, under the clock, but she got caught up in the crowd and found herself outside on the sidewalk. The heat was suffocating, the noise jarring, the horns, jackhammers, voices, buses.

Beads of sweat formed on Allicia's face. She thought she might vomit. Everything went gray and fuzzy as if she were about to faint. She put the plant down on the sidewalk in front of her and bent over it until the dizziness faded. Not a single person stopped. Everyone simply walked around her like the parting of the Red Sea.

Moments later—she wasn't sure how many—four sailors in their white sailor suits and caps noticed her distress and offered their assistance. Needing to come up with a reason for stopping, she mumbled, "Cab." In an instant, they'd hailed her a cab, deposited her in the back along with her plant, and tapped on the window to signal "all set." The driver took off with a jerk and she heard herself say "Michael's Pub" before falling back on the cool leather seat, stretching her legs, and pushing off her shoes.

It was only then that she realized, or remembered, that she'd been on the wagon. Also, she didn't need to take a cab anywhere, because Frank's office was above Grand Central. The noise, the chaos, the scorching heat, had all thrown her into confusion.

The cabby was an older gentleman in a suit coat over a white dress shirt. He had both hands on the steering wheel and his hands were notable. They looked worn, his fingers gnarly, the knuckles bulging. At the pub, he reached his open hand over the seat and said, "Fifty cents, ma'am." He had a strong southern accent. She gave him a dollar, looked at the plant and groaned. Giving her the change, he asked, "You need some help?" Without waiting for an answer, he got out and carried the plant into the restaurant.

Allicia slid off the seat and out of the cab, but from there she didn't move. Her plant was already inside. The cabby had gotten back into the car and was about to pull away, but the passenger door was still open. Inside Michael's was the relief of a drink; she could feel herself salivating. She got back into the cab. Confused, the driver said, "Are you all right? I brought your plant inside."

Allicia was holding her handkerchief, embroidered by her mother, on her forehead. "May I ask your name?"

"Joe Worley."

"Joe, have you ever found yourself doing or almost doing something, something that at one time you thought was normal and even good but not anymore? And it's as if you wake up, and you realize that you're in terrible trouble?"

Mr. Worley looked back at her. He had very dark skin, a kindly face and a warm, gentle smile. "Yes, ma'am, I have."

"It's like you're doing something you've always done, but this time you fear something bad will happen."

"You want me to go get your plant?"

"Yes, I do, Joe. Please."

In the elevator above Grand Central, she watched the number of floors climb to forty-eight. Just as the doors opened, she heard her daddy's words. She threw her shoulders back, sucked in her belly, took a deep seat and a long rein, and stepped out spurring.

"Hello, Mrs. Dominici," she said to Frank's secretary. "We finally meet. I am Mrs. Frank Rowan. You look just as I pictured you. I mean, from your voice. Anyway, please show me to my husband's office." Mrs. Dominici greeted Allicia, took the plant, and said she would buzz Mr. Rowan.

Seeing Frank's name on the door directly in front of her, Allicia took the plant back, marched right past Mrs. Dominici, and managed to open Frank's office door, with Mrs. Dominici scurrying behind her.

"Allicia?" Frank looked utterly caught off guard. "What are you doing here?" He dropped his pen and stood. "Is something wrong with the children? What's the matter?"

"Sweetie," she said, as casual and chipper as she could manage. She put the heavy plant on a table and pushed the door closed, shutting out Mrs. Dominici. "I wanted to see your office. I know, isn't it crazy that I've never been here? It's about time I added some necessary decorative touches. This plant is a good start." She gracefully lowered herself into the armchair across from Frank's desk and crossed one leg over the other without adjusting her skirt, so that her upper thigh was showing. "It's a philodendron. It'll do nicely here, I think. It doesn't need much light or water, and it will grow slowly over the years."

"Allicia, you could have gotten a florist to deliver it. Now you'll be flat on your back for a week in pain from carrying the thing. And I have work to do."

"Oh, Frank, you are a darling, and always so thoughtful. I know you have work to do and I would never want to interfere. I just thought it was high time I saw your office, to give it a woman's touch." She picked up a leaflet from the edge of Frank's desk, and used it to fan herself. It was the mailing from the UK, on Aberfan. Frank had planned on putting it on his bookcase, but hadn't gotten around to it, and in a way, he'd also kept it there as a reminder.

The cool plastic seat was a balm to her hot legs and she slipped out of her uncomfortable pumps. "Darling, your office is—well, how shall

I put this? It's boring. It needs spiffing, color, life. I'm getting ideas, though, so don't you worry." She stood and began walking around. "Let's see. We'll put your framed diploma right here." With her arms she made the shape of a large square. "Princeton University." Then she looked quizzically at him. "Honey, where is your diploma? I don't think I've ever seen it."

"I don't know where it is. I didn't go to my graduation. The university office keeps those records." Then, as if suddenly coming out of a daze, he blurted, "Allicia, are you smashed?"

With her mother's hanky she dabbed at the beads of sweat on her face. "Frank, I'm sober."

She sat down a little less expansively, forgetting for a moment her poise, defeat chipping away at her performance, and put the handkerchief in her purse. "I guess you don't keep track. I've been on the wagon for"—she counted—"fourteen days."

"No, I don't keep track. I thought you'd switched to vodka."

"Club soda and lime, if you must know."

He walked over to her and held out his hand. "Okay. I apologize. That was unkind."

She stood and took his hand. "Thank you, Frank." When she went to put her arms around him, though, he turned back to his desk and sat down.

"Allicia, you look bushed and you're overheated. You've come to the city on the hottest day of the year. How about you and I come in on a Saturday, make a day of it. We'll do some of those things you like to do, like museums. We'll stay in and have dinner. Get Loretta to watch the kids. But—"

"Oh, darling, that's all I wanted to hear. I love you so much and—"

"Right now, Allicia," his eyes got big, "I need to get back to work."

"But, Frank, what should I do?"

Tapping his fingers, he said, "Well, I have a lunch date in an hour with Vern—"

She blurted, "Why yes, I'd love to join you."

"We're eating at the Sky Club. Come back in an hour, and we'll go up together." At the door she blew a kiss and departed before he could change his mind.

For a long time, Frank stood and looked out the window. Mrs. Dominici had tapped lightly on his door and was waiting for him to notice her.

"Oh." He turned. "I didn't hear you. Have a seat." Then he turned back to the window.

Mrs. Dominici sat down, her pad and pen ready. She was wearing a black calf-length skirt, white button-down blouse, and gold cross necklace. She varied her attire little from day to day, changing it from black to blue to gray to brown. Her blouses were of the same plain type, differing only in color.

He was still looking out the window, even though she was poised and waiting, with her steno pad on her lap.

"Mrs. Dominici," he said, turning around briefly then turning back to the window, "do you know how squirrels survive the winter?"

"In the winter? No. I'm a city dweller, Mr. Rowan. I didn't even grow up near grass. Don't they hibernate or something?"

"No. They're not heterothermic. Squirrels are active in summer and winter. In the winter they have to find where they hid their stashes of nuts, sometimes months earlier. Did you know that it takes only two tries for a squirrel to learn to pull on a string to retrieve a nut from a glass tube?"

Mrs. Dominici put her pen down and cleared her throat. "No, I didn't, Mr. Rowan."

Still looking outside, he said, "And it's thought that squirrels dig holes and don't bury anything in them. They are just trying to trick other squirrels into thinking there are nuts there. It's a kind of decoy, a lure away from the goods. Do you know how squirrels find the nuts and acorns that they bury?"

"I guess I never thought about it." Mrs. Dominici had had trouble with bosses in the past. She had rich dark hair and large eyes, was tall and strong, and she was smart. She'd had to fight off a couple of her previous bosses, and that was why she'd now adopted her simple attire and the cross. Frank was not like those other bosses.

"They can smell them," he said. "They use their brains to trick other squirrels, they work hard to find their nuts, and if they're lucky, they may even find some extra ones. Squirrels know the three secrets to success."

Frank was thinking of strategies for this lunch and wondering if Allicia could actually be of help. Vern hadn't included Frank's father, and normally the three of them would have lunch together. Francis, Sr., if pushed, would always take Frank's side. There was no doubt that the subject of Otter Creek would come up. And even if it didn't, with Allicia there, Frank would bring it up. Vern was a puppy around

Allicia. Yes, having Allicia there might be a bit of luck.

Frank only had two months left. He had to come up with a plan to convince Vern that they needed an extension. If he told Vern that they were seeing a lot of progress, which was not the case, Vern would be more firmly entrenched in his position that six months was the limit. If he said there had been little progress and he needed more time, Vern might be discouraged and think the whole thing was a waste, and he'd never cough up more money. With Allicia there, Vern might be distracted enough that Frank just might be able to get more time, or more money, or hopefully both. He could only try.

Mrs. Dominici asked, "What are the secrets to success, Mr. Rowan?"

"Brains, hard work, and a little luck. No dictation today. Please reserve another seat at the Sky Club. Mrs. Rowan will be joining us."

Chapter 27

2019

My daughters, Adriene and Barnsley, were there when I got home from my trip to Kentucky. They'd driven together in Adriene's car from UConn, where they were students. Both were sweet and solicitous, helping me with my suitcase, probably because I'd complained about my back hurting from the long drive, and they'd cooked a delicious lentil soup for dinner.

I knew they were worried about me, and from upstairs I overheard them talking. Adriene, the older by two years, said she thought it was weird that I'd go to Kentucky. "She doesn't even know anyone in Kentucky." Then she asked, "Do you think she's depressed?"

Barnsley said she thought it was good that I was going places and not just sitting around crying. "Her marriage just broke up. If she's depressed, who can blame her? Although she needs to get angry."

Obviously, I hadn't told them the real reason for my trip, only that I wanted to see some beautiful country and that I needed diversion. Dr. Walker had been so encouraging about me taking a couple of days off. I'm the most senior hygienist there, and rarely take vacations. When he heard about Stephen walking out, that next day there were roses at my door.

I walked into the kitchen and assured them that I was fine, that the trip was fun and it got my mind off my problems. After dinner we went out for frozen yogurt and laughed a lot. We laughed at silly things, like trying to get a cell picture with all of us in it. We kept chopping off half of someone's face until we asked the waitress to take our picture.

I did feel lonely in the creaky house. Empty houses make noise. I never heard it before. It felt like half of my body was missing and without it, my insides might start leaching out everywhere. I was trying to learn to shop for one, cook for one. I scissor-kicked next to me in bed each morning, just to remind myself of the reality that it was cold, so I wouldn't get out of bed and think that I'd see him coming around the corner. Even so, throughout the day, I found myself glancing out the window, pushing the curtain farther back an extra inch, so that I wouldn't miss his car. And in my mind, I played the scene over and over: his return, our long talks, we'd go out more, we'd go away. It'd all be over—this nightmare.

But everything was going in the wrong direction. All communication between Stephen and me, which meant email because we weren't talking—he'd been avoiding my phone calls for months—now involved our mediator, one Clyde Sweltzer, whom Stephen had gotten through his lawyer and whom I'd met only once.

Sleazy Sweltzer reminded me of a reptile: skin like crepe paper, translucent, with the afternoon sun shining through his ears. Stephen's emails, no matter how insignificant, were always copied to him. His body was wedged between us.

Could I really have loved, slept with, and co-parented with this man for twenty years and not have a clue who he was? Or maybe going through divorce, like any huge life trauma, had changed him. Then it dawned on me that he'd been through this once before. I'd met Stephen a year after his first divorce. They'd only been married three years before breaking up, and he'd said it was because she didn't want kids. I never met his ex, and I put that whole marriage and divorce out of my mind. I truly forgot about it, never thinking it would happen to us.

As it turned out, it was there, waiting in the wings. I'd been trying harder and harder, making nicer meals, planning fun outings, redecorating the house, and he was growing more and more distant. What a fool I'd been.

How could I have just blotted out the things I didn't want to see? I'd clung desperately to the script after all the other actors had left the stage and gone home. I'd always had a vivid imagination; even as a kid I'd gotten all my classmates to believe in my imaginary people. Which made me worried about my future prospects for a relationship. Was I like the frog who just sits there in the pot of water as it gets hotter and hotter? Death by boiling seemed better than jumping, better than the unknown.

I looked again at my father's diaries. I reread the 1970 one very carefully, each page. And I came upon something else on January 25. He'd written, "Relegating happiness to heaven is too much of a gamble. I'm going to find it on Earth."

Why was I stupidly looking for this Sara person? I suppose Dad knew I loved him, even though I was so hard on him. Can't change the past. Can't change a failed marriage. And on that note, who were my friends? Sure, I could list some names, but the sad truth was that not one had come over after hearing of our separation. Not one. Okay, there were some concerned phone calls, but then radio silence. I knew I was in a giant hot tub of self-pity, but how could I get out?

My father had been a distant man, a man who represented a million things that were objectionable to me, or just unrelatable. Was I wrong? Probably, and that was at least part of what was motivating me. My stepmother, Jo Jo, could have lived a hundred years and I still don't think she would have been able to give me what I was searching for. I'm not sure how well she understood my father. How many people are lucky enough to spend a lifetime with a person they fall deeply in love with? I think my mother's alcoholism killed the love she and Dad once had. I didn't feel at all that it was Sara's fault, if indeed there was a Sara. I lived in that house. I saw what went on before 1970: my father staying downstairs, staring blankly at the TV, while my mother called for him, her drunken moans, from over the upstairs banister. I don't remember talking to Rose or Ray about those horrible nights. I think we were all in our own private miseries.

Other nights she'd stay up till all hours. Once she woke me before dawn, and quietly, so we wouldn't wake Rose, with whom I shared a room, we went downstairs to make manicotti. It was probably three or four in the morning, I don't recall for sure, but I may have had school the next day. Another time she woke me up a little closer to dawn, not yet light out, and we went for a long walk. She took me to a little back road she knew of. It was actually beautiful, the woods and hills and a little creek. She climbed down toward this creek and then she fell in— not totally in, but maybe up to her knees. I thought it was the funniest thing. Was she drunk then? I didn't think it at the time. Even if she was, it was a memory I treasured.

Had I ever really been in love with Stephen? All those years, but maybe I was just in love with my dream. I was the cheery cheerleader, the coach with the effervescent smile. I'd spent my entire life working so hard at trying to get things right, I never could fix what was wrong.

How do you hate someone while putting them on a pedestal? The many conflicting sides of my father. Of course, I didn't know him. I didn't even know myself. Whether I found out something or not, I had forgiven him already. What I really was trying to do was to forgive myself. I wanted to do something positive for a change. Something positive. Yes, I could help with the strike.

I decided to go back to Kentucky.

Chapter 28

1970

Allicia was getting dressed to go to Barbara Lovejoy's house. She'd met Barbara only once, briefly, at the club. Her husband was some hotshot attorney, on his way to being an ambassador or something. She hoped Flo would be there, but either way, these were people of consequence, and she counted herself lucky to be invited.

She put on her navy skirt that fell just above the knee, with a matching nautical short-waisted jacket and shoes dyed to match. She only had one or two bruises on her legs, which wouldn't show. She had no memory of bumping herself, but then she often had no memory of even getting into bed. The idea that she might be blacking out terrified her, and she quickly thought of something else.

Her many hiding places now depleted, she slipped downstairs without a sound. Frank was in the next room watching TV with the kids. With the precision of a surgeon, borne of practice, she got out her bottle, filled her flask, and took two hefty swallows, all without a single clink.

The Lovejoys lived in Belle Haven, a private community on Long Island Sound. Allicia stopped at the guardhouse and gave Barbara's name, and the man waved her on. The directions said to go straight for a half mile, then make a left on Trafalgar Drive. That sounded easy. The houses were all so spectacular that Allicia couldn't resist exploring a little.

She passed sloping green lawns, curving cobblestone driveways, fluted Ionic columns—she'd learned about them in an architecture book she'd gotten from the library—and fountains. She drove slowly, sipping absentmindedly. "Too-too," she said, and "I'm simply gaga." She wished she had a convertible; that would have made it perfect. When she finally remembered to look at the time, it was later than fashionably late. It was very late, and she was lost.

None of the roads looked familiar: Churchill, Somerset, Cornwall,

Avon, Devon. The neighborhood was a maze of silent, stately mansions, and not a soul in sight. Hardly any other cars passed, and the ones that did went too fast for her to signal. If she found the house now, she'd be thirty minutes late. But she couldn't even find the gatehouse. Finally, she saw a man raking leaves and asked him where Trafalgar Drive was. He didn't know but directed her back to the gatehouse.

At last, she found the Lovejoys' house, which sat on a five-acre estate. The water behind the house was bluer than the cloudless sky and filled with little whitecaps. A housekeeper led Allicia through a marble foyer with a winding stairway. Allicia peeked up as she walked by. She followed the housekeeper to a sunroom where the ladies were gathered. Rich peoples' houses had a certain smell; was it from the slate steps? Or the stone foundations? Perhaps it was the smell of old money hidden in the dirt, growing in the ground. She loved that smell, wished they'd bottle it so she could wear it as perfume. She was also thinking of how she would tell her sister about every detail, taking mental notes of the paint colors, the wallpaper, carpets, furnishings, and artwork.

"What would you like to drink?" Barbara asked.

A quick glance showed the ladies all drinking white wine. "I'll have what everyone's having," Allicia said. "I just got a little turned around. It's my first time in Belle Haven, so I gave myself *un petit tour*. What a lovely home you have, and a marvelous view."

Barbara mumbled a thanks and wandered off, absorbed with other guests. The housekeeper came back with Allicia's drink, which she downed in two swallows. Platters of hot hors d'oeuvres covered the table: pigs in blankets, little cheese things in tiny pastry shells, and something that looked to Allicia like honeybees stuck in piles of mud on small round crackers. There was a platter of drinks, and she helped herself to another and then a third, spinning around to down the drinks out of the view of the women.

Then she saw Florence—thank God—and joined her circle. Flo was chatting with Millie and Louise. Millie, a petite woman in a rust-colored cloche with a few wisps of white hair showing, asked, "Where are you from, Allicia? Oh, yes, New Mexico." She gave a little cough.

"Yes. I'm from Clovis," Allicia said cheerfully.

The other woman, Louise, who'd looked the other way when Allicia joined them, turned and asked, "Did you say Texas? I've never met anyone from Texas." She had dark brown hair piled high, with bangs that spread like thin frosting across her forehead.

Allicia didn't like the direction of the conversation. "It's near Texas."

"Clovis," Millie said. "Doesn't it have French roots? Wasn't Clovis that French warrior, or a king or something?"

Now Allicia was truly out of her element. She had studied up on artists, art history, and architecture, and had bought classical records to learn about composers, but European history? She hadn't a clue. They waited for Allicia to answer.

"It's, uh, Curry County, but I never heard why they called it Clovis. Probably French, yes. Isn't every good thing French?" she added with a smile.

They started talking about travel, and Barbara joined them. She was a large woman, all charged up, with an overtime smile. She looked as if she were plugged into a wall socket and if anyone accidentally tripped on the cord, she would fizzle to the floor in a heap.

"We're going to Boothbay next week," Barbara said. "Daniel loaned the *Princesa*, our schooner, to the University of Maine for a year. They're returning it. He's obsessed with that boat. I think he loves it more than me. Ha!" Her face had a tight expression, as if her smile had to gain release from the jail of her mouth.

Allicia went looking for the bathroom, but she found herself in the driveway instead. She told herself that was a good thing; those people bored her to death.

From behind her, someone said, "How about you and I get us some coffee at Delgado's Diner?"

It was Flo. Allicia lit up at the sight of her friend. "Flo! My dear friend, Flo." She embraced her. "I couldn't think of anything I'd like more right now."

Flo had two paper cups of coffee. She handed one to Allicia. "Sip this and follow my car. It's that white one," Flo said, pointing.

Allicia felt sleepy, but she dutifully drove behind Flo while sipping the coffee.

She didn't want to go home anyway. Sometimes she felt she'd rather be anywhere than at her own home. She didn't feel loved or appreciated by any of them, yet she loved them all so much, her eyes filled with tears just thinking about it. Funny, she thought, she wasn't thinking about that stupid party. She couldn't care less about Barbara Lovejoy or the others. What was breaking her heart was her family, the people she loved most in the world. Something was wrong and she didn't know what it was. Her husband was slipping away, and all her attempts to make things better had been useless.

They found a booth at the diner. Allicia's mascara was smudged from her tears, and her hair was a mess. Flo reached over to smooth it and gave her a tissue for her face. The waitress came by and gave them coffees, and they both added cream.

For a little while, neither said anything. Then Allicia broke the silence.

"Flo, I am so glad you suggested this. I was ready to leave that stupid party, but I didn't want to go home." She yawned. "I'm so tired."

"Barbara Lovejoy puts me to sleep. I don't know why I even go. I want to be included somewhere; I just wish there were some intelligent life forms to be had."

"Intelligent life forms! You're a hoot." Allicia laughed. "You'd do better to look on the moon."

They both laughed, but then Allicia got pensive.

"Flo, do you go to church? I'm Presbyterian; well, I was raised Presbyterian. And Frank—it's like there is no religion but Catholicism. I don't mind raising the children Catholic, but I'm not a Catholic. Sometimes, when I'm really feeling lost, I go to the Westminster Presbyterian church. It's really hard to tell people who introduce themselves to me that I have three children and a husband. They look at me like I'm a freak. The rule is: *You go to church with your family.* I feel so separate from my family, and I love them so much." She began to cry again.

Flo handed her a napkin. "We go to a Congregationalist church."

Allicia looked at her friend. "Flo, sometimes I feel I've been shut out of the club of happiness."

"Has there been more talking in his sleep?"

"No."

"Things are better since you went to his office?"

"Yes. He surprised me, to tell you the truth." Their waitress came by with refills. "He invited me to join him for a business lunch with his uncle. But—"

"What?"

"I've been a little worried. I get these bruises. I don't always remember going to bed. Maybe my drinking, but I don't know. The doctor said I should cut back, and he wants me to take some pills, but I won't. They put me right to sleep."

"Have you tried stopping for a while? The drinking, I mean?"

"A zillion times."

"What happens?"

"I start again. It's like I forget the reason I went on the wagon, or talk myself out of it. Sometimes it's like I don't think at all, I just start drinking."

"I know a good place where you can get expert care. And it's right in town."

"Place?"

"Well, a hospital, but it's lovely, a beautiful building."

"How do you know about it?"

"My sister had to go. She's been sober for seven years."

"Flo, you're such a good friend. There's no one else I could ever have told about this."

"Will you go?"

Allicia said she would. Then she said, "Give me your hand. I want to read your palm." Flo extended her hand, palm up, and Allicia traced the lines with two fingers. "Your heart line has only one line across it; that's your divorce. And see here? You're going to live a very long life."

After a few minutes, Allicia said, "Let's scoop the skin off our coffees. If you get it all on your spoon, that means you'll marry a millionaire."

"But we're already married."

"Who cares?"

Flo stirred her coffee and lifted her spoon with the whole skin of cream hanging off it. "Is this what you mean?"

Allicia did the same. "We're both gonna marry millionaires."

When Allicia told Frank that she thought she was having trouble cutting back on her drinking, Frank was enthusiastic and supportive. He brought her to a doctor in New York. The tests showed early signs of cirrhosis, abnormal blood work, and an enlarged heart, most likely, the doctor said, related to circulatory issues stemming from her drinking. The doctor recommended "a stay" at the Daniel Winstead Hospital.

"How long of a stay?" Allicia asked.

"They'll let you know."

What really convinced her to say okay and go along with them was that she'd lied about how much she'd been drinking. Knowing that she drank a whole lot more than what she told them scared her. The very next week, Frank walked Allicia up the sidewalk of the converted estate. He left her at the front door, and with her small suitcase she entered the Daniel Winstead Hospital.

Chapter 29

Sara walked Mandy in her stroller through the front door of Underwood's to wait for Pattie to get back from work. On the porch was the usual gauntlet of miners, disabled and discarded, with their black phlegm and bitterness.

Sara was enjoying her babysitting job, and with her earnings she'd gone on a shopping spree with Aunt Betts in Louisville. When Sara shopped by herself she'd look at two or three things, determine that they were the ugliest pieces of clothing ever to be invented, and would look for the quickest way out. But Aunt Betts, who had impeccable taste, could find things that Sara would never have found, and things that Sara loved. The rest of her earnings had gone into savings. Her nest egg was growing nicely and now had over five thousand dollars.

Sara perused the shelves, seeing the same old stuff she'd seen all her life: Bag Balm in the green tin, witch hazel, dusty stacks of toilet paper and Ivory soap. She listened to the old miners through the open windows.

"Fighting talk, so I heard."

"Well, it should be fighting talk. Punching out new mines with plenty of scabs to fill them."

"If the Number 5 walks out, they'll get a scab group to do the Winifred strip."

Strip! That perked up Sara's ears. Were they actually going to start strip mining? How could Frank let this happen? Did he know? He must know; he was the president.

She went out to speak to them. "They're starting the strip?"

They laughed. "Since when are you interested in mining?" one said.

It was true, everyone knew Sara Stone was the last person in the holler to show interest in mining news. She didn't want them to notice too big a change in her. She didn't want any suspicion. "I just didn't think they'd be starting the strip," she said. They laughed again.

Mimi Blackstone stepped onto the porch. "How are you, Sara

Stone? So's I heard it, you've got yourself a second job. Let me see that sweet thing." She bent over to coo at Mandy. "She's growing like a weed."

Mimi's stick-thin body was wrapped in a long gray shawl. She had sores and scrapes from bug bites and briars on her calves. It wasn't uncommon to see Mimi standing in the middle of a field looking for plants. Sara could hear wheezes and rattles from her heaving chest.

"Did you walk all the way here?" Sara asked.

"How else would I get here?" She was still making faces at Mandy, and Mandy, in turn, was doing her baby laugh, which was more of a hiccough and then a gasp, with a giant smile. Mimi said, "Just look how good I am with babies."

Sara nodded. She did not say that Mandy was born laughing, and made everyone feel that they were particularly good with babies.

Mimi then said she was in need of boric acid for fleas.

"I hear possums get rid of fleas," Sara followed her into the store. "Is that true?"

"Sure, they help some."

"Bonnie's scratching a lot."

Mimi placed a bottle of boric acid in Sara's hand and told her to rub a solution of it through Bonnie's fur. "One part boric acid to five parts water, four if the mites are bad. And possums are a might lot of trouble. Not the best at getting rid of mites."

"What is the best?"

"Guinea fowl."

"Oh."

"Got to worry about foxes, though. They'll come right out in front of you. Ever heard a fox bark? Wake up to that in the middle of the night—wooooo." Mimi shuddered.

Leon Underwood appeared, carrying a large open cardboard box, moving gingerly around the tight corners of the store. "How y'all doing?" He wore the same thing every day: a white shirt, black slacks, and a pair of falling-down brown leather tie shoes. Sara didn't know how old Underwood was, but somehow his shoes matched their owner, and both looked badly in need of retirement, yet both somehow showed up every day doing the same thing they did the day before. Rain or shine or snow, you could set your clock to Leon Underwood. She asked him once if he still worked forty hours a week. He'd said, "I'd be embarrassed to only work forty hours in a week."

Pulling a piece of paper from under her shawl, Mimi waved it at him. "I want to read you my letter to the governor."

Leon didn't look up from the soup cans he was arranging on the shelves with an unbroken two-handed tempo. Sara thought he must be able to do that in his sleep. But he did give Sara a quick wink, before saying, "The Governor's your boyfriend, right Mimi?"

"Go on. I don't have a boyfriend."

"You better get you one." He laughed.

"Now Leon, you got to hear it. It's important."

Leon mumbled, "That so? Did he write back?"

Sara decided it wouldn't hurt to show some curiosity. "I want to hear it."

Leon kicked the empty box away and opened another.

"I'll read it to you, Sara." Mimi began, "Dear Sir," and the words tumbled out and seemed to bounce off Sara's brain like a basketball off a backboard. "Dam collapse—people staying at the school—already been one flood—no one will listen—" It confirmed all her fears, and she'd always had a little gnawing doubt, thinking: *Maybe I'm wrong. Maybe it's not as bad as I think it is.*

Leon stood, his body rising off the floor in shifts, like a newborn horse standing for the first time. He flattened the boxes, then said, "You didn't get an answer, did you?"

"Yes. Said they'd would look into it." She put the letter somewhere back under her shawl and various layers of clothing.

"I'm glad you wrote it," Sara said. "Everyone wants to complain but not do a thing. Meanwhile we have these jokers driving around yelling, 'The dam's gonna blow!' We hear it so much that if it ever happened, no one would blink! We've got to do something."

Leon shook his head and mumbled, "Won't do a lick of good. Those politicians are all bought out, and you know it. And the UMW—that's a pure mess. Ain't worth the spit you put on that stamp." He had a wet line of sweat running down the middle of his back.

This talk gave Sara pins and needles in her legs. "Why should we sit back and do nothing? Just twiddle our thumbs? That's gonna look pretty stupid if there's another flood. That coal company is putting us in danger and we have a right to stand up to them. We have a right to live without fear, like any other American. Isn't that what you did? You didn't just sit back and let the coal company take your land. You fought back and won your case."

Leon was using a feather duster on the cans he'd just put on the shelves. Sara had always thought they got dusty from sitting. To her surprise they arrived dusty, and probably never sat long enough to gather any dust. He smiled, in a resolved, dispassionate way. "You can't swing at every fly buzzing around your head, now, Sara, can you? Do, and you'll go pure crazy."

"But The Big Lagoon goes on forever. I went up and—" She stopped herself and cringed because once again she'd opened her mouth too much.

Leon put his hand over his mouth and shook his head slowly. "Don't you be telling me this. Cuz I sure don't want to know."

Mimi said, "Just look at all those innocent children who died in Wales."

"What children died in Wales?" Sara asked.

"Aberfan, Wales, sweetie. The schoolchildren. Smothered. They had that mountain of mess above the school and it slid right down over them. Killing those babies while they were singing their hearts to God."

"Killed babies!" Aberfan, Wales. Sara repeated it to herself a few times, because she wanted to remember it. Mimi followed Leon, waving her letter, but just then the bell jingled. Pattie was there to retrieve her baby.

It was Tuesday, and Sara didn't have to work that evening, so she walked to the library only one mile each way, which was nothing for her. She got there just before closing, but Mrs. Bickford was still working and was happy to help Sara find all their articles on Aberfan. Just before leaving, she asked Sara to pull the door shut and make sure it was locked. "It's a little sticky, and the wind's been opening it," she said.

The Aberfan disaster had happened only four years earlier, in 1966. One hundred and sixteen children between the ages of seven and ten dead. Twenty adults dead. The gob pile—360,000 tons—had slid and crushed the school. The little children had suffocated to death. A hundred and sixteen children!

"No!" Sara cried.

How much was 360,000 tons of colliery waste? She wondered how many tons were in the gob pile up Hanson's Fork. The article went on to call the Aberfan gob pile "a moving mountain that went thirty to forty miles per hour." She'd heard once that a dog could run at top speed about thirty miles an hour, but no human could, certainly not a child. The children had been looking forward to their upcoming holiday. The gob pile had crushed houses, cars, and brick walls. The rescue workers, and basically everybody in the village, had dug and dug with shovels and even bare hands. Within twenty-four hours, a hundred and four bodies were found, fifty-two boys and fifty-two girls. Six of the children had died on the playground.

"Children died on the playground! Oh, shit!" Her tears fell. And this was just four years ago. If it happened then, it could happen now. She forced herself to read on.

The article said that "the National Coal Board had ignored concerns for years, and the mining debris had been deposited on top of underground springs." Underground springs! She paced the floor of the silent library. Water was the perfect material to create a slick foundation that would eventually give way. How was it she'd never heard of this? She thought of Mimi saying there'd already been a partial collapse and flood. It was hard to look at the pictures. She was so frozen in outrage she couldn't even wipe her tears. *All those beautiful little innocent children,* she thought. *And the officials had concerns for years, and did nothing!*

She stacked all the papers, turned off the lights, and pulled the door shut. During the walk home, she concocted a plan. Maybe it was crazy, but she had to do something. She'd tell her brothers and Todd that she was going to visit her aunt and uncle in Lexington. She was sure that Linda Lee would keep Mandy for a few days.

She'd get the bus to Lexington. From there she'd catch a train to New York City to see Frank. She had to get through to him that this was urgent. She'd leave tomorrow, but the bigger question was, should she call him or surprise him? She hadn't seen him for two months. Maybe he'd forgotten about her. But she didn't believe that.

She knew he traveled a lot, so calling him at work could get complicated. They'd ask her name, of course, and a reason for the call. She couldn't do that. And calling him at home was out of the question. But this was important. It had to do with lives, the very lives of the people in her holler.

She decided to take her chances on him being in town, and Friday seemed like a good day to get there. Things slowed down toward the end of August because a lot of people were on vacation. She'd look up the number for Rowan Coal in New York City when she got there.

Chapter 30

The next day, Sara took the bus as planned, debating the whole way what she would tell Aunt Betts and what she wouldn't tell her. When Aunt Betts picked her up, it turned out that, in response to her aunt's questions, she couldn't lie. "You're not going to like this, Aunt Betts."

"Okay, darling. That gives me an idea." Aunt Betts pulled off the road. "We'll have a proper chat." They walked down to the creek, where they took off their shoes and swirled their feet in the cold water.

"Ooooo, this water feels so good," Aunt Betts said, wiggling her toes. "Nothing cools like the river."

"You want me to cool off, huh?" Sara said. "You know what I'm going to tell you?"

"I'm guessing."

"It's about a man."

"That's what I thought."

"Aunt Betts, you always amaze me. How would you know?"

"I figured it was something like that when you were last up here buying clothes. Not the clothes; that's a natural part of growing up. But you had a faraway look. You were quieter than I've seen you. I knew something was up."

"But you said nothing. Never let on."

"I knew you would talk when you were ready."

"I guess I'm ready." Sara told her about Frank; who he was and how they'd met. "I've never felt like this before. It's just so wonderful to talk to someone about my dreams. He challenges me to do more with my life."

Aunt Betts asked what he did for a living. Sara told her that he was the head of Rowan Coal in New York, was thirty-six, married with three children. Aunt Betts sighed. Sara waited in dread for her response.

After a minute or two of silence, Aunt Betts said, "You're a grown woman, Sara. I expect you can make up your own mind. I just have one question. Do you love him?"

"I doubt that this is kind of it, if that's what you mean. I really like him, I think about him all the time, and the time we spend together is wonderful. But no, it's not what you're thinking."

Aunt Betts had that sweet look on her face, and a soft smile. She effused love. "I just hope you use your good sense, Sara. Falling in love, it can come upon you unaware. Just make sure you don't get in deeper than you'd like. As Uncle Shortie likes to say, 'It's easier to send your troops to battle than it is to bring them home.'"

"To be honest, I'm not sure I know whether I'm in love. But it's what I want right now. And to think that I could help our holler by knowing him."

"Help the holler?"

"Frank listens to me about the dams. He's making changes. He got them to stop the strip plans, and he's working on making the dams safer. But we need to do something faster. And that's what I'm going to do in New York. Tell him how urgent this is."

Sara was grateful for the understanding ear she always found in her aunt. Her aunt was sixty-four. She'd seen a lot. She and Uncle Shortie had raised four children, and Sara had heard bits and pieces of their adventures. There was little that could surprise Aunt Betts. Life hadn't hardened her; it was quite the opposite. Aunt Betts was like her brother Clay, Sara's dad. They were kind. "We'll have plenty of time to talk because we've got some shopping to do if you're going to New York."

"I'm fine for clothes, Aunt Betts."

"This time it'll be my treat."

"I'm more worried about Uncle Shortie."

"Oh, believe me, he's been broken in with our kids." They walked back to the car. "You're not the first to have a life, to have some adventures, to spread your wings."

"To make mistakes?"

They laughed. "Maybe that too. And one day I'll tell you about mine."

"Tell me now."

"Now we shop. But I will tell you some other time about how I left your Uncle Shortie, early in our marriage, and found a place to live above a funeral parlor."

"Oh, my gosh! Tell me now!"

"All right, come on."

They went shopping in Lexington and Sara got a gray wool skirt with a fitted short-waisted blazer and a dark pink blouse with glittery silver threads. And a black dress. Every woman should have a black dress, her aunt said. She also got a pair of burgundy shoes with a cute strap over the ankle, some hose and panties, a slip, and a simple white nightgown with eyelet lace at the top. Aunt Betts paid for everything.

Aunt Betts was such a mix of contrary things. She was a retired schoolteacher and lived in the woods, but never went out without a little lipstick and mascara. She always wore nice outfits that looked sharp and well-coordinated—the outfit, the shoes, the purse. But she could come home with more game on her back than grown men, including Uncle Shortie. Every night she washed her face with various creams, and she had taught Sara how to care for her skin, saying, "Only use the pad on the tip of your ring finger. It's the lightest finger and won't pull the skin. Always use an upward stroke, because gravity is doing enough pulling everything down."

Sara said, "Thank you for being so understanding."

"I try never to judge. You know what I always say; there's three sides to every situation."

"I know. There's your side, my side, and the right side." I knew my Aunt Betts's sayings, having heard them since I was a toddler. "And don't judge a man," I added, and here she chimed in with me, "till you've walked a mile in their shoes."

Sara had told her aunt about Aberfan and how it galvanized her into action. If anyone could get through to Rowan Coal, if anyone could improve the situation, she felt it was her, through Frank.

In a soft voice, Aunt Betts said, "It's rarely the case that one man has that much power. But I hope you're right." She turned on the radio. The male announcer was giving the weather report: partly cloudy, no chance of rain. After a few minutes, she asked, "Do you have a contingency plan in case he's not there? New York's a big city."

"Don't worry."

"You'll need money for a hotel, taxis, food. It may come to more than you've anticipated."

Sara told her how much she'd brought, but still Aunt Betts gave her a hundred dollars, saying, "Mad money. Put it in your shoe and forget about it. Promise me."

It was an overnight train that left late Thursday night. Sara would get there Friday morning.

When they hugged good bye, Aunt Betts held her tight the way she always did. With her scrunched up, loving eyes, she said, "I love you so much!"

After the sun had come up and the long train ride had nearly ended, everything suddenly went dark. Sara must have said something, because the woman next to her chuckled and said, "It's Grand Central, honey. We're in New York City." The tunnel seemed to go on forever, but eventually the train came to a stop and the doors opened. Sara stepped off and breathed in the warm air. It smelled gray. But she couldn't stand there long, despite her doubts as to which way she should go, because the tide of people picked her up and carried her along. Clutching her small overnight bag and purse and trying not to get trampled, she made her way inside the station. There everyone dispersed and she came to a dead halt.

She craned her neck to take it all in: the ceiling, the grandness, the mammoth size of the space. For a moment she forgot about the crowds, about everything, and stared. She stared at the ceiling with the zodiac paintings, then turned in a slow circle to look all around her at the terrific windows, the grand arches, and the marble floor. How could a train station be so beautiful? Her trance, however, was broken by a less lofty consideration. She needed a bathroom. So that was the first thing she did in New York. But even the bathroom was remarkable, so spacious and big, with a couch to sit on.

Upstairs, she sat for a long time watching the people, every kind of person imaginable was there. She imagined herself there, living there, and what it might be like. After almost two hours, she found a phone booth and called the Rowan Coal Company.

"Can I speak to Mr. Rowan, please?"

"Which Mr. Rowan?"

She tried to lower her voice and speak in a monotone. "Mr. Frank Rowan."

The woman asked for Sara's name and repeated it. "Miss Sara Stone. Would you kindly hold the line?"

Frank got on the phone. He talked in a fake, singsong voice. "Oh, so glad you're in town. Shall we meet for lunch?" Sara figured he was being listened to. She told him she was at Grand Central Station.

"Meet me by the clock at the information booth," he said. "I'll see you in fifteen minutes."

In less than fifteen minutes, he tapped her shoulder; she'd been looking the wrong way. They did not embrace, although she wanted to, wanted to take his hand, wanted to kiss him. He gave her a quick wink, took her arm and her bag, and before she knew it they were outside and stepping into a cab. In the cab, they hugged. Frank was concerned that something was wrong. "Has someone found out about us?"

"No, nothing like that."

"Okay. Well, are you hungry?"

"I am starved!"

He spoke to the driver and they were off. A short time later, they shuffled out of the cab. Again, Sara stood still to take it all in. "This is fantastic. It's the coolest building I've ever seen, squeezed onto this corner and with pillars."

"It's Delmonico's. Been here a hundred years. Great food. Let's go in."

Frank requested a table in the back, and Sara was dazzled as they walked through the restaurant, with its soft carpet, chandeliers, fashionable diners, and delicious smells.

As soon as they were tucked into their table in the back, the waiter brought menus and glasses of water. Frank reached for Sara's hand across the table. "Sara, are you sure everything's all right?"

"Yes and no," she answered, but before anything else, she needed the restroom again. She took a minute to look in the mirror. She had a perfectly almond-shaped face, smallish eyes, and a large forehead, but now, with makeup on and a little care to her looks, she looked so different to herself. That fanciful, impetuous girl by the river was gone, and she thought that was just fine.

Back at the table Frank said, "So, you're moving here? I know we talked about this, of course. But I guess I am a little surprised. Do you have some ideas about a job, or where you want to live?"

"No, Frank. I'm not moving. Well, not right now. I'm here for something else."

He exhaled loudly. "I must admit I'm a little relieved. It seemed somewhat abrupt. So, you came here to visit me?" He gave his dimpled smile.

The waiter came by for their orders. Frank ordered a roast beef sandwich with fries, but Sara was still reading the menu. Frank signaled to give them another minute. Eventually, after asking questions about terms such as "caramelized" and "braised," she chose the lobster Newburg and a Coke. Frank got a coffee.

For a time, neither spoke. Then Frank said, "You said you came here for something else. I doubt it's sightseeing, so what might that be? Is there a different problem? Something I can help with?"

"It may sound silly."

His face showed relief. He sat back and lit a cigarette. "I'm listening."

"I read about Aberfan."

"Aberfan. Yeah, it was terrible."

The waiter brought their drinks.

"And all those children who died."

"I'm familiar. You came here to talk about that?"

"Yes!" she shouted, but then regretted it. No one seemed to notice, though. She paused for a moment, sipped her drink. "Frank, I don't know if you're doing enough about the dams."

"Sara, do we really want to talk about this during lunch?"

"Yes!" she blurted again, this time paying no attention to what people around them did.

Frank sat perfectly still, but his eyes were severe. "I have given you my word that I'm doing everything that's in my power to do."

The waiter brought their food. They began eating, but then Sara stopped and in her emphatic voice, as if suddenly remembering, said, "But the lake is above the gob pile! Held back by gravel. I've seen it. I just want to hear again what you're doing. I know you have until October 25, but is that enough time?"

Frank put his fork down, and a sadness came over him, like a balloon losing all its air. "Is this all you're interested in?"

"Of course not."

"I'm throwing everything I can at this problem." He rubbed his eyes. "The problem is in Washington."

"Washington?"

"The laws coming out of Washington. A half dozen laws have led to this situation, along with some really bad decisions. And for years everyone's been looking the other way. It's—"

"Frank, there's been some talk of strip mining. I overheard it at Underwood's. Something about bringing in scabs."

"There won't be strip mining." Frank put his hand on hers. "I've told you that."

"Are you sure? That's all I want to know. Are you completely sure?"

Frank said, "I am, and the inspectors haven't even come. We have two months." He told her about the froth flotation, the new sludge dam, the pipes and grading work they'd done. "And we're releasing a lot of water, illegally, I might add."

"Why illegally?"

"It's black water. We'll be reported, fined, but that will just be added to a long list of violations. Which is good. More reason why we won't get a strip permit. Vern, my boss, can't go forward without a permit."

"Is there anything else, anything that'll work faster? Maybe spread the water in the mountains? Make more holes so it leaks faster?"

"They used to dump it in old mine shafts, but that's too risky. There've been cave-ins, and miners have drowned. There's nothing else we can do. If you're unhappy with me, I understand. I spend enough time unhappy with myself, that's for sure. Do you want me to take you back to the station?"

Sara hadn't had a definite idea of what she wanted from the trip, other than to have this conversation, which hadn't gone as well as she'd hoped.

The waiter came by, cleaned off the table, and left the tab. Frank put the cash on the table.

"Why would you say a thing like that?"

"Because I know I'm a disappointment to you."

She slid her hand into his. "It's not the only reason I came here."

Frank's face revealed a growing optimism. "Are you sure?"

"Let's go."

On the crowded street they maneuvered through the crowd, barely able to hold onto each other's hands. When they reached the corner, Frank stopped and pulled her close for a kiss.

After a few minutes, Frank said, "Sara, sweet Sara, I'm delighted if you want to spend time with me, but I want to be clear that I don't have anything to offer you, as far as any commitments of a personal nature."

"I know that, Frank."

He shrugged. "I don't want to see you upset, or disillusioned in me. I'm not the head of the company." Frank stroked her face.

After that they spent the whole day walking, exploring, window-shopping, and sightseeing. They didn't talk about anything serious, nothing to do with coal or the dams. They were just two people walking anonymously in a giant city, a city that continued to amaze Sara. It was so crowded, the buildings so giant, the streets so packed with cars, the sidewalks jammed with people; it seemed impossible that the whole thing ran so smoothly. They went to St. Patrick's Cathedral and Carnegie Hall and had pretzels on a bench in Central Park. That's when Frank pointed to a squirrel going up some steps, an apple in its mouth.

"Is that what they mean," Frank said, "by 'biting off more than you can chew'?"

They laughed.

"Good for him," Sara said, throwing bits of pretzel to the pigeons.
"You don't know what you can do until you try it."

"That's right," she said. "But you need courage."

Then Frank suggested they take the ferry to see the Statue of Liberty. "Ellis Island is where millions of courageous people first stepped on our shores."

Planes flew overhead, and tugboats were on the water. Sara, who had never seen the ocean, was spellbound. Inching away from the looming city, hanging over the rail, they each were mesmerized by curling white foam. Seagulls swooped in the ferry's choppy wake. Their kisses were warm in the chilly wind.

Upon their return, Frank said, "We need to plan dinner." His face grew serious.

"What just crossed your mind?"

"Well, whatever you want. You decide."

"Frank, I want to be with you."

"I want that too."

He had already told her about Allicia being in a special hospital. "I'll see if the babysitter can spend the night."

Chapter 31

Frank made his call, and then they took a cab through the evening traffic to the Upper East Side. As they walked along the tree-lined streets, Sara exclaimed, "Flower boxes. Ivy-covered buildings. Lampposts. This is not the New York I'd imagined."

In a small grocery store with a deli counter, they bought sandwiches and a bottle of orange juice. They walked up the five steps of one of the brownstones.

"Do you like it? We could always go to a hotel. There are many luxurious ones. But somehow I thought you'd like this better."

"Are you kidding? I love this. So romantic."

"It belongs to a friend." Frank found the hidden key, but he couldn't get the door open.

"Stuck?"

"Not only stuck, the key is jammed in there."

"Move over."

She pulled the key out ever so slightly, then wiggled it while pushing it. It opened. She handed him the key.

Before going in, his look changed—his brow furrowed.

"What is it?" she asked.

"I just want to check one more time, to make sure," he said. "Regardless of what you think I might want. I mean—"

"Frank," she said, taking his hand, "let's go in."

The narrow living room, with its bare wooden floor and a few upholstered chairs, smelled musty. "Look, they have handkerchiefs on the chairs. This looks like it was decorated by someone's grandmother."

"They look like nice antiques."

Past the living room was a curling set of narrow stairs, and beyond that a small kitchen. Frank said, "We have the whole place to ourselves, if you're comfortable here."

"Look at these stairs." Sara was ascending the curvy staircase. "They're steep as a ladder, and like a corkscrew."

Frank followed with her bag.

"I don't see how you could live here with children," she said at the first landing. "They'd break their necks!"

They picked the last bedroom because it had a private garden terrace. Sara immediately went out onto it. There were trees, flowers, and bushes, and a table with chairs. "I can't believe this. Tall trees, right in the middle of a giant city."

They sat for a while, shoes off, in mutual exhaustion. Dusk was closing in. After a while he said, "We have one last thing to explore. I noticed it as we walked by." In the bathroom he showed her an oversized tub. "Might fit us both."

"Worth a try."

The clock downstairs chimed eight times. They got undressed and into the tub, where Sara had also poured some foaming bubble bath that she'd found. What with the pouring water and their bodies displacing that water, and because the mixture was a lot more concentrated than Sara had expected, bubbles and water went over the top of the tub and onto the floor.

They jumped out, and were trying to clean it up while laughing. After they got most of it up, they had a bubble-covered hug, then, with the last dry towel, they dried the bubbles off each other's bodies. First Frank dried Sara, then Sara dried Frank. When she came out of the bathroom, the towel wrapped around her, Frank was sitting, naked, on the end of the bed. She walked to him and let the towel fall from her. He stood, took her hand, and said, "Have I told you how gorgeous you are?"

The next day they were glued to each other walking through Grand Central. Frank walked Sara to her train, and she got on but leaned out the doorway still holding his hand.

The bell rang and the train started moving. "When?" she shouted.

He waved, and she thought he said "Soon," but later she'd wondered if he'd said "Month."

She found a seat and looked out the window as the train started to move. Trains had always held a place of promise for Sara, her secret association. The hint of freedom, the hope of escape. This train was taking her away. Each inch and then each mile she'd be further from someone and something she'd never before known could be that sweet. She'd never known, never imagined, such a deep feeling of well-being, of love.

Staring out the window, she let her tears fall. It seemed they had a life of their own, these long held tears. They flowed from her body, the sadness being squeezed from her like a sponge. It wasn't all about Frank. She hadn't even known him that long. It was the long, long dry spell. The dark, dark nights. A moment, that's what it was, her time with Frank was a moment in the sun. A moment of magic, and this train was going farther away.

This man who'd shown such tenderness. This man who was so easy to talk to. They had so many differences, it seemed, yet much in common. They had fun together. She'd never have thought to pursue a man like Frank, and look what she would have missed. Inch by inch, mile by mile, over minutes and then hours, the leaving, the distance. Miles between her and Frank. Her tears fell.

She tried to picture his last word to her, from the platform. Was it "Soon!" Or did he say, "Month!"

Maybe it was "Goodbye!"

Chapter 32

Benny was in the kitchen when she got home. He said he'd called her at Aunt Betts's about a car that someone was selling that he thought she might like. An almost new bright red Pontiac. "A convertible, just beautiful, with white interior. Runs like a charm, great pickup."

"I didn't know I was looking for a car."

"Well, you're going places these days, getting dressed up. I thought you might want a car. You must be putting away a good bit of money with your two jobs." He walked by with his BLT on a plate and took a seat at the table. "You gonna tell me where you were?"

Still in the kitchen, she downed a glass of tap water. "You know where I was. And anyway, don't you think I can handle my own life without you butting in like some sort of bird dog?"

"Well, you did leave in kind of a hurry."

"I do everything in a hurry; haven't you noticed?" Sara had caught a bus directly after the train; she hadn't spoken with her aunt.

"Don't worry, Frisky," he said. "Aunt Betts covered for you, which was a dead giveaway. She didn't say where you were or when you'd be back." He took a swig of his PBR. "Who is this guy? Where'd you meet him?"

"Benny." She walked behind him and grabbed a shock of his hair, pulling his face up toward her. "My life is not your business."

"I just hope it isn't that joker, that scumbag, from Rowan Coal who shows up at Todd's."

She sat across from him, with her feet up on the chair beside her. She needed to change the subject. She wanted to act nonchalant, then put him on the defensive. "Why should I report to you, Benny? Aren't you tired of that game? I mean, who knows what you do every weekend?"

"Kind of curious, that's all."

"Maybe you're pushing to get rid of me, get me on out of here. That's it, isn't it? You and Darryl would be happy, so happy, if I got out of your hair. I'm just an albatross to you." She actually did fear this.

"An alba-what? Geez, you say the damnedest things. Where do you come up with all this?"

"Didn't you do any work in high school?"

"I skipped most of it," he said, around a mouthful of sandwich. "Anyway, why do you think we're trying to get rid of you? Where would we go? Darryl's not ready to marry. He hasn't put away enough money to get a place of his own, although I think he might be looking around. Sherry's not that easy to please. And I'm perfectly happy here. I might never marry. I'm kind of bummed it's not Pete, though. I know your thing about miners, and that's fine. But everyone knows Pete's not here for the long haul. He's here for some sort of adventure or something. But tell you what, that poor kid is crazy about you."

"Is that why you guys have him over all the time? Wasted effort."

"No. We like the dude. He talks too much but we're used to him now, and living with that old man can't be that thrilling. I still can't believe he bought that truck. Man, I thought he was smarter than that."

She looked around. "This place looks pretty clean. I'm impressed."

"We're moderately civilized. I'm heading out." Just before leaving, he turned back to her and, with a slight smile, he winked. "And I'm not telling where."

She waved him on. "Don't. I'm not asking."

Chapter 33

2019

I debated with myself about whether I should go. Finally, I decided, *Why not?* New sights, some spectacular vistas, and I'd been there before so I knew the route. Besides, hadn't they encouraged me to help with the strike?

This time, I decided, I wouldn't stay with Nancy. I would drop her a line saying only that I'd be back to help, with no mention of where I was staying. I also didn't feel comfortable staying at Todd's Motel, which I'd seen mentioned in my father's diaries. It gave me the willies thinking that he'd possibly stayed there with a lover.

I booked a room at the Cherry Tree Lodge, next to a state park; I figured it would be beautiful, and I planned to do some hiking.

When I told the girls my plan to help with a coal strike, they were excited for me, and proud, but they warned me that they couldn't bail me out of jail. "You're on your own, Mom." Funny how the tables turn.

I had absolutely zero idea or picture in my head about what helping with a strike entailed. Maybe carrying cartons of water and food, hauling trash, organizing provisions. Yes, I had my compunctions, and some guilt, about deceiving Nancy and some of the others, except for Leandra Blackstone, who could see right through me. But they said they needed help, and I could help. And getting out of the house was a good thing.

Sometime after Stephen walked out, my headaches had started. They weren't bad at first, mostly hurting when I bent over, but every day they got worse, to the point that I rarely turned my head quickly because of the shooting pains. My doctor gave me a prescription. She said it would help if my headaches were migraines. It didn't help. She also strongly advised that I go to a therapist. I did go to a therapist that my friend recommended. A woman who'd been practicing for decades. Almost as soon as I started talking, the tears fell, but not about my marriage. Not about my stupid trips to Kentucky. About Rose.

I thought the therapist would recommend grief counseling, or that other thing that's so popular—mindfulness. Actually, I needed mind-lessness, because I could hardly keep two thoughts going at the same time. But, to my surprise, the therapist recommended Al-Anon. She said it's for the family and friends of alcoholics.

"But my mom died in 1974," I said.

"It's a family disease," the therapist said.

I tried a couple of their meetings and chatted a little afterward. When I alluded to my father's possible extramarital affairs, the reactions were laughter. They certainly were a cheerful bunch, which really surprised me.

"That's often found on the buffet table of alcoholism." I was speaking with one of the women. Then she said, in a more serious tone, "The drunkalogues of this disease, the war stories, as they're called, get a lot worse than that."

I thought: *if ever there's a place to say this, it's here.* "Yeah, my mother died from it fairly young, well, very young."

Her face crinkled up. "That's exactly what I mean. Glad you're here. You came to the right place." She wrote her phone number on a piece of paper, as did a couple of other women, and gave it to me. "It's a phone list. Call anyone on that list. You're not alone. Do you want a hug?" They all wanted to hug me, but that was more touch than I'd had in a while. It was kind of nice, but it also felt fake, and made me want to find the exit quickly. I did keep her phone number, but never called.

Now, while driving, I found my mind going again to the past. I found it surprising that I wasn't thinking about Stephen, the years we were together, but seemed consumed with these half-submerged childhood scenes, events, and memories. They were sketchy and spotty, with big gaps. I remembered the early years as pretty innocuous, with a lot that was actually quite good: summer outings with Mom to the beach, museums, picnics. She took me to the opera in New York when I was seven. I could still picture the Metropolitan Opera House and the grand room with the chandeliered ceiling. The plays we put on in the living room on rainy days. She made sure we all had riding lessons; no child of hers wouldn't know how to handle a horse! I loved the smell of horses. I remembered the time Rose fell off and went in an ambulance to the hospital. She was fine, but that's when the lessons stopped, which was okay by me, because even though I loved horses, I was allergic.

Dad used to take us sledding, and he taught us to skate on the pond, but only after we'd had two weeks of twenty degrees or lower.

He took us to the drive-in, James Bond movies. We three paid no attention to the movie, just ran around getting food and playing in the playground, bugging dad with questions and knocking that speaker off the door each time. Then we fell asleep on the top of the station wagon on sleeping bags that my father had spread out.

But Mom wasn't there. Why wouldn't she have wanted to go to a drive-in movie? In fact, none of my memories had Dad and Mom together. I even remembered Dad taking us to Jones Beach on Long Island, with the big waves, but I didn't remember Mom being there. Dad took us to ball games and taught us to sing, "To hell, to hell with Pennsylvania. To hell with the U. of P. P. U.!" Mom wasn't there.

Remembering Christmases, little came to mind after the presents. Was that because her drinking increased as the hours passed? I had a lot of gaps in my memory. I tried to remember a time when the two of them had driven us anywhere together, but I couldn't. I just couldn't picture them together at all and then I put my recollections away as I parked at the Cherry Tree Lodge.

After getting settled, and getting the directions from the hotel clerk, I headed off to the nonprofit in charge of helping with the strike. Up a side road, off the beaten track, I found a small wooden sign: "Just Changes." I parked in the gravel drive and walked into the small white building. Four long tables, piled high with boxes and supplies, were pushed against the walls. In the center of this plethora of goods was a young woman in a T-shirt and shorts, filling brown grocery bags with food.

"Hi," I said. "I'm Aleena. Nancy Monroe sent me here to see if I could help out. This is a hidden-away place."

"Most people around here know where we are," she said, standing and offering her hand. "Welcome to Just Changes. I'm Sara, and thank you. We appreciate any help, and today I have someone out sick, so this is great."

Had she said "Sara"? For a minute I thought I'd imagined it. "You said—you said your name is Sara? Is that with an h?"

"No h. Named after my grandma."

I felt caught, exposed, and wondered for a moment if this was some sort of trick or joke. Taking my sweater off, I turned to compose myself. Sara was a common name. Yet I was also trying to do the math—if she were in her twenties, how old would her mother and her grandmother be? My brain was jelly, and math was never my strong suit. I lived by my calculator.

"Are you okay? You look pale. Where are you from? Was it a long drive?"

My hand was on my head and I didn't even know it. I was afraid the headaches would start. "Just a bit tired." I told her that I'd driven from Connecticut. Sara found some rice crackers, and I made myself a cup of tea in the small kitchen.

I'd done my research back at home. Kentucky had their vital statistics online for all counties. I'd checked births, deaths, and marriages, close to and approximating the relevant years. Of course, I didn't have my notes in front of me, but I'd found a Sara Stone born in 1949 in Whitfield County and no deaths by that name. There was also a Sara Stone marriage license to someone with the last name of Griffith or Griffen—I couldn't recall just then—within a year of the disaster.

"I hope you're okay. I could call my girlfriend, Joyce, she's an EMT. It's funny that you asked me how I spell my name. Not many people do. I don't really like my name."

"You don't?"

"No. Joyce likes it. She says it's old-fashioned. I prefer my middle name, Clay."

I sipped my tea and munched on the crackers.

She said, "We'd better get the bags into those boxes and the boxes in the van out front. Then we'll bring them to the strikers by the railroad tracks. It's only about three miles away."

"That's why I'm here, Clay."

"Thanks for calling me that. I like it. It fits, don't you think?"

I smiled in agreement. "I have two daughters about your age. They're in college, but I wish they'd have come. I think you'd all have gotten along really well."

We began carrying the boxes to the van. I liked the physical work, which temporarily stopped my mind. There were too many boxes for her van, so we began filling my Subaru. As we walked back and forth carrying boxes, I couldn't resist asking one more question. "What was your grandma's full name? I mean, her maiden name?"

"Are you a journalist? We've had a few of them show up, one from as far away as France."

I assured her I wasn't.

"My grandma was Sara Stone until she married my grandpa, Peter Griffith. She's probably down with the strikers. You might meet her today."

"I hope we don't have to go down a mountain. I still haven't recovered from trying to follow Nancy over that mountain months ago."

"Oh, I pity you. Nancy is notorious for her driving. She was the school bus driver for decades and could probably drive those mountain roads blindfolded." We pushed the doors closed. The cars were jammed tight with boxes. Clay said, "Do you know that people from as far away as D.C. have sent us food and school supplies? And now you've come here all the way from Connecticut. I swear, people are so nice."

Part of me wanted to go home and escape all of this, hide under my covers and eat peanut M&Ms, but my car was filled with boxes of food, so I was in fairly deep. One way or another, I was on my way to a coal strike where I might meet Sara, *the* Sara, and I had no idea what I would say.

When we got to the railroad tracks, the first thing that struck me was how small the strike was. I guess that being from the Northeast, where everything from concerts to baseball games tends to bring huge crowds, I'd expected something a bit bigger. A smattering of people, maybe fifty, stood around a couple of big tents, and there were numerous small tents. I saw some porta-potties lined up on the perimeter.

With a few extra hands recruited, all the bags were unloaded and distributed.

"Clay, can you explain to me again why they're here?"

She looked confused for a moment. Then she pointed way down the tracks. "To stop that train." She said it as if I were a little nutsy. "See their signs, 'No Pay We Stay'? That's because that train is loaded with the coal that they worked hard to get. It was about to head out and be sold, and these miners wouldn't get a penny of the money they earned."

"Right." I tried to sound as if it was all coming back to me.

We went to the kitchen tent, where some women were cooking burgers on a large grill. There was a sense of organization, and everything was neat. Somewhere along the way I lost track of Clay, and I couldn't see anyone who might be her grandma. My eyes searched for any possible candidates. I stood there looking around, feeling stupid and out of place, sipping Red Rose tea from a Styrofoam cup that a woman had kindly given me.

A few people stopped to say hello, and I got more details about the strike. Some of the miners had actually deposited their paychecks, but after a few days, the money had been literally pulled from their bank accounts, at least that's what they said. The mining company that went bankrupt was supposed to have a special reserve account, but apparently they didn't. Not only that, but the miners' retirement accounts were frozen. Some of the wives who talked to me had admitted that at first they were afraid to join the strike, but then they did because, as one woman said, "It's just plain wrong to steal."

I found out a woman had started the strike. She'd alerted a few miners that a train was getting ready to leave, full of coal, the coal they had mined. A couple of miners had gotten there in time to block the train on its tracks. *The New York Times* had been there, *Rolling Stone*, local TV crews had come there to cover the story.

At last Clay came back to the cook tent, along with a man. "Aleena, meet my terrific Uncle Benny Stone," she said.

"Not terrific," he said, jokingly. "Just great." He extended his hand with a smile.

I took his hand. "I think I know you. From Nancy's, right?"

"Yeah, you're right." He didn't seem at all like he was trying to recollect me.

Clay had said that her grandmother's maiden name was Stone. Benny was Sara's brother. Holy crap!

"Benny's my great-uncle," Clay said, confirming what I'd just realized. I couldn't believe how this whole thing was just opening before my eyes. It dawned on me that I'd never really expected to find Sara. Clearly, I was now in deeper than I'd ever imagined.

"That's right, and you better remember how great I am," Benny said, grinning.

Clay laughed. "You never let me forget it."

"I remember," I said. "You're the one who told me about the strike."

Benny said he remembered that also, and he thanked me for helping out.

My insides were in a knot. I didn't know what to do next. Should I nonchalantly slip away and drive home? Benny seemed to be giving me a weird look; my thoughts were tumbling through my brain like items on a conveyor belt gone haywire.

What happened next was the biggest surprise of all.

"Aleena, I thought I might treat you to a cup of coffee," Benny said. "There's a little coffee shop in town, nothing frou-frou with all those syrups. Just good coffee. Our way of saying thank you."

He knew something; I just felt it. Yet his face revealed nothing; it seemed casual, or matter of fact. My first impulse was to decline, but I did the opposite.

"No thanks needed," I said. "But I could go for a cup of coffee."
"Excellent. Let's take my car."
"But my car's here. Shouldn't I follow you?"
"It's not far. I'll give you a ride back."
"Okay."

Chapter 34

1970

Frank wasn't sure how he might influence the inspectors from the DNR and the Water Resource Council at their meeting that afternoon, but whatever their findings and conclusions, he hoped his presence would influence them to hold a harder line. Not long ago, he'd seen these inspectors as a nuisance, a pain in the butt. Today he prayed they'd just do their jobs.

Frank had asked Bill Emery, Rowan Coal's lawyer, to attend so he could also hear what the inspectors said. If Vern listened to anyone, he might listen to Emery. Vern wasn't concerned with fines or liability issues. But he was concerned about the press, the possible damage to the company's image.

Frank hoped he'd see Sara on this trip, but then he chided himself for that wish.

Her coming to New York had showed gumption, which didn't surprise him, but he knew the consequences she could face from their relationship. He didn't worry about pregnancy because they'd both used precautions, but her involvement with him could jeopardize her job, or worse.

What if her brothers found out? They'd probably wait for him by the river, put a bullet through the back of his head, and dump his body in a hole. The local deputy would probably help them or look the other way. Or they might not kill him. They might blackmail him. Despite appearances, he had very little saved. Most of his lifestyle was company-financed: club memberships, trips to the Greenbrier, fancy dinners with customers, liquor, all on his expense account. His big-ticket items right now were private school for the kids and treatment for Allicia— he couldn't believe what that hospital was charging. Few would believe he actually lived month to month.

He'd always prided himself on his decision-making abilities. Life was a series of problems that you had to solve. But all his logic, sound reason, and good judgment, what had they gotten him? A job he hated and an alcoholic wife. Then there was Sara. His better judgment said that getting involved with her was the most ridiculous, childish, and foolish thing he'd ever done. Yet he couldn't shake the feeling that, in a way, it was also the most meaningful thing he'd done.

If he could just see her and make sure that she was okay, that'd be enough.

His hands tightened around the steering wheel. He felt sweaty and cold. He lit a cigarette and tried the radio. Listening to the news was a way he could get mad at something other than himself. Politicians were an easy target, and the miles slid by.

When Frank arrived at the Otter Creek office, Sweeny had two pots of coffee going, extra mugs, and plenty of chairs. He told Frank the inspectors were out but should return shortly. Emery had arrived hours before and gone out to look at the dams. Sweeny had offered to drive him so he wouldn't get lost, but he'd preferred to go alone. He'd now been gone more than two hours, and Sweeny joked that he hoped he hadn't fallen in.

Frank gave him a hard stare. "Fill me in on the froth filtration, or flotation, or whatever the hell it's called."

Sweeny said it was at full strength, and they'd increased reuptake by twenty-five percent. The drain pipes were working as they should, and the sludge dam was reducing the filtration load on the big dam.

Just then Emery walked in. Frank poured him a coffee and handed it to him with raised eyebrows, saying, "Welcome to Otter Creek."

While Sweeny was on the phone, with a lowered voice Emery said, "I can see why you asked me to come here. To be honest, I wasn't expecting much, maybe something along the lines of twice as big as normal. That thing, that impoundment, goes beyond anything in my professional experience with mining, and I've been working in this field for thirty years. Quite frankly, I'm surprised it hasn't given way already. A natural disaster from that thing is a certainty."

Frank nodded.

The state inspectors arrived, and Sweeny made the introductions: Dub Brady, of the Reclamation Division of the Department of Natural Resources and Rex Tilley, from the Water Resource Council. They got their coffees and everyone took a seat.

Frank started them off. "All right, gentlemen, let's get down to business, shall we? My first question is: who makes the decision on the strip permit, you guys or the Feds?"

"We do," the inspectors said in unison.

Dub Brady added, "When all is said and done, the Feds tend to go with our recommendation."

"Huh." Frank wasn't sure if he believed that. "Let's hear what you've got."

Brady began reading from his clipboard. "Here's the list of violations: trailing cables, circuit breaker violations, improperly stored grease and oil—they must be in sealed containers—not enough bore holes, need another distinct passage for escape. Now, this is regarding the gob pile. Refuse Piles: Public Law 77.215: Refuse piles should be spread in layers." He glanced at Sweeny, then continued. "Refuse should not be deposited on a burning pile except to put the fire out."

Sweeny spoke up. "That's what we're doing. Trying to put the fire out."

"You don't put a fire out with flammable material!" Tilley blurted.

"Refuse piles should not impound water," Brady said, moving on with his list.

Again, Sweeny spoke up. "Ours doesn't."

"Tell me, then," Brady said, "how is all that water contained, if not by tailings?"

Sweeny considered this. Just as he started to say something, Frank interrupted.

"Give it up, Sweeny."

Frank then asked if he could look over the list. The thing went on and on. Roof control plan. Flame safety lamps. Anemometers, whatever the hell they were. Flame resistant brattice cloth. Frank handed the list to Emery.

In a measured voice, Tilley added, "In addition to that long catalog of violations, you'll be cited for dumping black water into Otter Creek."

Brady said the tipple was already at capacity—175,000 tons. Then he added, "With all the problems we've listed, and the preposterous state of that big dam, there is no way we will authorize a strip permit."

Sweeny tried to talk them into an extension. Apparently he was used to getting one. But they wouldn't budge.

"Not until we see a substantial number of these violations resolved." Brady was firm.

"Don't make the mistake of thinking the fines will not be substantial," Tilley told Frank. "They're drawing the line now. You'll be hearing from us in a few weeks."

"We'll straighten out the gob pile," Sweeny said. "Why not authorize the strip to start in a month or so?"

"Many of these violations go back a number of years already," Brady said. "We're just trying to do our jobs, man."

"And so am I," Sweeny snapped. Frank gave Sweeny a back off look.

The sun was on its decline and coming in the windows like a spotlight scaring up the dust that filled the air.

Frank stood. "Well, gentlemen, I thank you for your time. We'll review these things you've covered and address them. You probably have a long drive ahead of you, and are anxious to get on your way, so we won't detain you any longer." Before leaving, the inspectors left a carbon copy of the report.

Frank, Emery, and Sweeny mulled over the findings for a while.

"So, you're their lawyer?" Sweeny said to Emery.

He nodded.

"Need a good lawyer these days. Things are changing and that's for sure."

"Yes, that's true."

Sweeny said, "A guy in this holler had to find a good lawyer. He found one all the way up in Washington, D.C." He went into how Underwood had won his case for mineral rights on his land because he had that good lawyer.

"I wonder how they swung that?" Emery asked.

Frank seemed suddenly interested. "By the way, do you recall who won that case?"

Sweeny thought for a moment, but it seemed to be out of his reach. "Funny name."

Emery prompted, "The firm, perhaps?"

"Up in D.C. Shoe-something."

"Schoenwalder?"

"That's it! See, I said it was a funny name." He laughed, but no one else did.

Frank and Emery stepped outside. Emery said he thought there might be a loophole with the liability being limited to miners and company property, but he'd have to check. Also, he'd check about violations that weren't underground. He just couldn't believe Vern had agreed to purchase the mine, but Frank said it was sight unseen, and before they'd brought Warren on board. Frank asked Emery what he knew about the law firm and the case Sweeny had mentioned.

"Harvey Schoenwalder. I remember that case. They won the mineral rights for the landowner. They do liability and a lot of pro bono work, which I expect that was. Top notch firm."

Frank slapped Emery on the back. "No shysters, huh?"

"We're not *all* crooks, Frank."

"I guess there are exceptions," Frank said with a smile. They were walking toward Emery's rental car. "You're heading back to Lexington?"

"I'm not staying here, that's for sure." Emery's eyes were red and tired-looking. "You know, one word comes to mind about that impoundment."

"What's that?"

"Ominous."

Chapter 35

Dub Brady had a two-hour drive home. He lived an hour southeast of Lexington, but there were no major roads from Otter Creek to his home near Irvine. His stomach growled, but he knew his wife Laura always kept his plate warm. There weren't many cars on the road, no washed-out bridges or construction areas, so the drive should be smooth.

He took Stone Mountain Road to US-23. Then at Prestonsburg he'd take KY-114 north and west, then a smaller road to his home. Not long into his drive, however, it began to dawn on him that one car had, for some time, been behind him. Not just behind him, but at about the same distance. For sport, he tried speeding up and slowing, and still the lone car stayed the same distance behind. He kept checking in his rearview mirror; there the car appeared. Occasionally it would disappear, then reappear.

He decided to lose the car. He knew a lot of backroads. He waited until he didn't see the headlights when he made the turn, and now he could really put on the speed. The road was curvy but he knew it well. His entire body was pins and needles as he drove as fast as possible, without having the tires squeal. He was careful, knowing how to brake before curves and accelerate out of them.

He was trying to put out of his mind that someone might be after him. He told himself how silly he was and that it was all in his imagination. How could someone be after him? He was just an inspector. Although some people, when they want something very badly, were capable of . . . There his thoughts went again. He had to stop thinking like that!

He now had twenty miles left to go and there were no lights behind him. But after fifteen minutes, he spotted it. One lone car. He yanked the wheel right onto a dirt road that he knew and peeled around the corners, spewing gravel. There wasn't a light behind him when he barely made the left on to Juniper Road, then rejoined Mt. Sinai Road, before finally turning onto his street and his driveway. He turned off the engine and rested his head on the steering wheel until his heart stopped thumping. Maybe it was all his imagination. Maybe he'd been working too hard. Maybe they should go on vacation. It wasn't until then that he realized if someone was after him, surely they would know—or could easily find out—where he and his family lived.

He walked in his door and locked it. His German shepherd, Mac, rubbed against his legs. He leaned back against the door to let his heart calm down. His daughters ran up to him with their news, Katina about her basketball game and Caitlin about the tryouts. He followed the smell of pot roast into the kitchen, kissed Laura, and soon forgot about the lone car.

Out of a deep sleep, Dub Brady heard Mac growling. It was a low, fierce, snarling growl. That's when he remembered his drive home and the car. Without turning on the light, he leapt out of bed. Now the German shepherd was barking like a freight train. Laura mumbled something, and he told her he'd take care of it. He lied and said it probably was that porcupine again. Mac had attacked it in their garage a month earlier. He crept downstairs and, staying lower than the windows, went to the corner of one, where he could look out. Just as he did, he saw the taillights of a car driving away.

He lived at the end of a dead-end road.

Mac stopped barking. Dub's knees caved. He slipped to the floor, his pajama shirt wet with sweat.

"What was it, Dub?" Laura called.

He climbed the stairs on reserve strength, because the terror had drained every ounce of stamina from him. He whispered as he went back to bed, "It's gone now, whatever it was."

He didn't—couldn't—sleep, and sat up watching and listening to every creak and stir, to the chimes from the living room clock, each half hour and then hour. But there was no more noise.

In the morning, when Dub and Mac went outside to get the morning paper, he discovered, to his relief, that his tires were flat as pancakes.

He called Rex Tilley. "I think I was followed last night, and this morning I see that someone's slashed my tires."

"Mine too! I also thought I was being followed. Fuck, man. This is bad."

"We're lucky. Absolutely lucky."

"You say lucky! Are you out of your mind?" Tilley shouted into the phone.

"Yeah, man. It could have been something really bad."

"You know what this is about—Rowan Coal."

"Of course," said Dub. "But I'm surprised. What do they care about this small mine? They have bigger fish to fry."

"That's true. It's a piddly subsidiary. It's peanuts to them. I don't get it."

"Yeah, but we're the inspectors. Maybe they're trying to teach us a lesson, scare us. Who knows what they'll do next. I expect this is some kind of warning."

Rex said in a tremulous voice, "They've given me a warning. I'm no...I don't. I just can't deal with this kind of thing. This is just a job, man."

"Okay, Tilley, what are you thinking?"

"They're getting the permit."

Chapter 36

Early that morning, Sara's brothers had been talking about the inspectors who were due to arrive that day. Sara's ears had perked up, but she'd said nothing.

Now she paced the floor at Underwood's, rolling Mandy in the stroller while she waited for Pattie, who was late getting back from work. She knew Frank was in town; she'd seen his car, with the Connecticut plates. She wanted to see him, and she also wanted to find out what was happening with the inspectors.

She stayed close to the windows so she could hear the miners on the porch talking.

"We're losing jobs while that fat cat Boyle in Washington gets fatter. I should've moved out of here a long time ago."

"You're too old to move out of that chair, so you can forget leaving Otter Creek."

"You blame Boyle, but it started with Johnny L," another miner said. "He was the one, you know, who said 'You can't stop the clock.' I wish he were here now. I'd give him a piece of my mind."

"They just want to line their pockets while dishing out promises they know they won't keep."

"Not Joseph Yablonski. But it got him murdered, and his wife, and their poor daughter."

Sara couldn't see all the speakers because she didn't want them to see her, but she knew about the Yablonski killings. Everyone did. She felt shock now at how uninterested she'd been, how apathetic, almost as if she'd taken pride in her disdain.

"What do we have to rely on? Machines take our jobs, and the UMW, something my granddad died for us to join, is gone so corrupt they're killing each other."

"Big shot Boyle can kiss his big leather chair and picture window goodbye. They're gonna lock him up and throw away the key. And you can bet that with what'll happen to him in there, he'll be a'begging to be six feet under before the first week's out. Heh."

"They always leave a trail," someone else added.

After watching her father suffocate to death from black lung, maybe Sara had felt that nothing worse could possibly happen. In her child fantasy world, life provided some mechanism for fairness. Could things really go from bad to worse? Her detachment had allowed for her optimism, and her optimism had been a form of self-protection or even self-preservation.

But that was before she'd met Frank, before she'd seen the dams, before she'd read about the children smothered at school—when it had felt like there was nothing she could do to influence or change anything, and when the threat of the dams had seemed remote, pumped up by some teenagers out looking for trouble. There were the families staying at the school when it rained hard, but she'd easily shrugged that off, as did most people. The pieces of the puzzle never had fit together. Nothing seemed remote anymore.

Pattie still wasn't there. Sara asked Underwood if she could use his phone to call Todd to tell him she'd be late. When she got back from making the call, Pattie was at the door, and she looked to Sara to be in agony. Her head was kind of lowered, her hair was a mess, and she was very pale. Sara thought, for a minute, that she'd gotten into a car accident.

"I have to tell you this, before anyone else does."

Sara said, "It's not my brothers. Tell me they're okay." Pattie assured her they were fine. "It's not Baby Jake? Linda Lee? George?"

"No, no, no. Nothing at all about anyone. It's about me. Come get in my car."

Now Sara thought maybe Pattie was getting a divorce, or maybe she'd gotten fired or found out she had cancer and only six months to live.

As they got into Pattie's car, tucking sleeping Mandy into the place on the floor in front of Sara, Pattie said she had to drive. They pulled out, drove past Todd's, and turned out of the holler. She pulled off on a side road and turned off the engine. Sara said, "Just tell me, please. I can't stand this."

"God, I hate to have to say this." Without looking at Sara, she said, "I got busted."

Sara's hand went to her mouth. Her jaw had dropped open, and stayed there. "Is this some sort of joke? Busted? What kind of busted? Do you mean arrested? For what?"

"For taking pills. Well, not taking them. That's the word I used in my head. Geez. For stealing them. Stealing prescription pills from the hospital pharmacy."

"Jeezum crow, Pattie." Of all the people in the holler, Pattie was the last person Sara would have guessed would do something like this. She was no straight arrow, like Linda Lee, who'd probably never even had an overdue library book. But stealing! Stealing pills! Like Benny said, there was a lot she didn't know about her holler.

Pattie turned to face Sara. "Let me explain." She talked for a long time. She started by saying that Dr. Reilly and Sheriff Baker took her outside the hospital, one holding each of her arms. Then they'd told her to get in the car. Dr. Reilly's car, though, not the patrol car.

They busted her. They knew about the pills. She'd broken down crying, saying that she'd been so sad and nothing had helped and she knew how wrong it was, it just was too unbearable to go on feeling that way. She said she'd been crying every day since her pregnancy. It stopped for a little bit, but then came back. It was like her chest was pouring open, like the tears would drain the life out of her.

Dr. Reilly had been soft-spoken and not at all angry; in fact, he was sympathetic and kind. He spoke of doctors who were beginning to see this pattern. They said it may, for some women, be hormonal.

Pattie said she was so terrified she could hardly speak. She thought she would go to prison. But that's not what happened. They made her agree to go to a therapist and to some meetings. They took her inside and made her sign papers. She also told Sara that she was suspended from work.

"Suspended? I thought you could only get suspended from school, not work."

"And if I don't do what they say, I can't ever go back."

"But Dr. Reilly said it's connected to having a baby, right? You have every right to go back to your job."

"Not if I don't cooperate. I'm suspended and not in jail, thank God! And you don't have a babysitting job anymore. I'm sorry about that."

"Mandy's an angel. I would have done it for free. Can George keep her when you're at those meetings?"

"I may be desperate enough to call my mother. Now that is a punishment worse than death." They laughed.

Pattie drove Sara back to Todd's, and when she pulled in and parked, she was right next to Frank's car. Frank did not look over, but Sara felt the heat pumping into her neck and her face beginning to perspire.

"This happened before," Pattie said.

"What happened?"

"This time you can't deny it. I see the blood filling your cheeks. And I see him decidedly *not* looking over at us. Look at him, staring straight ahead, not moving."

"You're dreaming."

"And you're going to play this like there's nothing going on between the two of you, even after what I just told you?"

"Just because you told me something that you, basically, had to tell me because I'm no longer going to watch your baby, that means that I'm obligated to tell you whatever you want to hear? Is that right?"

Pattie said nothing. A sad, questioning expression came over her face. "Sara, I've always thought of you like a sister."

Sara stared for a moment. Did she hear that right? Had Pattie said "sister"? She had never had a sister. Linda Lee was kind but there'd always been a gulf, almost a generation gap. A sister, a close sister was something that Sara never dared dream of. Never thought would be possible for her. "You think of me as a sister?"

"Sara, what do you think? Yes!" They hugged. Sara's eyes welled with tears. Pattie went on, "If anyone hurts you, and I find out about it, I swear to God, there won't be much left for them to talk about. And whatever's left over, George will take care of that!"

"Please don't tell George. I don't think he'd understand." By this time, Frank had walked into the motel.

"Frisky, I'm not sure I understand. You haven't told me anything yet."

"If you want details, you can forget it!" They laughed. "But he's really great. Really nice, so nice to talk to. We've . . . I've been seeing him for a while."

"But please be careful. I will say that."

"I know what I'm doing, Pattie. I can handle my life."

Just then Todd walked out, giving one of his hairy looks.

Pattie said, "Now I wish I could give a dirty look like that."

"Shivers!"

They both laughed.

All evening, Sara noticed Todd's black, bushy eyebrows bearing down on her. She tried to convince herself she was imagining it, but she caught Todd staring at her too many times for it to be in her head. This was getting weird. First Benny, now Pattie, and maybe even Todd. What if he'd seen her going into or out of Frank's hotel room? That was why, during the busiest time of the evening, when all the tables were full, she slipped a small note into Frank's hand: "Meet me at the Big Hole, tomorrow, 5 a.m."

She woke in pitch dark, dressed, and was out the door by four o'clock. The night was still and silent, except for the groaning tipple; there were no cars, no trains, and no one awake. The air smelled of wet rocks and soggy moss. Not daring to walk on the gravel, she walked on the grassy shoulder. The going was slow because she couldn't use her flashlight until she was off the main road and on the trail.

Frank was there waiting. They hugged. She hung on to his jacket.

"You're out of breath," he said.

"Thank you for coming."

"Of course. I was happy to see your note and wanted very much to see you."

She slipped her cold hands into his pockets. "Something's changed. I can tell by your voice. What is it?"

"This is complicated and risky. Risky for you and risky for me."

"We've always known that."

They found a place to sit, a big rock that they shared.

"You know," Sara began, "if this were two days ago, I don't think I'd feel this way. But today I feel even less afraid of what other people think. I know you can't change people and they think what they think, but if there's anything that I feel bad about it's that you're married. Nothing else."

He gave a little tenuous smile. "Well, there are a lot of complicating factors here."

"But please, Frank, before anything else, tell me what happened with the inspectors."

He told her that they'd had a long list of violations. "There's no way we'll get a strip permit."

"Are you sure? Is it really true? They won't do the strip?"

"No, they won't. The violations poured out of them. You should have heard Sweeny; he was so out-gunned. I have the copy of the list in my car if you want to see it. And they said the Feds always go with their recommendations, which, as far as I know, is true."

"I don't need to see it."

Sara led Frank to a stand of pines where a break in the forest canopy let in enough light for a soft bed of grass to grow. There they made love to the sounds of summer crisping into fall. Leaves glowed red and orange in the muted dawn, and warblers flew south carrying the memory of their summer songs under their wings. Beyond them was the river with its constant refrain.

Dressed once again and folded in his arms, Sara said, "I wish I could stay like this and not let go. It was so hard for me when I left you in New York."

"I know what you mean. What a slender chance in the universe that you and I could have ever met. Sara, you are the woman of my dreams."

Sara didn't answer, thoughts swirling in her head, old desires to live some sort of fantasy life. "It's so wonderful to be together, and every time it has to end; it's hard."

"It's a gift, this moment. Just us being here as we are now."

They spent the day like that, talking of nothing important, warm in each other's arms. And when, years later, Sara looked back at that time, she only knew that the hours went by so slowly. It was a moment in time that seemed an eternity. The sun, the earth, the holler all faded. It was just the two of them, nothing else. And it stayed as one of the sweetest memories of her life.

Evening's chill was on when she hurried up the trail.

Frank didn't want to leave, though. He sat on the riverbank and watched the September leaves let loose, descending in slow motion. He watched the sashaying, the spinning and undulating, and with some, the free fall. Some fell stem first, as if fairies had launched out clinging to their umbrella handles, sailing slowly, defying gravity, then delicately touching down on black water. The fiery colors stretched from shore to shore. On the sliding, moving stream, the leaves would spin once, maybe twice, before being sucked away downstream.

Chapter 37

Another month passed and Sara hadn't seen Frank. She spent her spare time in the woods during those weeks, emerging with autumn bouquets of fall daisies, goldenrod, purple asters, and Queen Anne's lace. She made arrangements at home, mixing them with milk weed, cattails, and bittersweet along with twigs of flame-colored maple leaves.

Pattie seemed to have put her life back together, and that didn't include needing a babysitter. Her mother had come to live with them to help with Mandy. This was good, because Pattie had to go to her meetings in Pikeville two nights a week.

It was a Monday, and she got started on her walk in the late afternoon. The trail was a new one, and it meandered so far that by the time she got to a ridge, the sky was turning a myriad of colors. Pink and orange near the sun. In the distance was a deep purple and red. The clouds weren't bunchy but instead were long, thick brushstrokes. Sara was entranced. The trees in their autumn colors seemed to reflect the colors of the sky.

The world was quiet, except for the dropping leaves, which sounded like raindrops. Distant leafless trees were black against the vibrant sunset. She sat on a rock with an unobstructed view, hugging her knees, to enjoy the show. She sat until the veil of night closed in.

It was dark.

Damn! she said to herself. *That's what happens when the sun sets. It gets dark. Fuck!*

She lost the path early on, then pushed her way through for a hundred yards or so toward some brightness remaining in the sky, which she figured was westward. She quickened her pace with enthusiasm, helped on by an easier stretch, some briars that had more or less been flattened. Gaining momentum, what she didn't plan for was the boulder, covered by low shrubs. and the drop beyond it. For a moment she was in the air, and next she was on the ground in searing pain. She had stepped right off a boulder and fallen, she guessed, six to ten feet onto a heap of cedar bushes that luckily helped cushion her fall.

The pain in her knee was severe. She'd also hit the side of her head. She could feel blood trickling down her calf. She tried not to move, slowing her breath so she wouldn't throw up.

Eventually her brain began to work, and she realized that she was in a dire, possibly life-threatening situation. People died of exposure. Staying there was not an option. No one would ever find her.

Pulling herself up with the prickly branches, she began to hobble forward in the same direction, which she hoped was generally north and west. The going was slow. The new fear of never making it out alive took the focus from her pain. She hobbled and pulled herself along and made slow progress until she realized, with the darkness almost complete, that she had no idea where she was going.

Suddenly she could imagine her own death, and panic took over. Maybe some people, in those moments, experience peace or surrender. Not Sara. She had fight. When the panic was gone, a fire rose from her belly.

She was not going to die there. She would not allow that to happen.

She needed to find out where the houses were, and most houses had a dog. There were farm dogs, hunting dogs, domestic dogs. And dogs liked to bark, especially at other dogs. She began to bark.

She could do a good bark, vicious and growly. It had come in handy during high school to entertain friends. It got a response right away: a bark in return. Then more barking. She moved in that direction, kept up the barking, then listening. Eventually she got to a road. The houses were spread far apart and she couldn't go any farther. She lay down.

Pattie's car wasn't the first to pass her. No telling how many cars did or how long she lay there. But it was Pattie, on her way home from her evening meeting, who noticed the dark blob by the road. Sometimes people throw bags of garbage out their car window, but this was in a strange place. No mailboxes. Just the middle of a long country road. Pulling a U-turn, she went back to investigate.

From working in the hospital, Pattie knew all the town drunks, and she suspected this was one of them. She had a first aid kit in her car, and a flashlight. She approached the body and to her amazement, it was Sara.

"Sara!" she cried.

Sara was groggy, but awake. Pattie dropped to the ground next to her.

"Are you okay? What hurts? What happened?"

Sara told her she got lost. "Get me home. It's my knee. Everything else is okay."

"There's blood on your face." Pattie tried to convince her that she needed to go to the hospital.

"Just scratches, I promise. Please, Pattie, just take me home."

When they arrived, Pattie said, "I just want to ask one question: does this have anything to do with that operator?"

"My God, Pattie, are you kidding? NO! This was my own stupidity."

Pattie called out for help. Pete burst through the front door, with Benny following. Panic covered Pete's face. He ran to the car and helped Sara out, then carried her to the house.

Pattie knew exactly what to do, and she gave Benny his marching orders. "I'll need bandages or clean white cotton cloths, warm water to wash the wound, ice wrapped in a dishrag for the swelling, isopropyl alcohol—I hope you have it—and hard liquor if you don't. Oh, and scissors, and probably an Ace bandage but we won't use that until the swelling goes down, so forget the Ace bandage."

As Benny went to collect the items, Pattie looked carefully at Sara's head. She brushed aside some hair that was caked in blood. "You do have an abrasion and some swelling on your skull, Sara, but it's not on the temple."

"I didn't even feel my head because my knee hurt so much."

Benny returned with the scissors and Pattie cut Sara's jeans off above the knee and began to clean the wound.

"I think I could use a PBR," Sara said. Pete went to get it.

Benny, looking over Pattie's shoulder. "Good thing Pattie found you, Frisky. No telling how long you might have been laying up there. All night, maybe. Or you might have gotten hit by a drunk."

Pete said, "What were you doing over there? That's about fifteen miles away, isn't it?"

"That's fifteen miles by the road. This one goes through the woods. Takes animal paths mostly, don't you, Frisky?" Benny crouched right by her side.

"I was watching the sunset. It's true, though, I took a new path and it went forever before reaching a ridge. I really didn't know where I was, and then it got dark."

"That's what happens at sunset, kid," added Benny.

"Thanks. I'll remember that. But Pattie, you need to get home to Mandy."

"Don't worry about that. Mom's living with us. She might be worried, though. I'll give her a call in a minute. First, let's prop this leg up. Benny, I need three pillows and two aspirin."

"Aye, aye, captain." Walking by Pete, Benny said, "She could have been a medic in the Army Medical Corp."

After Sara was comfortable and had been to the bathroom, Pattie got Benny and Pete into the kitchen. She whispered, "She needs to be woken up every couple of hours. Her head is more of a concern to me than her knee. She likely has a mild concussion."

Benny said he'd made plans to be somewhere by nine. Pete said he could stay.

"Wake her until she responds coherently," Pattie instructed. "Ask her something: the name of a Beatles song, the name of the president or the governor. Ask her her phone number or address. Also, use a flashlight to see that her pupils dilate. That's the most important thing. If they don't dilate equally, rush her to the hospital."

"Every two hours?"

"Yes. For the next eight hours. You may want to start a pot of coffee brewing."

When Pattie went back into the living room, Sara reached her hand out. "Pattie, are you going? Thank you so much."

"You're welcome, sweetie."

"I love you."

"I love you too."

Pete pulled up a chair near Sara. "I'll be here with you. Don't worry about anything. You can rest, but Pattie said I'd have to wake you to check on you, okay?"

"I feel kind of cold."

Pete pulled up the blankets and tucked them around her. "Want some tea?"

Pattie was just going out the door, but heard this. She went back to take Sara's pulse. To Pete she said, "Put sugar in it, or honey. She might be hypoglycemic." To Sara she said, "Your pulse is okay. Are you sure you're not dizzy?"

"Not any more than I usually am. Now get outta here."

After making the tea and pouring in a lot of sugar, Pete adjusted Sara's pillows but still held the cup so she could sip. "Does it hurt very badly?"

"It's a lot better. Maybe the aspirin." She smiled up at him. "I've never felt so cared for in my life."

Still holding the cup near her lips, Pete said, "You're worth it."

"I never had a sister," Sara said, slipping into a groggy state, "but Pattie is the next best thing. She's almost my sister." She finished the tea, lay back, and closed her eyes.

Pete said in a whisper, "I'm so grateful Pattie found you. I can't even *think* of what could have happened if she hadn't. That's a lonely road out there. I hate to think of—"

"Then let's not think about it." She took his hand. And then, after a few minutes, she said, "Pete, you're so nice to stay."

"I'm glad to do it."

After a few more minutes, when she looked like she'd dozed off, because she'd let go of his hand, in a very groggy voice, she said, "Don't go, Pete."

"I'm here for the night, Sara. I've already called my grandpa. I have to make sure you're okay."

"Don't go into the mine." Then she began to snore.

Chapter 38

It was a quiet Friday afternoon in Otter Creek. Leaf piles bordered properties like moguls. Front yards were outfitted with black cats, witches, ghosts, and pumpkins on hay bales. Horizontal slivers of sunlight lanced the cold, purple clouds, resembling a Zorro signature, and fall flowers had faded from frosts in forgotten fields. Milkweed pods were empty, their scattered angel-hair seeds a memory. Cattails had gone brown. Blazing sumac leaflets were falling to the forest floor dotting the brown pine needles with their colors.

Sara was getting the mail before leaving for work, more to kill time than from any anticipation of finding something of interest. The flimsy mail consisted of a flyer about a shoe sale, an invitation to a bean supper at the Elliston Creek Free Will Methodist Church, and a letter addressed to her, with no return address. She almost didn't see the letter because it was stuck to the back of the shoe sale flyer. It looked like a nondescript commercial mailing, a legal-sized envelope with her name typed on it.

Inside the envelope was a handwritten note that said, in very messy writing, "It pounds my head. Chases my worries. Saturday, October 21st 5:30 a.m." No signature but it was postmarked from New York, so she knew it was from Frank. He must mean the Big Hole. She hurried back into the empty house as if someone could look over her shoulder, even though no one else was there. She hadn't seen his car, but he was probably in town and might be at Todd's for dinner. Today was Friday the twentieth.

She showered and got dressed, then put her hair up in a French twist.

It wasn't yet fully dark on her walk to Todd's, and she could tell that the clouds that had been purple were now black and lower and covered the sky. A storm was nearing, but she'd have no trouble getting a ride home. She arrived ten minutes early, and Todd said, "We need ground beef. Go get some. Ten pounds should be enough."

"Can I take the Jeep?"

"My Jeep?"

"It's about to pour."

"You know I don't let anyone drive my Jeep."

"Did you check the freezer, under the ice cream?"

"Sara, I know every ounce of food in that cooler and in the kitchen. Want me to list it all? There's forty-two pounds—"

"Todd, I didn't plan to go out walking in this weather."

"Pick up some ketchup too. Five of the large ones. The way we go through it, I swear they should pour it in a glass and drink it with a straw." Todd coughed and spat into his bright yellow Chock Full o' Nuts coffee can. Then he wiped his mouth with the back of his hand.

On the way to the store, she saw Frank's car at the hotel, but he might have gotten some food at Underwood's. When she arrived back at the diner, Frank wasn't there, and it was already busy, with more people still coming in.

"Took you long enough," Todd said. She put the cardboard box on the counter. Luckily, it hadn't started raining yet.

"Maybe you should have loaned me your car."

In a matter-of-fact voice, as if it happened all the time, Todd told her to put on an apron, that she'd be working the grill and he was going to wait tables.

She stood still, her hands on her hips, staring at him. "Are you kidding?"

"Tonight I'm waiting tables," he said, sipping his Coke.

"I didn't dress like this to stand at a smelly grill. And I work for tips."

"Sara, didn't I say when I hired you that you would be trained to do all jobs and duties regarding the operation of this diner?"

"Well, I'd appreciate it if you'd let me know I'll be cooking before I dress for work."

"Your uniform used to be good enough. I bought three of them. There's one hanging by the door if you want to change."

She was too angry to respond. He went out with a tray of food. If this was some sort of suspicion thing, it'd gone way too far. She went to the bathroom to try to compose herself. Her instinct told her to lay low, not to burn any bridges. Looking in the mirror, she pulled the barrette out of her hair, which fell in soft waves framing her almond-shaped face. She wore no makeup other than a little lipstick and mascara. She turned to the side and said, still looking at her reflection, "Todd, you pushed me a little too far."

Then she thought, in a sudden moment of clarity, *I'm better than this.*

The string of clothespins was filled with orders. Sara took it all in as if in slow motion: the stainless steel equipment, the dishes on open shelves, containers of food, and Todd standing there, not much taller than she, his back to her, working the grill in his wrinkly blue shirt and dark pants, flipping the burgers. He noticed her and grunted, "You thought they'd cook themselves?"

Of all the times she'd dreamt of it, imagined it, fantasized about it, and hoped for it, she'd never imagined it this way. She'd never thought that she could simply get her purse and coat and walk out. Yet that's exactly what she did. It was that easy. She didn't turn to look at him and she didn't say goodbye.

When she arrived home, Linda Lee was there with Baby Jake.

"I came by to bring you some leftover pumpkin cookies from our church's harvest fair. They're sugar cookies, but warning! The frosting will turn your mouth orange. The kids don't mind orange mouths, but I thought you might." She looked at her watch. "Wait a minute, aren't you supposed to be at work?"

"Life is about trying things and making mistakes, right? Living without making mistakes is not living." Sara bit into a large orange cookie. "I don't care about an orange mouth. Orange mouths are perfect." She demonstrated with a giant smile.

"You're talking crazy," Linda Lee said, "and you didn't quite answer my question." She was bouncing Jake, who kept spitting out his pacifier, which Linda Lee kept putting back in his mouth.

"I'll get some tea started," Sara went into the kitchen.

Linda Lee followed. "Okay. But tell me: what happened with work?"

"You might say Todd took my job from me. So I left."

"You quit? Is that what you mean? I can't believe it."

Sara picked up the baby from Linda Lee.

"Okay, tell me what's going on. I have all night."

And Sara did. First she told her about quitting her job at Todd's. Linda Lee was hanging on every word, and before she knew it, she was telling her about Frank and about the trip to New York. She left out the part about Frank being married.

After a long pause, Linda Lee began, "I'm concerned for you." Linda Lee waited and then said, "I assume he's married? Of course he's married. Sara, you'll just end up getting hurt. These things never work out. There are too many differences, different walks of life. What—what do you want from him?"

"Don't worry, Linda Lee. It's not really like that. Why do I need to want something? We've always known that after each time we're together, it could be the last."

Linda Lee was shaking her head. "Does he treat you well?"

"Oh my God, yes."

"I just don't want to see you falling in love, because—"

"I'm not." Sara couldn't explain about the dam. She'd tried to bring up topics of importance to Linda Lee, and they'd always fallen flat. Linda Lee never seemed to have a strong opinion about anything.

Benny came home and walked into the kitchen, where they were sitting. Linda Lee stood and whispered to him, "Maybe you could find someplace else to be for a while?"

Benny found a leftover chicken leg in the fridge, took a bite, and with his mouth full of meat, said to Sara, "Your mouth is orange, Frisky. And why aren't you at work? Got orange mouth disease?"

Without waiting for an answer, he went out the kitchen door to the backyard where he worked on his cars. Linda Lee picked up their conversation where they'd left off.

"Sara, I know you're too big for this holler. I've always known that. If you want to spread your wings, fine. I admire that. You're more courageous than me, and smarter. I know you'll land on your feet. I have faith in you. But you'll need money. Quitting your job shouldn't really be the first step; it should be the last step."

"Todd made it easy." Baby Jake started wailing, and Linda Lee needed to get him home.

Shortly after she left, Benny came back in.

"So, you quit?"

"I'm moving to Lexington. Can you take care of Bonnie for a while?"

"Depends on how long."

"C'mon."

"Course we will. But you're not moving in with that operator, are you?"

Sara stared at him. "How long have you known?"

"I put it together. Wasn't hard. The nights you weren't here coincided with him being in town. I didn't tell you, but Aunt Betts mentioned a train to New York when I called up there for you. Then, sweet as she is, she tried to cover for her mistake. You know that woman can't lie. She couldn't lie to save her life."

"I'm not moving in with 'the operator,' as you say. But he's a good guy and I wish you'd realize that."

"He's an operator. I wish you'd realize that."

"This has nothing to do with him, anyway; I'm doing this for me, and it's long overdue. I'm going to start my new life, Benny, and I hope you'll be glad for me. I'm going to find an apartment and a job, then apply to college."

"I am glad for you, Frisky. Not only the college part, but the other part too. And don't worry; I won't say anything."

She told him thanks. "Hey, could you look out for a car for me?"

"Oh, man. I know of three."

Chapter 39

Sara barely slept that night, worried that she might not wake in time. Long before the sun neared the horizon, she was off the main road and could use her flashlight sparingly, on her way to the Big Hole.

She was excited to see Frank, feeling stronger as a woman, stronger in herself, and wanting to share that with him.

Frank had seen her flashlight coming down the trail, and he blinked his a few times to let her know he was there. Without words, without the need for words, for a long time they hugged by the loud falls.

They waited, however, ten or so minutes to be sure that neither of them had been followed.

Sara said she had some things to tell him, but first, why did he want to meet? And wasn't he there because the six months were about over?

They found a place to sit that wasn't so close to the waterfall, so that they could talk quietly.

Frank began. "It's been like walking a tightrope to reduce the water level in the dam, to stay on Sweeny's back, and to distract Vern. Vern's my boss, I think I've mentioned that. Anyway, he's away fishing right now. I'm here with Warren and Emery, our engineer and lawyer, to get enough evidence, and to boost the argument for more time and more money to get this situation under control, or at least a lot less threatening. My hope is we'll be able to almost empty the dam. Anyway, the inspector's report put off the strip, and now I just have to get Vern to cough up some more money. He'll be back next week and I have a lunch planned, which I scheduled a number of weeks ago."

"What's the chance you can convince him?"

"Vern is callous and smart. A bad duo. I know enough not to count on his conscience, but he has to know, and Emery won't mince words, that if something were to happen, God forbid, it wouldn't get buried on page ten. Not anymore. Believe me, he won't want to risk that. That's the angle we're going to take. Sweeny's given me all the documents, we have the list of violations. He has to listen. I think he'll see that he's backed into a corner."

"How much are they down?"

"We're moving in the right direction. Well, to be honest, we haven't had the results I'd have liked. But we have a new plan. Warren came up with it today. The idea is to retrofit Dam 1 with concrete. After that, we'll drain the big dam by as much as we can. Later, when I get more money, we can retrofit the big dam the same way."

"The Big Lagoon hasn't gone down?"

"The pressure is reduced because the solids are down. That's good, believe me. I just wish the water level was lower."

"You saw it?'

"No."

"But you can't trust Sweeny. It could be worse than what he reported."

"Let's not split hairs. It's not good—we know that."

Sara told him that she was leaving the holler, moving to Lexington, and planned to apply to college to begin in January. She asked about his wife.

"The hospital didn't do any good, but I wasn't that hopeful. I ran out of hope a long time ago. She got drunk the first week out of that place. But Sara, I'm glad for you. This is really good news. And I guess," he paused a moment, "although I hate to say it, this is a good note on which to say goodbye."

"What about you? What will you do?"

"Vern can't get the permit, but he might sell. If he threatens to sell, I'll threaten with my resignation letter, which I wrote some time ago. It's my last card, but I don't think he wants to lose me."

"Sorry about your wife."

"I have my kids. Some people have it worse. No life is perfect."

They were quiet for a long time. At last Frank said, "You know, Sara, you've been a light for me. And knowing that you're moving forward in your life, it just means everything. It'll keep me going. I promise."

They hugged, and over Frank's shoulder Sara took in the sparkling orange and long sprays of yellow of the sunrise. Then kissed one last time.

Frank offered to drive her back to the Otter Creek bridge and she accepted. She had to get started on her move. Out on the main road, close to the turn for Otter Creek, they both noticed it. Smoke, grayish white smoke, coming out of the mountain.

"Someone's house is on fire," Frank said. "I hope they have a fire station nearby."

"There's no fire service up that way."

"Isn't that where—" Frank gasped.

Sara put her hand to her face. "Oh my God, it's not a fire! That's—that's—"

Frank said, "That bastard! That's the Winifred Seam."

"They're strip mining!"

Through clenched teeth Frank hissed, "Jesus Christ! That son of a bitch!" He pulled the car off the road and reached for her. She jerked away. "Sara, my God. You have to believe me. I had no part in this."

"How could he have started it without your knowledge? And why didn't Sweeny say something?"

Frank was shaking his head, staring in shock.

Sara smacked the dashboard. "Damn it Frank! Answer me!" She jumped out of the car like her legs were on fire and screamed, "How could you let this happen?" Her tears fell—hot, angry tears.

Frank got out too. "I just can't believe he got the permit. Those guys were clear. The list of violations a mile long." And then a new revelation dawned on him. "He must have paid them a pretty penny. Or worse."

"You mean, he had someone hurt them?"

"There are things you can do without hurting someone."

Neither spoke. The last of the season's leaves were sprinkled from the trees like crystals twisting in the morning light. Sara said, "Of all the fucked-up things. God-fucking-dammit!" She stamped her foot. "Why did you lead me to believe you could do something?"

"Oh, I am a fool here. Make no mistake. If I led you to believe anything, I apologize." Then looking off, he added, "I never thought he'd be capable of this. That miserable bastard."

The silent spectacle of smoke and all that it carried—the threat, the lives at risk, and their mutual helplessness—was now a wall between them.

After a time, she said, "You have to use your resignation letter. Will that convince him? You have to do something."

Frank grunted. "Believe me, I'll make Sweeny call this off right now. I'll break his neck if he doesn't. But Vern, that pathetic bastard, this order came from Vern. Don't worry, if he can play dirty, so can I. I'll take half of our customers with me, more than half. He won't want that."

She started walking away, but then turned back to him and said, "I know you tried, Frank." There were tears in her eyes.

Chapter 40

2019

After getting our coffees, and because he was hungry, Benny and I bought some sandwiches and then walked down a quiet street under a canopy of mature trees.

"So, did you really think that we'd just be open with you about someone in our holler, not knowing anything about you or why you wanted to know?" he asked.

His zinger question took all the wind from my sails. "Yeah, I guess I did. Pretty presumptuous."

"I'm glad you agree," he said. "It takes guts to own up. But you have to understand, in general, from where I stand, and I think it's pretty much true across the board in my holler, personal matters are just that—personal. What have you figured out so far?"

"Well, meeting Sara Clay today was the first thing that told me I might not be on a completely wild goose chase." He showed no reaction at all. Poker face. "I'd like to ask you some things."

"What do you want to know?"

"Well, for starters, why are you even talking to me now?"

He laughed and said, "That's a good question." Then he waved to someone driving by.

By the looks of him, I wasn't sure if he was going to answer or not, so I said, "It's because you know who I am, don't you?"

"Of course I do. I've known since the first time I met you at Nancy's. You have a license plate. But I found out more when I read your father's obituary."

"My license plate! Gosh, you have connections."

"Well, that could be; not too hard these days."

"And you've done some homework too. Why'd you bother?"

"Curious, I guess. Your dad's obit said he ran Hudson Coal but was the former president of Rowan Coal."

"Yeah. He started his own company called Hudson Valley Coal."

We'd been walking, but had come to a park, and Benny suggested we sit on a bench. I added, "My father quit before the disaster. I have all his desk diaries and I could tell you the exact date. Growing up, I always heard that he never got along with his uncle Vern. I never met the man. But I can tell you one thing, my father was anything but dumb."

"Ah. That's why he wasn't part of the court depositions or subcommittee hearings. But I remember him from Todd's. But how did the name Sara come up?"

"A little slip of paper that fell out of his desk diaries. You see, I inherited all of them, his desk diaries. I didn't even know they existed. My brother was in charge of the tangibles after my stepmother passed, and he just sent them to me. No warning or anything. I guess he figured it was send them to me or throw them out."

"But 1970 was fifty years ago. Who cares?" He didn't seem angry, but he looked protective and serious.

"It's hard to explain."

"Try."

"I blamed my father all my life—for my mother's death, everything. But it was my husband walking out, and getting those desk diaries out of the blue, that started me hunting—that's a bad word—looking for missing pieces of my life and history. My father died before I could apologize; nothing big, I was just a tough kid to raise. Well, I was a jerk to him, quite frankly. I fought with him a lot and criticized him. I went through some old letters recently, and in one of them he'd started with, 'I know you've never thought much about my opinion.' You know, as a kid, you don't realize that you're having an impact on your parents; it's all about what they're doing to you. In another letter he wrote the words, 'I love you, sweetie.' I'd have bet my right arm that he'd never said that. I had no memory of it. None.

"Anyway, I've seen a therapist recently and learned from some meetings that of course my mother's alcoholism wasn't my father's fault, wasn't my fault, and it hurt the whole family. In my marriage, I put so much effort into avoiding problems, any problems, that what we had was as solid as a house of cards. Stephen, my—I don't know what to call him—he simply took his ring off, put it on his dresser, and left. We're in mediation moving toward divorce. It's been like the Twilight Zone, but I'm getting used to it."

"No other woman?"

I shook my head. "That would have been much easier. Harder in the long run, though. Easier because I could be mad at her. Harder because I wouldn't have been looking at myself. This has really been a journey."

"Yeah, then you'd be stalking *her*."

"Do I really seem that pathetic?"

He scratched his head, scrunched his face in a *I hate to look* expression.

"Thanks a lot," but I had to chuckle. "Now it's time for you to take the hot seat. What are your pathetic confessions?"

"None. Can't you tell? I'm a cool ex-miner. I've got it all together."

"You were a miner?"

"Until the flood."

I asked him what he did for a living and he said he was a plumber and a farmer. I told him that sounded neat.

After another long pause—that guy could sure tolerate silence—and because I hoped to absolve myself, I said, "It's not like I wanted to dig up dirt on my dad, or *anyone*. It was the opposite. Seeing my mistakes gave me this new feeling of love for him, and regret that I'd been so hard on him. I had a desire to connect with him. But it's too late, of course. Chasing ghosts."

"Maybe. But other people aren't dead, that's the thing."

"I know. It was selfish of me and incredibly shortsighted. But why did you encourage me? You even said I should come help with the strike."

"I wanted your Connecticut friends and Connecticut money. Or maybe because you're kind of cute."

"That's nice. I guess I'll keep paying for my yoga and Pilates, then." We shared a smile.

"How old were you when your mother died?" Benny asked.

"Eleven."

"Whew, that's hard. Our mother walked out, and we never heard a word from her. In 2001, we got a death notice from the state of Texas. She died alone in her apartment. She did have some friends, though, who notified the sheriff because she hadn't been returning calls. Massive heart attack. I hope she didn't suffer. We all suffered enough from her leaving us."

After a moment, I said, "Nothing's been as hard as losing my sister. Talk about chasing ghosts, I drive to where she lived and I walk where we walked, and I pull over at the views that she loved. And I just stand there." My throat clamped and tears filled my eyes. After another silence, I said, "She wouldn't have approved of this thing I've been doing, by the way. Not at all. Quite frankly, I'm disgusted with myself."

"Not too much collateral damage," he said with a comforting smile. Then he said we needed to get going.

I was beginning to like him. "Benny, did you ever—I mean, are you married?"

"Never married. No kids. I have my farm, which in fact, ties you down more than children. It's called Benny's Farm. Got a website. My pumpkin patch is open on weekends, and we have hayrides. I have a Clydesdale to pull the wagon. Kentucky has a farm-to-school program that I'm involved in, so busloads of adults come to enjoy fine dining. Between the school kids and the adults, and all the work, I stay pretty busy."

"That is so cool."

"Well, I'll drive you back to your car."

I felt reluctant to finish the conversation. I liked being with him, but I also knew not to get ahead of myself. "Okay. Sure. Right."

I climbed into his truck, and the next thing he said really surprised me. "I can give you the address for my sister. She gave me her permission, said it's all right. She doesn't bite."

"Like you do?"

He looked at me with a sideways smile. "Do I?"

Chapter 41

1970

The night before Thanksgiving, there was a blowing, drenching rain. It drowned out the sound of Pattie's car and the sound of her climbing the porch steps. She couldn't knock because her hands were full of wet groceries and a wet baby, and when she got through the door, so did about a puddle of water.

"What a storm, and it's supposed to rain all night," Pattie said. "The way this wind is blowing, the water in our toilet bowl was sloshing around."

"Cripes, you're soaked. I'll get some towels, but first give me the squeaker."

Pattie handed Mandy over and then got out of her wet poncho and sweater. Mandy started wailing, her little mouth extending almost the width and length of her face. Bouncing her, Sara said, "Man, what a set of lungs on this kid."

Pattie took the baby and stuck a bottle in her mouth, which was apparently what she wanted because she vigorously went at it.

"You didn't need to bring groceries." Sara said. "I have everything: the bird, the stuffing, the veggies, the potatoes, the cornbread mix, and the cranberry sauce. That should do it."

"But I'm making an Italian Thanksgiving, if you don't mind."

"Why bother? I already got everything."

"Because I want to represent my mother's Italian heritage. So how many are coming?"

"Ten, if Benny brings a girl, and eleven if you include me."

"Why wouldn't we include you, silly girl?"

Pattie then mentioned that George was out with "Donny and them" looking at the dam.

Sara blurted, "Why? What have you heard? I mean, what did he say?" Every day she'd checked the Winifred Seam for strip mining. Since Frank had left, she hadn't seen any activity, no blasting and no trucks going up there.

"Beats me. I can't believe they'll be at that dam all night, and just because of a little rain."

Sara corrected her. "Pattie, it's been raining off and on for about two weeks now."

"When's Linda Lee arriving?"

"They'll get here after she's through making the pecan pie, and after Clay gets off. He's on second shift. Oh, she's bringing the sweet potatoes, but you won't find many potatoes under all those marshmallows." Still feeling concerned about the dams, Sara said, "They must be up there to the dams for some reason, other than just the rain. Aren't you worried?"

Pattie was looking down at her baby, still drinking but with her eyes closed. "I don't know, Sara. I go round and round about it. Sometimes I'm worried, and then I'm not. You can't live your life worrying. Would you start slicing garlic and chopping onions and green peppers and mushrooms?"

"We're going to have spaghetti with the turkey?"

"I told you. We're having an Italian Thanksgiving."

"Do they celebrate Thanksgiving in Italy?"

"Who cares about the details." She smiled at Sara. "I wanted to do eggplant Parmesan, but they didn't have good eggplants. I brought some penne instead."

Soon the garlic and onions were simmering in olive oil. Pattie put the sleeping baby in her carrier and joined Sara at the stove. She filled a large pot with cans of whole tomatoes and tomato paste. "You take your basil and oregano and sprinkle it so that it covers the entire pan." Pattie demonstrated with the spices while Sara watched. "How are your Aunt Betts and your Uncle—what's his name again? Smartie? Slim?"

"Shortie."

"Shortie! How are they doing? We should have invited them."

"They have their own kids. They're all doing good."

"Now we add the green pepper. Did your mother teach you to cook?"

"She hated cooking. I taught myself everything I know. Out of necessity."

"Stir these and make sure not to burn the green peppers. It's done when the onions are golden brown,"

"Golden brown," Sara repeated.

"I'll start the bird," Pattie said. "You have to put butter and herbs under the skin. Parsley, sage, rosemary, and thyme—just like the song."

The phone rang, so Sara went to get it.

When she came back to the kitchen she said it was George and that he wanted Pattie to leave right away.

"Oh, he's a worrywart," Pattie complained.

"No, I've never heard him like this," Sara said. "He was so serious. He thinks the road could wash out."

"All right, I'll go. You saw me do the spices, right? Now add the sauté and cook, very low, for a few hours. And here's my mother's family secret. You put in six anise seeds. It sweetens it. Don't tell anyone."

Sara was holding the door and helping Pattie with the baby under the poncho. "Go! George wants you home and I don't want him mad at me."

"Don't forget—stir the sauce so it doesn't burn."

"Bye, and call me when you get home."

Pattie stepped out, then turned and shouted in the pouring rain. "Don't tell anyone about the anise seeds."

Sara noticed the rain was mixed with sleet.

After cleaning the kitchen and putting the food in the fridge, she went to bed. Pattie never called.

Pattie did make a call, however, when she and Mandy arrived home. She called Todd's and spoke to George, who was there with Roger Painter and Donny Atkins, to let him know she'd made it home.

The men had been checking the dam every hour. At eleven, it was a foot from the top; at midnight it had been eleven inches. Now it was 12:40, and the rain was still pelting.

Painter was talking about The Big Lagoon being so soft he couldn't get the dozer on it, but he'd said that three times already.

"Yes, Painter, you told us already. It was too soft when I tried," George snarled. "Sons of bitches starting the strip with a shitload of violations. Bastards."

Donny asked, "But how'd they got the permit?"

Painter said, "But then they stopped the strip a few days later."

"Yeah, and someone gave Sweeny a nice shiner. That was something I've wanted to do for a long time. I think it was that operator who did it."

George barked, "No one's hitting anyone. We're just going to keep an eye on that dam and if we have to, sound the alarm to evacuate."

They waited in silence, just the three of them in the diner and the pouring rain outside. Todd had agreed to leave his place open all night. Donny picked up his yardstick. "It's one o'clock. Let's go."

They put the stick in at the same spot. The water was now ten inches from the top. Still rising an inch an hour.

Once they were back at Todd's, Mimi came in, drenched. She took off her hat and about three raincoats and left them by the door. Then she reported to the men that she'd gotten word out and some families were staying at the high school. She looked around at their worried faces. "Oh, heavens, if Honeycutt's here, I know you're finally taking this seriously. What are you seeing? What's going on? Why are you all so damn calm?"

They told her how they were measuring it and that it was rising every hour. She insisted that they tell the sheriff to call the National Guard.

"We're going to check it a few more times," Donny said.

Mimi said she wasn't surprised that they weren't listening to her, and that she was going to take matters into her own hands. She got on the phone and called Annie Underwood to tell Leon, her husband, what was happening.

Annie tried to wake her snoring husband. "Get up and out of that bed! You're gonna call Sheriff Baker. That dam's about to overtop. We need to get the Guard out here to evacuate."

"Who called you?" he said, yawning. "Not Mimi, I hope? Don't tell me you're listening to that horn-blower."

"You get up before I throw something at you."

"Now, woman, c'mon. What time is it? Can't you leave me in peace?"

The sleet made a tick, tick, tick sound on the windows. "Leon, hear that sleet? That dam is right near the top. They've been measuring it every hour. If you want to see each and every one of us float out of here on our mattresses, or end up in coffins, then you just go right back to sleep. But I guess I won't be seeing you in the by-and-by."

"Who's up there checking?"

"Honeycutt, Atkins, and Painter."

"Honeycutt! Why didn't you tell me?" He sat up and looked at Annie. She was glaring at him, her hands on her hips. "He don't rile easy." While pulling on his trousers, he said, "Fix me some coffee, Annie. I'll call."

Baker was doubtful. An election year was coming up, and he had to think of that. "Let's wait till the morning."

"Honeycutt is on The Big Lagoon every single day," Leon said. "You know he's not going to raise the alarm for nothing. That bulldozed slag is all that separates us from a half mile of water."

"You think I don't know that already?"

"And the water's been rising an inch an hour."

Baker called his deputy down at the jail and ordered him to call out the National Guard. Then he went back to sleep.

Leon Underwood went to Todd's and told them that Baker was notifying the Guard to start the evacuation. They continued to check the water levels, and each hour, the water had risen one inch.

At four o'clock the men piled into the car: Atkins with his yardstick, Painter, Honeycutt, and Underwood. They huddled together at the dam. Gusts of wind made the ice sting their faces. Atkins put the stick in the same place, and he saw something alarming. It was speeding up. The water had risen three inches in that one hour. It was now only five inches from the crest. Not knowing what else to do, they went back to Todd's to wait.

Sleet spat from the sky. The wind gave a low growl. The air was bone-chilling. At five, the men went up to check again. They could see before they even got out of the car that there was no need to measure. The entire monstrous structure was moving; it was undulating, swaying. It was a terrifying sight. The water lapped over the top and sides. Big fissures had emerged in the middle, with water pouring through. They couldn't go near it.

There was not a single car on the road. No National Guard. No evacuation plan. No evacuation warning.

The holler slept.

Chapter 42

Back at Todd's, Leon called Sheriff Baker again and found out that he had put it in the hands of the night deputy, who had called the duty sergeant at the Guard's headquarters, but the duty sergeant couldn't give the order because he had been calling the commanding officer and there was no answer. He'd called every thirty minutes.

"Mother of Jesus, call again!" Leon shouted. "Tell him to drive to the commanding officer's house and wake him up! The thing's about to overtop! It's about to go!"

The four men knew it was up to them to warn the almost four thousand people who lived in Otter Creek Hollow. Extra family members probably had arrived in town for Thanksgiving. Pups curled up on their mats, children were tucked in tight against the chill, and adults were for once relieved of work, looking forward to having a free day to eat a big meal and be with family. Turkeys were dressed and ready for the oven, stuffing and potatoes were cooked, pies and dinner rolls, green beans and gravy would be made tomorrow, when the TV would blare with football and periodic cheers and boos would rise to fill the air.

They jumped in their vehicles and sped off with horns blaring.

George first raced home to Pattie; a phone call might not have woken her, and he just had to see her. He told her to pack a bag with everything she'd need for Mandy for a week. She ran and got Mandy, while he used the bathroom.

"Don't put her down," he said urgently. "The thing is at the point of complete collapse. I think you'll be safe here, but don't move from this window. And whatever you do, do not put Mandy down. Keep your eyes on the driveway. If you see water coming, grab a blanket and climb the hill behind the cabin as fast and as far as you can."

"But George, stay here. You've got to stay here." She clung to his coat.

He looked deeply into her eyes. Her face crumpled. She knew he had to go. He was a soldier. He'd never stay when people were in harm's way.

In a quiet voice, he said, "I have to go."

"I know." They kissed and stayed there, faces touching, holding their lips together, lingering, breathing.

It took great effort for Pattie to manage a goodbye smile. But she gave him one, however weak. She made sure to send him off with her strength, her courage, her belief in him and in his return. She didn't know what he would have to face. Clutching Mandy to her chest, she watched him leave till his truck was out of sight, and quietly closed the door. Then the tears fell.

When he got back to Todd's, there were a number of cars there. Sweeny was at the counter drinking coffee. George marched in and told him that the water was over the top, that there was a wide, gaping separation, a gash thirty feet long and three feet wide in the center, that the whole thing was moving.

Sweeny scowled. "You're exaggerating. Go home to your wife, George. Everything's under control. I've already told Baker there is no emergency, and calling out the Guard is ridiculous and out of the question. Look at you, you're making a mess on the floor. I'll get some men shortly to install a few more pipes."

It was almost six o'clock.

"Sweeny, there's nothing left. It is going to blow!"

A few early-bird customers were drinking their coffees and listening intently.

George's tongue found the hole where he'd lost a tooth fighting those two cops when he'd first got back from 'Nam. One of them made the mistake of whacking him in the face with their pistol.

Sweeny was stirring some sugar into his coffee. "We're waiting on the pipes." He spoke in a casual tone. His mostly gray hair stuck up, disheveled, as if he'd left home in a hurry. "I'll have a crew there in an hour. Also need to pick up a few raincoats. So, like I said, it's under control."

"Pipes! You can't even walk on it. That'll be like a pin to a balloon."

"Are you questioning my qualifications? I'm a trained engineer, I'll have you know."

"You're a miserable, pathetic excuse for a human being."

George flew out the door and jumped into his truck. No use wasting valuable time. There was an enemy to fight, but it wasn't Sweeny's sorry ass. It was the monster at the top of the holler, with a half a mile of water in its mouth and thousands of sleeping innocents lying directly in its path. He raced up Otter Creek Road, blasting his horn the whole way. He stopped at Pete's house, jumped out, and banged on the door. "The dam's gonna break. Get out! Now!"

When a light came on, he sped on down the road, still blasting his horn.

Pete looked out his window and saw what looked to be Honeycutt's truck speeding away. Then he remembered dreaming of cars blasting their horns. Now he realized they weren't dreams. Had Honeycutt said the dam was going to break? Steady, sober Honeycutt?

He woke his grandfather and, ignoring his cursing and complaining, put a raincoat on him and then wrapped a blanket around him and dragged him out the back door. They hobbled up the little lane behind the house, Pete yelling to his neighbors all the while, "Get out! The dam's breaking!" He pulled his grandpa high above the railroad tracks, had him sit where he could lean on a tree, then tucked the blanket around him and told him not to move. His neighbors were getting in their vehicles, so they'd heard him. Pete went back for his grandpa's dog, who slept in a doghouse in a small pen next to the garage.

He was just about to the garage when, a few hundred yards up the street, there was a bright flash. The utility wires began shaking wildly, and sparks zoomed up the wires and into the air like fireworks. He thought maybe someone had hit a pole. Then there was a deafening explosion, like twenty bombs going off. He knew in that moment what had happened. The smoldering, burning gob pile, which was directly downhill from the dams, had been hit.

It was The Big Lagoon! The Big Lagoon had broken! The water had collided with the burning gob pile and was heading down the holler. He looked in the direction of the dams. In the predawn darkness, a giant gray mushroom cloud was filling the sky.

There was a split second of eerie quiet. He freed the dog, who was straining at his leash. It ran off in the direction of Pete's grandfather. Then he heard something in the distance: a thundering growl, growing in intensity with each passing second. A whirring roar, like a thousand engines. It sounded like approaching airplanes, dozens of airplanes, from all directions. He turned in circles to see where it was coming from, looking all around as it grew louder and louder.

His good sense, his sense of self-preservation and survival, did not overpower the mesmerizing pull, the gripping curiosity. He walked out to the street, and that's when he saw it. A black wave, rising, moving, swaying, a tower of black water, moving toward him, bearing down with a deafening, thundering roar.

He couldn't see that this wave had picked up the church, the Elliston Creek Free Will Methodist Church, where he and his grandfather went every Sunday at ten to sing and pray. He couldn't see that the monstrous wave had already swept away some of his neighbors, people drowned while sleeping, warm and comfortable in their beds on a dark, rainy Thanksgiving morning, a morning when icicles dripped from black branches.

And now this black thing, a raging thing, a murderous creature on a rampage, was coming toward him.

It had lifted up houses, the post office, and stores right off their foundations. Cars and telephone poles were mixed up with this constantly growing wave that was blackening the gray dawn. He saw it getting closer, taller than a city building. The noise was crushing. He had no idea how to make his legs work; he couldn't even feel his legs. He was frozen.

It wasn't even that he was afraid. It just didn't make any sense, this wave in the middle of the road. He stared on. Then he saw, rolling out from the black wave, as if the monster had spat it out, the steeple from the Elliston Creek church. The whole church had been taken up, and the steeple was bouncing around in this wave like a ping-pong ball. The giant mass of black water was still coming toward him. He looked a second longer, and then the big spire disappeared. Gone without a trace.

The wave lifted his neighbor's house, swept it up like a toy. Then his garage walls fell away and the water was upon him. He jumped into the bed of his pickup truck, grabbing the side rails. The truck was lifted, it swirled, and then was caught in the velocity of the water. The only thought he had, besides *I am going to die*, was *God, please save Sara.*

The truck rocked as it was carried away with the water. It remained upright at first, and Pete pleaded for his life. *Stay like this and I will live. Stay like this and I will live!* But in a flash, he was underwater, under his truck, gripping the rails and holding his breath. Over and over it turned. He breathed when it was upright and held his breath when it was under. Over and over and over. With great mental exertion, he kept his head and talked to himself: *Breathe! Hold. Breathe! Hold! Breathe!*

When he was under water, holding his breath, he'd count. One, two, three, until he got to ten, then fifteen. Even as the numbers mounted, counting gave him courage, a feeling of control. He could do this. The longest he was under was fifty-five seconds. It seemed like the end.

The truck flipped and he gasped and sucked at the air before going under again. Junk and debris kept hitting him. At last he grabbed at a plank of wood, let go of the truck, and pulled the wood until he could hug it to him with all his might. The truck floated away. He got pushed into a pile of wood, but by clinging and propping himself up he saw people running toward him. They pulled him out. He was naked, and his right arm was bent and bleeding; he vomited, then lost consciousness.

* * *

In her bed, Sara was in a deep sleep. She'd fallen asleep amidst the aroma of a homemade pasta sauce and the warm feeling of having plans for a Thanksgiving dinner with people she loved who loved her. It was the deep sleep of one who's known and loved, of one who isn't watching their goals slip by. A sleep that let true rest permeate her body and mind.

Her deepening trust in the women in her life, her plans to move and apply to school, the encouragement she'd received from her brothers, all helped to ease her worries. She'd done all she could for the holler. That time had passed, and instead of causing her alarm, it was a comfort that the men were now watching the dam. Her cause was now taken up by others. So, despite the rain that was pelting the ground, and the groaning wind, she slept peacefully.

And in this deep sleep she had a dream. It was the preacher from the revival, and he began calling. First it was faint, but he got closer and closer, coming down the aisle. "Come, Sister Sara! Come to the fountain!" The little sweaty preacher was next to her. "Sara, Sara." The preacher's voice got louder and louder, and then it turned into car horns.

She woke up. It was car horns! They were loud. Someone was yelling. Was it the pranksters again?

"The dam's gonna break! Get out! Now!"

Then the horns whizzed by. Then silence.

She didn't know that just seconds earlier Pete had made it to safety. She didn't know that the giant black wave had exploded into the gob pile and picked up burning slurry. She didn't know that this fiery wave, with icy water behind it, had ripped apart and carried away houses, cars, railroad trestles, churches, and telephone poles. She didn't know that in minutes it would do the same to her house.

But this wave was capricious. It didn't swallow all the houses. It moved and surged to the left and then to the right, hitting all the houses on one side of the street, then crossing to the other side and swallowing up those houses. So every once in a while a house would be left, the people in it watching in horror as their terrified neighbors, friends, and family members were swallowed to their grave.

All these, the houses, vehicles, telephone poles, were crushed to rubble. The wave took it all, sometimes slowing at a bridge, then tearing the bridge away. Sprung railroad tracks. It swallowed in its swirling might families who were just waking up to the smell of coffee, walking quietly in robes and slippers, feeding babies, or letting the dog out. People who woke just in time to scream their way to death. People stood at their windows and watched a screaming, naked little boy float by on a piece of wood, then watched him go under. The wave ripped the clothes and the skin off bodies, severed limbs, and filled people's lungs with burning black tar, leaving them begging for the end.

She could hear it now, the engines, the warplanes, all around her house. She grabbed her robe, ran to the front door, and flung it open.

"What the hell?"

The family next door was piling into their truck, screaming, "Get out! The dam broke! Get out!"

The noise was increasing each second, a whooshing roar, as if from the sky, bearing down on her house, like the Earth was rising up growling, a giant monster. Neighbors were screaming. "Run! Get your family and run!" She ran to the street and saw it coming. A wall—a black moving wall, undulating. Coming toward her.

She went screaming through the house. Linda Lee came out in pajamas, and Clay followed with wide-eyed Jake in his arms. Panic was in their eyes. Panic and confusion. Clay put his arm around Linda Lee, who was bent over trying to breathe. Darryl came out in boxers. Sherry hadn't been with him.

"Where's Benny?" Sara yelled over the increasing cacophony.

Then Darryl saw it. They all saw it. Water had crept halfway up their living room window. "Oh my God!"

They huddled together for what seemed to Sara like an eternity but was only seconds. Linda Lee's legs gave out. Clay grabbed her, while Baby Jake crawled up his daddy like a cat up a tree, scratching at Clay's face and yanking his hair and wailing from the deafening noise. Linda Lee started screaming. Sara grabbed Baby Jake. Darryl yelled for them to go upstairs but it was too late. The windows broke. The glass flew at them. The roof came off and the walls melted away with the water. The water smacked Sara and her family, sucked them away. An eerily high-pitched plea reached Sara's ears over the thundering, crushing water: "Save my baby!"

Sara, twisting and turning with the current and crushing that baby to her chest, kicked with Herculean strength. Her legs fought wildly to keep her head up and Jake's head out of the water.

Something hard hit her shoulder. Something else tore at her legs. Then she was pulled under, kicking harder and harder with every bit of her strength, unable to see, just trying desperately to hold the baby up. Her head went under many times, but she kept kicking herself back up, straight arms holding him high. *Breathe, Jake, breathe!* She couldn't hear his screams. Had they stopped? Was he alive?

She banged into debris, spinning and being pushed under. Kicking, kicking, kicking, kicking. She'd gasp for air before being pulled under again, her arms stiff around Jake, pushing him high. But she couldn't feel them and wasn't even sure if she still held the baby.

Kicking, kicking, kicking. Her lungs were on fire. All her might went to her arms. *Up! Hold him up! The baby! The baby!* But she was being pushed down. Kicking, gasping. Where was Jake?

Baby Jake!

A piece of wood hit her in the face. She was able to grab it and hold on. Using it to prop herself up, in an instant she made a decision. She saw people, not that far away on the shore. With some sort of superhuman strength, she threw Baby Jake toward them. Immediately, she was swept away again.

Kicking, keep kicking.

Her feet at last found earth. She crawled as far as she could. A thin layer of ice coated the mud. She collapsed halfway out of the water.

The next thing she knew, someone was with her. She could feel their warm breath on her face. She didn't know where she was and she couldn't seem to open her eyes.

"Baby Jake?" She struggled to form the words, then coughed. The person shook her and spoke loudly, but she didn't respond.

* * *

"Sara, are you okay? Sara? Can you hear me? It's me. Benny."

She was aware of searing pain. Her whole body hurt. She was afraid to move. She tried to open her eyes. Through chattering teeth, she managed to say, "Baby Jake?"

Benny tucked the blankets tighter around her. "Jake is alive," he whispered. "The helicopter took him to the hospital."

"Benny, is that you?"

"Yes, Frisky, it's me. And Baby Jake is going to be okay. You saved his life."

He's alive, he's alive, he's alive. She began to gasp and weep. One eye was swollen shut, and she had cuts and bruises all over her face and body.

"Be still, Sara. Baby Jake's alive, be still."

Chapter 43

When she woke again, Benny was still there. They were in the high school gym. He asked her if she could move her legs and arms, which she could do. He'd been told by the nurses to periodically check that she had feeling in her fingers and toes. She did. He checked her leg wound. The bleeding had stopped. Her clothes were torn. She had gashes in her arms. She could only take short breaths in between coughing and spitting black gunk. He kept an ice pack on her head, as he'd been instructed to do.

He flagged a woman volunteer to help because Sara nodded that she thought she could go to the bathroom. Leaning on the volunteer and Benny, she went to the restroom, where the volunteer took over. She led Sara to the toilet, and afterward she gently dripped warm water on Sara's sores, which were filled with black tar and grit. Then the volunteer helped her get into a hospital gown and wrapped a blanket around her.

The post-storm fog surrounded the gym like smoke. Sara asked Benny for the time. He said it was going on two and that he had to leave her for a while. He wanted to look for Clay, Linda Lee, and Darryl. He'd been asking people if they'd seen them, but everyone was asking about their own loved ones. No one knew anything. Holding her hand, Benny said, "Just rest; you've been a hero. You saved Jake's life. But I need to go out looking."

They hugged goodbye. Still holding his jacket, she asked, "How will I know you're okay? What if you don't come back?"

"Sara, there are a million National Guard out there, and medics. I will come back. I'll be back before seven. That, I promise."

Sara was improving. She could sit in a chair, and they'd given her something for the pain, an antibiotic, and a tetanus shot. She'd eaten something and could hobble to the bathroom now on her own.

Not long after Benny left, Sara opened her dozing eyes. She thought she saw—but then again, it might have been a mirage or a hallucination. She tried to focus through her burning eyes. The man was wearing his red-checked jacket. She saw the cigarette, and then she knew it was him. It was Frank.

He looked at her, his eyes intent, waiting.

She got up gingerly. Moving slowly, she'd only gone a few steps when she heard a little boy speaking to his mother. He asked if this is the end of the world.

The mother, whom she recognized to be Mrs. Morgan, said, "No darling. This is not the end of the world. We are here and we love you and we're going to be all right."

Sara stopped to speak and quickly realized that Mickey wasn't there.

"Mickey?" she asked quietly.

Mrs. Morgan couldn't answer. She was white as a sheet. She sat back down and hugged her two boys.

Their father, who didn't get up from the bench, said, "Mickey got up early. Must have thought it was a school morning. Went outside." He broke down crying; his two sons looked at him with terror in their eyes. "He just wanted to go to school."

Sara hugged the grieving father, and whispered, "You've got to be strong for your boys."

She kept walking toward Frank, but with her swollen face she had no peripheral vision, so she was startled when Pete was right next to her.

"Sara!" he said. "Oh, thank God, thank God!" He was limping and his arm was in a sling, but with his good arm he leaned in to embrace her gently. "I'm so glad you're alive. But your face! Your eye. Are you okay? You should see the doctor. There's one here, I'll get him!"

"No, the nurses have seen me. There are way too many people worse off than me."

His shoulder had been dislocated, he said, but they'd yanked it back. She noticed his bandages, but he looked okay. His grandfather was fine, and his dog had survived. She told him about Baby Jake having been flown to Louisville, that Benny was fine, but he'd gone back to look for Darryl and Clay and Linda Lee. Pete asked about Bonnie, and she said, "I don't know."

Their conversation couldn't have taken more than a few minutes, when Sara looked again for Frank, but he was gone.

"I've got to go," she said.

Pete had seen Frank too, although in the crowd, Frank blended in, wearing his red plaid woolen shirt jacket. What Pete did notice was that Frank was walking toward Sara.

"That operator? Do not go with him, Sara. This is his fault!"

"Pete, you don't understand. He tried to stop this. He—he—" She was stumbling for words.

Pete looked crushed. He stepped back and shook his head.

She hurried toward the door and caught up with Frank. She touched his coat.

He turned. "Oh, Sara. Darling, I'm just so grateful that you're okay." He kept repeating it, his eyes filling with tears. "I came here to make sure you were okay. I didn't know what else to do. I—"

"Where's your car? I need to call my aunt."

He supported her as they made their way to the door. Once outside, she paused and looked around her. Otter Creek was gone. There were helicopters overhead, and chaos everywhere. Smoldering bare earth, buildings and bridges, churches and homes now in giant piles, smashed into rubbish heaps on top of one another, nothing but charred earth. There was nothing left, not a tree, not anything standing. A blackened, smoking wasteland. The homes gone. Smashed cars with broken buildings on top of them. The stores gone. The road gone. Utility poles snapped, wires everywhere. Railroad tracks bent like licorice. Rescue workers hustling gurneys with patients under bloodstained sheets.

Frank helped her into the car and then got the heat going. Her teeth were chattering, and he held her until she warmed and calmed.

He drove slowly toward the Miner's Market outside of Otter Creek. National Guard vehicles, a long line of them, were approaching. Frank helped her to the pay phone.

Aunt Betts burst into tears when she heard Sara's voice. She was sobbing so loudly she couldn't speak. Uncle Shortie asked the questions. Sara reassured them about Baby Jake, Benny, and herself. But that was all she could tell. She promised to call as soon as she knew anything.

Back in the car, she turned to face Frank. She was shivering.

"It was so horrible, Frank."

Frank's eyes welled up again. "I know. I couldn't stay away. I had to see you."

"But my family. Little Mickey. He just wanted to go to school. Everybody. My whole world." She was looking out the window. "It's gone."

"I quit, Sara. I resigned. And started my own company." His face pleading, gesturing with his hands. "They stopped the strip that last day I saw you. I made sure of that. Got that weasel Sweeny up against the wall and about knocked him out. Waited until he gave the order to stop the strip. It was Emery, our attorney, who put it to Vern. Emery told him the liability would finish him. That Rowan Coal would never recover if there was a disaster."

Sara was still looking out the window. "I just want you to promise that you'll remember this."

"Sara, my darling. How could I forget? I'm horrified and I want to help you." He handed her a piece of paper. "I brought you this. It's the name of an attorney. I know you can't think of this now, but you'll need to soon. Very soon. Representatives from Rowan Coal will be here before you know it and they'll want you, everyone, to sign a settlement form. Listen to me," he said. She looked at him, her swollen eye tearing up. "Do not sign anything. Call this number and ask for Harvey Shoenwalder. I've also written down my new office phone number and address. Tell Shoenwalder to call me. I'll tell him everything. I'll give him anything he wants, documents, everything."

Frank tenderly brushed her hair from her face. "Let me drive you to the hospital. Your eye looks very bad. You need medical care."

"I need to go back. I have to go back. Benny will be back before seven. He's searching for my family. My two brothers and my sister-in-law—" Her voice choked up. "Oh my God, what time is it?"

"It's 4:45. Does your eye hurt? What can I do?" He took out his handkerchief and lightly dabbed her cheek. The cuts were oozing, and her teeth chattering, even though the car was warm. He gave her his handkerchief. "Take this. You can use it for your face." Then he took his coat off and tucked it over her. He implored her to let him drive her to the nearest hospital, but she said no. She had to get back to the high school.

Helicopters thudded overhead, emergency vehicles with lights swirling, people and rescue workers carrying stretchers. Commotion everywhere.

"I failed you, Sara. I failed so badly."

"You tried. I know you did. This was bigger than you and bigger than me."

"I had to walk such a fine line with Vern, scaring him enough to cough up money, and leading him to believe that we were making progress. And we *were* making steady improvement. I just never thought he'd go around me and give the order."

Sara said, "I was such a fool. My aunt told me that one man rarely has all the power. But I suppose you were a fool too."

"That slimy bastard," Frank said through gritted teeth.

"He *is* a bastard. All them are. Sweeny, Curley and Simpson."

Frank reached into his pocket. "I brought you some money. It's for your new life and college expenses. It would make me happy if you took it." She didn't move. "It's just a gift, Sara."

She took it and Frank drove her back.

There was someone, a deputy, outside their car blowing his whistle. There were cops and people and mayhem as far as the eye could see. Their shouting penetrated the car. Sara began to open her door.

Frank rushed around and helped her out. "My fair Sara."

They hugged and then he watched her until she disappeared through the door.

Chapter 44

2019

Never had this idea seemed so preposterous as it did when I found myself at her house. I followed her into her living room. Her home was neat and cozy, light and airy. I sat on the floral upholstered couch. The windows let in light through the sheer curtains. I let myself take in the nurturing atmosphere.

"Benny told me you'd be coming by. I think you know who I am," she said, "but I'll tell you anyway. My name is Sara Stone Griffith."

"I guess you want to know who I am, or why I'm here."

She gave a light chuckle and half smile. "I could tell you were his daughter as soon as I saw you. And you found my name in his desk diary. Hmm."

My cheeks flushed, and I didn't know what to say. She had a kind face, and there was no sign of impatience, no tone of condemnation.

"You're not upset, I hope. I don't want to cause any trouble."

"No, it's not a problem. I'm surprised, but not offended." Then she popped up and chided herself for not offering me anything. She said she'd get some tea, and I went with her, offering to help. It felt better in the kitchen, more relaxed. I opened cupboards and quickly found the cups while she filled the kettle.

"Aleena, I have no hard feelings toward your father and no grudges. He tried, as any man could have. That I know. The dam was preposterously big when Rowan Coal bought Otter Creek Mining. Rowan only owned it eleven months before the collapse."

"He tried? What did he do?"

"To prevent the flood? Oh golly." We went back into the living room with our tea. "I don't remember the specifics, but he would tell me about all the things he'd done."

"God, I'm just so sorry."

She passed me a plate of cookies.

After a pause, she said, "We lost Clay and Linda Lee, my brother and sister-in-law. I adopted their son B.J., and Pete and I raised him. We called him Baby Jake at the time. He got helicoptered out, and for a while there we weren't sure if he'd lose his leg. It was almost completely severed. But they saved it. He's a systems engineer with the Tennessee Valley Authority. We're real proud of him."

"Must have been hard to raise a child all of a sudden in your grief. You must have been pretty young, too."

"I married Pete soon after. Turns out I was in love with him and didn't know it. Later, we had our daughter, Linda Lee."

"Linda Lee. The mother of Sara Clay?" She nodded. "What does Linda Lee do?"

"She's an attorney in DC. She works for the Environmental Law Institute."

"That's very cool."

"Well, I used to drag her along when I worked for the Fish and Wildlife department. My division tracked fish populations, so we were out in the woods a lot. She wants to make a difference in the world, which I respect."

"I did kind of want to ask about my father. Strange, right? Because he was my father, so you'd think I'd know about him. But I don't. I don't think I ever knew my father." I couldn't think of how to ask what I needed to ask.

"Your father was a unique man, I'd say. I suppose there was that tough businessman side of him, but that's not the side he showed me. Our time together was kind of separate from the world." She was quiet a minute, and I sensed there was a lot that she wouldn't say. But she added, "He had a good heart."

"That's really good to hear." I sipped my tea. "And that's kind of all I really hoped to hear." Sara's eyes were filled with warmth.

We talked for a long time. She told me that Pete, her husband, worked as an urban planner. She said his hours were crazy, with tons of overtime. For twenty years he'd also been a volunteer fireman, going to emergencies at all times of the day and night. She mentioned that he missed meals or could be out at a fire for the entire night and then work straight through the next day. I tried to detect sadness about this, or loneliness, or a trace of marital discord, but there was none. If anything, there was pride.

Then she said she had to get something and disappeared to the back of the house, saying she'd return in a moment. I walked around the living room looking at the family pictures on the tables and what looked to be a handmade quilt next to the hearth.

When she came back, she was still looking, opening drawers in a cabinet in the dining room while muttering to herself.

I was walking to the front door when she exclaimed, "I found it!" She was holding a small piece of white cloth. "This belonged to your father. He gave it to me the day of the disaster. He drove to the holler to make sure I was all right. I want you to have it."

The handkerchief had been rolled up. I gently unrolled it. Clean white linen with his initials embroidered on it, FRR. I ran my fingers over the letters.

"When he passed, I didn't want anything of his. So, if fact, this is the only thing of his that I have."

"Except his desk diaries."

"Yes. Except his desk diaries. But really, this means so much. Thank you."

"I'm glad for you to have it. He was your daddy." She opened the door.

My daddy, I repeated to myself, because I liked the sound of it.

"Why not come back tomorrow for dinner? You and Benny can come up in one car. Here's his number." She gave me a piece of paper with his phone number, and hers, on it. "I'll call Pattie and George and invite them. Pattie makes the best lasagna. Maybe Darryl and Sherry can come too. And you can meet Pete."

"If there's no fire." We laughed.

I thanked her again, especially for the handkerchief, then headed down her front walk.

This long journey, which seemed so foolish, had such a surprising result. I felt like I'd been given a father, the one I'd always wanted, my dad. He was a complicated man, but a loving one. I put his handkerchief in my purse. The warm, wet ground, with layers of mold and decay, smelled rich and full of life.

—THE END—

Chapter 28

Acknowledgments

Thank you to my editor, Grace Albritton, and the editorial staff of Belle Isle Books for your guidance and commitment to this novel.

Heartfelt thanks to readers: Sarah Gribbin, Ed Henegar, Fred Chappell, David Noble, Lorraine Nelson, Lynn Travis, and Susan Hutton. A special thanks to: Jane Benesch, Lee Smith, Elizabeth Tackett, Judy Goldman, and Kimberly Macdonald. Thanks to Karin Borg who braved the Beckley Exhibition Coal Mine in West Virginia with me. Thanks to Gertie Moore, who loves her mountains.

To my teachers along the way: Mark Sarvas, your guidance and encouragement has meant so much. The Table Rock Writers Workshop, the Appalachian Writer's Conference, and the North Carolina Writers Network all have helped me to hone my craft through their dedicated faculty and community of writers.

Thank you also to the Lesley University MFA Dylan Thomas International Program in Wales. Thanks to the Duke University Special Collections, particularly Carson Holloway, to the Buffalo Creek Memorial Library, and to Christian at Kinkos on 9th Street.

Most deep and heartfelt appreciation goes to my abiding family, for their love and encouragement all along the way. And to Rylee.

About the Author

Isabel Reddy began her career in clinical research as a science writer. She has been a guest columnist for numerous newspapers, and she is working on her MFA in Writing at Goddard College. Ms. Reddy lives in North Carolina with her husband and German shepherd, Mac. This is her first novel.

CPSIA information can be obtained
at www.ICGtesting.com
Printed in the USA
LVHW031920030223
738627LV00004B/14